Sherlock Holmes

The Selected Cases of Doctor Watson

Martin Daley

Hardcover ISBN 978-1-80424-321-3
Paperback ISBN 978-1-80424-322-0
ePub ISBN 978-1-80424-323-7
PDF ISBN 978-1-80424-324-4

Published by MX Publishing
335 Princess Park Manor, Royal Drive,
London, N11 3GX
www.mxpublishing.co.uk
Cover design by Brian Belanger

Contents

Foreword

Of all the adventures my original literary agent presented to the editor of the *Strand* magazine that involved the singular talents of my friend Mr. Sherlock Holmes, I left it to the two of them to decide which were deserving of publication. I should stress this is not a criticism of either man's judgement, or indeed of that wonderful publication. After all, it was no small task in selecting each appropriate investigation, as I have personally been involved in – or have had knowledge of – over a hundred cases during my acquaintance with Holmes. What is more, he once stated that he had been involved in five hundred cases of capital importance, most of which took place before we even met. Decisions had to be made therefore as to which adventures were worthy of publication and I believe the judgements made were as good as any.

Having stated that, I recently had cause to visit the vaults of my bank, Cox and Co. at Charing Cross. I had misplaced a keepsake given to me by my beloved Mary not long after we first met and I suddenly remembered I had placed it with other valuables in the vault of the bank. While I was there, I could not fail to be tempted by the contents of my old, battered despatch-box, containing the notes of my adventures with the great consulting detective. I sat for over two hours glancing through the piles of papers, recalling every possible emotion experienced during my association with Sherlock Holmes. Some investigations I had completely forgotten about; some brought feelings of great satisfaction, while others triggered feelings of tremendous sadness or discomfort.

I later discussed the afternoon in question with an acquaintance of mine who persuaded me to choose several cases that might be suitably grouped together in one volume. After much consideration therefore, I selected a collection that, for varying reasons affected me greatly, either at the time or still now, many years later. I hope my ever-loyal readership can enjoy them as much as the previously published adventures.

JOHN H. WATSON M.D.

Dial Square

Chapter I

By my recollection, there have only been a handful of cases in my friend's illustrious career where any sort of sporting activity formed the backdrop to his investigation. Sherlock Holmes once told me that, apart from fencing and boxing, he had little interest in any form of athletic activity. As for my own sporting prowess, Rugby Football was one of my great passions in my early years. But I was recently reminded of one of only two cases as I can remember, when Sherlock Holmes became involved in a matter relating to Association Football. I must confess that I had always considered it a rather crude form of the game; that was until my friend received a commission to investigate a series of thefts from the munitions factory at Woolwich. As I review my notes of the case, I recall, in turn, that this would be the first of two investigations Holmes would undertake at the Woolwich Arsenal.

It was late autumn in 1886 – not a particularly pleasant time of year for myself as invariably, that wretched Jezail bullet would torment me during the damp stormy season. During the third week of November however, the rains ceased, the fallen leaves dried and a watery sun drew me out for an afternoon stroll.

Despite the desperately cold temperature, I enjoyed the exercise immensely and returned to our rooms looking forward to a pot of coffee by the welcoming fire. I was to be surprised and – I must confess – a little disappointed however, for when I arrived, I found that we had a visitor.

"Good afternoon, Holmes – Oh, I'm sorry, I didn't realise you had company."

"Come in my dear fellow," replied Holmes rising from his own chair on the other side of the hearth. "You couldn't have come at a better time. This is Mr. John Parker. Mr. Parker, may I introduce my friend and colleague Dr. Watson."

"How do you do sir?" said a young fresh-faced man, rising from his chair and tentatively offering a hand.

"Pleased to meet you Mr. Parker."

"Mr. Parker called speculatively while you were out," said Holmes, "Fortunately for him, I am between cases and he now has the opportunity to fill that gap in my schedule."

Holmes reached down into the fire with the tongs and clamped a glowing coal, with which he lit his pipe; re-taking his seat, he smiled at our visitor, "Now Mr. Parker, tell us what brings you to Baker Street."

"Well, Mr. Holmes, I have been sent by my father Joe Parker. He is the manager of Dial Square, which is the workshop at the munitions factory in Woolwich. I work as an assistant there. It has come to my father's attention that some boxes of ammunition have been taken from the factory and they appear to have gone from the workshop itself."

"Why hasn't the matter been brought to the attention of the police?"

"My father is a very proud man Mr. Holmes. He has worked at the factory all his life. If it were to transpire that such losses had occurred under his nose, his reputation, not to mention his position, would be in jeopardy. He learned of your name after your involvement in the Worthington gang matter on Brook Street. Hayward's cousin works at the factory and the place was rife with rumours about what had happened. When my father heard of your great skills, he was hoping that you could investigate the matter without it coming to the attention of either the police or the government."

7

"That may be unavoidable, I'm afraid," said Holmes. "You say the theft came to your father's attention – how?"

The young man fidgeted in his seat. "There was a consignment of ammunition, ready for transportation to Aldershot. When the crates came to be loaded onto the vehicle, the number of boxes did not match the inventory."

I found Parker's manner a little odd: there was hardly any eye contact with either of us when he spoke and he continually twisted his cap in his hands as though he was ringing a wet towel. Holmes ignored such behaviour however, as he continued his preliminary questioning.

"Could there have simply been a mistake on the inventory?"

"No, Mr. Holmes, the consignments go through a strict check in three parts before being released for distribution."

"So, who could have had access to the crates?"

Parker fidgeted again, "Well that is probably the area with which my father is most concerned, as many people in the workshop could in theory have access to the boxes, given that they are stacked close to the main loading area."

"Does your father suspect anyone?"

"A name has been brought to his attention but rather than accuse the man on the say-so of another and potentially cause unrest within the factory, he would like you to look into the matter and provide him with a definitive explanation before deciding on what action to take."

"Well in that case," announced my friend rising from his chair to signify the end of the interview, "I shall be delighted to help your father with his little problem. Doctor Watson and myself will meet you at the main entrance to the factory tomorrow morning at ten o'clock" – he turned to me as though it was an afterthought – "that's if you are free my dear fellow?"

"Of course," I replied.

"That's settled, then," he said as he ushered our guest towards the door, "until tomorrow, Mr. Parker."

I watched Parker from our window as he crossed Baker Street.

"An unusual young man," I said, half to myself.

"Um?" replied my friend retaking his seat and picking up the newspaper, "yes, and an unusual circumstance. An employee who is prepared to fund an investigation from his own pocket. It should prove an interesting little problem."

At the appointed hour the following morning, Holmes and I found ourselves outside the imposing main entrance of the munitions factory. Within seconds of our arrival, our visitor from the previous day appeared.

"Good morning, Mr. Holmes, Doctor. Thank you for coming. If you would like to follow me, I will take you to my father's office in the workshop."

He led us through several wide, hollow corridors, each separated by large timber doors, until we arrived in Dial Square, the workshop at the centre of the factory, which was to be the focus of Holmes's investigation; the workshop itself was vast. The intense heat generated by the giant forges, coupled with the deafening noise and the almost overwhelming smell of cordite instantly transported me back to that hellish day six years earlier at Maiwand.

Young Parker kept shouting over his shoulder – presumably trying to tell us about the various processes involved in the production – but it was impossible to hear what he was saying. We followed him across the workshop floor to a set of timber stairs that led to a row of offices which were situated overlooking the operation. After having apparently arrived at our destination, Parker knocked on the door of one of the offices and entered. He closed the heavy door behind us, blocking out a lot of a noise, before he introduced us.

"Dad, this is Mr. Sherlock Holmes and his friend Dr. Watson. Gentlemen, this is my father, Joe Parker."

The manager of the workshop got up from behind his desk, revealing his stockily built frame and, wearing an expression of intense relief, offered a large hand to greet us.

"Mr. Holmes, Doctor Watson, thank you for coming at such short notice. I think John has told you already that I wanted to be as discreet as I could be, regarding this matter. I haven't told Mr. Cavendish about the thefts and I don't want the police involved if we can help it – it would be a national scandal if it got out that ammunition was going missing from the factory."

The man was clearly nervous about the situation and his own position. He was clearly someone who had worked hard all his life to get the position he was in, but I had the impression that he was more used to overalls and dirty hands than the shirt and tie he now wore. I have often seen the self-made man retain a level of insecurity when raised above his immediate circle and I sensed this was the case with Parker.

"How long have you been the manager of the workshop Mr. Parker?" asked Holmes.

The question took Parker by surprise, "Erm…five years now," he said.

"I'm sure you have nothing to worry about," replied Holmes reassuringly, "Mr. Cavendish would not have appointed you to such a position and left you there for five years if he did not have the complete faith in your abilities."

"I suppose not," said the man in reflexion.

"When were the boxes of ammunition taken?"

"It was just over the weekend, probably because it was quieter than during the week."

"And do you have any theory on who the thieves might be?"

"Well, I do have one name that's been put to me" – Holmes's raised eyebrows prompted Parker to continue – "David Danskin, one of our engineers."

"And presumably this man was working over the weekend?"

"He was," replied the manager with some conviction.

"And why would this person steal anything from the factory?"

"We have a lot of Celtic immigrants working here Mr. Holmes. They come to London from Ireland and Scotland looking for work and often end up in large factories like this. The theory is that Danskin and few of his friends have sympathies with those Fenian anarchists and would look to supply them with ammunition for their seditious activities."

"Where is Danskin from?"

"Fife in Scotland."

"Hardly a hotbed of anarchism," commented Holmes, almost to himself. "How long has Danskin been with you Mr. Parker?"

"He's only been here a year Mr. Holmes. Seems to be an extremely outgoing sort of a chap – makes friends easily and can be quite influential."

"Has he caused any trouble for you in the time that he has been here?"

Parker paused and rubbed his chin in thought, "Well, I don't suppose he has really, now you mention it."

"So why do you suspect him?"

"Well, when we discovered the theft, his foreman told me that he'd recently heard what he thought was seditious gossip on the factory floor."

"Is the foreman on duty now? Can I speak with him?"

"Yes, certainly," said Parker signalling to his son to summon the man.

Some minutes later young Parker appeared with a jolly looking chap in his mid-thirties.

11

"This is Clive Irwin," said the manager, "he's been with us since he was an apprentice and one of our finest."

"Mr. Holmes, Doctor Watson," said Irwin, unable to disguise his enthusiasm, as he wiped his hands on his overalls before offering a formal greeting, "it's a great pleasure to meet you both."

"Mr. Irwin," said Holmes, "talk about your suspicions regarding this Mr. Danskin."

"Well sir," said Irwin, looking a little embarrassed, "it's not really for me to cast aspersions about people but I have been hearing a bit of gossip recently on the workshop floor about these anarchists that seem to be all over the place right now. Danskin is a bit of a popular figure in the brief time he's been here and everybody seems to buzz round him as if they were bees 'round a honeypot."

Holmes smiled at the analogy. "Mr. Parker here tells me that Danskin has only been here for a year."

"Yes, that's right sir. Decent worker but if I were a betting man, I reckon he'll be involved somewhere along the line. He lives on the same street as me and I regularly see lads from the workshop going in and out of the house where he stays – they all live round about themselves."

"I see," said Holmes. My friend then paused his questioning and stared into the middle-distance, tapping his chin lightly with his cane, before announcing, "Well I think our Mr. Danskin is certainly worthy of interest."

Both Parker and Irwin appeared satisfied that their suspicions were justified.

"Would you like me to go and get him then, sir?" asked Irwin.

"No, that won't be necessary just yet," replied Holmes, much to the surprise of those present, "I think we should carry out just a little more investigation before we pounce."

"Very good, sir, as you wish."

"Tell me Mr. Parker, who supplies the coal for the workshop?"

It was such an unusual question, I even found myself a little surprised. Parker spluttered a little as he racked his brains.

"It's Sykes and Sons, the coal merchant at the back of Taylor's Buildings."

"They must have a large operation?"

"Yes, I suppose they do," said Parker, still coming to terms with the strange deviation in Holmes's line of questioning, "as well as the factory, they supply coal to all of the houses in the area."

"I see," said Holmes nodding slowly. "Well then gentleman! I think this morning has been quite productive. Mr. Parker, I am confident we will have the matter resolved in a few days, although I believe the involvement of the official authorities may be unavoidable."

"I feared as much," said the chagrined workshop manager, "at least if you can solve the matter Mr. Holmes, it will lessen any scandal."

"I knew Mr. Holmes would sort it out!" said Irwin, looking at me with great enthusiasm, "I told Mr. Parker here 'if I were a betting man, Mr. Holmes is the man to sort it out.'"

Holmes also turned to me, "Watson, I need to conduct an errand. Can I trust you to look into something before you leave?" – he looked across to the workshop manager – "with your permission of course, Mr. Parker?"

"Of course," repeated the bewildered Parker.

"Excellent! Watson, get me the address of Mr. Danskin and the friends Mr. Irwin suspects of being in league with him."

"John will be able to help you with that Doctor," said Parker.

"No, I can do that Joe," said the enthusiastic Irwin, "perhaps John could show Mr. Holmes out?"

Parker shrugged and nodded his assent.

"Oh, and one more thing," said Holmes turning, as he reached the door, "I would like to know if there has been any change in personnel in the Accounts Office."

"Yes, there has been as a matter of fact," said Parker, "Bob Elliot who worked in there, died suddenly a couple of weeks ago – tragedy it was. He jumped in a pond at Hampstead Heath to save a young lad and got into trouble himself. The boy escaped but poor Bob drowned. Sad business. He was replaced by a young lad in the Accounts Office – I can't remember his name now but I'll get it for you."

"That's right, now you mention it," agreed Irwin, as he clicked his fingers in an attempt to recollect, "Got it! Elijah Watkins, they call that young lad. If I'm not mistaken, I've seen him knocking about Danskin's place an' all."

"That is also interesting. Thank you, gentlemen. Watson, I will see you back in Baker Street this afternoon."

"I'll show you out Mr. Holmes," said John Parker.

Chapter II

By the time I returned to Baker Street that afternoon, Holmes was already there, wading through some old newspapers.

"Ah, Watson, this *is* an interesting little problem," he announced as I entered our sitting room.

"I got the information you wanted Holmes but before we got through it, I wonder if I could get Mrs. Hudson to make us a sandwich?"

"Of course, my dear fellow, you must be famished! Besides, we can do nothing until tomorrow."

"What will happen tomorrow?"

"Later, Watson, later. Let us impose on our landlady first."

The ever-obliging Mrs. Hudson duly arrived some minutes later with an appetising tray of sandwiches and a pot of tea.

Afterwards, I shared the names and addresses of Danskin's friends. "Danskin himself is a lodger at the home of a Mrs. Harrandon on Holgate Street. Apparently, he is also engaged to be married to his landlady's daughter – 'a real cracker' – by all accounts, according to Irwin."

"Really Watson, you're getting as bad as the factory workers for your gossip!" announced Holmes with a smile.

"I'm only relaying what I heard," I replied with a smile of my own. "And I have to say that it is not the only bit of tittle-tattle I have returned with."

"Oh?"

"Clive Irwin gave me his theory as to why Joe Parker was trying to keep this all under his hat. It turns out that young John Parker fell in with the wrong crowd a few years ago and at one point, found himself on the wrong side of the law. Irwin told me that to get him on the straight and narrow, his father convinced Mr. Cavendish to take him on a in the factory. Apparently, Cavendish was unsure at the time but Parker assured him that he would not regret it."

"That would certainly explain why young Parker gave himself that rather non-descript title of 'assistant' when he visited us yesterday," said Holmes.

"Yes, that is what I thought. And clearly his father does not want to highlight the matter in case his son is somehow implicated and his own judgement is therefore called into question.

"When young Parker then escorted me out of the factory, he had his retort on Irwin by suggesting he was a bit of a 'ladies' man.' I'm not sure there is much love lost between the two."

"Perhaps," Holmes said evenly, as he lit a pipe and added with a chuckle, "they certainly seem like a happy workforce."

I showed Holmes the list I had taken from the factory. "Apparently they are all men from the workshop who live in neighbouring streets."

Holmes referred to the piece of paper, "Argyll Road, Bunton Street, Holgate Street...yes I recognise these names," tapping the paper with the stem of his pipe.

"How could you possibly know these streets?" I asked.

"No matter," said my friend infuriatingly, "you have done some fine work in my absence."

I satisfied myself with the rare compliment, "What next?" I asked.

"There isn't much we can do today," he replied, "but the matter should become clearer as the week goes on. Starting tomorrow, Watson. I propose we spend an afternoon in Rochester."

"Rochester?" I asked incredulously, "what on earth can we do there?"

"I'm sure you are not averse to a little sporting flutter."

"Well, no," I stammered. "But haven't we got work to do on the case?"

"We will be working my dear fellow. There is a race meeting in Rochester tomorrow that may clear the fog of our case a little."

He refused to elaborate on the comment until we were in our carriage on the eleven-thirty from St Pancras, the following day. As our train pulled out on that crisp autumn morning, I ask Holmes again.

"Much as I can be amused by a day's horse racing, Holmes, I fail to see how it can help us with the case."

"We are going to Rochester, to speak with a bookie who may be able to help us. You may recall that when we visited Dial Square yesterday, Parker informed us that someone in the accounts department had died tragically around two weeks ago. His name was Bob Elliot and according to the newspaper reports of his death, as well as working at the munitions factory, he was also a bookmaker's clerk for one Isaac Hooper. It is Mr. Hooper we are going to see."

"I see," I said, even though I didn't really see at all. Reluctant as I was to appear even more obtuse, I kept my counsel for the remainder of our journey.

The day was bright and the fine weather had drawn out a large crowd on what was due to be the last meeting of the year. The hustle and bustle of such an event created an excited atmosphere and by the time we entered the track, I was quite looking forward to the day. On the train journey, I had read up on the recent records of those competing and had made a list of horses I would risk a little wager. Meanwhile, Holmes wasn't interested in the going, the form, or the crowds; as soon as we entered, he scanned the long line of bookies until he spotted his man.

"Ha!" he exclaimed with a tap of my arm and a sharp glance.

He indicated towards the line of bookmakers with his cane and I followed him through the burgeoning, noisy crowd until we arrived at the stall under a large sign with the legend *Isaac Hooper, Turf Accountant.* A young man was marking the odds for the horses in the first race on a large chalk board, while an older man I presumed to be Mr. Hooper, called out the latest prices following his tic-tacing to colleagues further along the line. Holmes finally made it to the front of the queue and the bookie broke off from his gesticulating.

"Two shillings on *Spanish Dancer*, please!" called Holmes above the din.

"Two shillings on Spanish Dancer, sir!" repeated the bookie for the benefit of his young colleague.

"I see you have a new clerk, Mr. Hooper," shouted Holmes, "the last time I was here, you had that chap Elliot working for you. I was so sorry to hear of his untimely demise."

The man looked at Holmes questioningly, as though trying to place him. Having decided that he did not recognise him and therefore accepting him at face value simply as a regular racegoer, he responded to my friend's comment.

"Well, he wasn't working for me by the time he met his end," he said, apparently with an air of some resentment, "I had to let him go. Fell in with the wrong crowd he did and, in the end, he was more trouble than he was worth."

"Oh, I'm sorry to hear that," said Holmes taking his betting ticket from the man.

"Well, R.I.P., eh?" said the bookie, clearly bringing the short exchange to its conclusion as the customers behind Holmes waved their money at him.

"Would you like to sit in the grandstand Holmes?" I asked as we extricated ourselves from the throng.

"No, I think I will remain here for the afternoon Watson. You go ahead and watch the racing."

"You mean you're not even going to watch? You've come all this way, just to ask one question?"

"Oh, I will be watching," he replied cryptically, "watching and observing."

I knew it was futile to try and dissuade him from his course of action, so I left him to it.

It proved to be a profitable afternoon for us both. I enjoyed three winners and a second place; by the time I found Holmes again – standing next to a pillar not far from where I had left him – he wore an equally satisfied expression.

"Success Holmes?" I asked.

"Indeed," he replied with a smile. "Now, back to Baker Street."

That evening over dinner Holmes dismissed my attempts to discuss the case in any great detail. The only thing I could get out of him was:

"Tomorrow should see some significant developments. I must go out quite early and will be away for most of the day."

"Can I be of any assistance?"

"No, it's a day for clandestine operations and as useful as you have been so far, I'm afraid my trusted comrade will have to be patient on this occasion until I return."

I satisfied myself with Holmes's affable mood and his complimentary remarks about my contribution to the case. We spoke little more about it for the rest of the evening and by the time I went down to our sitting room for breakfast the next morning, he had already left.

Once Mrs. Hudson cleared my dishes away, she informed me that she too was leaving for the day, to visit a friend in Islington who had fallen ill. I was therefore left alone to idle the day away; I caught up on some reading and went out at one point for a stroll. As I wandered aimlessly around the bustling streets that encircled our lodgings, I couldn't help wondering what my friend was up to. When my absentmindedness almost caused me to be run over by a fast-moving hansom on Marylebone Road – much to the displeasure of the cabbie – I decided it was time to return home and simply wait for Holmes's reappearance. It came around four o'clock and was one I am hardly likely to forget.

I had been dozing over the newspaper in front of the fire when I heard the front door opening. Hearing a heavy footstep on the stairs I raised myself from my slumber; as I folded my paper the door opened.

"Good afternoon," said my friend matter-of-factly.

I stared in disbelief at the sight. Holmes had revealed himself with his greeting but had he not done so, it's unlikely I would have recognised him. He wore large hob-nail boots, knee-length gaiters, a longer leather smock and coalman's backing hat which reached the middle of his back. His hands a face was blackened with soot and as he removed his hat, the almost comical sight of a perfectly clean ring around his forehead appeared.

"Holmes what have you been doing?" As soon as the question had left my lips, even I realised the absurdity of it.

"I have been on my rounds, Watson," said my friend, continuing to lever himself out of his disguise.

At this moment, the questions that filled my mind and had been hitherto jostling for attention, were set to one side as I realised Holmes had trailed a film of soot through the room and no doubt up the stairs.

"What about Mrs. Hudson?" I asked incredulously.

My comment seemed to take Holmes aback as he stopped what he was doing momentarily, "Mrs. Hudson? What's wrong with Mrs. Hudson?"

"Nothing at the moment, but I'm sure that will change as soon as she sees this mess."

For the first time, Holmes looked at the floor and the trail he had left.

"Yes, I suppose I have created a little work for her," he said in a typically carefree manner.

"*A little work!* Where have you been?" I asked, returning to the matter at hand.

"I have been back to Woolwich. When I left you at the factory the other day, I visited Sykes and Sons, the coal suppliers in the area. I was told that today was the delivery day for the streets you identified when I left you. As Mr. Danskin and his confederates live in that area, it was a perfect opportunity to learn a little more about these characters. A small bribe to the working man is rarely refused Watson and the shift manager at Sykes and Sons was no exception. He allowed me to carry out the delivery this week and here I am," – he placed his fists in the small of his back and stretched – "a little stiff perhaps and a bit worse for wear but satisfied nonetheless at another productive days' work."

Before I could question him further, I heard the front door again.

"That will be Mrs. Hudson," I said in a hushed tone.

"Ah, excellent," announce Holmes, "I will impose on her to organise a bath for me."

I stood for a moment, looking at the man in disbelief before accepting that as an invitation to withdraw.

"Well, I'll leave to you to it. You enjoy your bath and I will resume our conversation later."

I crept out of our sitting room and tip-toed up the stairs to my bedroom, just as I heard the first gasp from Mrs. Hudson in the hall below.

"*Mr. Holmes!*" I heard her cry as I closed my bedroom door quietly.

For the next two hours I remained quiet, listening to the exasperating muffled cries of the most patient landlady in

London. Finally, at shortly after six o'clock, I ventured downstairs again to our sitting room. I found Holmes sitting in his chair, bathed and already changed into his night shirt and long dressing gown; his uncreamed hair flopped over his brow and he was staring into the fire. I glanced round the room and couldn't see a spec of soot anywhere.

"Everything all right?" I asked.

"Ah, yes I feel much better after a nice hot bath, thank you."

"And Mrs. Hudson?"

"Mrs. Hudson? Why do you keep asking about Mrs. Hudson? Is something wrong with her?"

"Never mind," I said.

"She will be up shortly with our dinner. I will tell you all about my day's adventures then."

He tossed his cigarette into the fire just as our landlady entered with a tray, containing a pot of tea and two silver domes.

"Good evening, Mrs. Hudson," I said, "did you enjoy your visit to your friend? I do hope she is feeling better."

"Yes, she is Doctor, thank you. The most upsetting part of the day was when I returned home." The latter comment was made looking at Holmes, who remained oblivious to the poor woman's lot.

"Oh dear," I said trying to sound as ignorant about the situation as possible.

Once she had left, I then returned to the subject of the case.

"So, to whom did you speak today?"

"Everyone I wanted to. My first call was on Holgate Street to the home of Mrs. Harrandon, Danskin's landlady. When I knocked, a younger woman answered the door – what a pretty young thing she was."

I raised my eyebrows at such an uncharacteristic comment.

"It turned out to be Danskin's fiancée, Miss Georgina Harrandon. She was as pleasant as she was pretty, offering to make me a cup of tea on such a chilly morning."

"'Go on then Miss,' I said, 'I wouldn't say no. I'll just get the other bag.'"

"I carried two bags down the lane adjacent to the house and deposited them by the bunker in the back yard of the house.

"'I don't think you've been round here before?'" she asked, as she brought two mugs out of the kitchen.

"'No Miss, I'm fairly new to this round.'"

"We chatted for a while and I offered to load the coal into the bunker. Before she could reply, a man came out into the yard – it was none other than the man himself, Mr. Danskin. He isn't particularly tall but he's a well-built man with jet-black hair and a matching moustache."

"'Naw, a'll dee it, pal,' he said, overhearing my offer.

"'If you like.'

"He gave his fiancé an affectionate squeeze. 'Awright hen?'

"'Hello Davey, good night was it?'

"'Aye, no bad, a'm looking forward to ma bed mind you.'

"'Been on the night shift I take it,' I asked.

"'Aye just at the factory round the corner,' he replied.

"'You sound as though you are a long way from home?'

"'Aye, cem down frae Scotland last year.'

"'And how'd you find it being down here?'"

"'Aye, it's grand, the footba's good and women are nice,' he said with a smile, giving his fiancé another squeeze and a peck on the check, for which he received a playing pat on the arm.

"'*You!*' she said, laughing, 'you think more of the daft football than you do of me!'

"'Well, thanks for the tea, Miss,' I said draining my mug and handing in back, 'I'll bid you both a good morning.'

"Danskin certainly seems a charismatic figure. I can see how people are drawn to him. I left them both in jovial spirits and carried on with my round. I visited all of the main cast in our little play, either speaking to them personally and their respective landladies. It is quite remarkable the things you can pick up from people through seemingly meaningless, polite conversation. The trick is to never let them think their information can be of the slightest importance to you; if they think they are demonstrating their superior knowledge, or that they are simply participating in backstreet gossip, you are likely to get everything you need to know. I even called in at the Royal Oak public house where I learned Danskin and his friends meet. The landlord was a garrulous fellow!" concluded Holmes with a laugh.

"So, it sounds like a productive day?" I asked.

"Yes, all in all, it was a very productive day," said Holmes, as he lifted the dome from his plate.

Chapter III

The following day was a slow day with not much to occupy my friend's great mind. The last thing he told me the previous evening was that he was expecting some correspondence from the munitions factory that should prove to be the last piece of the puzzle. Being a Sunday, it was unlikely he would receive this vital piece of information for another twenty-four hours at least. He spent most of the morning impatiently drumming his fingers on the arm of his chair and grinding his teeth. The atmosphere of our sitting room gradually became thicker and thicker with the smoke from his strong coarse tobacco until I could barely see him on the other side of the hearth.

"Why don't we go outside and you can clear your head, Holmes?" I suggested after lunch.

Holmes snorted his contempt.

"This is doing you no good," I persisted, "you are just torturing yourself unnecessarily."

He reached for the Persian slipper once more and found it empty. Slumping back into his seat and glancing round the room, he finally relented.

"I suppose you are right, there is little else we can do on such a stagnant day as this."

Getting away from the fug of our sitting room did us both the world of good and even Holmes's mood brightened somewhat. We walked through Hyde Park, where a group of hardy souls were sitting around the bandstand, being entertained by a military ensemble. Young couples walked arm in arm and found themselves giving way on the wide pathways to the occasional carriage or cyclist who rode past. It was when Holmes saw a young man playing ball with his son that he broached the subject of the case for the first time.

"Amongst other things on my round, I discovered that our man Danskin has arranged a meeting with his confederates on Wednesday at the Royal Oak Inn."

"What do you propose to do?" I asked.

"We shall be there too. And much to Mr. Parker's chagrin, I shall be forced to invite Inspector Lestrade."

"I see. And what about the correspondence you are waiting for?"

"I expect it to be a mere confirmation of what I believe already. Providing we receive it tomorrow, I fully expect to have the matter concluded on Wednesday."

Holmes was to have his satisfaction the following day. The young page came up to our room around eleven o'clock.

"Letter for you Mr. Holmes."

"Thank you, Billy!" replied Holmes, leaping from his chair, snatching the jack-knife from the mantlepiece, taking the letter from the silver tray and slitting open the envelope all in one flowing movement. "*Ha!* Just as I thought."

"So, you will be reaching out to Lestrade then?" I asked.

"I will," he said. "*Billy?*" he shouted after the boy who was descending the stairs to resume his duties.

"Yes, sir," shouted Billy eagerly as he ran back along the landing.

Holmes was now seated at his desk scribbling two telegrams. He handed them to the page-boy, "See that these are sent immediately. Then come back to me this afternoon when I will have another letter for you to deliver."

"Right away, sir," replied to the young lad, who was already on the half turn as he took the first two notes.

"Now what?" I asked.

"We wait," said Holmes, "there is little we can do for another forty-eight hours."

He spent some time writing the third note he had referred to and even had the decency to explain that, whereas the first two were to Parker and Lestrade, asking to meet us at the Royal Oak on Wednesday, this more detailed missive was again to the policeman. This time however, he was giving Lestrade more details about the case that would allow him to effect an arrest.

Holmes then refilled his pipe and sat contentedly by the fire. One of the many traits I have notice in my friend during the years we have spent together is his strange attitude towards waiting. When he is waiting for information that is not forthcoming, he can be irritable and rude; when he is simply waiting for the denouement of a case, however, he can be the polar opposite: patient and sanguine.

So, it was for the next two days. Apart from receiving replies to his two telegrams, Holmes barely moved from his chair, sitting with his eyes closed and a contented smile upon his face. Then, at the appointed hour on Wednesday 1st December, we donned our outdoor wear once more and set off for Woolwich.

The temperature had dropped, as if to usher in the first day of winter and as we crossed Westminster Bridge, I noticed a carpet of mist had covered the river. Big Ben struck two o'clock.

"Our munitions workers should be filling their tankards and taking their seats about now," said Holmes, "I asked Lestrade and Parker to meet us at half past outside the inn."

Our cab gradually took us away from the activity of the capital towards the narrow, labyrinthine streets, beside which incongruously stood the largest munitions factory in the Empire. As we neared our destination, the blackened buildings – some of which were plastered with faded old newspaper advertisements – acted as supports for lines of lank washing that drooped from one side of the street to the other. We eventually arrived at the Royal Oak Public House at twenty-five past two. Parker, the manager from

Dial Square, his son and his foreman, Irwin were already there waiting for us.

"Excellent!" Holmes said flashing a glance to me as we alighted the cab. "Good afternoon, gentlemen!"

"Mr. Holmes; Doctor." Parker's tone was a mixture of nerves and relief that the matter was about to be resolved.

"Ah!" cried Holmes, looking down the street, "and here comes Inspector Lestrade now."

The inspector climbed down from the horse drawn police wagon and proceeded to walk towards us with one of his uniformed officers.

"He'll need more than that," I heard the eager Irwin say to young Parker under his breath.

"Good afternoon, Inspector!" said Holmes as Lestrade approached.

"Mr. Holmes; Doctor; gentlemen."

"Now, is everything in place?"

"I think so, Mr. Holmes. I received your correspondence, so providing what you tell me is true, there should be no difficulty."

"Excellent!" repeated Holmes.

There was then a pause in the proceedings that could only have lasted a few seconds, but somehow strangely felt longer. I looked across the street through the window of the inn and wondered how many men were in there. The same thought must have crossed the mind of Joe Parker who asked rather nervously.

"Far be it from me to tell you your business, Mr. Holmes, but won't the Inspector need more than one officer and a small Wagon, to round these villains up?"

"Yes, what time's the raiding party turning up?" asked Irwin with a smile of anticipation.

"Oh, we won't be going into the public house ourselves," said Holmes, casually.

We all turned as one to look at the consulting detective.

"Not going in?" repeated Parker.

"There is no need," said Holmes, himself, looking across the street at the establishment.

"I don't understand," said the manager of the workshop.

"There is no need, my dear Parker, because the perpetrator of the thefts that have been the cause of your immeasurable discomfort is right here."

"I don't..." the phrase died on Parker's lips.

"I must apologise, my dear fellow but Watson here will tell you that I never can resist a touch of the dramatic. You see there *has* been a conspiracy to steal ammunition from the factory – but it is not Mr. Danskin and *his* confederates who are guilty, it was Mr. Irwin here and *his*. Or should I say, confederate, singular."

Everyone in turn looked at Irwin, whose expression had changed from one of smugness to one of nervous improvisation.

"What?" he bluffed unconvincingly, "what nonsense. If I were a betting m-"

"If you were a betting man, Mr. Irwin?" interrupted Holmes, "that appears to be one of your favourite phrases is it not? But the truth of course, is that you *are* a betting man. Very fond of betting but sadly, not particularly good *at* it."

"That's..." Irwin could offer nothing in reply.

"That's quite enough," announced Holmes, "no more lies. Inspector, I suggest you take this man away."

Lestrade nodded to his constable who handcuffed the workshop foreman and led him away towards the small wagon.

"Gentlemen," said Lestrade as he touched the brim of his hat and followed the two.

Joe Parker stood bemused, watching the prisoner being led away. "I don't understand Mr. Holmes."

29

I had every sympathy with the man. Although Holmes had surely solved the case there was almost a feeling of anti-climax about the whole thing.

"Could I make a suggestion?" asked Holmes, "why don't we impose on our landlord opposite and I will explain the chain of events that have brought us to this point."

The three of us agreed and crossed the street to the Royal Oak. I had almost forgotten about the meeting of the Dial Square workers which I thought was the purpose of our visit. We entered and around twenty of the men were gathered in the far corner of the establishment. They were deep in their own conversation and didn't notice us enter; Holmes suggested we sit away from the men and leave them to their business, while he would share with us the series of events that led to Irwin's arrest.

Before he could, the landlord came over and asked what we would like to drink.

"Four glasses of beer if you please," said Parker, "I think this is my treat."

"Certainly gentlemen," said the landlord. As he turned, he stopped and looked at Holmes, "I'm sorry sir, but do I know you from somewhere?"

"I don't think so, landlord," said my friend with an enigmatic smile.

"My apologies, sir," said the man turning away with a headshake and a knitted brow. "Must have mistaken you for someone else."

"Now Holmes," I said, "you have kept us in suspense long enough."

"Quite right," he said as he began his narrative. "When I left you the other day in the office, young John here escorted me back out of the factory. On the way I asked if I could meet Elijah Watkins, the man who took over from Bob Elliot in the Accounts Office following his sudden demise.

"Watkins informed me that, although it appeared that the boxes of ammunition had been removed over the weekend as you suggested Mr. Parker, it was actually part of a consignment that had been delayed for over a month. So, the missing boxes had been stolen some weeks earlier, but the loss hadn't been discovered until the final paperwork had been signed off and returned to the office. It was then that Watkins discovered the discrepancy. I asked him to go back through the records for two years to see if there were any similar discrepancies. He found no fewer than eight."

"Presumably, this was the letter you were waiting for on Monday?" I asked.

"Indeed," confirmed Holmes. "This was the final piece of information I needed to alert Lestrade.

"I can't believe it," said Parker, "Clive Irwin's been with us for years. I've known him since he was a young apprentice. How could he fiddle the paperwork without being found out? And why would he?"

"This is where the mystery deepens and becomes a little more sinister, Mr. Parker. The main instigator of this larceny was not actually Irwin, it was Elliot, the man who was Watkins's predecessor in the Accounts Office. His avarice and stupidity had led him to become entangled with some particularly unsavoury characters.

Our talkative landlord here told me the other day that Elliot used to meet one such character in here on a regular basis."

"I thought you said you didn't know the landlord," asked Parker.

Holmes waved the question off as an irrelevance and continued his narrative.

"From his description of the man Elliot met, I believe him to be Grigory Yubkin. He is a Russian dissident and a key agent in the huge criminal underworld of London; he is also suspected of sourcing and supplying illegal arms and munitions to various anarchist groups on behalf of greater minds than his. By weaving his web around Elliot, he had the perfect channel to the factory, through which he could obtain a seemingly endless supply of munitions."

"So, Elliot would falsify the records?" I said.

"But he needed someone on the workshop floor to help him conceal and despatch the boxes themselves," added Parker.

"Excellent gentlemen!" cried Holmes, "Excellent. And of course, he found such an ally in our man Irwin. With the vast quantities of munitions being produced to fight our seemingly endless wars, Elliot and Irwin concentrated on small amounts, just one or two boxes that could be easily concealed and lost among the reams and reams of paperwork that facilitate such an operation."

The landlord brought over our drinks and laid them on the table in front of us, all the while peering at Holmes with a curious expression, as if he were trying to place him. He walked away again shaking his head, as my smiling friend rasped a match against the side of the box and lit a cigarette.

"When Watson and I went to the race meeting in Rochester, I spoke with Mr. Hooper, the bookmaker with whom Elliot worked for as a clerk in his spare time. I had suspected that Elliot's death wasn't quite as sudden as newspaper reports would have you believe and completely unprompted, Hooper voiced his own suspicions regarding his former clerk's demise. I believe that Elliot crossed the wrong people too often and paid for it with his life."

"But the newspaper reports said he died saving the young boy," said Parker.

"What young boy?" asked Holmes, "I found that no young boy or his family were ever identified and there were no witnesses to the incident. And why would Elliot be at Hampstead Heath in the first place when it is well over ten miles from his lodgings in Woolwich? No, no, my dear fellow. The stories would have been an act of convenience and distraction – concocted by the people of influence who had Elliot removed. Elliot dies a hero and the perpetrators of this crime and others go about their business completely unsuspected."

"So how do you think Irwin became involved?" I asked.

"While I was standing observing the crowd," resumed Holmes, "none other than our friend Irwin appeared at the stall of Mr. Hooper. As their discussion became quite animated, I moved closer to hear what was being said. Despite the hub-hub of the crowd, their raised voices told me enough of what I needed to know: Irwin had accumulated significant gambling debts. With the income from his nefarious activity with Elliot now cut off, he had resorted to asking for credit, not only from Hooper – who presumably knew him through his association with his former clerk and was now giving him summary treatment – but from the other bookies along the line as well."

"But it was Clive who brought the theft to my attention in the first place," said Parker, still struggling to come to terms with the apparent betrayal of his friend and colleague.

"It was actually Elijah Watkins who brought it to *his* attention," replied Holmes. "Watkins discovered Elliot's falsification of the records from a month earlier and checked with Irwin how many boxes had been dispatched. Once Irwin was struck with the realisation that the batch had been delayed and the implications of the discovery, he knew he had to act to divert attention away from Elliot and ultimately himself. This is when he raised the matter with you my dear Parker and planted the seed of doubt regarding the honourable Mr. Danskin over there." Holmes indicated the man in the far corner of the inn who – oblivious to our presence – appeared to be holding the attention of his colleagues.

"But why Danskin?" I asked.

"Why not?" asked Holmes, "Irwin needed someone to implicate in the crime and Danskin was as good as anyone. He was relatively new to the factory and Irwin was jealous of how popular he had become in such a short space of time."

"He was also jealous of his fiancé," added young John Parker, the first time he had spoken. "He often spoke of her and lucky how the Scotsman was. If *I* were a betting man, I would say he had designs on her too."

Holmes laughed at young Parker's comment before resuming, "So by removing Danskin he would divert attention away from himself and clear the way to indulge in his other vulgar pastime."

The workshop manager then satisfied himself that Danskin could not possibly have been involved.

"And because Watkins discovered discrepancies going back at least two years, there is no way Danskin could have been involved, given that he has only been with us for twelve months."

"Precisely," said Holmes.

"The irony is that it was Irwin who suggested I kept it away from a police enquiry," said Parker. "That's when I thought of you Mr. Holmes after reading of your work."

"*Ha!* He would have been better suggesting that the police should get involved – that way he would have had a greater chance of evading capture!"

"Now I have the unenviable task of approaching Mr. Cavendish with the whole sordid affair," said the workshop manager.

"If he is the reasonable man, I believe him to be," said Holmes, "I'm sure he will not apportion any blame to yourself or young John here. And besides, you are not giving him a problem, you are clearing up a problem."

"It still leaves the issue of the missing ammunition, Holmes," I said.

"That is a much bigger issue, Watson. The network into which the munitions disappeared cannot be unravelled over a glass of beer in Woolwich. That considerable task will have to wait for another day," – he raised his glass – "let us be satisfied that we have resolved this little problem."

"I'll drink to that," said Parker, prompting his son and myself to follow suit.

"There is one other thing, Holmes," I asked, looking over towards the munitions workers who were still deep in conversation, "if Danskin and his friends are not here as conspirators, what *are* they doing?

Holmes smiled.

"Something that is completely innocent and unconnected, Watson. Mr. Danskin is a keen player of Association Football," – he turned to Parker – "you are probably not aware Mr. Parker that he is attempting to organise a team that will represent the workshop and the factory."

"Well, I'll be!" said the workshop manager scratching his head, "it's been a day of surprises all round."

Two weeks after our visit to the Royal Oak, I returned to Baker Street after having carried out a little Christmas shopping. I found Holmes at his chemistry table, working on some malodorous experiment. I sat in front of the fire and leafed through the morning paper.

"Holmes" I declared, "remember our encounter with Mr. Danskin at Woolwich? Well, he must have been successful in raising that team you were telling me about. Listen to this:

The recently formed Dial Square Football Club played its first fixture on Saturday against Eastern Wanderers. It proved a successful start for the team from the munitions factory in Woolwich who ran out

6-0 winners in the encounter on the Isle of Dogs. The victorious team was captained by their Scottish defender David Danskin, who works as an engineer at the factory.

"How wonderful!" I declared, "good old Danskin."

"Each man to his own interest, I suppose," was my friend's disinterested reply.

The Continental Conspiracy

Chapter I

Sherlock Holmes became involved in many political cases during his long and illustrious career, many of which could not be related at the time because of their sensitive nature. Perhaps the most sensitive of all was the case that took him to the Continent in the spring of '87. The investigation would have significant ramifications for the government in London and its counterparts in virtually all the capitals of Europe.

After many years and given that most of those involved are no longer living, I feel as though I am now on safe ground laying out part of the narrative regarding this incredibly complex and intricate case. I would stress that what I am about to relate is only one thread of a tangled skein in which Holmes found himself embroiled. The particular loose end that my friend discovered, eventually led to the unravelling of the whole conspiracy and resulted in Holmes becoming the toast of Europe. Such acknowledgement, however, almost came at the highest possible cost to his own wellbeing.

The early months of the particular year in question proved physically and mentally draining for both Holmes and myself but for very different reasons. I had caught a chill during the preceding Christmas holidays that gradually worsened and developed into a nasty bout of pneumonia. I knew that I would need complete rest and specialized treatment, so I therefore made some enquiries and received permission to return to the Royal Victoria at Netley for a brief period of recuperation.

Little did I know at the time that the period would be one of several weeks, as my condition initially showed little sign of improvement; and then finally, when I did begin to recover, it was at a glacial pace.

During my convalescence I was unable to keep in touch with Holmes and was therefore unaware of any adventure in which he may have found himself. It was only when I returned to London in early April that I learned that he had left for the Continent and had been gone for several weeks. Feeling much better myself, it was on the morning of the 14th when I was reading the newspaper full of the resignation of the Secretary of State for Foreign Affairs, that I received the telegram informing me that Holmes was ill and needed my assistance in Lyon. I made arrangements to catch the Continental Express later that night.

I have previously described the desperate condition in which I found him and I was keen to get him back to London. I gathered up the carpet of congratulatory telegrams and stuffed them into a bag, bundled Holmes into a cab and headed for the station, intent on getting us back to London as soon as possible.

No sooner had we arrived than it occurred to me to accept the open invitation from my old comrade, Colonel Hayter, to stay with him in his home in Reigate. I convinced Holmes that it would do us both the world of good and – drained as he was, after his mammoth investigation – he reluctantly agreed with a gesture. I emptied the bag of telegrams and crammed them into my old despatch box, fully intending to read them upon our return. Returning the bag to Holmes and packing one for myself, off we went. Little did I know however, that our trip would result in yet another case for Holmes but thankfully, it turned out to be a blessing in disguise as it proved once again that the best stimulant for the consulting detective was *work*.

We returned to London invigorated by our sojourn to Surrey and again, I tried to ask Holmes about his investigations in France.

"Not right now," he replied darkly, "let's leave that for another day."

Through long experience I had learned the wisdom of obedience and I respected his comment by never mentioning it again. Imagine my surprise when Holmes himself raised the matter a year-and-a-half later, following the investigation into the unfortunate Mr. Melas. That case had been brought to Holmes by his brother Mycroft whom I had met for the first time. As if the revelation in learning of Holmes's brother wasn't enough, when we were back in our sitting room, I was further surprised when Sherlock Holmes informed me that he had regular contact with Mycroft over the years, and the two had discussed many a case together.

"Take the Continental affair last year," he remarked casually.

"The one that took you to France?"

"Not only to France, but also to Amsterdam and Geneva."

He explained that a few days after I had left to convalesce at Netley, Mycroft summoned him to the Diogenes Club and demanded that he investigate, "'...a matter of national importance!'" Holmes lit a pipe and waved an arm as he imitated his brother with a flourish. Sir Richard Rosendale, the British Ambassador to France had been assassinated while at an official function in a Paris hotel.

"I had read of the killing in the newspaper and asked my brother why it was not a matter for the French police and Scotland Yard."

"'That is just the point, my dear boy,' was his reply, 'The French authorities are refusing to involve Scotland Yard, claiming the poor man's demise is strictly a domestic matter. The Prime Minister doesn't want to kick up a fuss and cause an international scandal in his first twelve months in office but equally, he is deeply mistrustful of the French and wants someone from this side of the Channel to investigate the ambassador's death. He wants the matter dealt with as discreetly as possible Sherlock, and I know that you are just the man!'"

"So that was me," said Holmes, as he prepared to tell me of his adventure, "bags packed and off to Paris. Little did I know at the time that the case would take me into three countries and last over two months.

"Apparently, the killing took place when the ambassador excused himself from his table during the function. When the alarm was raised, people rushed to the cloakroom to find him lying in a pool of blood, dead from gunshot wounds. There were no apparent witnesses and a Moroccan waiter was quickly arrested and charged with the murder."

"On what grounds?" I asked.

"Basically, on the grounds that he was a Moroccan waiter!" Holmes was not being facetious. "He lived on his own in a modest dwelling; he had no family in Paris and certainly had no motive to murder a British diplomat or anyone else for that matter.

"The staff in the hotel had a little area where they kept their personal possessions. When our man's belongings were searched, a gun was found among them. He claimed to know nothing about it but that didn't stop the enthusiastic – if easily led – *Sûreté* to arrest him and charge him immediately with the murder. Fortunately for him, the detective assigned to the case was Francois Le Villard, who I subsequently met for the first time. Of equal good fortune to the poor immigrant was the appointment of Monsieur Duclos to represent him as his lawyer – one of the few honest and decent men of that profession in Paris.

"Mycroft had wired ahead to Duclos through the British Embassy and he had managed to delay any thought of a hasty trial – and presumably conviction – pending further investigation. By the time I arrived there, almost a week after the assassination, Le Villard and Duclos had virtually unpicked the allegation against our Moroccan friend. The case fell apart within days; not only was it proven that he did not own the gun that was found amongst his things, but the gun itself still had a full chamber and showed no signs of being fired – hardly the work of a master criminal. Inference? It was planted by some incompetent buffoon, who was seeking to set up an innocent, vulnerable bystander. The prosecutor quite rightly dismissed the case."

I contemplated this fantastic adventure I had missed. It seemed that – at the time – political assassinations had become a scourge around the world and on the face of it, Sir Richard had just been the latest victim of some anarchist or disgruntled extremist. But there was another line of enquiry that interested the British Government. Prior to Holmes's departure, Mycroft had appraised his brother of a letter written by Sir Richard's personal aid – a man called Winterburn – to a friend of his in the Home Office.

In it, Winterburn expressed his concerns for Sir Richard's safety. The ambassador had apparently discovered some unusual activity involving a shipping company based in Amsterdam who had major trade routes to the Far East. Without elaborating on his thoughts and before Sir Richard could make his findings official – after all, why would the ambassador to France be concerned with a shipping company in the Netherlands? – he was murdered. The letter from Winterburn had been brought to the attention of the Prime Minister who wanted to know if the ambassador's findings and his murder were connected in any way.

This had all taken place while I was in my hospital bed at Netley and I was completely oblivious to the complexities of the matter. I was full of curiosity, "So what happened next?"

"Duclos's work was done, but I then formed an interesting working relationship with Le Villard. I must say I was impressed by the young man's enthusiasm. His observational and deduction skills are excellent; this, coupled with a basic common sense and a willingness to learn, makes me believe there is the makings of a fine detective there.

"It was obvious that the Moroccan did not murder the ambassador, but who did? By the time I arrived in Paris, Le Villard already had the guest list of those attending the dinner, waiting for me. The event was an annual gala hosted by the French Government to which officials from all the foreign consulates and embassies in Paris were invited."

"Who discovered the body of Sir Richard?" I asked.

"Excellent, Watson!"

It was one of those occasions when I could never quite work out if Holmes was being complimentary or condescending. I ignored his exclamation however and encouraged him to continue.

"It was an official from the French Foreign Ministry who discovered the body."

"What did this official report to the police?"

"He stated that he was just passing the cloakroom when he discovered the body."

"*Passing* the cloakroom and yet the body was *inside* the cloakroom."

"All a little too convenient, wouldn't you say? It was the same man who suggested the waiter may have been the assassin."

"Despite him not witnessing the incident."

"Indeed."

"Did anyone else hear shots fired?"

"Watson, you are on scintillating form today! No, they did not, and that is a very distinctive point. By acting with such enthusiastic haste, the French official only succeeded in attracting attention to himself. It seems thereafter that poor Le Villard was warned off from digging too deeply into the individual by some of his superiors."

"But that didn't stop *you*."

Holmes glanced across at me and smiled, "It would have been a pity to go all that way for nothing."

Chapter II

Holmes's Continental investigation would eventually lead to the arrest and conviction of one of the most notorious criminals in Europe. Neither he, nor anyone else, could have predicted such an eventuality however, as the detective set out from London on that late winter morning.

It would be the vague letter sent by the ambassador's aid – and shared with Holmes by his brother Mycroft – that would provide my friend with a thread to pick at, and one which would ultimately unravel numerous illicit schemes and plots around Europe, where the lines between officialdom and crime organisations became so blurred, they became almost indecipherable.

The public is now aware that, following Holmes's work, the Netherland-Sumatra Company was established by the Germanic-Franco-Dutch nobleman Baron Maupertuis. He took advantage of the confusion caused by the war between the Dutch and their colony in the East Indies to start his own illicit trade route between the Far East and Europe. Illegal goods were shipped between the two continents; war and a lack of regulation at one end, bribery and corruption at the other, each created a perfect channel for the villain to exploit. With his status and initial reputation for success, Maupertuis had no difficulty attracting backers for the venture and within five years of its launch, the vast profits being made by the company for its *shareholders*, as he called them, began to attract the attention of governments around the continent.

However, instead of performing even the most rudimentary of checks into the practices of the company, and instead of conducting any robust audit of the accounts, the profits being generated for the benefits of the investors sadly created a wilful blindness amongst the authorities of Europe.

Although he had *heard* of Maupertuis, Holmes was completely unaware of the extent of the wrongdoing perpetrated by the villain and his network of activity when he set out for the Continent to investigate the killing of the British Ambassador. But as history teaches us – regardless of duration – such schemes only have a finite period and inevitably in the case of Maupertuis, the time came when the wrongdoing and malpractice generated by those associated with the Netherland-Sumatra Company couldn't be concealed any longer – that time came with the killing of Sir Richard Rosendale.

Once in Paris – thanks to Mycroft's influence – Holmes gained access to the ambassador's residence within the British Embassy.

"I questioned Winterburn, the aid, and asked him about the letter he wrote."

"'Well sir, I don't really know. Sir Richard confided in me that he had come by some information that could have some consequences for the Foreign Office.' The man was frightened, Watson.

"'Consequences?' I asked.

"Winterburn was hesitant, 'Well I don't really know the details, sir. I would regularly join him in his study for a night cap after the staff had all turned in. Over a drink we would chat about various issues. I think he saw it as a kind of therapy – a way of unburdening himself from the troubles of the role.'

"'And what troubles was he dealing with?'

"'Well, that's just the thing, sir. In the week before he died' – Winterburn had to pause for a moment and compose himself, his distress still evident – 'I had the impression that he wanted to tell me something about the information he had obtained but he dare not. It was most unlike him. Then on the night of the gala dinner itself, he almost seemed reluctant to go. Perhaps I am reading too much into it with the benefit of hindsight but I remember his wife was ready before he was, which was an extremely unusual occurrence.'

'"Almost as though he expected danger?'

'"Well, that's how it looks to me now Mr. Holmes, but maybe I am guilty of fitting the question to the answer rather than the other way around.'

'"Perhaps Mr. Winterburn, but it seems a plausible hypothesis, given what we now know. Speaking of Lady Rosendale, where is she now?'

'"She returned to Berkshire sir, to stay with family.' He reflected and shook his head, 'poor woman, they were devoted to each other. I don't know what she will do now.'

'"Did anyone visit the embassy shortly after the assassination?'

"Winterburn's demeanour changed markedly. He snapped out of his reverie thinking about Lady Rosendale, and a saturnine expression came over him.

'"Yes, sir. The morning following the murder – just as we were all learning of the killing – officials claiming to be from the French government came to the embassy and asked to see Sir Richard's office and apartment. We were all in a state of shock and confusion as to what was happening and looking back, I must confess that I mistakenly allowed them free reign. I never thought anything of it at the time. I didn't know what was going on but now I think about it, it was if they knew exactly what they were looking for. They weren't here very long and left with a box full of papers. I was surprised when Inspector Le Villard came along later that morning. I told him of the officials earlier visit and it seemed clear to me that he had not authorised it. When the inspector and I entered Sir Richard's study, it was obvious that it had been thoroughly searched as the draws were all open and papers were strewn across his desk. I couldn't be sure exactly what they had seized but after the inspector left, I went up to Sir Richard's sitting room and was relieved to find his personal journal was still there. I couldn't bring myself to read it but it may be of some use.'

"'I think that will be extremely useful, Mr. Winterburn,' I said as he handed it to me, 'thank you for your time and assistance.'"

Holmes left Winterburn and went to speak with Le Villard. When he asked the French detective about the matter, he confirmed Winterburn's story and said he knew nothing about the confiscation. The local man questioned his colleagues and confirmed to Holmes that no one connected with the investigation into the murder had removed anything from the ambassador's quarters.

"This was suggestive, Watson," said Holmes, re-filling his pipe, "if it wasn't the police who removed the items, it could only have been someone from the French diplomatic service. The items removed would have been of no interest to common thieves and no one else other than government officials could ever wish to gain access to the embassy."

I followed Holmes's train of thought, "The suggestion being that there was something among Sir Richard's papers that someone wanted kept hidden. And you obviously suspected these characters of carrying out this brazen sequestration? Did Winterburn get any names or give you any description of the men?" Holmes looked at me with an expression of abject disappointment. No words were necessary. "Well, he would no doubt be in a terrible state of shock that morning," I said in Winterburn's defence, having myself been the subject of the detective's discontentment in the past."

"No doubt," he mumbled. "The only word he used to describe them was '*menacing*,' which I thought was interesting."

"It sounds as though poor Winterburn was frightened for his own safety," I commented.

Holmes affirmed my supposition with an "Mm. I immediately contacted Mycroft at this point and appraised him of my findings." He broke off from his narrative and chuckled to himself as he reflected on his brother for a moment, "I sometimes wonder if Mycroft's influence is somewhat greater than he would have others believe.

"After reporting my discoveries to him, he in turn approached the Prime Minister who summoned the French Ambassador to Downing Street. It was then that Le Villard in Paris who told me that the ramifications of the London meeting were being felt all over the French capital. Every station and government office had been briefed about the 'theft' as it had been termed from the British Government, and searches were ordered. This was a significant development, as it confirmed that the French Government were not involved in any wrongdoing on an official level."

"But unofficially?" I asked.

Holmes smiled, "Exactly – *unofficially*. It suggested that rogue diplomats or politicians were acting independently, presumably for their own personal advantage. Returning to the murder itself, the interesting point was this question about the noise – or should I say, *lack* of noise – made by the gun."

"*Lack* of noise?" I repeated.

"Yes, apparent silence, in fact. You yourself commented that it was unusual that no one had heard any gunshots. When questioned, even the waiter and the other hotel staff swore that they didn't hear anything."

"How can that be explained?"

Holmes looked intensely at me. "I had previously heard of a man called Von Herder – he is a blind German mechanic who turned his skills to gun making some years ago; it is said that his touch and feel is like that of the most skilled watchmaker. Appropriate perhaps, as although he learned his skills in Berlin, he has spent that last ten years living in Geneva."

"What has *he* got to do with all of this?"

"The reason I knew about Von Herder was because I discovered he had been developing and experimenting with a noiseless device that is fitted to the end of a pistol, thus rendering it virtually silent when fired."

"That's surely too fanciful to be believed!" As a former army man and someone who had handled weapons most of his adult life, I couldn't see how such a contraption could be possible.

"With imagination and skill, Watson, nothing is beyond the cleverest minds and hands. Sadly, too often, those skills are used for nefarious purposes. If it were true that Von Herder had been successful with his development, it could change the course of firearms development in the future. Just think of the damage such silent devices could do when fitted to various kinds of pistols and rifles. It seems the more modern the world develops, the crueller it becomes."

"So, if this silent gun was used," I asked, "where is it now."

"If such a weapon existed, it would almost certainly be used by a skilled assassin. This would be no random killing; therefore, it would have been planned to the point where the killer would be admitted to the event and aided in his escape."

"So, he must have had an accomplice." I was being drawn into Holmes's narrative with every revelation. "Who could it be?"

"I immediately suspected the French official, Monsieur Lionel Brossard. He was either an innocent guest himself who was simply unfortunate enough to make the gruesome discovery; or he participated in the assassination in some way. I suspected the latter of the two alternatives before pausing to reconsider. You'll recall my hasty conclusions in the case at the Munro household."

"Norbury," I said with a chuckle, recalling Holmes's request to whisper the word to him when I thought he was getting a little overconfident in his powers.

"Norbury, indeed. I asked Le Villard what he thought of the individual concerned. He informed me that Monsieur Brossard was an aid in the French Foreign Office. He had been in his current position for over five years. Le Villard amusingly described him as 'a person of interest.'" Holmes laughed at his recollection.

"It's plausible that he may have been disgruntled," I commented, "but could such a feeling of injustice extend to murder?"

"That is what I had to find out. And given the lack of material evidence, I used it as a working hypothesis.

"Undoubtedly, the most interesting characteristic of the murder – given that it was carried out with a gun – was this apparent lack of a sound. When Le Villard informed me of this oddity, I immediately thought of Von Herder. Unfortunately, my French colleague could not leave his duties in Paris but I was free to travel the length and breadth of France and beyond its borders in search of answers to the assassination."

This was made all the easier for my friend as he was fluent in the language. He informed me that he left Le Villard in Paris and made the long journey across the border into Switzerland. Some discreet inquiries in Geneva eventually took him to the door of the afore mentioned Von Herder.

"I appeared in the guise of an assassin based in southern France with connections in Corsica. I was gambling that if he *had* successfully manufactured the noiseless appendage, it would be just such a character for whom he would be manufacturing it. My assumption proved accurate.

"'Are you connected to Bardet?' he asked when I explained the purpose of my visit. Before I could answer he added, "He came here last month and took the only one that has been a success so far.'

"'Yes, it was Bardet who put me on to you. He obviously didn't realise that you had only made the one to date.'

"'He told me he had a job in Paris,' said the craftsman, 'but was reluctant to tell me who his client was, mind you. Not that I was much interested. I'm only interested in my work and the money it makes for me.'

"'Yes, of course, that's where I saw him. I came straight here from there. He said it had been an enormous success.'

"'No doubt he will be back in Marseilles by now,' commented Von Herder, thus giving me the information I was looking for – a name and where I might find him.

"I travelled back across the border and headed south to the port city. It's a dangerous place, Watson. Seldom have I been so concerned for my own safety but those dark alleys and taverns along the waterfront must constitute the vilest murder-trap in the whole of France."

Rarely had I heard Holmes speak with such gravity regarding the dangers involved in his chosen profession and I kept having to remind myself that this had all taken place while I was incapacitated in my hospital bed. My dearest friend could have been murdered in that far off place and I would never have known. "What did you do?" I asked.

"You have complimented me on my acting skills in the past, Watson – they were certainly required on this occasion." He continued in response to my questioning expression. "Still in the guise of a dangerous ruffian myself, I made some discrete enquiries as to the whereabouts of this Bardet character" –"He didn't take a lot of finding in such a cesspool of villainy. He lodged in a small garret above a dingy barber's shop on the waterfront."

"Surely you didn't confront him?"

"No" – Holmes paused, I'm sure for dramatic effect – "I waited and watched until he left and broke into his lodgings."

I was incredulous, "Holmes that was damned irresponsible – had he caught you your life would not have been worth a farthing!"

"Calm yourself, my dear fellow. It was a calculated risk and I've always found that the bigger the risk, the greater the reward."

"Your venture was successful then?" I asked after composing myself once more.

"It was indeed. Amongst the detritus in Bardet's room, I found a telegram from none other than Monsieur Brossard."

"The Foreign Office official?"

"The very same. And he was advising Bardet of the date, time and location of the event at which Sir Richard Rosendale was subsequently shot and killed. So, there you had it – within ten days of being in France, I had established the probable assassin and the likely weapon he used to carry out the killing. The next step was to establish the motive for murdering the British Ambassador.

Chapter III

While I was still taking in Holmes's incredible tale, our landlady knocked and entered with our afternoon refreshment.

"I thought you might like some coffee and crumpets, gentlemen."

"That's wonderful, Mrs. Hudson," I said taking the tray and setting it down. Pouring the coffee for us both and retaking my seat with a plate swimming in warm butter, I steered Holmes back to his continental investigation.

"By good fortune I arrived back in Paris from Marseilles on the morning that the box of papers taken from Sir Richard's study were found."

"Where *were* they found?"

Holmes smiled and replaced his cup on its saucer, "In a box in a small office of the *Gendarmerie* hidden away in an obscure suburb in southwest Paris."

"How was that explained?"

"The finding had all the clumsy, amateurish hallmarks of the individuals who planted the gun among the Moroccan waiter's belongings. Upon being met by Le Villard at the Gare de Lyon, he informed me of the finding and we went straight to the site. I discovered that a window to the office had been forced from the outside – they had actually broken *in*, to plant the box of papers, apparently to implicate the local *Gendarmerie* and distance themselves from the potential scandal!"

"How ridiculous!" I cried, "Why on earth would the local *Gendarmerie* have stolen the papers?"

"Precisely. Such incompetence on the part of my adversaries gradually succeeded in making my investigation simpler. It was clear that the officers at the station knew nothing about the papers, as they reported the incident upon discovering the box when they opened the station the following morning."

"Did you see the contents?"

"Indeed, I did, Watson and this proved a significant episode of that enormous investigation."

Sir Richard had somehow obtained details of British Government dealings with the now infamous Netherland-Sumatra Company. Among the papers were trading accounts, with Sir Richard's annotations pointing out various discrepancies; there were false balance sheets; evidence of dividends being drawn by individuals from what appeared to be capital investment. Losses had been written down as profits, and unaudited references had been made to dubious expenses and use of petty cash.

"The ambassador's journal, given to me by Winterburn, was perhaps the most damning of all," continued Holmes. "In it, he mused over how deep into the heart of government this suspected wrongdoing ran; he expressed his uncertainty as to whether he should raise the matter and further questioned himself as to whom he should raise it *with*."

"Poor chap," I said, "he must have been in emotional turmoil. This is obviously what was on his mind when he spoke to Winterburn. Why did the thieves not just destroy the papers?"

I was taken aback by Holmes bursting into a roar of laughter. "I pride myself on my own detective skills, Watson," he said after composing himself, "and I must say I am impressed by the work of the young Le Villard, but I must concede that in this line of work, one does need to have a little luck at times. Fortunately, on this occasion, I was dealing with a gang of villains whose incompetence appeared to know no bounds. You will recall that the chamber of the gun planted to implicate the Moroccan was full for some bizarre reason, indicating that it could not have been the gun that killed the ambassador.

"Regarding the papers, the British Government protested in the strongest possible terms to the French that they considered the removal of documents from the embassy as theft. Failure to recover them would result in an international incident. Rather than destroy the documents therefore, those responsible decided to dispose of the evidence by breaking into the small suburban station to shift the attention of the investigation elsewhere and away from themselves."

"Without much success it would appear," I added, joining in Holmes's amusement. I thought for a while and then asked, "How did Sir Richard come by these incriminating documents in the first place?"

Holmes exploded into another fit of laughter, "The ridiculous act of trying to secrete the box took place during the night when there was no one on duty. Such buffoonery was preceded and surpassed however by the original act of misplacing the papers in the first instance. Whoever gathered the documents together presumably employed one of their lackeys to take the papers to the German Embassy for the attention of *their* ambassador; instead, the imbecile took them to the *British* Embassy, where they naturally – if unintentionally – came into the possession of Sir Richard."

"So, the German Ambassador participated in the conspiracy?"

Holmes finally calmed down and took a drink of coffee, "Conspiracy is the word, Watson. He and his chief advisor were guilty of channelling funds from the German Government into the coffers of Maupertuis to invest in his nefarious activities. Not only German but Italian officials were also ultimately exposed as being involved in funding the Neapolitan Camorra and the Sicilian Mafia through their dealings with the Baron. Governments and royal houses from virtually every country in Europe had indirectly been drawn into the villain's web. Once he had his claws in individuals connected to these great institutions, blackmail, embezzlement and any other heinous act you care to think of became reasonably straight forward.

"In effect they all became agents of Maupertuis – initially blinded by greed but then snared to the point where it was impossible to extricate themselves from his vast international crime empire. As a result, the countries they represented became unknowingly drawn into the conspiracy."

I paused, reluctant to ask the obvious question; Holmes shot a glance at me without moving his head and read my thoughts, "Yes, Watson, sadly the tentacles of Maupertuis spread to these shores also. Before Sir Richard could expose the wrongdoing in London however, he was murdered.

"Of course, Maupertuis never got his own hands dirty with such activity. But his world of crime grew to such an extent that it became unwieldy and ultimately spiralled out of control and it was poetic justice that this proved to be his downfall. As we have discovered, he developed many allegiances and generated various illicit schemes around the world, but they became so vast that it was impossible to control and oversee all the activity that was taking place. As a result, individuals were left to their own devices. So, when Brossard realised that evidence relating to an illegitimate alliance between government officials in London, Berlin, Amsterdam and Paris had fallen into the hands of the innocent Sir Richard Rosendale, he took matters into his own hands and had him killed by the Marseilles assassin Bardet.

"The evidence against Bardet included the telegram received from Brossard and was sufficient for our friend Le

Villard to approach the prosecutor in charge of the case and have the Marseilles man arrested. I provided his address and he was taken into custody and transported to Paris for questioning. It was under this scrutiny that he implicated Brossard, telling Le Villard that he had been hired to kill the Englishman: Brossard let Bardet into the hotel on the night of the murder and then helped him make his escape before the body of Sir Richard was properly discovered.

"Following the questioning of the killer, Brossard was arrested" – Holmes broke off in more laughter – "the effrontery of the man, he tried to claim diplomatic immunity from any criminal investigation!

"Upon further study of Sir Richard's papers, his annotations included several references to 'LB' and his involvement with two British officials in the Foreign Office, Small and Featherstone. They had been responsible for what appeared to be a legitimate British investment in this Netherland-Sumatra Company. What was unknown to investors however was that, far from making profits through lawful means, the profits made by the company came from embezzling, smuggling and piracy. Shareholders were paid their return, while other monies were used to set up phantom companies in Switzerland. These *companies"* – Holmes spat out the word – "would then use various accounts in Geneva banks which would, in effect, make the money appear quite unsullied. That money was then re-invested into companies in Britain."

"For what purpose?" I asked, struggling to keep up with the incredible scheme.

Holmes smiled, "For the purpose of lining the pockets of the British officials who had invested other people's money in the first place. It was no surprise to learn that they were major shareholders in the companies involved."

I sat and pondered the villainy for a few moments, "Remarkable."

"The more complex these schemes were, the harder they were to detect. And when it is considered that government officials themselves were involved in some, it became virtually impossible to uncover some of the wrongdoing. The likelihood is that there will be other illegal ventures that remain, and will forever remain, unsolved."

Afternoon had turned to evening and Holmes informed me that he needed to go out. I remained in our rooms and after dinner, spent the rest of the evening writing up the details of what Holmes had told me of his continental adventure so far. I was determined to find out more the following day.

Chapter IV

It was a beautiful September morning as I opened the curtains of my room. I had struggled to get to sleep the previous night; my mind had raced with what Holmes had told me of his case over twelve months earlier. I looked forward to pressing him on its denouement. I was to be initially disappointed however, when I went downstairs and found our sitting room empty. Mrs. Hudson informed me that my companion had left earlier that morning. It would be shortly after lunch before he returned.

"Where have you been, Holmes? If Mrs. Hudson hadn't informed me of your early departure, I would have believed you had been out all night."

Holmes chuckled, "No, two separate matters, Watson. Nothing that my biographer need worry himself with." He removed his hat and coat and rubbed his hands together, "I must say I am starving."

"I will make a deal with you Holmes – I will go and ask Mrs. Hudson to make you a sandwich and you must tell me the rest of your tale from yesterday."

"Very well."

I believed Holmes was enjoying teasing me with his adventure. Mrs. Hudson duly arrived with a tray and I allowed him to eat his lunch unhindered. For my part, I sat in silence, reading and re-reading the front page of *The Times,* unable to concentrate and tortured with impatience as I waited for him to resume his narrative. Finally, he did so.

"I alerted Mycroft to Small and Featherstone, the two government individuals in the Foreign Office and he made arrangements with Scotland Yard to have them arrested. The matter would ultimately result in the resignation of the Foreign Secretary himself; although not personally implicated in any wrongdoing, he did the honourable thing as he had personally appointed the two diplomats."

"Yes, I remember reading about it in the newspaper. But why didn't you return to London?"

"As I had found the first chink in the armour of Maupertuis's empire, word began to circulate around the capitals of Europe about their own possible involvement. Representation was therefore made to London to see if the success that the British had enjoyed, could be replicated."

"So, Mycroft commissioned you to stay and see whatever else you could uncover?" Again, Holmes looked up and smiled at my perspicacity. "Although I would imagine you took little convincing, given such a challenge."

"You know me all too well, Watson."

"So, what *did* you uncover?"

"I first went to Amsterdam to see what I could find out about this so-called shipping company. I presented myself as a senior official of the British Maritime Association."

"I've never heard of such an organisation."

"That's because it doesn't exist! It is yet another example of the complacency that exists in this parallel world of crime. There are so many acts of wrongdoing perpetrated by so many different parties from so many countries, it has become almost impossible for one element to keep track of – or even be aware of – what is happening elsewhere. In my case, I simply mentioned the names of James Small and Ronald Featherstone from London and this gave me free access to the records of the wretched Netherlands-Sumatra Company.

"The first thing I discovered was that Small and Featherston had invested tens of thousands of British monies in the company. I would later discover in Geneva that they were personally benefitting to the tune of several hundred thousand pounds in return for their unlawful investments."

Holmes then learned that Maupertuis himself was looking to expand his empire still further and was currently in transit on his way home from the Americas, where no doubt he would have had his eye on the blends and spices of Columbia and Brazil.

"This gave me some time to investigate the various arms of his operation virtually unhindered. Because some of them had become so large and had been in existence for so long, there were little or no barriers required to hide the operation."

"And I suppose," I ventured, "if various branches of officialdom were themselves involved, there would be no incentive to monitor what was happening."

"You are correct." Holmes lit a post-lunch pipe and settled back into his chair, "Power and greed are a potent combination among those in positions of authority. Small and Featherstone in London proved to be the tip of an exceptionally large iceberg. The procurement of goods and services – with their ridiculously complex processes and high levels of interaction between public officials and private businesses – leaves any government vulnerable to corruption. And so it proved across Europe at the orchestration of the Baron.

"Those private companies meanwhile would simply misinform their shareholders as to their activities and even go as far as to registering their dealings in another country. Any cursory investigation into such dealings could never hope to uncover the true extent of the wrongdoing.

"Even some of those in the various European insurance agencies were not beyond temptation when it came to the giant conspiracy. The war between the Dutch and its colonies in the southern oceans also provided an ideal opportunity to distract and hide suspicious activity.

"Piracy is rife in the southern seas and when raids were not being perpetrated on legitimate vessels, they were being staged by vessels attached to the company to defraud the insurance companies of thousands. From what I could find out, this had been going on ever since the wretched company had been founded. One vessel – the *SS Zealand* – had been the subject of at least twelve insurance claims over the past five years. In wandering around the port, I discovered the ship had been in dry dock for the past eighteen months! It appears as though anyone who took an overactive interest in the company and its subsidiaries' activities, could usually have their curiosity rectified with a bribe."

"And if it didn't?"

Holmes looked at me earnestly once more. "I discovered no fewer than forty-three murders and more than a dozen kidnappings, running parallel to the innumerable financial crimes, which could be traced back to, or connected with, the giant web created by Baron Maupertuis."

From Amsterdam, Holmes travelled to Lyon and took a suite at the Hotel Dulong. The city's proximity to the Swiss border and Geneva just beyond it, gave him the perfect location from which he could conduct the remainder of his enquiries. It was not long before he discovered that it was the same city from where Maupertuis himself conducted much of his operation, presumably for the same geographical reason.

"Each time I conducted a line of enquiry," remarked Holmes, "the same name would invariably crop up – that of Lionel Brossard."

"The official from the French Foreign Ministry?"

"The very same. His clumsy handling of the ambassador's killing inadvertently led to the uncovering of the Maupertuis empire. Brossard himself proved to be a man of great wealth, raking in thousands from his association with the Baron. His account in the Credit Lyonnais was worth a king's ransom alone. But invariably complacency sets in with such individuals and the trick is to follow the money, Watson. As this whole underworld of nefarious activity gradually became known over the following weeks, it transpired that Brossard had counterparts in Germany, Italy, Belgium and Greece. And all the while, the giant financial houses of Europe – Deutsche Bank, Banca Monte dei Paschi di Siena, Banque Nagelmackers, the National Bank of Greece – had all unknowingly facilitated illegally-obtained money through their grand old institutions. Hundreds of accounts in scores of cities across the continent provided the perfect cover for the giant operation. Those in authority who weren't part of the enormous conspiracy were simply oblivious to its workings, such was its vastness."

"It is incredible that the conspiracy lasted so long without detection," I said.

"Being entirely without any scruples or sense of loyalty," Holmes replied, "Maupertuis wouldn't hesitate to dispose of one of his generals if he believed him to be too careless and risking the exposure of his operations. Take Brossard for example. His bungling in the handling of the papers which led to the assassination of Sir Richard would certainly have led to his own killing had Maupertuis been in the country at the time."

"And so, Brossard ended up in a prison cell as opposed to a coffin."

Holmes laughed, "It is as though you have adopted the language of the continental villain, Watson! But yes, you are correct. And once Brossard was taken into custody – in an effort to save his own skin – he began to confess, not only to his part in planning the assassination, but also in the various schemes of which he was aware. His compliance with the investigation ultimately saved him from the *guillotine* as, one by one, his connections with his associates in various other countries led to each of their

63

arrests. As each card began to fall, the evidence against Maupertuis ultimately became overwhelming. He was arrested and charged with hundreds of crimes for which I am pleased to say, he has been convicted."

Suddenly, Holmes fell into a brown study and he silently stared into the fire. I was instantly reminded of the state I found my friend in when I travelled to Lyon to accompany him home. On that occasion he was drawn and paler than usual, as if he hadn't eaten or slept for days. Over twelve months after the events described on that September afternoon, I finally plucked up the courage to ask him about his final days in France before Maupertuis's apprehension.

"I can't help feeling you are holding something from me Holmes. I understand it had been a lengthy investigation, but its ultimate success and the adulation you received upon its completion seem to be at odds with the condition I found you in, when I arrived at your hotel. You appeared not only exhausted but...*frightened*." I couldn't think of another word.

My friend looked up at me from the fire, "You are not wrong, Watson. Danger is part of my trade but rarely has a case presented so *much* intensity and danger over a prolonged period. The truth is that I had to endure not one but two attempts on my life towards the conclusion of the investigation."

"Holmes!" I exclaimed, unaware of what my friend had coped with. "Had anything happened to you, I would never have forgiven myself."

"My dear fellow, there is nothing you or anyone else could do. Living on one's wits in enemy territory will always be exhausting and hazardous. It is not only within his own organisation that Maupertuis demonstrates a ruthlessness – it also applies to those with whom he finds himself in competition *and* opposition."

It was this latter category within which Holmes found himself and he explained that when the Baron arrived back from the Americas, he began to discover that all was not well within his European empire. From Copenhagen to Athens, from Vienna to Lisbon, hairline cracks were starting to appear. Once those cracks developed into noticeable fissures, he suspected something was amiss. Through his network of agents, it wasn't long before he found out about a British agent who was dismantling areas of his organisation, following the debacle involving Sir Richard.

"It was at this point that I knew my life would be in danger. The Baron had rarely been questioned, let alone seriously opposed, regarding his activities and I was aware that he was not about to begin at that moment.

"The first attempt to rid me from his world came when I was making one of the numerous journeys back to Lyon from Geneva. We were crossing the border and I was passing through one of the carriages. Suddenly, one of the doors slid open with some force and two ruffians emerged into the narrow passageway. They managed to overpower me to the extent that I was bundled into the compartment from which they had sprung. I was thrown to the floor and had to act quickly from being completely incapacitated. I managed to roll away from a kick aimed by one of the ruffians and at the same time, grab his foot and send him careering into his associate. This allowed me to regain my feet and even the contest somewhat by connecting with a straight left to the other flailing lout.

"I then had enough time to hastily exit the compartment and raise the alarm. The train was halted but the two leapt from the external door within the compartment and fled into the night. Upon the recommencement of our journey, it became apparent why they had waited to make their assault – the train passed over a giant viaduct. Had I not extricated myself and made my escape when I did, I have no doubt that I would have been overpowered and thrown from the train at that very point."

"You said that was not the only attempt." I was still coming to terms with the thought of losing my friend without even knowing it.

Holmes sunk his chin into his chest, his voice almost becoming a lament, "Yes," he paused. "That is the saddest part of the whole tale, Watson. Once I arrived back in Lyon, Le Villard asked me to return to Paris to share my latest findings with the prosecutor who was by this time, building the irrefutable case against Maupertuis. After our meeting with the prosecutor, Le Villard and I were leaving the *Palais de Justice* in the company of two young *Gendarmes.* At one point, Le Villard stumbled on the steps and I moved to assist him at the very moment a shot rang out from across the square. When we both regained our footing, I turned to see that one of the young officers who was standing behind me had been shot in the head. He died instantly and lay there bleeding on the steps of the highest court in the land."

"The bullet had been intended for you."

Holmes nodded sadly, "I later learned that the young man had recently become a father. His wife would be left to bring up their child alone. More victims of the web spun by this wretched creature. It made me even more determined to bring the matter to a swift end; I craved seeing Maupertuis's empire come crashing down and him being brought to justice.

"In light of the most recent atrocity, the prosecutor gave permission to use whatever resources were needed to apprehend the villain. Le Villard accompanied me back to Lyon where we intended to bring down the final curtain on the whole repugnant affair. Dozens of officers surrounded his chateau, south of the city; as it was, his apprehension proved much simpler than we had anticipated. As the order was given to rush the building, it was found that the Baron was virtually unguarded, save for the two characters I had encountered on the train some days earlier. They and their master were all taken into custody there and then. It was over."

"Did you get to speak with the villain?" I asked, knowing my friend's habitual liking for confronting his vanquished opponent.

"No words were exchanged," replied Holmes as his gaze returned to the fire and he brought his pipe back to life. "You are the military man, Watson, not I, but Wellington's quote after Waterloo came to mind, as Maupertuis was led away: *nothing except a battle lost can be half so melancholy as a battle won.*

"I was completely exhausted after weeks of seemingly endless days of travelling, detection and at times, self-preservation." In recollection of his painful experience Holmes's voice lowered almost to a whisper, "As he was led towards the police vehicle, he paused and looked at me – clearly knowing who I was. He was a thick set individual with thinning dark hair that was creamed heavily against his scalp. His complexion suggested more of a Mediterranean origin than northern European. But I'm sure I speak for all his adversaries when I say it was his black, evil eyes that left a deep, unsettling impression. Clearly the man had no conscience.

"I did not have the energy or the inclination to converse and before *he* could do so, two of the *Gendarmes* – no doubt aware of their colleague's murder in the capital a few days earlier – bundled him unceremoniously into the back of the wagon. Le Villard then escorted me back to my hotel where I asked him to send a message to you."

He finally looked up and I – exhausted myself after listening to my friend's adventure – slumped back in my seat, on the edge of which I had been perched, transfixed for the best part of two days.

"Good heavens! When I discovered the condition you were in upon my arrival in Lyon, I thought little of the cause – I was simply interested in getting you back home. Now that you explain the series of events that led to such a state, I am only surprised and thankful that medically, you were not in a worse circumstance."

We sat in silence for a while longer before another thought occurred to me.

"Holmes, I wasn't aware of any recognition from the government for your efforts regarding the matter?" My friend sneered his contempt at such a suggestion, but I persisted with my point, "Lesser men have received knighthoods for simply attending Parliament!"

"And they are welcome to their awards; and to telling each other how great they are and how they serve their country so well." Holmes made no effort to hide his cynicism, "No doubt, those same men will impose on my brother once more, who in turn will call on me the next time there is a difficult problem to solve."

The Dulwich Solicitor

Chapter I

It was late September 1888 and Holmes had then only recently completed the strange case of Mr. Jonathan Small and the great Agra treasure. During his investigation, I met the sweet and sensitive Miss Mary Morstan for the first time, and once the case had been concluded I was delighted when Mary accepted me as her husband in prospective. A few days' later I received a letter from her inviting me to be a guest of hers and that of her employer Mrs. Forrester's family at their home in Lower Camberwell. I am not ashamed to admit that my heart skipped with joy upon receiving the letter and I had no hesitation in accepting.

As a matter of courtesy, I asked Holmes if he could do without my assistance for a few days. He had been lukewarm at the news of my engagement and further demonstrated a lack of feeling as he barely looked up from his newspaper and sent me off with a dismissive wave, announcing, "I have all the company I need in the form of the cocaine-bottle."

Ignoring the reference to this foul habit, I left and enjoyed enormously a wonderful week in the company of Mary and her employer who had clearly become more of a friend during the years Miss Morstan had worked for her. In fact, the affection they had for one another could easily have one mistaking them for mother and daughter – an embrace here, a whispered conversation there, followed by mischievous laughter between the two. There was a part of me that carried a certain amount of guilt, given that I was proposing to take Mary away from this heart-warming idyll. But Mrs. Forrester wouldn't hear of it – this graceful woman couldn't hide her joy at Mary finding such happiness and was fully supportive of our match.

I experienced a wonderful week and was even more delighted to find that Mary enjoyed my company just as much as I did hers. On the final day of my holiday, she gave me a signet ring belonging to her father, which was apparently a gift to him from her mother on the day of their wedding. I was touched that she would even consider parting with such a memento and was honoured to accept it.

My heart was full of joy as I returned to a blustery autumnal Baker Street the following morning. Clouds raced across a brooding sky, while fallen leaves swirled and eddied up and down the street, giving the road cleaner who was trying to sweep them up, a virtually impossible task. Our normally bustling thoroughfare was congested still further as the road was being repaired outside our quarters; this resulted in half the street being cordoned off, which in turn saw traffic in each direction jostling for the same space on one side of the road. Frustrated drivers, unsettled horses and the noise from the workmen all made for a chaotic scene.

But such was my cheerful disposition, nothing could dull my feelings – as far as I was concerned it could have been the first week of glorious May without a cloud in the sky or a murmur of noise from the street.

"Just drop me here cabbie," I called, tapping my cain on the roof of the hansom, after seeing the commotion further along the street.

"Very good, sir," he appeared as happy as I was to end our journey slightly early; he took his fair, touched the brim of his hat and spun his horse around, heading in the direction from which we came, thus avoiding the congestion up ahead.

As I passed the antiquarian bookshop, its owner tapped on the window and beckoned me inside, "Doctor Watson, I'm pleased I saw you," said he as I entered, "I wonder if I could ask a favour?"

Such was my disposition that morning, I believe I would have obliged anyone, "Certainly, Mr. Morten, how can I help?"

"Mr. Holmes asked about a particular volume a couple of weeks ago but I haven't seen him since. Could you tell him that I have discovered a copy if he is still interested?"

He gave me a piece of paper with the details: "*Discourse on the Method of Rightly Conducting One's Reason and of Seeking Truth in the Sciences* by René Descartes." I smiled to myself at my friend's taste in literature. Above the noise from outside, I added, "I will certainly pass the message on. How are you coping with all this disruption?"

"Oh, it's dreadful. It's been going on for days. I don't even know what they are doing, other than creating upset amongst everyone on the street, that is."

I bid the shopkeeper a good morning and went on my way. Despite the commotion on the street, I didn't think anything could disturb the joyous mood I found myself in. That was soon to change however upon entering our old rooms at 221b. Such was my demeanour that I virtually bounded up the stairs, eager to see my friend and share the news of my holiday. Not for the first time however, I was to be disappointed.

"Morning Holmes!" I shouted from the landing as I hung up my hat and coat on the stand. There was no reply.

I entered our sitting room only to find it littered with discarded newspapers and engulfed in a cloud of thick pipe smoke. Coughing and waving in futility, I made my way over to the window and raised the sash. After regaining some composure, I looked across the room to see my friend with his eyes closed, sitting in the wicker chair by the fire. He was in his grey dressing gown and sat with his knees up under his chin. Protruding from his mouth was what I often thought of as his counsellor – the small oily clay pipe he would invariably turn to when he was in a pensive mood.

In trying to get some of the smoke out of the room, by opening the window, I had allowed the cacophony of banging and clattering from the street below into our sitting room. Holmes never flinched and I smiled as I recalled Mr. Morten's comment about everyone being upset by the disruption: I would wager that Holmes was the only person on the street who was totally oblivious to the work going on outside his very door.

"Good *morning,* Holmes," I repeated, "I spoke to Mr. Morten on the way in and he asked me to tell you the book you enquired about is available if you are still interested."

Raised eyebrows and a creased forehead were all that I received by way of a response. Already feeling my jovial mood dissipating, I began collecting up the strewn newspapers. In doing so, I noticed that many were yellowed and dated back months and even years. I piled them on Holmes's desk and sat down opposite him, snapping open the most recent journal as loud as I could to illicit some form of acknowledgement. Again, I was to be disappointed.

My eyes inevitably travelled towards the Persian slipper which hung to one side of the fire, and then to the Morocco case I knew contained a hypodermic syringe, sitting on the mantlepiece above it. I was appalled at the thought of Holmes stagnating like this over the past week.

The newspaper I held was open at the obituaries page. It was one of the few pages which was not dominated by the two stories that had horrified the nation over the previous few weeks: the theft of the favourite for the Wessex Cup and the tragic murder of its trainer was now rivalled by the recent dreadful murders in Whitechapel. I wondered if either of these matters were the cause of my friend's non-communicative mood. Without remembering the detail, I did recall him making some comment about the first of the

Whitechapel murders some weeks earlier but when he was not consulted by Scotland Yard on the matter, and then when the case which was brought to our door by Miss Morstan took the following three weeks to complete, his attention and mine were naturally focussed elsewhere.

No sooner had Holmes embarked on the case that I subsequently titled *The Sign of the Four*, when another brutal murder took place in Spitalfields. Little did we know that the following week would see a further two horrific attacks. Again, I wondered if Holmes was reproaching himself for not getting involved in the matter.

Just then, there was a loud peal from the doorbell and my friend instantaneously leapt from his chair, as if propelled by a giant spring hidden under the wicker seat.

"Ha!" he cried, *"Mrs. Hudson – MRS. HUDSON!"*

He practically sang the name of our long-suffering landlady and I could hear the footsteps of the poor woman hurrying up the stairs as Holmes made it to the door.

"Yes, yes, Mr. Holmes," she said as she turned and hurried across the landing. Handing a telegram to Holmes at the threshold of the room, she saw me and attempted to add, "Oh, hello Doctor, I didn't hear you come–."

But the poor woman was gone, the door of the sitting room having been closed in her face by surely the most infuriating lodger in London. Completely oblivious to his rudeness, Holmes was ripping open the telegram.

"Excellent!" he cried, "Watson, back into your coat, we have work to do!" He headed towards his own room to collect his outdoor wear but stopped in the doorway and turned, "Oh and by the way, no, I wasn't contemplating the actions of the Whitechapel maniac when you entered – nor indeed the interesting developments at King's Pyland."

I stood there for the umpteenth time, open-mouthed. "How on earth…" I began and then realised there was no point in trying to extricate myself from the mischievous trap I had fallen into yet again. Holmes turned again towards his room with that familiar twinkle in his eye. Among the thousands of words I have written over the years to describe my friend, the one I mentioned earlier deserves a prominent place – infuriating.

Chapter II

We retraced my steps of an hour earlier to the bottom of Baker Street before we hailed a cab.

"Where are we going?" I asked as our hansom pulled away.

"First we must call at the Post Office on Marylebone Road," replied Holmes, "and then it is on to Dulwich; we are going to Dulwich to trap a villain who is more cunning than Roylott and more cold-hearted than Rucastle."

"Good heavens!" I was shocked by the reputation afforded to this man by Holmes. After gaining some composure I couldn't resist adding icily, "I'm pleased you haven't spent the whole time locked away with your cocaine and tobacco."

A brief smile plucked at the corners of my friend's mouth as he prepared to tell me about the matter.

"You will remember when I employed the Irregulars to find the steamboat *Aurora* two weeks ago during the Jonathan Small case?"

"Of course," I replied "I've never seen such a group of sad, grubby looking characters. What their lives have been like to date, I cannot begin to imagine."

"And that brings us to the point at hand Watson," Holmes leant forward to elaborate on his narrative. "When the boys entered our sitting room, did you notice any*one* or anyth*ing* in particular?"

"Not particularly," I said, "they all descended like a plague of locusts! I remember poor Mrs. Hudson was none too pleased at the intrusion."

Holmes smiled at his recollection of the event. "Yes, but among the excitement there was one boy who stood out from the rest."

"You mean Wiggins? *He* seemed to be doing all the talking."

"No, no. Like the rest of his companions, Wiggins had naked feet, rags for clothes and an eager sparkle in his eye, attracted as he was by the prospect of earning himself a guinea. But there was one boy who was distinct from the rest. He was the last to enter, he stood slightly apart from the others, as if he didn't really know them. Most distinctive of all was his appearance: he wore shoes, his clothes were not as worn as his friends and his skin and hair were not as pitted with the grime and filth of London as the other poor wretches."

"I can't say I particularly noticed," I said, not for the first time in my long association with my friend.

Holmes widened his nostrils and exhaled loudly in disappointment at my failure. "No," he drew out the word before continuing. "The sight of the boy troubled me and I later called Wiggins back to ask about him. It transpired that he had only been with Wiggins and his associates for little more than a week prior to us receiving them in Baker Street.

"'He's called Simon,' said Wiggins, 'Simon Rutherford. I found him begging down Rotherhithe way, where I had a bit of business.'

"A bit of business indeed!" Holmes threw is head back and roared with laughter as he recalled the conversation, "the little tyke!"

"Simon Rutherford?" I questioned, "hardly the moniker of your average street urchin."

"Exactly, Watson. His name, his appearance, everything was incongruous with the situation he found himself in. It transpired that the boy was recently orphaned. Wiggins told me he thought he was from a quite well-to-do family but his parents died leaving him destitute."

"Surely a decent middle-class family would have provided for their offspring with a Will?"

"And this is what intrigued me still further. In the absence of my trusted biographer, I resolved to conduct some further research into the matter and discovered that the boy's father had died suddenly within six months of his mother, and he did indeed leave a Will."

Holmes reached into his inside pocket and brought out a piece of newspaper torn from *The Times*. It was part of the obituaries page and recorded:

> *Sudden passing of Mr. Gerald Rutherford of 13 Tewkesbury Avenue, Dulwich. Husband of the late Sarah Rutherford and father of Simon James Rutherford. The reading of the Will is due to take place at the offices of solicitor Mr. Silas Wagstaff on 15th August 1888.*

"So presumably this took place and as a result the poor child received nothing and was kicked out onto the street?" I asked with some alarm.

"I am certain of it," replied Holmes through gritted teeth. "There is something quite despicable about crimes against the most vulnerable of our society, Watson, and they are invariably perpetrated by the wealthy and privileged."

"And you obviously suspect this Wagstaff is guilty of wrongdoing against the boy Rutherford?"

Holmes looked squarely at me, "I know it Watson, I know it."

At that moment, our hansom drew to a halt outside the Post Office and Holmes leapt from the vehicle onto the pavement and into the building in a single movement. I saw him through the window speaking with the Postmaster behind the counter and he took an envelope from him, in exchange for some form of payment. Within seconds he was back in the hansom and with a rap on the inside of the roof with his cane, we lurched back up to speed.

"I know it my dear Watson because of this," he announced showing me the envelope he had just collected, "it is the final piece in the puzzle of evidence against this wretched creature."

The envelope was addressed to a Mr. John Radford c/o Marylebone Road Post Office NW1. "I don't understand," I said, "who is Mr. John Radford and how have you come to receive his mail?"

Holmes once again flashed me a mischievous glance of his before announcing, "*I* am Mr. Radford. I have already visited Wagstaff during your absence Watson and this letter is the result."

Naturally, I was at a complete loss as to what Holmes was up to and asked my friend to elaborate.

"Every fibre in my body told me that there was something sinister concerning the passing of Gerald Rutherford, so from the newspaper room at the British Library I went straight to the Registrar's Office in Dulwich to view the recorded deaths. In Rutherford's case, the cause of death was listed as a heart attack and organ failure."

"What age was he?" I asked.

"Forty-six," replied Holmes, "an unusually young age for one's organs to completely shut down wouldn't you say Doctor?"

"Indeed."

"And less than ten entries before that of Gerald Rutherford was the recording of his wife's passing. The cause of her death was typhoid fever.

"I leafed through the ledger still further and found no less than six entries during the previous three years where causes of death were listed as either a heart attack, or organ failure or both. Six weeks prior to each death, the respective spouses of the deceased had also passed away. I made a list of the names concerned and then visited neighbouring Registry Offices. I found a similar pattern of spousal deaths in Norwood, Kensington and Norbury: one passing away first and the surviving spouse outliving them by no more than two or three months. All enough to form a pattern but not enough to particularly arouse any suspicion of wrongdoing.

"From there I returned to the library to discover that in each case, there were children orphaned by their parents' passing and of those cases that were heard at a Coroner's Inquest, it was judged that the deaths were as indicated on the respective death certificates."

"You naturally do not believe this?"

"I do not," Holmes said gravely, as our cab rattled over Waterloo Bridge, "and in each case, the solicitor involved in dealing with the deceased's estate was the same."

"Silas Wagstaff."

"Precisely."

"But surely it should be a matter for the police, Holmes," I suggested, "after all, no one has actually commissioned your services in the matter."

"I am not interested in money when it comes to such matters, Watson. There are some cases worth pursuing simply because it is the correct thing to do. If this ends up with this odious character being brought to justice then that will be my reward.

"But you are correct about the police; the telegram I received earlier was from Inspector Athelney Jones who has obtained a magistrate's warrant and will meet us at Wagstaff's offices this morning. And following a telegram of my own sent earlier this week, I hope we can snare another criminal at the same time."

Chapter III

For the remainder of the journey, Holmes completed the gaps in his narrative concerning his meeting with Silas Wagstaff.

"I first contacted him claiming to be Mr. Radford who had recently lost his wife. As it was too painful for my young daughter and myself to remain in the family home in Dulwich, we had moved out and were temporarily staying with friends north of the river. I explained that I had not made a Will and my dear wife's sudden passing had prompted me to give the matter some serious thought. Not surprisingly, he was all too willing to help. I visited him first last Monday in the guise of the grieving widower."

Having witnessed – and been taken in by – many of Holmes's disguises over the years, I could picture him playing the part to perfection. I have thought on many occasion that the stage lost one of the finest actors when Holmes turned his attentions to the art of detection.

"Like most villains of his kind," resumed my friend, "Wagstaff is certainly a plausible character. You have often complimented me on my thespian qualities in the past Watson, I must grudgingly pay tribute to his.

"'Come in my dear Mr. Radford," he said when we first met, "and let me express my heartfelt condolences to you and your daughter for your devastating loss.'

"'Thank you, Mr. Wagstaff, it has been an extremely difficult time for us both.'

"'Let me get us some refreshment. *Mr. Kent!'*

"The solicitor's clerk answered his employer's call.

"'Ah, Kent, would you be so kind as to bring us some refreshment please, there's a good chap.'

"'Very good sir,' replied the clerk with a nod.

"He returned some moments later with a tray upon which was a pot of tea and two cups, and a plate of what looked like a most appetizing fruit loaf, cut into slices.

"'Oh, how lovely Kent, thank you,' said Wagstaff when he saw the tray, 'and we've got some of my dear wife's beautiful recipe; we are in for a real treat Mr. Radford.'

"Kent placed the tray carefully on the corner of Wagstaff's desk, 'Would you like me to pour sir?' he asked.

"'No, I'll deal with it myself Kent, thank you,' said his employer. 'Now, Mr. Radford,' he said turning back to me, 'you would like to make a Will. May I ask how much your estate is worth?'

"'Well, I'm not really sure – a reasonable amount I suppose as I do own my own house on Hartington Place and I have some savings.'

"I saw Wagstaff's eyes glisten behind the lenses of his spectacles. 'And presumably you want to secure your daughter's future in case something unthinkable happens to yourself?' he asked.

"'That's right, but I don't know what I can do, which is why I contacted you. I remember a neighbour said how kind you were after her husband passed away. Your assistance appeared timely as sadly, she herself died shortly afterwards. Thank goodness she managed to put things in place to protect her young son.'

"'Well, I can't talk about individual clients you understand,' said Wagstaff bowing and shaking his head, 'but it is true that I have experienced such tragic affairs.'

"'What would you recommend in my case?' I asked.

"'I think the sensible thing to ensure that little…erm?'

"'Katy,'

"'Of course, Katy, how delightful. To ensure that little Katy's inheritance is secured.'

"'That sounds perfect,' I said.

"'What I suggest therefore is that we make your Will and list Katy as the sole beneficiary. In the unlikely event of your passing, your estate will be held by a Trust called the Dulwich Children's Fund until Katy reaches an appropriate age where she can access her inheritance. In the meantime, the Trust would identify a family home in the area where Katy would be raised commensurate with the high standards demonstrated by yourself and your dear late wife.'

"'I see,' I said, rubbing my chin in thought. 'In the unthinkable event of myself *and* Katy passing away, what would happen to my estate?'

"'I have known clients in the past requesting that their estate be given to the fund to continue their excellent work in supporting orphaned children.'

"'I suppose that would be as good a solution as any, although I'm sure that doesn't happen very often.'

"'Oh no, no, no, hardly ever,' replied Wagstaff, 'The tragic events involving your neighbour is the only occasion I can ever remember. Oh, perhaps I shouldn't have said that – client confidentiality and all,' he added in mock horror with a chuckle."

Holmes broke off momentarily from his narrative, "I must say Watson he is amongst the most wicked of creatures."

He resumed.

"'There is one thing I would like to alter,' I said in the role of Radford.

"Wagstaff looked slightly chagrined at this revelation. 'Alter?' he repeated.

"'Yes, I was speaking with the friend Katy and I are currently staying with, and he suggested that he could act as Katy's guardian in the unlikely event of me passing away before my daughter comes of age. I wonder if we could include that into the Will?'

"Wagstaff sat down and was silent for a while. 'Yes, I don't see why not,' he said at last.

"'Oh, thank you Mr. Wagstaff, that would be most kind and a great relief to me. I would therefore like you to make the necessary arrangements to that effect.'

"'Excellent, excellent,' cried the solicitor, now let's have some tea.'

"He poured the tea and delicately put two slices of loaf on to separate plates.

"'I have a model Will here, Mr. Radford,' said Wagstaff, bringing a document out of his desk drawer. He offered it to me and then reached across to the tray. He put a cup of tea and a slice of loaf in front of me and attempted to do the same for himself. As he did so however, the saucer of his cup collided with the tea pot causing him to spill the contents over his own piece of loaf and part of the blotting pad that covered half of his desk.

"'Oh dear!' he cried, 'I am so clumsy. Do forgive me Mr. Radford, I will go and get a cloth to clean this mess up. In the meantime, please continue reading the document and don't stand on ceremony when it comes to your refreshment. I will return shortly.'

"During Wagstaff's absence I folded the piece of loaf on my plate and another from the cut slices, into a handkerchief. I also poured a small sample of tea from my cup into a vile I was carrying and poured the remainder back into the pot.

"As I was doing so, I heard a commotion in the hall outside. It was difficult to establish exactly what was being said but there was a raised voice and clearly threats were being made. The dispute subsided and was followed by the slamming of the front door. I looked out onto the street to see who had left and saw none other than Teddy Taylor striding past the window. He is a dangerous character from Brixton with a history of violence and extortion. I he was one of the villains hired by Messrs Latimer and Kemp to abduct and assault the unfortunate Paul Kratides in September, and I had previously encountered him in a case before your time involving an elderly pawn broker in Lewisham."

"What on earth was a character like that doing at Wagstaff's offices?" I asked.

"What indeed!" I saw the familiar twinkle in Holmes's eye, "sadly, the man is solid bone from the neck up which makes him extremely dangerous – not someone anyone should be on the wrong side of. He has a brother who has a little more about him but they can't possibly be working on their own initiative, so the question is – who are they representing? One thing is for sure, the Taylors' involvement raises the case above the commonplace.

"Shortly after Taylor's departure, the solicitor returned, looking a little less self-assured than when he left ten minutes earlier.

"'Sorry about that Mr. Radford, I was looking for the maid. How are we getting on?' he asked as he started dabbing away at the excess liquid.

"'Yes, I'm sure that will do fine," I gestured towards the sample Will.

"'Good, good. And I see you have enjoyed your refreshment in my absence?'

"'Yes, it was delicious, please compliment your wife on her wonderful baking. I hope you don't mind but I helped myself to a second piece.' I indicated to the plate which was still on the tray containing the remainder of the sliced loaf.

"'Oh, no, not at all, sir.' Wagstaff seemed positively excited. Then observing my empty cup, he asked, 'Can I get you some more tea?'

"'No thank you, it was most refreshing. Quite a distinctive flavour.'

"'Yes, I particularly like it – that is when I'm not spilling it all over my desk you understand,' he laughed at his own supposed stupidity, no doubt inwardly amused by his apparent deception. Then referring to the Will itself, he rubbed his hands together lightly, 'Splendid, splendid. Could I make a suggestion? If you give me the details of your friend, I will write out the Will and invite you back to have it signed up. I can ask my clerk and maid to act as witnesses. You could even bring your friend along.'

"'Yes, that's a good idea, thank you.' I gave Wagstaff details of my fictitious friend Robert Wilson and he told me that he would hope to have the document completed for the end of the week."

"'Excellent, excellent. One thing I should add, in the interest of fairness and disclosure. I am one of the Trustees of the Children's Fund, along with three other solicitors.'

"Wagstaff gave me a piece of paper with three names listed and then added, 'We could be listed as your Executors if that would be convenient. I appreciate that I appear slightly older than yourself but two of my colleagues are considerably younger and therefore the chances of everyone pre-deceasing you are extremely remote.'

"Once again, I assumed Wagstaff was amusing himself at this last comment as he would make sure that he would not pre-decease me, but I played along at face value. 'Yes, that sounds like a good idea also.'

"'Wonderful. In that case, I will draw the documents together. Would it be convenient to call again towards the end of the week?'

"'Yes, I suppose that would be fine.'

"I gave Wagstaff all my details as John Radford and – given my supposed temporary living arrangements – asked him to correspond with me via the Post Office on Marylebone Road.

'"I will indeed my dear sir; I will confirm it by letter but let us provisionally say Friday morning at ten o'clock?'

'"That would be ideal Mr. Wagstaff,' I said shaking his hand heartily, 'I will look forward to hopefully seeing you then.'"

Chapter IV

The great city went about its business: pavements crowded with the great throng of humanity; streets and bridges echoing to the rattling of wheels and neighing of horses; all oblivious to the story my friend was telling inside our tiny cab as we made our way towards Dulwich.

"My task in your absence Watson, was to look into this so-called Dulwich Children's Fund and the involvement – however unlikely – that villain Taylor and his brother had in all of this.

"It transpires that the Fund *is* listed in the index of London Charities but that is where any legitimacy begins and ends. The three names of fellow-Trustees given to me by Wagstaff turn out to be a deceased gas-lighter, a retired tailor who knew nothing about the matter and a plumber's mate from Bermondsey. *Ha!* The effrontery of the man!

"The most interesting part of my research however was the discovery that the original documentation relating to the setting up of the bogus charity was attributed to the solicitors' firm of Wagstaff and Clegg."

"He had a partner?"

"That is correct Watson – *had* a partner. Wagstaff and Clegg had a modest office in Brixton, no doubt where they met Teddy Taylor and his brother. The back editions of *The Times* informed me that the body of Jonas Clegg, said solicitor from Brixton, was fished from the Thames five years ago. Initial reports suspected foul play but without sufficient evidence the coroner recorded an open verdict."

"So Wagstaff appears to have gone up in the world by moving to Dulwich and setting up his own practice."

"Precisely so – the question is how could he fund such a venture?"

"You obviously don't believe the official verdict of the coroner regarding Clegg?"

"Not a bit of it."

"Do you think Wagstaff had some part in his partner's demise."

"Whether he had direct involvement in the killing is unlikely. What is *more* likely is that Taylor was involved. I would imagine if someone were inclined to threaten, kidnap or violently assault, they would find the final step to murder is a relatively short one."

"But why would Taylor murder Clegg?" I was finding Holmes's line of reasoning more confusing by the moment.

"At the time of his death, Clegg and his partner Wagstaff were acting in the conveyancing of a development of warehouses at the docks in Rotherhithe. When the council papers of the time are studied in detail, discrepancies in some of the finances become apparent. The developer turned out to be Robert Taylor, the brother of our friend Teddy."

"But surely if there were some manipulations of funds, it would have been picked up by the council officials who were overseeing the development?"

"These people can be bought, Watson. Whenever there is money and personal gain to be had, too many people in authority are ready to take advantage and abuse their position. If my theory is correct, the officials you speak of were probably benefiting from Taylor's bribes, while separately taking advantage of Clegg's misdemeanours."

"Ah, so the inference is that Clegg was somehow embezzling funds from the project and once the Taylors found out, they took retribution?"

"When the individual threads are identified and stated as I have, it is certainly plausible."

"But what about the council officials – should they not be investigated for their suspected wrongdoing?"

"Many of them will be gone. Bear in mind this would be over five years ago and the reform act of earlier this year has seen further changes to local councils."

"So, if your theory about Clegg stealing from the Taylors is true, then why wasn't Wagstaff also disposed of?"

"This is a question that I haven't found the answer to yet. It could be that Clegg was working independently without his partner's knowledge. Alternatively, the Taylors may have seen Wagstaff as an opportunity to make money. The circumstantial evidence appears to suggest that both Clegg and Wagstaff were less than honourable in their profession from the beginning. Although Teddy Taylor would not have the basic intelligence to realise Wagstaff could be useful in the future, his brother Robert certainly did. By pressuring Wagstaff into paying them part of his ill-gotten gains, they would be guaranteed a regular income while always having a hold on him with knowledge of his various wrongdoings."

"Which has developed into making orphans of children and stealing their inheritance in the process," I concluded. We continued in silence for a while and I reflected on Holmes's incredible tale before saying, almost to myself, "I'm sure all of Wagstaff's other victims were too grief-stricken to think so lucidly."

"Indeed," said my friend as our cab slowed to its destination, "now let us see how he reacts to someone who is."

The office of Silas Wagstaff was on Wyndham Avenue, a stylish Regency thoroughfare with a long sweeping crescent and trees either side of the road. It was this elegant tranquillity which afforded the solicitor a perfect cover which allowed him to carry out his heinous activities unmolested and unsuspected.

We climbed the few steps to the front door and Holmes rang the bell. Moments later a tall thin man with a ramrod straight back opened the door. Upon seeing my friend his self-assured demeanour appeared to alter slightly. I assumed from this that he recognised my companion from his previous visit but – knowing my friend as I do – no doubt Holmes had altered his own attire and demeanour to confuse and distract his opponent.

"Good morning, Mr. Kent," Holmes ignored the clerk's uncertainty and strode past him with characteristic confidence across the hallway, "I assume Mr. Wagstaff is in his office?"

I followed Holmes across the reception area towards the door at its furthest point. Kent came scampering behind us and as Holmes entered, the clerk bundled past us to announce, with some uncertainty, the arrival of his employer's client.

Silas Wagstaff was a short, rotund man of around sixty, with a high forehead and a wide nose on which were perched a pair of tortoise shell spectacles. As he looked up from his desk, his expression mirrored that of his clerk some moments earlier.

"Mr....Radford," he said hesitantly, "and this must be your friend, Mr. Wilson." He rose from his desk and appeared to regain some composure. "Gentlemen please sit down. Kent, please bring us some refreshment."

The clerk left and we remained standing. Again, Wagstaff attempted to break the uncomfortable silence, "Please gentlemen sit down, I have drafted your Will, Mr. Radford and I think you'll find everything is in order, including Mr. Wilson here acting as Katy's guardian in the event of your unlikely passing." He had a strange manner of speaking which was both obsequious and patronising; all the while I sensed that he was inwardly amusing himself by deliberately misleading his vulnerable clients.

"Unlikely?" questioned Holmes, "come, come Mr. Wagstaff, I think my passing would be extremely likely if I continued to allow you to act for me."

"I'm sorry, I don't understand," said the solicitor whose disposition appeared to be changing from one of uncertainty to one of concern.

At that point Kent entered with a tray on which there was a steaming pot with three cups and a plate containing what appeared to be slices of fruit loaf.

"Ah, please come in Kent," said Holmes, "I see you have some of that distinctive loaf I so enjoyed on my last visit."

"Kent put the tray on Wagstaff's desk and, with a dismissive nod from his master, left the room.

"Shall I pour the tea Mr. Wagstaff?" asked my friend, "I wouldn't want you to accidentally spill it again?"

The solicitor sat in silence, unsure of how to respond, as Holmes poured one cup of tea and placed it in front of him. He then lifted one slice of the loaf onto a plate with the serving tongs and put it beside the tea.

"I don't think I am particularly hungry actually," spluttered Wagstaff.

He reached down to the bottom draw of his desk, as if to retrieve some papers that were pertinent to the matter, but Holmes was alive to his intentions – he slammed down his cane on Wagstaff's wrist, trapping it in the open draw. Under the solicitor's splayed fingers, I saw a revolver.

Holmes eyes darted from the weapon to its owner, "A pretty affair this is turning out to be Mr. Wagstaff."

"Who are you? What is this all about?" Wagstaff attempted to keep up the façade of confidence and authority but it was draining away by the minute.

Holmes moved his cane from the solicitor's wrist to under his chin and pushed him back in his seat, closing the drawer with his foot as he did so. "My name is Sherlock Holmes and this is my friend and colleague Dr. Watson."

Wagstaff's eyes flashed wide behind his thick lenses.

"I see my name is familiar to you," added Holmes.

"You have deceived me," Wagstaff tried his best to sound like the wronged party.

"I salute your effrontery but it simply won't do. *You* are the deceiver; the thief; and the murderer."

Rarely have I seen Holmes so angry as he jabbed his cane under Wagstaff's chin to emphasise each accusation.

"I…I don't know what you are talking about," Wagstaff was desperate now.

Holmes released the cane and took a calming breath, "I notice you haven't eaten your cake," he said. "Of course, neither of us should be surprised by that; while you left the room during my previous visit, I wrapped some up and took it away with me, along with the tea you served. It was not made by your wife as you claimed, amongst other things I discovered that you are unmarried. I tested the…*refreshment* and confirmed my suspicion that it was poisoned – both laced with aconitine.

"What a nice person you are Wagstaff; you pray on the bereaved by poisoning them and stealing their estate, while leaving their children starving and destitute."

"That is a serious charge," blustered the solicitor.

"One that you can discuss at length with Inspector Jones of Scotland Yard who has a warrant for your arrest," replied Holmes.

Before Wagstaff could protest further, our attention was taken by the sound of a commotion in the hallway and the door of the office burst open to reveal a tall, strongly built evil looking lout: he had the dark eyes of a scheming villain and a hard, pockmarked face with a misshapen nose that was evidence of many a bruising battle, most no doubt, bare-knuckled and illegal. His teeth snarled at us from behind his fat ugly lips as he looked from one to the other. His appearance prompted me to grip my cain tighter.

"Taylor, what...?" such was Wagstaff's confused and panicked state, the question died on his lips.

"I'm sorry, sir," said Kent over the intruder's shoulder, "I couldn't do anything to stop him."

"What's this – you ordering me to come here?" Taylor barked at Wagstaff and waved a telegram above his head, "Who do you think you are?"

"I didn't demand anything," spluttered Wagstaff, now openly sweating with fear.

"No, that was my handiwork," said Holmes, casually, "it would be much easier if we were all here together."

"Who are you?" shouted Taylor, turning his vitriol towards my friend, "and easier for what?"

"Who I am is not important, what *is* important are those who are about to join us."

As if on cue, I heard a heavy police vehicle pull up outside and a kafuffle in the hallway resulted in Athelney Jones entering the office with three uniformed men.

"Good morning, Mr. Holmes; Doctor," said the inspector and then turning his attention to the seated Wagstaff, "so this is the man you informed me of Mr. Holmes? And who's this pleasant looking character?"

Taylor had involuntarily made his way into a corner of the room as the policemen entered.

"This is Mr. Edward Taylor, Inspector. He is in league with Mr. Wagstaff and I am confident there is enough evidence to charge him with blackmail and murder."

"Murder?" cried Taylor, "who am I supposed to have murdered?"

"Mr. Jonas Clegg. Hardly the bastion of honesty and integrity himself but nevertheless, he still perished at your hand."

"I never met the man, you can't prove that I done him in, or anyone else for that matter."

"No, but *I* can," came a voice from behind the group of policemen. Kent, Wagstaff's clerk made his way into the room. "I witnessed what happened that night."

Taylor stared at the clerk with hard eyes, wondering what he was going to say next. "You didn't see anything," he snarled.

"I believe I am in enough trouble already with him," Kent threw a contemptable nod towards his employer, "I'll be damned if I'm going to swing for the likes of you."

"What do you have to tell us, Mr. Kent?" asked Holmes.

"Mr. Clegg asked me to accompany him to a meeting he had with this man's brother Robert Taylor on the night he died. He was overseeing the conveyancing of a large development in Rotherhithe. He had been called to a meeting on the site and told me he was a little uneasy about going unaccompanied. I therefore went along. I remember it was an eerie, moonless night and the river looked menacing as our hansom pulled up outside the Angel Pub. Mr. Clegg checked his watch and told the driver to pull round the corner out of sight while he would look for Taylor. He told me to wait in our cab.

"After several minutes of feeling extremely uneasy, I heard voices in the distance; unsure as to whether they were simply people coming out of the pub or not, I decided to leave the cab and walk towards the road end. I stayed out of sight but leaned around the corner and saw Mr. Clegg about a hundred paces away by the steps that led down to the foreshore, in animated conversation with both of them," – again Kent indicated towards Taylor – "the conversation appeared to get more and more heated and I saw this one pull out a knife – I could see it glinting in the dark. His brother seemed to remonstrate with him and he put it away, grabbing Mr. Clegg by the collar instead and dragging him down the steps. His brother meanwhile disappeared in the other direction. I heard Mr. Clegg's fearful cries and found myself paralysed with terror. I despise myself for my own cowardice."

Kent dropped his head momentarily before concluding his tale.

"He dragged Mr. Clegg to the river and held him under until the futile thrashing stopped. He simply waded out and went on his way. I sent the cabbie away and wandered the streets all night in a daze at what I had just witnessed."

The room was in complete silence throughout Kent's recollection of the horrific event.

"Why didn't you say anything?" It was Wagstaff who broke the silence.

"How could I? What was the point? The wrongdoing that you and he were both up to would have all been exposed and I would be incriminating myself by my own involvement, or at least my knowledge of it. I couldn't go to the police; I couldn't confront Taylor; much to my shame I decided the best course was to say nothing and keep my job."

"Well, this is a pretty little picture, isn't it?"

"It is indeed Jones," replied my friend to the policeman's comment. Holmes proceeded to repeat his findings to the inspector concerning Wagstaff and informed him of the solicitor's *modus operandi*, including handing over the letter he had picked up from the Post Office that morning.

"Thank you, Mr. Holmes, another triumph!" cried Jones, "Two for the price of one in fact! I've arranged for this Taylor's brother to be arrested as well, so we'll take it from here."

His constables marched all three men out in handcuffs and we returned to Baker Street. As we sank back into our chairs I reflected on the case:

"Holmes? I can't help feeling that the case is somehow incomplete. What about the fraudulent activity regarding Taylor's building development – how can the monies be recovered? And then there are the corrupt corporation officials that allowed it to happen and who presumably benefitted from it – how can we identify them and bring them to justice? And as for Wagstaff and Clegg's other activities – we have only addressed the wrongdoing we know about, what else have they been involved in?"

Holmes, who was sitting back with his eyes closed, interrupted me with a calming gesture, "Watson, my dear fellow, don't torture yourself. Such is the criminal nature of such a vast metropolis like ours. Wagstaff, Clegg and Taylor are simply the minute hands that turn and keep the giant timepiece of corruption moving. The unseen wheels and mainsprings are the mechanisms which make the chronometer work. While the other smaller parts can, and will, be replaced, *they* invariably remain intact, never seen, always innovating and adapting their methods to the passing of time." He looked at me kindly, "We can never hope to complete cases like this to any degree of satisfaction, Watson. All we can do is bring certain pieces of villainy to an end – if that inconveniences others in the meantime, that we must view that as an added satisfaction. One thing is guaranteed however – we will never see an end to our line of work.

In the weeks that followed the Wagstaff case, the body of the unfortunate Gerald Rutherford was exhumed along with three other suspected victims. As Holmes had predicted, traces of aconitine were found in each body and it was enough to convict Wagstaff who went to the gallows as Holmes had hoped for.

His clerk was found guilty as an accessory and sentenced to hard labour, after it was established that – after Wagstaff had murdered the surviving parent in each case – Kent had taken the orphaned child and discarded them in some far corner of London to fend for themselves. As despicable as his actions were, the authorities took into consideration his assisting with the prosecution of Taylor. *His* fate mirrored Wagstaff's after he was found guilty of murdering Jonas Clegg and dumping his body in the river. Much to Holmes's annoyance, Taylor's brother escaped the clutches of Scotland Yard after some confusion amongst Inspector Jones's colleagues – apparently, they raided the wrong house allowing the older Taylor to flee. He was never seen or heard of again.

In the days following the conclusion of the case, I read in the *Pall Mall Gazette* of the latest atrocity in the Eastend and it struck me for the first time that two such killers were operating in various parts of London simultaneously. The methods of Wagstaff and the affluent setting of South London may have been quite different from the horror and violence perpetrated by the so-called Ripper in the slums of Whitechapel, but the net result was the same: multiple deaths of innocent people. Unfortunately, the latter murderer has yet to be apprehended, but at least the good people of South London have had *their* threat removed.

As for Holmes, I recall him commenting of his exhaustion following the Jonathan Small case and that of the Dulwich Solicitor, and how he would welcome an escape from London for a while. We would be in luck as the following weeks would be taken up by not one, but two cases in the fresh air and spectacular setting of Dartmoor.

The Baroda Silver

Chapter I

"Ah, a client, I perceive!" I was standing by our window, idly looking down onto Baker Street when I made my grand announcement. It had been a slow, dull few weeks for my friend and by association, for myself. I always dreaded such periods of inaction during my days at our lodgings, for fear of my friend Sherlock Holmes reverting to his foul drug habit, used in order to supplant the stimulus gained from his unique profession. So, the sight of someone hurrying along, studying the numbers on the doors of each house – clearly looking for a particular residence – came as somewhat of a relief.

It was a pleasant late spring morning – the last Saturday in May – with a gentle breeze cooling the warm sun. Birds twittered under the eaves of our roof, while down below, Baker Street was bustling into life, preparing for a new day.

I had spotted the fellow, who was the subject of my exclamation, some minutes earlier and watched as he hurried between buildings before stopping in front of each one briefly and then moving on. From what I could make out under his cap, he appeared to be a middle-aged man with a sallow complexion. Whenever he looked up, he seemed to have an expression of some consternation. Underneath his arm he carried a rolled-up package, while a seemingly bulky sack was strapped to his back. Surely it was 221b he was looking for, seeking out Sherlock Holmes to help solve the cause of his concern.

At my announcement, Holmes rose lazily from the chair in which he had been lounging and came to stand by my side. With his hands in the pockets of his dressing gown, he followed my gaze and smiled as he saw the interested personage approaching our door.

"I knew it!" I exclaimed, triumphantly, at the pealing of the front doorbell. I couldn't resist going onto the landing to greet our visitor, so pleased was I with my own cleverness. Hearing the exchange between the man and Mrs. Hudson in the hallway however, I was soon to return to our sitting room disappointed.

"It was Johnson, the butcher from Edgeware Road, Watson," announced Holmes, who hadn't left his spot by the window. "His delivery lad was taken ill and the poor man has been forced to carry out his own errands."

"Yes," I commented, somewhat chagrined, "Mrs. Hudson ordered a cold joint of mutton apparently."

Holmes chuckled, without moving. "I suspect you are not wrong however, in your prediction of a client." I re-joined him by the window. "The man opposite," he indicated with an upward nod.

"The soldier?"

"Cavalryman, I believe."

"Indeed," I confirmed, observing the officer's blue tunic, matching overalls with two yellow stripes that ran down to his mess spurs.

He was standing beside the lamppost on the opposite side of the street, apparently oblivious to the other occupants who went about their business: the flower seller; the passing cabs; and the young newspaper boy, who was trying to inform his prospective customers about the latest arrangements for the forthcoming Diamond Jubilee but was failing miserably to make himself heard above the increasing hubbub. Even two off-duty infantrymen, distinct in their red tunics, passed and appeared to motion an acknowledgement to their fellow serviceman, but no response was garnered, as the cavalryman stared straight ahead.

Finally, he picked his way across the street and the doorbell of 221b echoed through the house for the second time in as many minutes. Hurried feet could be heard on the stairs and Mrs. Hudson duly appeared and announced, "A gentleman to see you Mr. Holmes. A soldier."

Holmes acknowledged our landlady and indicated that she should show him in. Moments later, the finest figure of a man anyone could behold entered our quarters and I couldn't help but stretch my back to attention in his presence. My friend had no such inclination of course. "Good morning," he said simply to our visitor.

"Mr. Sherlock Holmes?" – Holmes confirmed with a sharp nod – "My name is Lieutenant Robert Fenton of the 17th Lancers. We would like to engage your services in an extremely delicate matter."

Holmes indicated our visitor to sit on the couch as he casually rasped a match and lit a cigarette before slumping into his chair by the fire. Fenton removed his cap and perched himself on the edge of the couch, barely creasing his immaculate uniform as he did so. "This is my friend and colleague Dr. Watson. He is more of a military man than I, it may be useful that he remains."

"Indeed, Doctor," said the soldier turning to me as I took the seat opposite Holmes. "It was a mutual acquaintance of ours who suggested we approach Mr. Holmes. I believe you know Simon Woodward from Afghanistan?"

"Of course!" I cried, "although I haven't seen him since we dined together one Christmas, several years ago."

"Well, Woodward's son, George, is also in the Seventeenth. It was a combination of the two who suggested Mr. Holmes may be able to help."

"Lieutenant Fenton, you have a skill for prevarication!" cried Holmes, "Help with *what?*"

The officer was clearly not used to being spoken to in such a fashion by a civilian and had to compose himself.

"We have had a great treasure stolen from our depot headquarters in Canterbury," he explained. "The regiment is preparing to celebrate the fortieth anniversary of its actions during the Indian Mutiny and its most prized spoils from the campaign have been taken."

"They are?" Holmes appeared disinterested, even dismissive.

"The regiment chased one of the ring leaders of the Mutiny around the jungles of Central India for nine months. When they caught up with him at Baroda, they charged, and routed his army. It virtually signalled the end of the hostilities. He had a cache of silver, passed down from the Mughal Emperors – coins, charms, elephant rings – worth thousands. They've been held at the depot ever since and are displayed whenever there is an anniversary. Now, on the eve of the biggest one of all, they've been stolen."

Lieutenant Fenton spoke with a clipped tone and remained perfectly still – his back, ramrod straight – throughout his brief narrative.

"When were they taken?" asked Holmes.

"Last Tuesday night. I was away from the depot myself at the time but when I returned the following morning, I discovered the theft."

"Where were they stolen from?"

"Beside the officers' quarters is the Mess, at the rear of which is an anti-chamber where the regimental colours are displayed. Adjacent is a storeroom where various campaign trophies are kept when not on display. It seems to be from this room that the Baroda silver was taken."

"What are the items kept in?"

"There is a large trunk or chest containing the various trinkets." The cavalryman indicated the approximate size of the container with his arms.

"Who has access to this area?"

101

"Well, that's the mystery, Mr. Holmes. Very few people other than the officers of the regiment would ordinarily access the area. There may be some cleaning or serving staff I suppose, but it would be unlikely that thieves would make their way in there."

"And yet someone did, and then made their way out of the depot with a large trunk, without being seen." Holmes's tone was cynical and disinterested.

"I understand it doesn't reflect terribly well on the regiment Mr. Holmes, but that is the situation we find ourselves in."

"Tell me your suspicions, Lieutenant Fenton."

"Well, there are two witnesses who reported they saw a Sikh in and around the depot on the night of the theft."

Holmes looked up, "A Sikh?"

"Yes, sir. It could be that he had something to do with it."

"In what way?"

"Well, there are a lot of Indians over here for the Queen's Jubilee – one theory we have is that maybe a group of them want to steal what they feel is rightfully theirs."

"Have you notified the local police?"

"No, not as yet."

"Why have you waited over two days to seek help with the theft?"

"The colonel hoped that we could resolve the matter internally before approaching anyone. It was only when our own internal investigation turned up nothing that Woodward suggested we approach yourself and Doctor Watson for help. I should add that the colonel wants to keep the matter as discreet as possible, in order to limit any reputational damage."

"Ha!"

"If you think this is beneath you Mr. Holmes, I can go elsewhere." Fenton was clearly getting impatient with Holmes's disrespect for what was clearly an important issue. After a moment's pause Holmes relented and threw his cigarette into the fire.

"Very well, Lieutenant Fenton, I shall take your case."

"I'm sure the colonel will be pleased," replied the soldier, not appearing terribly impressed himself. "When can you come to the depot?"

"We shall be on the eight-twenty out of Victoria on Monday morning. Perhaps you could have someone meet us in Canterbury?"

Lieutenant Fenton stood up and made to leave. "I will. Thank you, Mr. Holmes, Doctor Watson. I will show myself out."

With that, he was gone.

The following Monday morning, having packed a clean collar and an overnight bag, we found ourselves being met at Canterbury Station by a private from the regiment, who had a horse-drawn cart waiting for us. With a salute and an introduction, he took what luggage we had and loaded it on to the vehicle. We climbed aboard and twenty minutes later, Private Thomas was showing us into Lieutenant Fenton's office within the regimental depot.

"Good morning, gentlemen, I'll take you to meet the C.O."

We followed the Lieutenant across the large parade ground and he pointed out the Officers' Quarters on the far side. Holmes stopped, forcing our host to do the same. He studied the layout of the depot from where we were standing, balancing his cane on the tips of his gloved hand, as if it were a weathervane gently turning in the breeze. He studied the six wide pathways that led away from the square. "Not exactly a labyrinth," – his muttered observation was addressed to himself rather than to either Fenton or me – "but enough passages and dark corners for someone to move around unseen, especially at night."

With a nod of permission, Holmes indicated to Fenton that we could move on. The officer took us into the building on the other side of the parade ground and up a flight of stairs, at the top of which sat another man in uniform behind a desk on a large open landing area. Upon seeing his superior officer, the young man immediately stood to attention.

"Stand easy, Davis. Is the colonel in?"

"Yes, sir," replied the private, "he's expecting you."

Fenton knocked on the door marked Lieutenant General Sir Darcy Harris-Baxendale, K.C.B. Colonel, 17th. Lancers. We both read the nameplate and Holmes shot me a mischievous glance, the corners of his mouth being plucked into a half smile.

"Come!" came a command from inside.

We followed Fenton into the spacious office that had a large window overlooking the parade ground and was decorated with memorabilia from the regiment and its adventures: pictures of famous battles, portraits of previous commanding officers, models and a collection of books displayed in a beautiful oak panelled bookcase that lined one of the walls. As we entered, the colonel rose from behind the large matching desk. He was a man who appeared to be in his late sixties; his thinning white hair barely covered a large dome of a head, while his eyes and mouth gave the impression that they were being pulled down by heavy, sagging jowls, themselves covered with grey side-whiskers.

Fenton saluted his C.O. "The gentlemen from London, sir."

"Good morning," he said curtly and continued, without waiting for a reply, "I have to say immediately that I have little time for amateurs, Mr. Holmes. If it wasn't for young Woodward who talked me into hiring your services, you wouldn't be here at all."

"And yet, here I am," said Holmes coolly. "I suspect it is not the army way to make the theft public and formally go to the police, so it appears that I am your only option. That said, I do have other matters to attend to if my presence here is such an inconvenience?"

My friend's gaze never left the colonel who clearly had never been spoken to in such a manner under any circumstance, let alone in his own office. I sensed Fenton's discomfort and must confess that I had to bite my gum to save breaking into a smirk.

The colonel cleared his throat and eased his neck uncomfortably in his collar, "No," he said at last, "we appreciate your help, I'm sure. Can't have those damn 21st making us the laughingstock of the army." This final comment was almost mumbled to himself. His tone then became more conciliatory, "Perhaps we could offer you some refreshment?"

"No, that won't be necessary, Colonel. Tell me, what steps have been taken so far?"

"All leave has been cancelled until the silver is found," – the colonel made no attempt to hide his indignation – "we have searched the depot high and low without success and this Indian chap seems to have disappeared into thin air!"

"Well in that case," said Holmes, "I would prefer to inspect the area where the silver was taken from."

"Of course, of course."

With a gesture, he indicated to Fenton that the meeting was over and he should acquiesce to Holmes's suggestion.

Chapter II

We retraced our steps out into the parade ground, where we had to pause while a troop of six cavalrymen walked their horses back towards the stables, apparently having returned from exercising their mounts.

"Feels a bit lame B," called one of the riders, as he indicated his mount to Lieutenant Fenton.

Fenton acknowledged, "Take him straight to the Farrier, Burns."

"Sir."

The rider peeled away from his colleagues and walked his horse towards one of the pathways Holmes had studied earlier. We continued across the parade ground and Fenton took out a set of keys to let us into a corridor that led to the anti-chamber he described in Baker Street two days earlier. The room was decorated with flags and banners from the various campaigns that the regiment had participated in over the past century. A guard in full uniform, armed with a lance, stood at ease by the colours; he stood to attention at the appearance of his superior officer.

"As you were," said Fenton and the private resumed his position.

Fenton then took another key from the set and opened the door to the storeroom. Holmes immediately crouched down to inspect the keyhole: he took a small lens from his vest pocket and grunted his frustration at the gloomy light. Striking a match, he held it up to the keyhole and peered into the small aperture through the lens.

"Is this room normally guarded?"

"Not usually, Mr. Holmes," replied Fenton, "but the C.O. has ordered it since the theft."

Holmes went through several matches before he appeared happy with his observations and finally crossed the threshold of the room itself. The detective then glanced round focusing his attention on the one window in the room. Moving towards it he gave it a cursory examination. Running his gloved fingers along the sill, studying the latch he gave a quiet "Hmm" to himself. Almost as an afterthought Holmes then looked at some of the items within the room itself.

I have observed on many occasions that my friend pays little regard for the cleanliness of his clothes or the condition of any material items when he is on a case. Countless times, I have witnessed him wade fully clothed into water, crawl on hands and knees through mud or sift through the dust and ashes in an uncleaned fireplace, in an effort to find that vital clue. It was with little surprise therefore that I saw my friend climbing over boxes, throwing items away after studying them and generally treating the regimental trophies with disregard, almost contempt. I could not help being amused by Fenton's reaction to the detective's behaviour. Discomfort gradually turned to horror as he witnessed Holmes carelessly manhandle mementos from campaigns dating back to the regiment's formation and brought back from all four corners of the globe. The poor man was beside himself as he followed Holmes around the room, recovering discarded items, full in the knowledge that he would be held responsible for any damage.

The almost comical scene culminated in Holmes spotting a bugle that was mounted in a glass case. Fenton swiftly positioned himself between the detective and the object in case Holmes decided to inspect it further. "That is the bugle that sounded the charge at Balaclava. It remains in its case."

Holmes shrugged his disinterest. After some minutes he appeared to grow tired of his search and announced, "I have seen enough, we can leave now. I think we should turn our attention to this mysterious Sikh and in particular, to the men who claim to have seen him."

"Yes certainly," said Fenton, "he was seen from across the parade ground in the Sergeants' Mess and then by the guard at the south gate. If you would like to follow me to the Mess, I will introduce you to the man who saw him first. Perhaps I could suggest a little lunch first as Quartermaster Sergeant McCabe is on duty."

Holmes was unable to object, given the man's immediate unavailability, so we followed Fenton back across the parade ground to the canteen where he arranged a sandwich and a pot of tea. He then left us to eat our lunch while he went to look for the QSM. Holmes said little and ate nothing as we waited. After half an hour or so, Fenton returned and informed us that the QSM was now available when we were ready.

"Excellent!" cried Holmes rising to follow Fenton once more and giving no thought for what remained of my sandwich.

I hurriedly took a final bite and gulped a mouthful of tea, whilst wrestling with my hat and coat, as I attempted to keep pace with Holmes and Fenton. The lieutenant led us up another flight of stairs to an office apparently shared by the sergeants. As we entered, a mountain of a man rose from his chair; he had a ramrod straight back, dark slicked back hair with a matching handlebar moustache.

"Mr. Holmes, Doctor Watson, this is Quartermaster Sergeant McCabe. He was in the mess on the night in question and saw the Indian from afar."

Holmes addressed the man who stood well more than six feet tall, "Sergeant, can you describe the man for me?"

"It was strange, sir. As Lieutenant Fenton said, I was in the Mess," – McCabe thought for a moment – "I reckon it would be about eight o'clock. I was standing by the window and just happened to glance across the parade ground for no particular reason. There he was, on the far side, near the Officers' Quarters."

"Can you describe him?"

"It was difficult to see his features sir, at such a distance. He was distinctive by his orange turban. I think he had a beard. That was about it I'm afraid, sir. It was just a fleeting glance and he would be over a hundred yards away."

"Where exactly were you standing?"

McCabe took us through to the main hall of the Mess that had six windows that all looked out onto the parade ground. "I was standing here in front of this window, sir."

"So, it is likely that the man would have seen you too from his position?"

"I suppose so, sir, although I never really thought of it like that."

"Did you report the sighting?"

"I did, sir. I immediately turned away to speak with a colleague about the sighting, but when I turned back, he had disappeared. I then left the Mess and hurried over to where the man had been standing, but there was no sign of him.

"Just then, Private Richards appeared. Richards had been guarding the south gate of the depot and he claimed he had also seen the man. When Richards saw me, his face dropped as he knew he would be in trouble for leaving his post."

"Leaving his post?"

"Yes, sir. Those on guard duty are instructed to never leave their post."

"What did you then do?"

"I ordered Richards back to his position and carried out a search of the area to see if I could find the man, but I found nothing. I then raised the matter with Captain White who was the officer in charge that night."

"And what was Captain White's reaction?"

"He was in the Officers' Mess, sir. He just told me to ensure all the gates were guarded and to carry on. I then informed Lieutenant Fenton of the incident upon his return the following day and entered it in the diary."

I sensed a slight tension in McCabe as he spoke of this Captain White and wondered if that is why he also mentioned the matter to Lieutenant Fenton.

"Where do you suspect the man went?" asked Holmes.

"Well sir, the only explanation was that he hid out of sight and when Richards left his post, he sneaked out the south gate unchallenged."

"Thank you, Sergeant, if you could let me see the diary you refer to, that would be extremely helpful," said Holmes drawing the interview to an end.

"Certainly, sir," replied the QSM, standing to attention, "I'll get that for you now."

As the interview with McCabe was drawing to a close, raised voices could be heard outside. A moment later, a figure I took to be Captain White not so much entered as burst in.

"Mr. Holmes? Which one of you is Mr. Holmes?"

"That is my pleasure. This is my friend and colleague Dr. Watson. Now you have us at a disadvantage," Holmes added, knowing full well who he was addressing.

Ignoring me completely the man confirmed his identity, "I am Captain Clive White. Why do you not wish to speak with *me* regarding this most serious of matters?"

"Oh, I do apologise Captain, I did not realize you had some vital information that would help solve this mystery." There was more than a hint of sarcasm in Holmes's tone. This was however, lost on White and once more I found myself amused at Holmes's attitude towards the rather senior military personnel.

"Vital information? Vital information? I was the officer in charge of the depot on the night of the theft," asserted White.

"How long have you held your current rank?"

The captain was taken aback by Holmes's question, "Since February of this year. Why do you ask?"

Holmes ignored the question. "Approximately two months. And how many times have you been the officer in charge of the depot?"

"Twi- ", suddenly it dawned on White that he had dug a rather large hole for himself. His haughty air and arrogant tone instantly disappeared. "Well, I wasn't personally on guard myself," he said, rather pathetically.

"No, but you still maintain overall responsibility for the safety and security of your Regimental Depot." There was an uncomfortable silence before Holmes dismissed the officer curtly, "Still I'm sure no one blames you personally Captain. Thank you for your time. If I need any further information from you, I know where to find you." White left the room quietly. 'Another one full of his own importance,' sneered Holmes, after him.

"Quite an unusual pair," I said, "him and the quartermaster sergeant. I got the impression that there wasn't much love lost between the two."

At that moment, McCabe returned with the Regimental Diary, which Holmes leafed through for several minutes before announcing, "I think I would like to speak with your friend's son."

"Woodward?"

"Yes, I think he will be extremely helpful with the matter."

I failed to see Holmes's train of thought but Fenton arranged for Lieutenant Charles Woodward to speak with Holmes. After introducing us, Fenton once again excused himself and carried on with his other duties.

"Doctor Watson," said Woodward, "my father has spoken very highly of you in the past, it's a pleasure to meet you."

"The feeling is mutual I'm sure Lieutenant, I had dinner with your father on Christmas Eve, some years ago. It was wonderful to see him again, although I must say we have lost touch again since then."

"He's doing well. I'll be sure to pass on your regards."

"Please do."

The occasion I referred to was a gala dinner Simon Woodward invited me to at the Café Royal on Christmas Eve. It was an event that deserves documenting in its own right, as it resulted in Holmes preventing an attempt on the life of my old military comrade and others who were present at the occasion. As Holmes foiled the plot without Woodward, or anyone else knowing anything about it, I did not feel it was necessary to raise the matter, either at the time, nor now in the company of my former colleague's son. Instead, I stepped back and allowed Holmes to question the junior officer on the matter at hand.

"Lieutenant Woodward, tell me what you know about the theft."

"Not much, sir, to be quite honest. I wasn't on duty on the night in question and only learned about it the following day."

Holmes paused, "Lieutenant, I must ask you some delicate questions regarding your colleagues. I assure you your responses will be kept in the strictest confidence, but I do feel it is important for me to know a little more about the individuals I am working with and their relations with one another."

I was aware that Holmes was asking a lot of the young man, it wasn't the done thing to speak with people from outside about the workings of any regiment. Woodward was hesitant.

"Come now, Lieutenant," Holmes sought to reassure him, "I only want to recover the silver and prevent any embarrassment to the regiment."

After some further thought, Woodward appeared suitably placated. "Who in particular would you like to know about?"

"Well let us start with the individuals I have met so far, Lieutenant Fenton, Quartermaster Sergeant McCabe and Captain White."

"Well, beginning with B...or...Bob...well...Lieutenant Fenton that is – he's a fine chap; really popular with all the men; always first into the action."

"How long have you been fellow lieutenants?"

"Well, I won my promotion only last year, sir. Bob on the other hand has been on the rank for quite a few years," – Woodward paused momentarily – "must be five or six years I suppose. I think B is an ambitious lad but the cards just never seem to have fallen his way. Unlike Captain White, meanwhile, he knows just what to do to get ahead." It was as though Woodward had crossed his own Rubicon and was now prepared to speak freely about his colleagues.

"Really?" questioned Holmes in reference to Captain White.

"Yes, he hasn't been with the regiment that long and within a couple of years, finds himself climbing the officer ranks at pace. Hasn't gone down too well with the men if I'm honest who prefer their own lads who have come up through the ranks and who have fought alongside them."

"That was certainly the impression I got from the QSM," Holmes flashed a sly glance my way after using the army abbreviation, "your influence, Watson."

"Yes, the QSM is a bit old school, sir. Like many he doesn't really approve of someone coming in and wanting to take over without having served a bit of time in the regiment."

"And the private soldiers, Richards and Thomas?"

"Yes, they are both decent lads, sir. Richards got into a bit of hot water last week when he left his post. He's been relieved of guard duties and placed in the guard house pending the investigation later this week."

"Tell me Lieutenant, what is the process for cleaning the uniforms at the depot?"

Woodward appeared surprised by Holmes's change of subject, "Well, the men are responsible for cleaning their own uniforms, sir. The officers' uniforms are slightly different, they are not actually cleaned in the depot itself. There is a local tailor in the town who takes them, organises the cleaning and carries out any repairs – the repairs could also be the rank and file as well as the officers."

"And when does he collect them?"

"He doesn't actually collect them himself, sir. Every Wednesday afternoon, one of our men usually takes them down in a cart."

"Is it the same private who transports the items?"

"It is usually Private Thomas, the lad who collected you at the station."

"Could you give me the address of this tailor?"

"Yes, I suppose so, sir." Woodward reached in a draw for a piece of paper. Writing down the details, he handed it to Holmes.

"Gilmour's Tailor and Gentlemen's Outfitters, Green Street, Canterbury. That has been most informative Lieutenant Woodward, thank you for your help. Perhaps I could speak with Private Richards?"

"Certainly, sir, I will ask the QSM to show you to the guardhouse."

Holmes then turned to me whilst putting on his hat and coat, "Watson, I think I would like to pay Mr. Gilmour a visit following my chat with Richards. In the meantime, perhaps you could impose on Lieutenant Woodward again to carry out an inventory of the uniforms that have gone in and out of the depot during the last three weeks."

"Three weeks?" I repeated.

"Yes," he replied as he reached the door, "and perhaps it would be useful to speak with Private Thomas. I shall see you later this afternoon."

Woodward followed him out, whilst reflecting my own slightly bemused expression at Holmes's instructions. A few minutes later, the young lieutenant returned and, consenting to Holmes's request, took me to the armoury. The large atrium was an impressive sight with the walls lined with racks of lances, swords and carbines. At the far end of the store were rows of uniforms hanging like sentries, waiting for duty.

"Doctor, I will leave you in the capable hands of Corporal Round," – he indicated the man behind the desk who stood as we entered – "Corporal, this is Dr. Watson, a guest of the regiment who would like to inspect the inventory of uniforms."

"Certainly, sir," said Round, without questioning the unusual request, whilst at the same time, offering a nod of acknowledgment to me.

"In the meantime," said Woodward, "I will go and find Private Thomas and ask him to come down."

"What records do you want to see exactly, sir?" asked Round once Woodward had left.

It was a good question, to which I wasn't really sure of the answer. Following Holmes's instruction, I asked if he had a uniform inventory for the previous three weeks.

"Certainly, sir." Round reached into a cabinet behind him and produced a large leatherbound ledger that landed on his desk with a thump. "Take my seat, sir. He opened the book at the most recent entry, "Just work back as far as you want to go, sir. I have some labelling to do, so just give me a shout if you need any assistance."

"Thank you, Corporal," I said as Round disappeared into the regiment of tunics and overalls.

The ledger clearly listed the items being sent to Gilmour's: what was required for cleaning; what was required for repair, and details of the repair; who the item of uniform had been assigned to; and who had submitted the item for attention – in every case, the individual was one and the same person. Over the previous three weeks, the numbers of items being transported to the tailor had been reasonably consistent:

Wednesday 5th May '87
Officers: fifteen service dress for cleaning.
Other ranks: twelve tunics and ten sets of overalls for repair.
Wednesday 12th May '87
Officers: twenty mess dress uniforms for cleaning.
Other ranks: fourteen tunics and ten sets of overalls for repair.
Wednesday 19th May '87
Officers: thirteen service dress for cleaning; one ceremonial frock coat for repair.
Other ranks: ten tunics and ten sets of overall for repair.

Just then, Private Thomas appeared, "Lieutenant Woodward said you wanted to see me, sir?"

"Yes, Private Thomas, thank you for taking the time to come," although I must confess at that stage, I wasn't entirely sure what Holmes wanted me to ask the young man. I decided to start with the obvious question, "I believe you take the boxes of uniforms to the tailor for cleaning and repair?"

"Yes, that's right, sir. I just load the trunks onto a cart and take them down – it's not far away, just a couple of miles into town."

"And is that every Wednesday?"

"Yes, that's right, sir."

"Where to you collect them from?" I asked, rather floundering in my thought process.

"Usually from here at the armoury, sir, where George – Corporal Round – has some that need to go, or from the Officers' Quarters as there are always some officer uniforms that require attention."

"And where did you collect them from last Wednesday?"

Thomas thought for a while, "I think it was over at the officers' quarters, sir."

"And you simply take them to this tailor Gilmour in Canterbury?"

"Yes, that's right, sir. Old Gilly has worked with the army as long as regiments have been stationed here, I believe. Not a bad bloke, although he's a lad for his horse racing – always got a tip or two for me every time I go. I never win anything mind you," the private lamented to himself.

"Is there anything else unusual about your recent visits to Mr. Gilmour?"

Thomas pondered a little more, "I don't think so, sir. There were one or two more trunks last week than normal I suppose but it's not unknown for there to be a few more."

"How many do you usually transport?"

"Well, it's usually just two or three but last week I think it was five…no actually, I think it was six because I remember thinking to myself it equalled the record."

"The record?"

Thomas initially paused, as though he had said too much, but then explained, "Just my little tally, sir. There was a bit of a raucous do in the Officers' Mess in January. A lot of the uniforms had to be cleaned afterwards. Sorry sir, I hope I'm not speaking out of turn."

"Don't worry about it, Thomas," I said with a smile, knowing how some officers can behave at times, "your indiscretion is safe with me."

Not knowing what else to ask, I dismissed Thomas, thanking him for his assistance. I sat for about ten minutes turning the thing over in my mind and trying to find some possible explanation for the whole thing. The more I tried to adopt Holmes's method of reasoning, the less the strange series of events appeared to make any sense. I was still puzzling over the matter when Corporal Round appeared once again from the forest of uniforms.

"I heard Thomas come in sir, was that useful?" he asked.

"Yes, I think so," I replied, rather embarrassed by my own obtuseness. I closed the large ledger that sat before me and prepared to hand it back to Round, when a sudden thought occurred to me. "Thomas said there was a particular occasion in January when there were more uniforms than normal to take for cleaning?"

Round smiled, "Yes, sir, some of the young officers got a little boisterous at one of their dinners and the result was several of their Mess uniforms had to be sent for cleaning. I seem to remember it led to a real dressing down by the C.O. at the time – no pun intended, sir."

"Can you remember the date?" I asked.

"Yes, I do as a matter of fact, sir. It was Burns' Night – one of the officers comes from Glasgow and he organised it. Do you want me to find him for you Doctor?"

"No that won't be necessary, Corporal Round," I said, re-opening the ledger. Having enjoyed many a Burns' Nights in my younger days, I knew the exact date I was looking for. I leafed back through the large parchment pages until I found the 25th of January, which was a Monday. Turning the pages to the following Wednesday, I found the entry:

Wednesday 27ᵗʰ January '87
Officers: fifteen service dress and thirty Mess dress for cleaning; nineteen Mess dress items for repair.
Other ranks: eleven tunics and ten sets of overalls for repair.

Thomas had just told me on that occasion in January, he had transported six trunks full of uniforms for cleaning or repair. I then turned back to the most recent entry:
Tuesday 25ᵗʰ May '87
Officers: fourteen service dress for cleaning; two Mess dress for cleaning
Other ranks: twelve tunics and nine sets of overalls for repair.

The numbers didn't compare. It was at that moment when I suddenly realised what Holmes had been getting at with his interest in the uniforms and the tailor. Something else struck me for the first time upon re-reading the ledger.

"Corporal, the entry made for last week was made on a Tuesday, as opposed to a Wednesday. Why was that?"

"Yes, that is unusual, sir. I just received a note to have whatever uniforms recorded by Tuesday."

"Who gave you the note?"

"I'm not sure, sir, it just appeared on the Monday morning. I probably still have it here if it would be of any use?" he added looking through one of the desk drawers. "Yes, here it is."

Taking it from Corporal Round, I read: "*Gilmour requires consignment first thing Wednesday morning. Have rank and file uniforms deposited in anti-chamber no later than three o'clock Tuesday.* Thomas didn't say anything about taking the consignment early," I added to myself.

"I'm not sure, sir. I think he still took them on the Wednesday morning, it was just earlier than normal.

119

Usually, by the time he gets everything together, it is after lunch when he sets off. You can keep that note if you might think it will be of some use."

"I will Corporal, thank you, and thanks you for your time."

It was shortly after six o'clock when Holmes returned to the depot. We had only just greeted each other when Lieutenant Fenton appeared looking agitated and eager for news.

"The colonel is keen to learn of your findings Mr. Holmes."

"All in good time, Fenton. Would it be possible for Dr. Watson and myself to find some accommodation for the evening?"

"Yes, of course," replied the lieutenant, "I'll arrange for rooms to be made up in the Officers' Quarters. Have you some news? Should I inform the colonel?"

"No, that would be premature. I would prefer to share my findings with you first."

"Very well, perhaps you could come to my office?"

"Not tonight, I think tomorrow would be better."

"Very well, shall we say nine o'clock?"

"That will do nicely," said Holmes, then turning to me, "Doctor, I suggest we find something to eat and have an early night."

It was clear Holmes had no intention of divulging his findings, either to Fenton or to me. I, on the other hand, was keen to share my own deductions with him. It was during our excellent steak and a glass of the finest claret in the Mess that I decided to raise the matter.

"Holmes, I think I know how the silver was taken."

"Really?"

"When Private Thomas made his weekly journey to Gilmour the tailor last Wednesday, I would wager that the treasure was packed in the trunks with the uniforms. Thomas told me that he normally transported two or three of the containers, whereas last week he carried six. However, when I checked the inventory, there were no more uniforms for cleaning and repair than normal."

"Excellent, Watson. I was thinking the very same thing myself."

"What is more," I said, producing the note given to me by Round earlier, "this instruction was received into the armoury a week ago."

Holmes studied the note, "You really have done some excellent work this afternoon, my dear fellow. I must congratulate you."

"Thank you," I replied, a little taken aback by the generosity seldom shown by my friend. "There is one thing, however. If our hypothesis is true, that Indian chap who was seen the night before was nothing to do with the robbery. Therefore, the question remains, who was he and what was he doing here?"

"I'm sure we will find out soon enough," was Holmes's enigmatic reply.

Chapter III

The following morning, we were seated in Lieutenant Fenton's office at the appointed hour.

"Well, Mr. Holmes, do you think you can throw any light on the matter?"

"Yes, but before I do, Lieutenant, tell me about your life and career with the 17th Lancers."

Fenton was not the only one to be taken aback by Holmes's strange question. "I…I don't understand," he stammered.

"Well, where were you born? What is your background? How long have you been with the regiment?"

Fenton flashed a glance at me that was a mixture of confusion and suspicion. Not understanding the relevance of Holmes's question myself, I was unable to offer the soldier any clarification, so he finally turned his attention back to my friend.

"Well, my family come from Derbyshire, where I was born," said Fenton, hesitatingly, not really sure as to the relevance of what he was saying. "My father was a mill worker. I was always a curious lad and wanted to do something different, so I joined up as a boy soldier back in '69. Served in India and Ireland, charged with the regiment at Ulundi during the war with the Zulus, before returning home."

"So, you are due to retire from service in two years' time having served thirty years?"

I could not see where Holmes was going with his questioning but I sensed that Fenton was becoming increasingly nervous. "That's correct," he said.

"And what do you have to show for your long service and loyalty to the regiment? Not even a Captaincy."

"I still don't understand what you are getting at Mr. Holmes."

"Oh, I think you do, Lieutenant," – Holmes's voice lowered to a most serious tone – "if you work with me, I can save your own reputation and that of your regiment. If you work against me, I must expose you as the thief of the Baroda silver."

"*Holmes!*" I exclaimed, not believing what I was hearing. My gaze of astonishment then shot across to look at Fenton, who was staring at my friend intently. "Lieutenant Fenton?"

The officer ignored my question but continued to stare at Holmes. "What do you mean?" His tone was measured, without any indication of offence or surprise.

"Upon questioning your colleagues, I learned that for more than ten years now, you have tried to gain promotion but have been passed over at least three times. Popular with the men but *'not officer material'* as your senior colleagues might put it. Risking your life for the regiment and your country is still not good enough in the eyes of some if you are not from the right background or you did not attend the right schools. Your most recent disappointment came earlier this year when you were overlooked in favour of Captain White, someone with little experience and even less affiliation to the regiment which you have dedicated your whole life to.

"Something else your superiors no doubt looked down upon was your proclivity for enjoying the company of your rank and file colleagues in the local hostelries. It was on one such occasion, when you found yourself in the company of Josiah Gilmour, the tailor who deals with the regiment's uniforms. Whereas some of the men knew he liked a sporting flutter, few knew the extent to which he was in debt through his reckless gambling. The night when you found yourself sitting beside Gilmour and listening to his tale of financial despair, was the very night that the devil took hold of you. You had just been overlooked for promotion yet again and saw an opportunity to make both you and Gilmour a fortune. In doing so, he would alleviate his debts and you would not only gain some revenge on those you feel have wronged you over the years, but you would make yourself financially secure for the rest of your life, following your forthcoming retirement. You set about hatching a plan with Gilmour that would see you remove the silver and have it transported to his shop. He, in turn, would make arrangements to have it whisked away to be melted down, thus earning you both a small fortune and at the same time seeing the evidence destroyed.

"Your weeks of planning culminated in the events of last Tuesday. You were one of the few officers who did not attend the dinner in the Mess; you made it known to as many people as possible that you were visiting a sick relative in Deal. But the truth was that you do not have any family in Kent; you yourself said your family hale from Derbyshire. Your fabrication was simply an excuse for you not to attend the dinner with your colleagues. Instead, you mixed a little lime-cream with some boot polish, disguised yourself as a Sikh and made sure you were seen by a few colleagues, who – once the silver was found to be missing – would suspect the mysterious Indian of stealing the treasure to avenge his ancestors from forty years earlier."

"*You* were the mysterious Sikh?" I cried, turning to Fenton, whose expression remained impassive, his eyes never leaving Holmes for a moment.

Holmes continued, "You succeeded in planting a seed with your colonel that the mysterious figure must have perpetrated the theft that night, while the whole of the depot was distracted. But the silver was never moved on that Tuesday night – not by you or anyone else. It lay waiting to be transported out of the depot the following day, from under the noses of the whole regiment. You, meanwhile, in the guise of the Sikh, cleverly positioned yourself at a distance from those who saw you, so they could never identify you personally in the role. The purpose of your guise was simply to arouse suspicion amongst those witnesses which allowed you to create the elaborate story of a group of vengeful rebel-Indians. The reality was that you were always within just a few yards of your own quarters into which you could disappear and assume your normal person. If anyone saw you as yourself – once you had rid yourself of your disguise – you could simply explain that you had just returned from your so-called mission of mercy to Deal."

"But if that is true," I asked, "how did the silver come to be missing?"

"This is where your plan became very dangerous, Lieutenant Fenton," said Holmes, replying to my question but addressing his answer to the officer. "Once you had left this note in the armoury," – he produced the note I had passed to him the previous evening – "you had to work quickly to wrap the silver."

"Wrap the silver?" I repeated.

"Yes. What uniforms were due for repair were brought across on Tuesday afternoon, not on the usual Wednesday morning. Without a guard in place, you took the boxes into the storeroom, where you had emptied a further three trunks in preparation for your nefarious operation. You proceeded to wrap the coins and treasures into the uniforms and distributed them evenly within the six boxes, making sure that no one trunk was any heavier than the next, and significantly, the silver would not be felt or heard by Private Thomas as he lifted the trunks and transported his weekly cargo.

Gilmour would then take receipt of the boxes from the oblivious Thomas. The tailor's role was then to unwrap the

125

silver and arrange through a contact in his desperate world of money lending and repayment to have the silver melted down. He would then take a percentage of your profit following the completion of the operation.

"You were aware of Gilmour's gambling debts which made him a willing ally. What you couldn't possibly have known however was the extent to which Gilmour was in financial difficulty. With a dreadful stroke of luck as far as you were both concerned, the very afternoon he took receipt of the trunks of uniforms and the silver, bailiffs arrived and seized all his assets, including everything in his shop."

Holmes looked at Fenton intently, "*Including* the trunks containing the uniforms – *and* the Baroda silver. Also contained within one of the trunks were items of clothing, when arranged and worn correctly, could easily be mistaken at a distance for that of a Sikh prince. Confirmation of this ruse came with the long piece of orange cloth that you fashioned as a turban. Dark marks were still present on the edges where the cloth had rubbed against your face that was covered with the mixture you concocted. It is an effective method of darkening the pigmentation of the skin, one that I have used myself on more than one occasion.

"When I spoke with Private Richards, who is currently under house arrest – like QSM McCabe – he told me that he saw what he thought was a male Sikh from across the parade ground.

"'I thought I was seeing things at first,' he told me. 'I was sure no one had entered past me at the south gate. I assumed therefore, that he must have somehow got in through the main entrance on the other side of the depot. I'm not sure what made me turn round but when I did, there he was, near the Officers' Quarters. He was just standing there in his white robes and orange turban. The funny thing was, he made no attempt to move – it's almost as though he wanted to be seen. I quickly checked the perimeter as far as I was able to and when I looked back, the man had disappeared.'

"*It's almost as though he wanted to be seen,*" repeated Holmes. Richards was quite perceptive with this comment, as that is exactly what you wanted – you wanted to be seen to add credibility to the subsequent theory about a group of Indians seeking revenge. As Richards turned away, and as McCabe left the window to come down and investigate, it gave you the little time you needed to slip into your quarters unseen and rid yourself of your disguise."

At last – at the conclusion of Holmes's narrative – Fenton spoke while being extremely circumspect with his question, "If this is all true, how could you possibly access items that were now in the possession of the authorities?"

I noted that he did not refute any of Holmes's allegations.

"I have connections in government – a telegram between here and Whitehall gave me all the permission I needed to inspect the contents of the sequestration. Once I had confirmed my suspicions and discovered the silver, Mr. Gilmour had little choice but to confess all."

It was only then that Fenton broke and his demeanour completely changed; his head sunk in shame at the sudden realisation of what he had done. "I am finished," he mumbled.

After a long, uncomfortable silence, Holmes spoke again, "Not necessarily Lieutenant Fenton. The connections I have in government extend beyond the exchange of telegrams. I am confident that I will be able to recover the boxes of silver and pardon you and your conspirator in the process."

Fenton looked up in surprise, "Why would...? I would be deeply indebted to you Mr. Holmes if you would consider -"

Holmes cut him off with a raise of the hand, "I will make the necessary arrangements."

Chapter IV

And so it was. Sherlock Holmes somehow, through the contact in government he referred to, effected the release of the trunks containing the stolen silver from the clutches of the authorities who had seized the assets of Mr. Gilmour following his descent into bankruptcy. That afternoon, upon Holmes's instruction, Fenton ordered Private Thomas to retrieve them from the impound, without revealing their contents and transport them back to the depot. They were taken back to the room from where they were packed and Fenton repositioned them in their rightful home. At four o'clock, we entered the colonel's office to appraise him of the good news.

"I don't understand," said the Commanding Officer, "How can the silver be back in its rightful place all of a sudden?"

"It was simply a misunderstanding. As the silver was being prepared for your *Mutiny celebrations* – Holmes couldn't resist emphasising the words in a condescending manner – "the boxes they were contained within were mistakenly mixed with some other containers that were due for removal from the depot. Fortunately, they were recovered and returned to their rightful place."

"It all seems a bit strange to me," mumbled Colonel Harris-Baxendale from under his whiskers. "Who was responsible? I'll have them on a charge!"

"No one person could be held accountable. It was a series of collective oversights and bizarre coincidences."

"What about this Indian chap who was seen on the night of the theft?"

"Inexplicable, Colonel. Perhaps one of the coincidences that I referred to: QSM McCabe and Private Richards thought they saw the same man, or perhaps there was such a character who got lost and strayed unknowingly into the depot. Either way, I suggest you have Private Richards released from his confinement immediately and celebrate the fact that you have recovered your treasure; and with it you have succeeded in avoiding any further scandal. I shall arrange to have my fee settled through Lieutenant Fenton. Good day." With that, Holmes headed for the door.

It was once we were back in Baker Street that I broached the subject of Holmes's decision not to expose Fenton as the thief.

"I almost have a certain sympathy with him," Holmes explained as he thumbed his favourite black tobacco into the bowl of his cherrywood pipe and we settled by the fire. "The man had dedicated his life to the army and for what? It seems that Fenton is popular with his subordinates but much of his work has gone unrecognised by his superiors. Woodward described him as 'ambitious,' and yet it appears his ambitions were never realised. This could only result in an element of resentment as he approached retirement."

"But how were you alerted to him?"

"I suspected something was amiss before we even left Baker Street. Fenton stood opposite our lodgings on Saturday morning for over ten minutes before knocking. Why would anyone do that when they were desperate to have a matter resolved."

"But why would he come at all if he knew there was a chance you could solve the mystery?"

Holmes looked disapproving at me, "*Chance?* Ha! If you recall Watson, it was not Fenton who suggested commissioning our services but the son of your friend Woodward. Once the suggestion was made to Colonel Harris-Baxendale, he ordered Fenton to visit us in Baker Street and even then, he waited over two days before making his reluctant journey to London.

"It was highly unlikely that someone could have broken into the depot, identified exactly where the silver was and successfully made off with it without being challenged. Therefore, it had to be arranged from inside the depot itself. Things became a little clearer when I read the Regimental Diary. There were several entries concerning the transportation in and out of the depot of munitions, food, general supplies; but there was only one regular event: that which saw boxes being taken out."

"Thomas's transportation of the uniforms each Wednesday," I announced.

"Precisely! This was the best hypothesis that would meet the facts. When you yourself worked out the irregular numbers of trunks to transport the number of uniforms, the matter was settled beyond doubt. My interview with Gilmour simply confirmed my suspicion that it was Fenton who instigated the theft."

"Remarkable! I suppose the great irony was that his plan to steal the silver became academic when the treasure was seized as part of Gilmour's assets."

"It was fortunate for Fenton that it was," replied Holmes. "Had he made good on his intention to have the silver sold into the criminal fraternity – where it would have certainly been melted down – I would not have been able to save him. Moreover, given the characters Gilmour had associated himself with, it is unlikely that he or Fenton would have seen any financial return for the stolen booty. Instead, I believed I have helped him get away with an even greater treasure – that of liberty, freedom and an unblemished reputation.

The Dowager Lady Isobel Frobisher

Chapter I

I have recorded elsewhere how young Doctor Verner purchased my Kensington practice upon Holmes's reappearance and my subsequent return to join my friend in our old quarters in Baker Street. I was extremely proud of the practice that I had developed and part of me was loathed to let it go. However, the years prior to my decision had not been without pain – first my belief that I had lost Holmes and then the all too real passing of my darling Mary. When the time came therefore, it was with a sense of optimism that I agreed to the sale, believing a fresh start would do me good. And so, it would prove over the years following, although I was delighted when Verner asked me to act as his *locum* on occasion when he was unavailable.

I recall one such instance when the young man spent a couple of weeks in France visiting some distant relatives of his. As I would be due to be back at my old desk for two weeks and given that the surgery was almost three miles from our Baker Street lodgings, it made sense to stay in the living quarters which held such bitter-sweet memories for me. Both Verner and I agreed it was the sensible option, so I packed a bag and left Holmes to his latest chemical experiment.

It had been a relatively quiet few weeks for my friend and as I left, I couldn't help but glance at his desk drawer, hoping that it would remain firmly locked during my absence. Holmes was hunched over a microscope analysing some insect he had been telling me about the previous evening, while a test tube containing a strange non-descript coloured liquid bubbled and smoked beside him.

"With some of the aromas omitted from my experiments," said Holmes, apparently reading my mind, "I don't think there will be need for any artificial stimulants. Be on your way, Watson, and attend to your duties." He gestured towards the door without looking up from his work.

"You know where I am if you need me. Otherwise, I shall see you in a fortnight."

The following week proved to be an interesting, even enjoyable period, as I reacquainted myself with some of my old patients and took great satisfaction from engaging my professional skills once more. Little did I know that my final days as *locum tenens* would see my two worlds overlap.

It was the Thursday of the second week, with Verner due to return from France the following weekend. The maid wakened me and informed me that a telegram had been received from the home of Lady Isobel Frobisher, and I was being asked to attend urgently. I groggily looked at my watch on the bedside table: it was just after half past seven.

I wasn't familiar with the name of the patient so, after hurriedly washing, shaving and dressing, I leafed through the patient files in Verner's surgery. There was no sign of any Isobel Frobisher. Rather than waste more time, I climbed into the hansom that the maid had waiting for me and set off. The address was one in the beautiful rows of stucco townhouses in the heart of Belgravia. I wasn't under the illusion that it would be an ordinary house call, but if I were, any such thoughts would have been dispelled as the cab pulled up. A small crowd had gathered and were being shepherded away from the white steps of the property by a uniformed policeman. Another of his colleagues appeared to be standing guard at the front door. There was a police wagon ominously parked along the street.

I identified myself to the officers and was shown into the house, "Just in there, sir, third room on the right," said the constable pointing down the hall.

From the doorway of the room indicated, I immediately saw the body of an elderly woman slumped over the dining table. There was another constable standing with his back to the window opposite and with a nod, he consented to allow me forward to approach the body – it was clear that she was already dead.

"We are both too late, I'm afraid Doctor," said a familiar voice behind me.

I turned to see Holmes and Inspector Athelney Jones standing on the other side of the room.

"Holmes! What on earth-"

"Later Watson," interrupted my friend. He wore an expression I seldom saw in all our years together – that of a defeated man. "Do your professional duties and I will explain later."

I turned my attention to the deceased. She was fully dressed and had fallen forward in her chair to the point where her head hung over the empty dinner plate in front of her. It appeared as though the large table had not been cleared from the previous evening as dirty crockery and cutlery were still present around the five place settings. The fingernails and the lips of the corpse had a slight hint of blue while the skin felt clammy; the advanced stage of *rigor mortis* had set in. I looked up from my preliminary examination at the sound of someone entering the room.

"Mr. Brotherton," said Inspector Jones upon the man's appearance, "the Dowager's butler, I believe?"

"Yes, sir," said the man without taking his eyes from the body, as though transfixed.

"We have met already," said Holmes to the policeman, "I would like to ask Mr. Brotherton some questions.

Brotherton was oblivious to the exchange and stared at his mistress. Holmes sought to ease his distress, "Come, Mr. Brotherton, let us move to the other room where we can speak a little easier – with your permission of course," he added to the inspector almost as an afterthought. Jones nodded. Holmes then turned to me, "Watson, if there is nothing more you can do right now, perhaps you would join us?"

"Certainly. Other than pronouncing the death and estimating the time of death around midnight, I can't confirm anything else until after the *post-mortem.*" I certainly had my suspicions about the cause of death but didn't feel it appropriate to speculate with Brotherton and some of the junior constables present.

I followed Holmes and the butler into an adjacent sitting room, while Jones commenced arrangements with his men to have the body removed.

"Now Mr. Brotherton," began Holmes after the butler had composed himself, "how long have you been in Lady Isobel's employ?"

"Martha, erm…Mrs. Brotherton and I have been in the service of the late Lord and his wife for more than twenty years now."

"Your wife is the cook?"

"That's right sir, and also lady's maid, I suppose. When Lord Frobisher died some of the staff were let go because they weren't really needed anymore. Martha and I were retained as we had been with them for such a long time."

"Are there any other staff here now?"

"No sir, there is a footman and groom back at the country residence in Berkshire but it was only Martha and I who accompanied Lady Isobel into town."

Holmes looked round the room. "Does Lady Isobel own any other properties?"

"No sir, not anymore, just this house and the family estate. The Earl used to have quite a few properties but when he became ill, I think he made sure he had everything sorted for his wife. He sold most of his assets to make life as easy as possible for her Ladyship."

"Who discovered the body?"

"I did, sir. My wife and I have rooms downstairs in the basement, so we don't really hear much once we are down there. It would have been unusual for Lady Isobel to be up so early," Brotherton paused as he tried to gather himself, "so, when I came upstairs this morning, I didn't go into the dining room initially. As Martha prepared her ladyship's breakfast, I went to wake her. I knocked a few times but received no reply. I announced that I would enter but when I did, I found that it was empty and the bed had not been slept in. I then came back downstairs to find Lady Isobel slumped over the table, where she had been sitting the previous evening."

Brotherton put his head in his hands, clearly distressed by what he had found. His wife was equally so; her sobs could be heard in an adjacent room where someone – a neighbour as it turned out – was comforting her. He continued by telling us that his wife had been alerted to the tragedy by her husband's cries. Rushing into the dining room, the housekeeper let out a shriek at the grim scene.

"And what time was this?" asked Holmes.

The butler inhaled deeply, "I would say about seven o'clock, sir. That's when I called for you Mr. Holmes."

Holmes took out his watch and flipped open the lid: it was now a quarter past nine.

"Called for you?" I asked my friend and then turning to the butler, "Why did you call for Mr. Holmes and not myself or the police?"

"I-" Brotherton began, but Holmes interrupted and waved away my question.

"Tell me about last night." I was surprised by his question; it was if he had some prior knowledge as to the events of the previous evening.

"Lady Isobel hosted a dinner party for members of her family."

"And who was in attendance?"

"It was just a small gathering – Lady Isobel and the late Earl's niece Miss Celia Frobisher, Lady Isobel's brother-in-law Mr. Noel Lytollis, her *own* cousin Reverend Laidlaw and the cousin of her late husband, Mr. Simon Frobisher." I thought I sensed a half smile from Holmes, as though he could have listed the group himself. "They were all the family she had left, and now this. What a terrible way to go."

Brotherton continued saying that the gathering had sat up quite late and Lady Isobel excused him and his wife from the duties telling them that they could clear up in the morning.

"What time was this?"

The butler thrust out a lip as he pondered, "I would say around eleven o'clock sir. I had ordered a coach to take her ladyship's guests home around midnight." He nodded to himself, "Yes, so Martha and I must have left them to it around eleven."

"And you suggested the time of death somewhere between twelve and one," Holmes checked with me. I nodded my confirmation. "So, the events between eleven o'clock and one o'clock are of interest," he added to himself.

I think it was only then that Brotherton realised that if there had been foul play, he – and his wife for that matter – must be considered as one of the handful of suspects.

"Yes," he said simply, almost to *him*self. And then, "As I said earlier, we don't hear that much from downstairs but one thing I thought I heard at one point was the dining room door opening. I probably thought that was Lady Isobel going to bed."

"What time was this?"

"Well, I'm not sure, it would be sometime after her guests had left." Brotherton thought a little longer, "In fact come to think of it, yes, I heard the dining room door open – the hinge has a distinctive creak that I should have attended to before now – but a couple of minutes later it opened and closed again. It struck me as a little unusual at the time but I thought nothing more about it until it just now came to mind. Probably nothing." As he spoke, the butler looked into the middle distance, clearly trying to recall the events of the previous evening and make some sense of them. "If only I had come upstairs to check. I didn't know anything until this morning – that's when I notified you, Mr. Holmes, knowing that you had been working for her ladyship. We also thought it best to summon the police and Dr. Verner, although I didn't realise he was away."

He looked at me when he made the last point, as if to answer the question I asked earlier. My instinct told me that it was unlikely he or his wife would be involved in any wrongdoing but I understood that Holmes had to pursue the line of enquiry anyway, as gently as he could.

"Would you describe Lady Isobel as a good employer?"

"I would, sir," said Brotherton firmly, focussing back on the detective, "a real lady in every sense of the word. Never had a cross word with either of us. Nor did her husband before her, Lord Frobisher was a true gentleman. We've both been very happy working for them and they have always treated us well."

"Can you give me a few more details of the family members who attended last night?"

"Yes sir. There was the niece, Miss Celia. She only moved back to England last year after her father – Lord Frobisher's younger brother – committed suicide.

138

Apparently, he had got into some financial difficulty and couldn't take it anymore. Had to sell his big house in Norbury at one point but it didn't do any good. He kept losing money and it seemingly all got too much for him. Left his widow virtually penniless and she married some acquaintance of her husband. They planned to honeymoon in America but tragically during the crossing, there was a fire in the engine room of the liner and it went down with all passengers and crew. Miss Celia then moved back here after she was living on the continent, as her aunt was then her only living relative."

"And the others?"

"Mr. Lytollis is Lady Isobel's brother-in-law. Poor chap was blinded in a house fire in which his wife, her ladyship's twin sister, perished. Apparently, he fought to save his wife but to no avail. What a tragedy," Brotherton lamented, shaking his head, "She was such a hansom woman just like her sister, they were like peas in a pod. What a shame – Lady Isobel took that really hard."

After a reflective pause, Brotherton continued. "Then there was the Reverend Laidlaw from St Bartholomew's. He is Lady Isobel's cousin. And finally, Mr. Frobisher, the *Earl's* cousin."

"What were their respective relationships like with your employer?"

"It's difficult to say, sir," answered Brotherton, "she didn't seem to see much of them but in fairness, they have all rallied 'round since the Earl passed away. They have all been fairly regular visitors to Lady Isobel since then. I may be speaking out of turn but Martha reckons young Celia can be a 'right little madam'! The others I only showed in at the door so I couldn't really judge." I was amused at Brotherton's last comment as he proceeded to do just that. "Mr. Lytollis was a bit of a sullen chap, although after losing his wife and his sight I'm not surprised. The

Reverend was a bit of a cold fish I suppose – difficult to read. And if I'm honest, I was surprised her ladyship welcomed Mr. Simon Frobisher as I had never heard him spoken of before the Earl's death, let alone come to the house. But then it was none of our business, I suppose. We just looked after Lady Isobel."

"Thank you, Brotherton," concluded Holmes, "I will probably need to speak with you and your wife again but I think that will do for now."

Once the butler left us, Holmes sat in silence for a few minutes before we made to leave. We met Inspector Jones again in the hallway and Holmes gave him the names and addresses of Lady Isobel's relatives, "I suggest you inform them of the Dowager's passing."

"Do you suggest I bring them in for questioning?" asked the policeman.

"No, I don't think that will be necessary at this stage. Wait until the *post-mortem* confirms the cause of death and tell them that the reading of Lady Isobel's Will will take place on the afternoon of her funeral – date still to be confirmed. I don't think any of them will be going anywhere in the meantime." He bid the Inspector good morning and then turned to me, "Are you free later this afternoon, Watson?"

I knew it was irrelevant as to whether I was free or not in Holmes's view. "Nothing I couldn't postpone," I said.

"Meet me back at Baker Street at four o'clock where I shall tell you a little more about this strange case."

Chapter II

I met Holmes outside our lodgings at the appointed hour as he was just stepping out of a hansom. Back in our sitting room, he lit a pipe and then used the match to bring the fire Mrs. Hudson had prepared for us to life, before taking his favourite chair. Once I was positioned opposite in my usual station, he began to tell me of his investigations in my absence. On the very afternoon I had left, Holmes had received an extremely brief letter from Lady Isobel; he pointed to the envelope on the mantlepiece. It ran thus:

Eaton Square, SW 1

Dear Mr. Holmes

I wish to commission your services in a delicate family matter. I fear that my life is in danger. I would be obliged if you would call at my residence tomorrow morning at ten o'clock.

Sincerely yours

Isobel Frobisher

I looked up from the note and Holmes took up the story.
"As I had no current engagements I was intrigued by the invitation and naturally went along. Brotherton met me at the door and showed me into the room where we interviewed him this morning. Lady Isobel was waiting and proceeded to tell me of her fears."
Holmes related how the Dowager had lost her husband two years earlier and she was now in the sole possession of

their extremely wealthy estate. They hadn't any children of their own and their only living relatives were the people who Brotherton had informed us had been with Lady Isobel last night.

"'I have my concerns and suspicions about them all, Mr. Holmes,' Lady Isobel had said to me, 'my husband Geoffrey was a proud, honourable man and I would hate to think his memory would be sullied in any way after I am gone.'

"'You speak as though that is imminent, Madam.'"

"'No one is sure what the future holds,' said the Dowager cryptically. She referred to possible criminal behaviour perpetrated by her family members and asked me to investigate their various backgrounds. 'My husband's niece for example, Celia Frobisher. I fear that she has done nothing but bring the family name into disrepute all her adult life. Her father Richard was a good man – he worked hard to achieve a certain standing for him and his family. Yet it seems to me that his daughter repaid him by endlessly demanding funds to indulge her frivolous escapades in Monte Carlo, Venice and Constantinople with her unscrupulous friends. Richard told Geoffrey that he believed she not only wasted *his* money but she was also involved in embezzling some as well, and much of what she spent it on was illegal. The one thing that Richard was guilty of was his inability to refuse his daughter. The poor man couldn't take it anymore and ended up blowing his brains out.

"'Then there is the pathetic creature, Noel Lytollis...' Lady Isobel proceeded to relate quite a bit about him, which I shall share with you in a minute. She then stopped herself stating, 'No, this isn't fair, I should say no more. I want you to act with complete impartiality Mr. Holmes. If there is nothing to find and no wrongdoing then so be it. If, however, my fears are confirmed, I want your complete candour in the matter.'

"The first person I visited was Lady Isobel's niece Miss Celia Brotherton."

"And did she turn out to be a 'right little madam'?" I asked.

"Ha!" cried Holmes, recalling Brotherton's comment from earlier, "I'm afraid she was! I presented myself as Mr. Smike, a colleague of her late father's solicitor. With a wig, false nose – at the end of which balanced precariously a *Pince-Nez* – and a stoop, I enjoyed my visit immensely.

"'I don't know why you want to speak with *me!*' she announced haughtily, after I had finally tracked her down to a friend's house south of the river.

"Because when your father died last year, there was some confusion,' I replied. 'We are trying to establish if some funds that have come to light were part of his estate.'

"Her eyes flashed and her attitude changed immediately, 'Oh, in that case you better sit down, would you like some tea?'

"'That's very kind of you, thank you.'

"She disappeared momentarily and returned with a tray. Her hands were shaking with anticipation as she poured. 'Oh, I do love a nice cup of tea,' I said, 'it tends to reinvigorate one in the afternoon, don't you find?'

"'Yes, now what is this business you spoke of regarding my father's estate?'

"'Ah, yes.' I interrupted myself as I peered out of the window into the garden. 'Is that a rose bush, Miss Frobisher?' I rose from my seat and walked over to get a better look.

"'What? Oh, yes...I suppose so...I don't know. Come and get your tea before it gets cold.'

"'What a beautiful thing. I'm somewhat of a rose fancier myself you know – it looks like *Rosa Damascena* if I'm not mistaken. My dear wife always encourages me to display them at those rather grand flower shows but I don't think I have the confidence. They seem so very knowledgeable at these events, don't you find? I would hate to make a fool of myself.'"

I was amused by Holmes's narrative, picturing him playing the hapless buffoon – and referring to a wife! – much to the irritation of Celia Frobisher.

"'Mr. Smike, will you please come and sit down and tell me about my father's money!'

"'Well, that is just the thing Miss Frobisher,' I said retaking my seat, 'We are not sure if it is proper to your late father or not. Apparently, there were some shares belonging to your grandfather that don't appear to have been allocated to your late uncle Lord Frobisher for some reason. As he passed away before your father – his younger brother – we are just informing all relevant parties of our investigations in trying to establish if they were bequeathed to anyone and if they were not, trying to establish if they are proper to your father and his descendants, or to Lord Frobisher's widow, the Dowager, Lady Isobel.'

"'How much are we talking about?'

"'Oh, I would say there will be several thousand pounds' worth.'

"She almost spilled her tea into her lap," recalled Holmes with a roar of laughter, "just managing to catch the spillage in her saucer."

"'Tell me Miss Frobisher, did you attend the reading of your grandfather's Will when he passed away?'

"'No, I was just a child. He left me some money as his only grandchild but that is all I know.'

"'I see. And the reading of your uncle's Will, Lord Frobisher?"

"'No, I think I was a way in Monte Carlo at the time of his death.'

"'Did you not think to visit?'

"'Why should I want to visit?' she replied lighting a cigarette, 'there was nothing I could do.'

"'Perhaps show a little compassion for your uncle and his widow,' I ventured with a straight face.

"She didn't reply but simply looked at me with distain."

I have witnessed Holmes enjoying the discomfort of many an interviewee in the past and clearly this was one such encounter. He continued.

"'So, you didn't actually return to England until your own father died last year?'

"'Yes, that is correct, Daddy was funding my stay in Venice, so I had to return. I must say Mr. Smike, your questioning is more like that of a policeman than a solicitor.'

"'Heaven forbids, Miss Frobisher! I apologise if I am giving the wrong impression. I am only trying to establish the chronology of the events so that any outstanding monies can be allocated to the correct individual.' Reverting to the subject of money appeared to refocus the young lady's mind.

"'Of course, of course.'

"From my deadpan expression, I don't think she could work out whether I was being sarcastic or genuine. Realising that she had not shown much sorrow at the loss of her parents or at her uncle's passing, she made no reply and turned her head away to look out into the garden at nothing in particular.

"'I will leave you to admire that beautiful rose bush Miss Frobisher, good afternoon.'"

"She was staying not too far from St Bartholomew's in Greenwich, so I took the opportunity to visit the Reverend Christopher Laidlaw in the same guise. The vicar was a slightly built man with a sallow complexion. His facial expression upon my arrival had me puzzling over what word you might use to describe him in your flowery tales, Watson – I settled on, '*shifty*'."

"'I don't suppose anyone in the family ever mentioned the shares to yourself Reverend?' I asked once I had explained the purpose of my visit.'

"'No, I am not particularly close to my cousin Isobel,' was the clergyman's curt reply, 'I have never had the opportunity to visit.'

"'Never? How long have you been back in the area?'

"The vicar's eyes flashed with concern at my apparent knowledge. He was wondering how I knew he had been *away* from the area. If I knew that, what else did I know? He decided not to pursue his own questions.

"'About twelve months I suppose. I've been extremely busy and we were never that close in our younger days. She had completely gone out of my mind if I'm honest."

"'Yes, well honesty is always the best policy,' I said with a smile. 'Tell me, do you know of any other relatives of the Frobisher's in the area? Perhaps I could ask for their help too.'

"'I would hardly describe them as *relatives*, Mr. Smike. There is a niece of Isobel's husband' – he thought for a while 'yes, Celia, that's her name. Absolute wastrel if I recall, always flitting around the country, and when she wasn't doing that, she was off galivanting abroad. And then there is that poor wretch, Lytollis, I think I had only ever met him once before, on his wedding day. He is the husband of Isobel's sister who died in a house fire. I think that's about it.'

"'Did I hear something about a cousin of the late Earl?'

"'Oh yes, now you mention it, I think there is. I'm afraid I couldn't tell you anything about him however.'

"'Not to worry Reverend Laidlaw, it has been kind of you to spare me some of your time. Our investigation will continue and if there is any news, I will be sure to pass it on.'"

When Holmes had finished his narrative, I asked, "How did you know Laidlaw had been out of the area?"

"As part of my preliminary investigation, it transpired that the Reverend Christopher Laidlaw was not quite as reverential after all. This devious *clergyman*" – Holmes spat the word out – "is guilty of stealing monies from charities connected to his former parish in Lancashire; what he got away with earlier in his career can only be imagined. The bishop was obliged to call the police in but rather than risk the reputational damage to the parish and the diocese, he decided not to press charges against Laidlaw. Instead, and in agreement with the Archbishop of Canterbury himself, it was arranged to have him moved out of the diocese and back to London where it was felt he could do less damage."

"Good Lord, it's almost so fanciful to be unimaginable!"

"You will always remain a kind soul, Watson," said my friend with a smile, "but money and power do strange things to people, even those in the most trusted of positions."

"How such a man can put his head on the pillow at night, having abused his position is quite beyond me. Should have been defrocked if you ask me." After the shock of listening to Holmes's narrative regarding the Reverend Laidlaw, he them moved on to the tale regarding Noel Lytollis.

"'Laidlaw had described Lytollis as a 'poor wretch;' I understood why when I met him. A seemingly once handsome man had been reduced to a stooped cripple, shuffling along behind a tapping white stick which cleared his dark path.

"'You must forgive me Mr. Smike, I'm not as light as I once was,' he said as he led me into a sitting room.

"'Don't worry about that, Mr. Lytollis, I will try not to fatigue you.'"

"'I'm not sure I can be of any great help in the matter, as I am technically the in-law of the family. But obviously if there is any light I can shed, I would be happy to do so.' Lytollis lowered himself into a wingback chair by the fire, "'Well Lady Isobel will need all the support she can get no doubt, at this confusing time.'

"'Yes indeed, very confusing. I must try to visit more often.'

"'How often do you visit the Dowager.?'

"'Not very often, I'm afraid. Isobel took the loss of her sister very badly and seemed to blame me. I not only lost my wife in the fire but everything else I owned as well as my sight. Whatever compensation I received has been virtually exhausted in the few years since.'

"'Yes, such a terrible tragedy. Please accept my, belated condolences for your loss. I remember reading about the tragedy in the newspapers at the time, with their wicked rumours.'

"Lytollis shuffled uncomfortably in his seat. 'Yes, people can be so cruel.' He looked in my general direction with a pleading expression, 'I wasn't aware that my wife was in the house at the time of the accident. I simply knocked over an oil lamp after returning home late from a business trip. The flame skittered across the carpet and caught the hem of the curtain; from there the fire gradually got out of control and I had to get out of the house. It was only then that I heard my dear wife screaming – she had been asleep in bed the whole time. By the time I ran through the flames and into her bedroom, it was too late. I had to leap through the first-floor window to make my own escape. The creature you see before you is the result Mr. Smike.'"

"A detailed account," I commented, as Holmes paused his narrative.

"Yes, and one which I never asked for. My Shakespeare is a trifle rusty but I feel I am reminded of Hamlet."

"*'Me thinks he doth protest too much,'* to paraphrase."

"Exactly. As I mentioned, when I visited Lady Isobel for the first time, she shared with me her suspicions and relayed a very different version of events.

"'What my darling sister Evie saw in that gambling rake I will never know!' she told me. 'The day she died, she was due to come and spend a few days with me. Lytollis meanwhile was already away from home, no doubt at the track or in the bed of another man's wife. What he didn't know is that Evie took ill and didn't travel as scheduled; instead, she decided to stay at home and travel the following day. She told me that Lytollis's gambling debts were mounting up and I suspect that in order to raise some funds, he came up with the hair-brained scheme to defraud his insurance company by perpetrating an arson attack on his own home. When he returned that night, he assumed the house was empty and it was only when he heard Evie screaming through the fire that he realised she had been asleep in her bed. His attempts to save her failed and he was left in the state you saw before you – poetic justice I suppose, but it will never bring my darling Evie back.'"

I was startled by Holmes's recollection of what Lady Isobel had told him, "A very serious allegation."

"Yes, but not without foundation," Holmes replied. "After I spoke with Lytollis, I made some further enquiries into his background and confirmed what Lady Isobel had told me. He had indeed accumulated considerable debts and on the day of the fire, his 'business trip' had consisted of an afternoon spent in an East End brothel he was known to frequent regularly. The circumstances of the fire were also suspicious as the Dowager suggested. The report into the fire – which even made the newspapers – stated that there was a strong smell of coal oil around the perimeter of the

149

house, suggesting that the fire had been started outside and not inside as Lytollis claimed. He may have been ultimately blinded by the fire, but Scotland Yard appear to have been blinded by the tragedy – and to the man's guilt, as established by additional evidence I have accumulated. The insurance company remained unconvinced and only issued a quarter of the policy total, something which Lytollis didn't challenge."

"Incredible." I sat shaking my head in disbelief. "Hang on! There was a fourth relative wasn't there?"

"Hah! Of course, the feckless Simon Frobisher, cousin of the late Earl. A bigger imbecile never walked the streets of London! I shall be interested in the mutual reaction when we introduce him to our friends at Scotland Yard." We both roared with laughter at Holmes's mischief. "The sum of his contribution to his family's legacy was to attempt to impersonate his cousin on not one, but two occasions: once to gain entry to the Tankerville Club and another to gain entry to the Royal Enclosure at the Epsom Derby! On both occasions, the Earl had to rescue his cousin and his own reputation in the process – at great expense apparently – to keep the matter out of the courts. I also discovered several other illegal impersonations on his part.

"I visited Lady Isobel to present my findings."

"And what was her reaction?"

"She was disappointed but not surprised. It seems my investigation had simply confirmed her own instincts about her family members."

We sat in silence for a while. "Holmes?" I hesitated but had to ask anyway, "do you think your investigation endangered her life?"

He sucked on his pipe, "I would be lying if I denied that it was the first thing that crossed my mind when I was summoned this morning. You probably picked up the strange vinegar-smell from the Dowager's table?"

"Yes, I did. You suspect poison?"

"Unfortunately, I did not have the opportunity of carrying out a thorough inspection of the scene as Jones and his herd of elephants arrived at almost the same time. I am still considering the question following my enquiries this afternoon."

"This afternoon?"

"Yes, I retraced my steps and visited three of those present last night. Miss Frobisher looked at me with a hint of recognition but obviously couldn't place me. I did not waste time in referring to my previous visit. Instead, I was suitably vague about my identity and succeeded in giving her the impression that I was working with the official police force."

"How did she appear in light of the news of the Dowager's passing?"

"Ambivalent," replied Holmes, "I asked about the evening.

"'What time did you leave your aunt's house?'

"'It would be around about midnight I suppose. We all left together.'

"'And how did she seem when you left her?"

"'Absolutely fine,' she snapped, clearly bored with such meaningless questions, 'I hope you don't suspect me of doing anything.'

"'Why would I suspect you, Miss Frobisher? I'm simply trying to piece together what happened last night.'

"'Of course. It is quite shocking news that's all.'

"'If you don't mind me saying, notwithstanding your family connection, you appear to be a slightly diverse group to be having dinner. What was the purpose of the gathering?'

"'Aunt Isobel said she had been looking into her affairs and she wanted to seek our views."

"'Seek your views? In what way?'

'"Well, as we are…*were*, her only relatives, I thought she wanted to share with us what she intended to do with her estate.'

'"And did she?'

'"Not particularly. Every time I raised the subject, she would deflect my question and simply say how much she adored her family. I think the old girl was losing her marbles if you ask me.'

'"Well, sadly not anymore, Miss Frobisher. I will leave you to deal with your loss,' I said rising to leave.

'"Do you know when the reading of the Will is due to take place?'

'"I'm sure you will be informed once the body is released for burial. Good afternoon.'

"No question as to where her main concerns are," I commented when Holmes paused, "Did you find out anything from the others?"

"The Reverend Laidlaw appeared as disinterested in the Dowager's passing as her niece had been. 'How did everything seem last night?' I asked.

'"Perfectly fine. Isobel appeared to be in perfect health when we left.'

'"Did you all leave together?'

'"Yes, it must have been around midnight I suppose. Her butler had arranged for us to share a four-wheeler. I got back to the vicarage at about a quarter to one. I have the luxury of a telephone here and it was this morning when I received a call from your police colleagues informing me of her death.' Naturally, I didn't bother correcting his assumption.

'"What did you talk about on the way home?'

'Nothing in particular; the usual inane chit-chat which one participates in during such circumstances. Much like the rest of the evening.'

'"You don't seem as though you were terribly enthusiastic about your cousin's invitation?" I noted.

'"I wasn't particularly, I had to cancel choir practice."

"Why didn't you just tell her you couldn't go?"

Reverend Laidlaw hesitated. "I…I just thought it would be the kind thing to do, given that she wanted some assistance with her affairs."

'"Yes, exceedingly kind I'm sure," I said as I rose to leave. 'Thank you for your time, Reverend, no doubt I will be in touch.'

"Lytollis greeted my visit with the most enthusiasm, unlike the previous two, he hadn't yet heard about his sister-in-law's death – not that prompted him to feign any form of loss. He launched straight into questions about the estate and the Will. His enthusiasm was dampened a little when I informed him that I was there specifically to ask about the events of the previous evening.

'"What did you eat and drink at the dinner?'

"He was obviously taken aback by the question, 'I obviously couldn't swear to it but I assume we all had the same thing: Isobel's cook produced a beautiful leg of lamb that was complemented by a fine claret; it was followed by a steam pudding. Why do you ask?'

'"Because Mr. Lytollis, your sister-in-law appears to have been poisoned.'

"I could almost see his devious mind working overtime.

'"I didn't go anywhere near the kitchen – besides, in my case, I couldn't possibly have done such a thing.'

'"I am not accusing you or anyone else of anything, Mr. Lytollis. I am simply trying to establish the fact of what happened and when.'

'"Of course, of course,' he said, clearly relieved.

"What about the other person, this Simon Frobisher?" I asked.

"He was missing unfortunately, so I never had the chance to speak to him."

"They all seem a delightful group," I commented.

"You are getting very cynical these days, Watson," replied Holmes with a smile, "It really doesn't suit you. Nevertheless, there is more than an element of truth in what you state. I am confident that they will all be available when the Will is read.

We sat in silence for a moment and I checked my watch: it was just after five. I heard a foot on the stair and assumed it was Mrs. Hudson with some afternoon refreshment; instead, there was a light knock on the door and Billy the page entered with his silver card tray.

"Letter for you Mr. Holmes," he said, standing to attention and offering the tray, "came earlier, sir when you were out."

"Thank you, Billy," Holmes looked unsure suddenly, as he slid the long cream envelope from the tray; it was as though he knew what the item was.

"What is it – were you expecting something?" I asked, as the page closed the door behind him. I sensed that all was not well with my friend and noticed that the elegant cream stationary appeared to match the one I had handled earlier.

He stood up and very deliberately removed the jack-knife from the mantelpiece; slitting open the envelope, he removed the contents and inspected the two items with his usual thoroughness before slumping back into his chair, almost letting the items drop to the floor as he held them delicately between the tips of his fingers.

"Holmes, what is it?"

Without looking up from the fire, he gestured for me to take the papers from him. As he had taken the two items out of the envelope, I had observed that one was a cheque.

"Good heavens!" I cried when I now saw the amount was for ten thousand pounds,

"Holmes, this is a king's ransom!" My friend snorted his derision.

The other item was a letter:

Eaton Square, SW1

Dear Mr. Holmes

I assume that we will not meet again so I am writing to express my sincere thanks for your work and to apologise for deceiving you. You completed your commission with the utmost thoroughness and confirmed my worst fears about the people I am ashamed to call family members. What I failed to disclose to you however is that some months ago, after feeling a certain discomfort, my doctor, Verner, referred me to a specialist in Harley Street who diagnosed me with an aggressive cancer that could not be treated. I insisted that no one was to know about this, not even Dr. Verner and my faithful and loyal staff Mr. and Mrs. Brotherton.

Over the past few months, I have been self-administering morphine to ease the pain. As the pain has gradually increased, so has my dosage. It has now reached a point where I can't bear my condition and fear of worse to come has brought me to the conclusion that now is the time to draw a curtain over the matter.

I should state categorically that I am ashamed to be associated with the people you investigated on my behalf; they are the epitome of avarice, profligacy and duplicity. I would encourage the authorities to investigate their misdemeanours further and take whatever action is appropriate.

It is mischievous of me to intimate that one or all of them will also be responsible for my demise, but I

155

must state in the interest of fairness that, to the best of my knowledge, they are not murderers, not in my case at least. My death will be at my own hand. Whoever clears my home should find an empty vile in the top drawer of my dresser. This vile contained the morphine with which I contaminated – or should that be, will contaminate – my own wine. The purpose of your investigation was to confirm my worst fears before I commit what some may view as a crime against human decency – I can only hope anyone who judges me does not have to suffer the same illness themselves.

I would be obliged if you would carry out two further tasks as part of your commission. First, I have arranged for my solicitor to read my Will seven days after my death. I would like you to attend on my behalf and subdue any disputes that may arise. Second, you have my permission to hand your findings regarding my family members' actions over to the police, where I hope they will take the appropriate action. I hope the enclosed cheque will suitably recompense you for your work and any further inconvenience.

Once again Mr. Holmes, thank you for your marvellous work and I again beg your forgiveness regarding my necessary subterfuge. Do not think too harshly of me and believe me to be-

Very sincerely yours,

Isobel Frobisher

As I read, Holmes continued to stare into the fire that crackled and sparked – the only thing which broke the silence in the room. I sat back down and I looked at the postmark on the envelope – it was dated the previous day.

"What a remarkable woman. She must have posted this yesterday, knowing what events were to follow later that night." Holmes did not respond. "Will you adhere to her final two wishes?"

He was clearly angry, "This is a new nadir, Watson. I have been reduced to police messenger and arbiter to squabbling families. I can promise her one of her wishes, but not the other."

Chapter III

Two days following the revelation, the results of the *post-mortem* confirmed that the cause of death was excessive amounts of morphine in the body. I mused that Lady Isobel must have organised the dinner party as a final act of revenge against those who had wronged her, to mislead them into believing they were in line to inherit her fortune, whilst at the same time, casting suspicion on them regarding her pending death.

Holmes did not disagree with any of my conclusions but showed little interest in discussing the case further. Since receiving the Dowager's final letter which solved the mystery of her death and, despite the financial recompense received from his former client he gradually sunk into one of his dark fits of depression as the week went on, clearly wanting nothing more to do with the matter.

On several occasions during our many years together, Holmes has asked me to represent him and conduct investigations on his behalf, as he claimed to be unavailable. On this occasion, he requested I go along to the solicitor's office of Lady Isobel and be present for the reading of her Will.

I therefore acceded to his request and attended the offices of William James who had apparently been Lord and Lady Frobisher's solicitor for years. It was on the seventh day following the Dowager's death that I joined a group of people in the anti-room of his chambers, waiting to be admitted. Looking around the room, it was obvious to me from the descriptions given by Holmes who those present were. Mr. and Mrs. Brotherton were also present at the instruction of Mr. James. Brotherton and I acknowledged each other when I arrived, much to the surprise and confusion of the others who had never set eyes on me. Everyone sat in uncomfortable silence, alone with their thoughts.

I decided it was appropriate to speak and cleared my throat, "Erm, good morning, everyone, I assume you are all here to hear the reading of Lady Isobel's Will. Perhaps I could introduce myself as a matter of courtesy. My name is Doctor John Watson. I am the *locum* doctor who was called to the home of the Dowager on the morning she died."

"So, what are you doing here?" asked the haughty young woman, shamelessly smoking a cigarette – presumably, Celia Frobisher.

"I was asked to attend."

"By whom?"

I was saved from further whittering by Mr. William James who appeared at his office door, "Sorry to keep you all waiting, you can come through now."

I waited for the others to enter the spacious office and brought up the rear. As I did so – and naturally unseen by the others – Inspector Jones and four of his constables came through the main entrance and took their seats in the waiting room.

Holmes's last contribution to the case had been to hand his findings over to Scotland Yard, the previous day. Jones and I nodded at one another before I entered Mr. James's office and closed the door behind me.

The solicitor took his seat, "Good morning, everyone. Just to confirm that my name is William James and I am Lady Isobel's solicitor and Executor of her Will, which is the reason we are all here today.

"I don't know why *they* should be here," said the young woman I took to be Celia Frobisher, tossing an insulting head towards Brotherton and his wife, "surely it should be family only."

"All those present are at the request of your aunt, Miss Frobisher," said the solicitor, calmly. "Now if you would all be seated, we will cover the contents of Lady Isobel's Will.

He proceeded to cover the peripheral and procedural points of the document before delivering the news that hit the room like a shell:

"I bequeath the whole of my estate in its entirety to Robert and Martha Brotherton."

There was an audible gasp. Before anyone could respond, Mr. James added:

"I wish to exclude from my Will the following people: my niece Celia Frobisher, my cousin Christopher Laidlaw, my brother-in-law Noel Lytollis and my late husband's cousin Simon Frobisher."

"This is *outrageous*!" shrieked Celia Frobisher. "She must have been coerced into this nonsense. They obviously poisoned her!" She speared an accusing finger in the direction of the named beneficiaries.

Martha Brotherton began to sob into a handkerchief, while her husband sat there looking shocked at what had just happened.

"There, you see!" continued Miss Frobisher, "proof of their guilt!"

"Your aunt changed her Will only a fortnight ago, Miss Frobisher and added a codicil, giving the reasons for her amendments."

This momentarily prompted silence in the room and allowed the solicitor to produce the document from the bottom of the pile of papers. He read:

"The reason for my decision is that Mr. Robert Brotherton and his wife Martha, have been faithful servants and friends (yes, friends) of both myself and my late husband for many years. I have found their loyalty and selflessness

humbling and their behaviour should be held up as an example to all.

"Equally, I exclude the few family members I have remaining, as their behaviour is the opposite to that which is demonstrated by my deserving beneficiaries. I shall leave it to Scotland Yard to decide whether previous actions perpetrated by those excluded from my Will constitute criminal behaviour."

After the shock of the announcement, there was a silence in the room which hung like a dead weight. It was the clearly nervous Reverend Christopher Laidlaw who broke it by asking, "What evidence does the Dowager have of *criminal behaviour?*"

"Perhaps you could help in that regard, Doctor Watson," said Mr. James.

With that, everyone turned to look at me; I had been sitting quietly to the side of William James's desk.

"Certainly, and perhaps I could invite Inspector Jones to join us." I called Jones into the office before continuing; his arrival seemed to cause an element of discomfort as those present shuffled in their seats. "I introduced myself earlier as Lady Isobel's *locum* doctor which is perfectly true; but I am also the associate of Mr. Sherlock Holmes who is a private consulting detective. Lady Isobel commissioned Mr. Holmes two weeks ago to investigate the crimes that she suspected you of committing."

"I was aware of no investigation!" Celia Frobisher's tone had weakened somewhat signalling a diminishing of confidence.

"That is what you *can* be aware of when Mr. Holmes carries out his work." I must confess I did enjoy the statement. "You may remember being visited by Mr. Holmes under the guise of a 'Mr. Smike'." The sense of realisation in the room was palpable and Laidlaw bowed his head.

"What I can confirm is that all family members here present are perfectly innocent of any wrongdoing as far as the health of Lady Isobel is concerned, either before the night of the gathering, or on the night itself."

"There! That proves it! It must have been Brotherton that did it!"

"Be quiet you idiot!" It was Christopher Laidlaw who rebuked his cousin.

I continued, "What none of you knew was that Lady Isobel had been suffering with cancer for more than a year and had been taking morphine to alleviate the increasing pain. At a recent consultation she was told that her condition was terminal and that she only had a few months left at most. Therefore, she got her affairs in order and changed her Will, something that she hadn't done since the death of the Earl.

"She then knowingly self-administered an excessive draught of morphine after you all left the other night." Again, there was silence, "I am afraid that Lady Frobisher was ashamed of you all."

"Where is your proof of that?" Celia Frobisher's confidence was deserting her as she clutched at her final straw.

"Mr. Holmes reported his findings to the Dowager and with that, she ended his commission. Following her death, Holmes received a letter from her, revealing her illness and her feelings towards you all.

"Regarding yourself, Miss Frobisher: your aunt told Mr. Holmes that you did nothing but bring the family name into disrepute, squandering your father's money and even using some of it as collateral in a conspiracy to embezzle funds from financial agents both here and abroad – which he confirmed.

"Then there is you, Reverend Laidlaw." All eyes moved from one to the other. "The bishop and archbishop may have forgiven your sins, but I'm not sure the authorities may be quite so understanding.

"As for Mr. Lytollis," – he must have felt the collective stare of those present boring into him – "Mr. Holmes found evidence that the fire which took the life of the Dowager's sister could only have been started deliberately from *outside* the house and not by accident from inside as you claimed. You are therefore directly responsible for the death of your wife."

"Finally, Mr. Frobisher. Not only was it discovered that you tried to impersonate your cousin, the late Earl, on more than one occasion, you actually posed as Inspector George Lestrade in an attempt to gain entry to the Christmas Ball at Windsor Castle last year." At this, Inspector Jones – who hitherto had had been unaware of this last revelation – managed to disguise a snorted laugh as an unexpected coughing fit.

"Lady Isobel asked Mr. Holmes to turn over his findings to the police who will decide on the appropriate action, so I will now invite Inspector Jones to take over."

Jones called on his uniformed officers to enter before addressing his suspects, "I would like the four of you to accompany us to Scotland Yard for questioning."

As they were being escorted out, Mr. Brotherton – who had been sitting quietly throughout – asked:

"What about my wife and myself, Doctor Watson?"

"You, Mr. Brotherton? I suggest you both enjoy your newfound wealth."

Barstobrick House

Chapter I

As I reflect on the many thousands of cases I associate with my friend Sherlock Holmes, I am aware that many cannot find their way into print due to their particularly sensitive or confidential nature. Holmes himself has forbidden me to publish certain investigations and there have been other occasions when I have given a pledge to a client that I would only consider publication if those involved were to pre-decease my friend.

In recalling the surprise telegram, I received from Holmes, encouraging me to tell the story of what he called "The Cornish Horror," my mind strayed to another case later that year that I, *myself* had deliberately withheld. It is only now, many years later, and having considered how others have permitted me to recount their own strange and curious problems, that I feel it only proper that I should publish a case that arguably had the greatest effect on me personally. It began upon receipt of a letter from a dear friend, three days after my forty-fifth birthday.

As I have chronicled elsewhere, Holmes's health had suffered at the start of the year through overwork, but his inability to rest had resulted in him keeping up a relentless pace that had shown no signs of abating as the year had progressed. Up to that point, he had already been involved in cases that had seen him journey, not only to Cornwall, but to Kent and Staffordshire, as well as solving mysteries involving Colonel Carruthers, the Dowager Lady Isobel and the disappearance of the one-legged Hurdy Gurdy man on Bond Street.

Finally, as we entered mid-summer, his workload had eased somewhat and by August, he found himself either wandering restively around our apartment, or curled up on the sofa under a cloud of blue pipe-smoke.

His mood wasn't lightened by the usual summer temperature. August was its regular oppressive self: an airless heat was trapped within the streets of the capital while the bleached buildings opposite our rooms in Baker Street reflected the mid-morning light upon our windows as if someone were playing a spiteful trick with a giant magnifying glass.

"Anything of interest, Mrs. Hudson?" asked Holmes, as our landlady entered with the morning's post.

"Not for you, sir I'm afraid," she replied, causing my friend to slink back into his languid position on the sofa, "just something for the good doctor."

"Thank you, Mrs. Hudson," I said, taking the letter from her, while feeling secretly contented that for once it was I that was the centre of someone's attention. "Good heavens!" I cried upon opening it, "it's from Jeannie!"

"Attracting the fairer sex once again, Watson?" asked Holmes from the sofa with a mischievous expression.

Ignoring my friend's impish comment I explained, "Jeannie is a childhood friend, who I haven't seen in..." – I paused to recollect – "...Good heavens, it must be over twenty years." She wrote:

Kirkcudbright, Scotland

My Dearest John

It has been almost ten years since we last corresponded and more than twice as long since we were together. Your birthday prompted me to write and make two requests of you.

Firstly, it is my own 40th birthday next month and my parents are insisting that we hold a small celebration. As darling Hugh is unable to attend and as we haven't seen each other in so long, I would love it if you would consider coming home for a short stay and join us. There is plenty of room here and it would be wonderful to see you again. My second request – regardless of your availability for our celebration next month – is that we can see a little more of each other in the future. As I get older, I think increasingly of our childhood and the wonderful times the three of us spent together.

My father is still the gamekeeper on the Queenshill Estate where you used to visit. It would be wonderful to see you again, please write and say you will come.

Affectionately yours,

Jeannie

"Well, I never," I said to the room in general. I appraised Holmes of the letter, more out of courtesy than anything else, not believing he would be remotely interested.

"You should go," said Holmes as he blew pipe-smoke upwards, dispersing the blue rings that were attempting to reach the ceiling.

"Oh, I don't know," I said turning back to the letter, 'it's been such a long time."

"Yes, it will do you good to take a break from the heat of London. I shall come with you."

My eyes shot up from the page, my expression of incredulity obviously speaking volumes.

166

"Don't look so surprised," said Holmes, clearly amused, "you have supported me all these years, friend Watson, I have a feeling that you may need a little support of your own, once you start delving into your past."

As I hold my pen today, with the rather unsteady hand of recollection, it was if Holmes were anticipating the profound affect the trip would have on me.

"Are you sure?" I asked.

"Of course," he replied, as if taking a casual leisure trip to the country or the seaside was the most natural thing in the world for him, "when is it?"

"Jeannie's birthday is the 12th of September, which is a Sunday, so it would mean travelling up the day before. We would then stay for a few days afterwards I suppose."

"Perfect!"

For the remainder of the day, I could not help myself from glancing over the top of my newspaper at my friend, as I tried – like I had on countless other occasions – to fathom the workings of that great mind.

The following day, after composing my reply to Jeannie, I paused as I went to post my letter. "Are you *sure* about going to Scotland?" I asked.

"Of course," my friend looked up with a smile, "I would love to see where it all began for my trusty biographer."

We spoke little of the matter during the following month until a few days before we were due to leave, I raised the topic again with Holmes and found his apparent enthusiasm hadn't abated. The day before my friend's birthday we set off from Euston on the long journey.

There was little conversation between us as our train rattled north. As usual on such a journey, Holmes spent most of the time in a meditative state while I struggled to concentrate on the various newspaper stories, I found myself reading and re-reading. Anticipation, excitement and a strange feeling of foreboding combined to make my journey uncomfortable and it wasn't until our train sat breathing heavily in Carlisle station, prior to the final leg of our journey, that Holmes sought to assuage my feelings.

"You seem troubled," he said from beneath his drooping eyelids.

"I suppose I am. I never thought such a trip would affect me so."

"What are you afraid of?"

"That's the thing, I don't really know! It's just been such a long time. I haven't been home – if it is appropriate to call it home – since I left for medical school over twenty-five years ago."

"I sense you are concerned about raking up old memories."

"They do say, some things from the past should stay in the past."

"And yet you seemed happy with the arrival of your friend's invitation."

I knew that Holmes had already deduced the reason for my discomfort.

"Yes," I replied, "Jeannie is a dear friend of ours from childhood."

"Ours?" Holmes let the word hang there.

"Indeed. My mother was childhood friends with her mother Elen. When Aunt Elen met William McFadden of Kirkcudbright, she moved east along the Galloway Coast from Stranraer. He was – and still is – the gamekeeper on the Queenshill estate near Kirkcudbright. It is owned by the Neilson family, steel magnates from Glasgow. While Elen and William had Jeannie, my parents had Hugh and myself and we would go on family holidays to visit them every year. It's a beautiful place."

"And I take it that your friend and your brother were particularly close?"

I smiled thinly at Holmes's perception.

"Indeed. Even though Hugh was seven years Jeannie's senior and I am closer in age to her, it was the two of them who became closer as we all grew. As I left to travel south, I believed and hoped that there would be a happy ending for them both."

"But alas, your brother fell on hard times."

"Yes," I replied, somehow finding a kind of catharsis in speaking of my brother, "I always maintain he was the cleverer of the two of us and could have been a doctor himself had he put his mind to it. But he went to Edinburgh and seemed to drift from one job to another, unable to find what he was looking for. I'm ashamed to say I gradually lost touch with him as I launched my career and went abroad."

"And it was your friend Jeannie who sent you his watch upon his passing."

"Yes. I didn't realise that the two remained so close and when Hugh died, his goods and chattels were sent to Jeannie."

"Don't torture yourself old friend. However much we care for others, everyone must take responsibility for the paths they choose."

I knew Holmes's summary was perfectly logical but I couldn't help thinking about our carefree childhood days when Hugh would look after his little brother. This led to the inevitable feelings of guilt at being oblivious to the extent of his troubles in adulthood and being unable to offer the help he no doubt craved.

I did feel a little better however, after articulating my feelings and as we crossed the border, I found myself looking forward to our journey's end.

Chapter II

Kirkcudbright's tiny station was as pretty as I had remembered it. When we stepped down from the train, it was as though I had been transported back in time to my childhood. The large round clock still hung above the westbound platform, which was furnished with gas lamps that stood like sentries at twenty-yard intervals; from their posts hung decorative baskets, flush with brightly coloured chrysanthemums and wisps of heather.

"*John! John!*"

My reverie was broken by the familiar Galloway accent, calling from the other end of the platform. Jeannie looked as lovely as ever, her beautiful chestnut-coloured hair peeping out from under her bonnet. We rushed towards each other.

"Jeannie, it's so wonderful to see you again. It's been so long."

"Thank you for coming John, it means a great deal to me. I have been so looking forward to your stay."

"How are your parents? The estate? What have you been up to?"

I was giddy with excitement at the sight of my dear friend and had completely forgotten about Holmes who had followed me along the platform at a more reserved pace. Jeannie however, looked past me and gave a slightly embarrassed cough.

"Oh, I'm so sorry!" I said to them both, "Jeannie, this is Mr. Sherlock Holmes, my friend from London. Holmes, this is Jeannie McFadden."

"Miss McFadden," Holmes touched the brim of his hat, "it's a pleasure to meet such a dear friend of the doctor. Thank you for inviting us to share in your special celebration."

"Thank you for coming Mr. Holmes, it's lovely to meet you. Now, let's get you both to your lodgings, you must be exhausted after such a long trip."

We followed her to a four-wheeled dog cart which had clearly doubled as a working vehicle over the years.

"Thank you, Robert," Jeannie said as the driver climbed down to help us with our bags.

Queenshill Estate was four miles inland from the little harbour town. It consisted of a large working farm and acres and acres of forestry. The nearest property to the road was the large farmhouse in which Jeannie and her parents lived. Further along the driveway was the original gamekeeper's cottage, which was too small for the McFaddens and so was now occupied by Mr. Neilson's butler and his wife. Then further still was Barstobrick House, named after the large hill, which towered above the estate, and the family home of Neilson and his family.

Elen and William McFadden were just as I remembered them – it was if time had stood still in this idyllic place. I had to stop myself from calling Jeannie's mother *Aunt* Elen and attempted Mrs. McFadden before both she and her husband insisted on me using their Christian names. That didn't stop William from instinctively lapsing back to his use of the adjective 'wee' when referring to me, as he had with my brother and I we were children. Every time he used the term 'wee' John, I swear I saw the hint of a smile pluck at Holmes's lips.

Elen made a wonderful meal from the produce of the farm and after some further reminiscing over a dram, Holmes and I made our excuses and retired early to our separate rooms, shattered after such a long day. Before I turned in, I peered out of the window at the black sky, another feature of this wonderful part of the country. I thought how I'd missed this, and yet on the other hand, of all the adventures I had experienced instead. There was almost an innocence about this place – untouched by the war and villainy I had encountered since leaving all those years ago. Uncertain as to whether I had made the right decisions, I turned out the light and let myself be engulfed by the blackness and the silence.

I enjoyed a wonderful night's sleep and awoke to an autumnal sunshine filtering through the curtains. Unaware of the time, I prepared my toilet, dressed and went downstairs in search of some breakfast. To my surprise, the house was deserted, until Elen appeared into the kitchen from the rear entrance, carrying a bowl full of eggs.

"Morning, John, sleep well?"

"Good morning, Elen, I did thank you," then looking around "where is everyone?"

"Oh, you must have been sleeping like a log because there were all sorts of activity during the night. There has been a fire at the big house. William and Mr. Wallace – that's Mr. Neilson's man – managed to put it out before it took hold. Thankfully, there's not much damage. Jeannie's up there helping clear up the mess and Mr. Holmes followed them when he learned of the excitement."

"That's dreadful news," I said, "hopefully no one was hurt?"

"No, thankfully not. The house is virtually empty as Mr. and Mrs. Neilson are visiting family in America. Apparently Mr. Wallace discovered the fire quite early and raised the alarm. No major damage done thankfully."

"Good heavens! I'll go along and see what I can do."

"Would you like some breakfast before you go?"

"No, that's really kind, Elen, but hopefully I can get something later."

I hurried along the sweeping, tree-lined drive to what those on the estate and throughout the area referred to as 'the big house.' I found William and another man removing sodden sheets from the building through a large sunroom which was attached to one side of the building. Some of the glass panes had broken and others were blackened with soot. Fortunately – as Elen had suggested – the main body of Barstobrick House appeared undamaged.

"Ah, morning wee John!" called William as he saw me approaching.

"Good morning, William, how did it happen? Why didn't you wake me?"

"*Argh*, there was no need, once Mrs. Wallace woke me, I hurried along to help Mr. Wallace here and between us we managed to dampen it down before it got started." William then realised that I hadn't met the man he was referring to, "Oh by the way, this is Mr. Wallace; this is John Watson a friend of Jeannie's who used to come and stay along with his brother when they were wee boys."

"Pleased to meet you," I said, "although it's a pity it is in such difficult circumstances."

"Yes, well at least there was no great damage done and no one was hurt," said Wallace. I wondered if the sad expression he wore was permanent or had simply been prompted by the night's events.

"I suppose the fact that the house was empty is both a blessing and a curse," I suggested. "On the one hand there was no one there to get hurt, but on the other – had the fire taken hold – the whole house could have been destroyed."

"Well, the cook and her daughter stay at the other end of the house," said Wallace, "but, as you say, they were unharmed as the fire was virtually confined to the sunroom."

"Jeannie's helping them to clean up," added William.

I looked past him to see the three blurred figures through the damaged glass sweeping and gathering up damaged items. Before I could resume the questioning, an approaching voice cried out from behind me:

"Good morning, Watson! I trust you slept well?"

"Holmes!" I exclaimed, turning round, "where have you been?"

"It would seem adventure has even followed us to this little tranquil corner of the world," he said ignoring my question.

Holmes had obviously met Mr. Wallace earlier, as – without further hesitation – he resumed questioning the man.

"You said that your wife heard something, shortly before you discovered the fire?"

"Yes," said the butler, "my wife's a very light sleeper and our bedroom faces the drive. She woke me, telling me that she thought something was wrong – just instinct I suppose. When I went out to investigate, I looked back and saw the flames in the sunroom taking hold. It was then that I asked my wife to fetch Mr. McFadden and between us, we managed to get water from the byre and douse it down."

"What exactly had caught fire?" I asked.

"Excellent Watson!" said Holmes before Wallace could answer, "I was just about to ask that myself."

"While Mr. and Mrs. Neilson are away, they are taking the opportunity to have the house decorated," explained the butler. "The painters had delivered their equipment only yesterday and stacked most of it in the sunroom in preparation to start work tomorrow. There were pots of paint, dustsheets, cleaning fluids, any of which could have caught fire."

"Does your master have any enemies Mr. Wallace?" asked Holmes.

"Not that I particularly know of, sir," he replied after a little thought. "I suppose there is always the type who are jealous of other people's success, but I'm not aware of any great feud with anyone."

"Yet someone may have known that the house would be empty."

"Everyone knows each other's business round here, Mr. Holmes," said William, a little confused by my friend's question, "it would have been common knowledge that they were away."

"Do you mind if I take a look at the sunroom door?

"Yes, by all means. Be careful as there is quite a bit of broken glass but certainly, you can have a look if you like."

"Thank you," said my friend.

I followed him to the entrance where we almost bumped into Jeannie who was exiting with a box of breakages.

"Good morning, Miss McFadden and a very happy birthday," said Holmes.

In all the excitement, I had completely forgotten about the reason for our visit.

"Jeannie, I can't apologise enough – I'm mortified!" I cried, "many happy returns."

"Don't worry, John," she said with a characteristic gentleness, "it's not uppermost in my mind either right now."

She put down the box and we hugged.

"I do have a card and a gift for you back at the house," I added apologetically.

Holmes meanwhile had taken a small lens from his inside pocket and was examining the lock of the sunroom door. Although the upper pane had been blown out, the lower, timber part of the door was still intact, if a little blackened. The annex itself was about fifteen feet wide and led to the side door of the main house; beside *it* was a small window. Holmes addressed the two staff who were still sweeping up shards of glass.

"Good morning, ladies. Could I ask if either of you heard anything prior to Mr. Wallace raising the alarm?"

"No sir," said the elder of the two.

"And this door was locked I assume?" he asked pointing to the large side door.

"Yes sir, that's always locked, as is the tradesman's door round the back. While he and his wife were away, Mr. Neilson gave the painters permission to use this entrance."

"May I see inside?"

"Yes, sir."

I followed Holmes into a small hallway which led into the main entrance to the house. It occurred to me that in all my visits to the estate as a child, I had never set foot in the big house until this moment. There was further evidence of the work that was about to commence as scaffolding was stacked on the floor awaiting construction. William and the butler had followed us in and joined us at the foot of the grand staircase which was the centrepiece of the entrance hall. Holmes addressed the butler:

"Mr. Wallace, has anything of note recently come into the possession of Mr. Neilson?"

"Yes, as a matter of fact, there has," he replied. "Mr. Neilson has recently purchased a painting by the famous local artist Edward Hornel, you've probably heard of him."

"No – and this painting is of great value?"

I was both amused and a little embarrassed by Holmes's dismissal of the artist and his reputation.

Wallace was a little taken aback but continued anyway, "Oh, well Hornel is thought to be one of the best artists in the world. Mr. Neilson successfully bid for one of his most famous works at an auction house in Glasgow last month."

"Was this widely reported?"

"Yes, the story of this major work returning home, as it were, was in the local paper for a few days running."

"May I see the painting?"

"Yes, I suppose so," said Wallace, a little confused, "if you just follow me, it will be in Mr. Neilson's study.

Wallace took a set of keys from his pocket and opened one of the three doors that opened directly from the entrance hall. We followed him into the room.

"That's the one, sir," said the butler, pointing to a large, rather abstract oil in pride of place behind a large walnut desk.

"Ah," said Holmes softly to himself and then to us all, "gentlemen, there may be more to this unfortunate incident than meets the eye." But he refused to elaborate.

Chapter III

Amidst all the disruption caused by the morning's events, I felt so sorry for Jeannie whose big day had almost been completely overlooked as a result. Generous soul that she is, however, she never made a fuss and continued helping clean up the mess.

"There have been plenty of birthdays in the past, John," she said with a smile, when I raised the point, "hopefully, they'll be plenty more in the future."

As she and the others got on with restoring the big house to its condition of 24 hours earlier, her mother continued in her kitchen making a cake and preparing the rest of the food for that evening's celebration.

The day progressed and I commented to William that the official services were conspicuous by their absence. The gamekeeper laughed:

"Aye, there's not much round here, son. There's only two or three part-time policemen and a similar number of volunteer firemen. Once we got on top of the fire, there was no need to bother them. Besides, being slightly out of the way up here, I don't know how long it would have taken them to get here – the whole place would have been up in flames!"

"Still, I think it should still be reported to the authorities as a matter of course."

"Aye, I'll have a word with Mr. Wallace and next time he's in town, he can pop into the police station and let them know."

It was typical of the slow, *laissez-faire* attitude which pervaded among the people of the Galloway Coast, and not for the first time, it was as though I was taken back in time to my childhood, and how things used to be in that simpler time.

The day past without further incident and, as afternoon turned into evening, people gradually started to gather for Jeannie's party, oblivious to the morning's events. Friends and neighbours from farms and hamlets around the area enjoyed the night's festivities, dancing to the music produced by a couple of young men skilled on the fiddle and squeeze box. When she wasn't being dragged onto the make-shift dancefloor by various friends, Jeannie spent most of the night going from table to table, laughing, joking and generally sharing stories about her forty years amongst these good people. I watched her from afar and was pleased that she enjoyed the life she had chosen; I also felt proud and privileged to know someone so gentle and kind.

Holmes spent most of the evening sitting in the corner with his pipe, observing those present. Although it was lovely to be part of such an event, it was neither mine, nor his idea of a relaxing evening and we made a polite exit earlier than most. Before I retired, Jeannie said we would spend the following day together on the estate as we hadn't had an opportunity to properly catch-up. I agreed it was a splendid idea and went to my room. I imagined Holmes propped upright for most of the night smoking endless pipes as he contemplated the events of earlier that morning. Either way, it was almost certain neither of us would enjoy a good night's sleep with all the raucous activity downstairs.

I must have fallen to sleep sometime in the small hours and woke around nine o'clock. As I descended the stairs, I heard Holmes in conversation with Jeannie.

"You can come with us Mr. Holmes – John and I are going to spend the day walking on the estate."

"That's very kind Miss McFadden but I shall politely decline. I intend to visit the beautiful little town you introduced us to upon our arrival."

"Ah, Watson, good morning," he continued as I appeared, "I trust you slept well? I'm sure you will have a fine day in this wonderful Scottish air. I shall see you both later."

With that, and a touch of the brim of his hat to Jeannie, he left, leaving our host somewhat bemused.

"Don't worry," I said, "he can be very unpredictable at times."

Like Jeannie, I had no idea exactly where my friend was going or what he was up to. My curiosity gradually dissipated as we enjoyed a wonderful day idly wandering round the vast estate and catching up on old times; times that in one respect seemed like a lifetime ago, while in another were so vivid, they could have been only yesterday. None more so than when we climbed to the top of Barstobrick Hill. The panoramic view was spectacular, with Kirkcudbright in the distance and the sea beyond, glistening like a vast field of diamonds in the low sun. The autumn colours of the fields and valleys in between were equally as stunning – as the sun moved round, violet turned to russet browns, to orange and then to yellow. At the bottom of the hill, Barstobrick House stood, seemingly unharmed from the accident the previous day. I couldn't stop smiling at the scene. Jeannie must have read my mind.

"Do you ever see yourself returning, John?"

"Oh, I don't think so, as beautiful as it is. I've been in London now for almost twenty years. I probably have more roots there than anywhere else. When Mary passed away, I thought about moving and making a fresh start; but where to? I had built up my practice, I had my patients and whatever friends I had left, there. Present company accepted, of course," I added with a smile.

"And not forgetting your adventures with Mr. Holmes," said Jeannie, teasingly.

Again, I smiled with slight embarrassment, "It's true. Holmes was away for a few years and when he returned, we resumed our friendship and if I am honest, I would have to say that filled a rather large void in my life." I resumed taking in the view,

"Having said all that, I would love to visit again; I'd forgotten how beautiful it is here."

"Well, you're always welcome," said Jeannie, linking my arm, "remember I asked for two things in my letter."

We left it at that and made our way back down the hill, where we were met by Jeannie's father who was wheeling an empty barrow.

"What are you two *bairns* up to?" he asked, much to our amusement.

"We've just been catching up on old times," said Jeannie, "I've been reacquainting John with the estate."

"I'm just off to the garden to pick some vegetables if you want to come along?"

"Yes, I haven't shown you the walled garden yet," she said, turning to me.

We walked further along a path that led from the big house to a high wall with what seemed like a disproportionately small wooden door at its centre. William opened the door, wheeled his barrow through and we both followed. Inside, I could see that the wall formed a perfect square approximately two hundred yards in each direction; uniform rows of plants and produce covered the ground in front of us and led to a long, elegant glass house at the far end of the garden.

"What a beautiful place," I exclaimed.

"Yes, it's probably my favourite spot," said Jeannie, "I come here a quite a bit."

"It was never here when I was a boy."

"No, it was built about fifteen years ago. Hugh paid for it."

Jeannie's words didn't register at first and I looked at her for clarification, "My Hugh?" I stammered.

"Aye," said William, "he was a generous laddie was wee Hughie."

Jeannie added, "Hugh's fortunes fluctuated wildly and he came to stay often. Dad wanted somewhere to grow produce and develop plants for the estate but Mr. Neilson was never interested – it's not that when it comes to daft paintings," she added under her breath. "Anyway, when Hugh was down here one time, he had had a particularly successful period and insisted on having a walled garden built. He paid for it all."

"I didn't want anything as big," explained William, "but he insisted. He had a local builder come round and build it for us."

As Jeannie helped her father harvest some of his produce, I sat on a bench and contemplated the beauty of the place; the colours and birdsong; and above all else the revelation that my brother had financed the whole space. My reverie was broken by the clanking of the iron ring that opened the door.

"Holmes! What are you doing here?"

"Good afternoon, Watson," said my friend, also touching his hat in the direction of Jeannie and William, "I arrived back at the farmhouse and Mrs. McFadden said I might find you all here."

"What have you been up to?"

"I must say I am beginning to really enjoy our little sojourn. I have spent a very informative day in Kirkcudbright."

"It's a beautiful little town, isn't it?"

"I can't say I really noticed; I was more testing a theory than taking in the sights."

"And what theory was that?"

"That the little incident the other night was not the innocent accident that everyone believed. It may well have been an accident, but the fire didn't start by itself, it was caused by the clumsiness of someone breaking in."

I looked at Holmes and suddenly realised to what he was referring, "The painting," I said.

"My first suspicion that it was no ordinary accident came on Sunday morning immediately after the break-in." Holmes broke off from his narrative and lit a cigarette.

"Among all the footprints on the soft drive were a distinctive set. Whereas most were heading towards the house, these were deeper but showed no showed no heel, and were heading in the opposite direction away from the house. Inference? Someone was either on tip toes or more likely…?"

"…Was running away!"

"Precisely. My suspicions were confirmed when I found the marks of a dog cart which had been standing for some time on the soft ground outside the entrance to the estate. The tracks made by the wheels and its horse were quite distinct from any other vehicles that had made continuous and uninterrupted tracks as they passed by. The running man's tracks finished at the dog cart and it pulled away.

"I believe it was the sound of this man running past the butler's cottage that disturbed Mrs. Wallace from her slumber, although she didn't realise it at the time.

"When I inspected the lock on the sunroom door, it was clear it had been tampered with. The burglar must have forced the lock. He would not have known that the decorators' equipment was stacked just inside and he has almost immediately disturbed it and inadvertently started a small fire in the process. Then he panicked and ran."

"What did you find out in town?" I asked.

"I spent the morning in the library, leafing through the back editions of the local newspaper." He drew on his cigarette and exhaled lengthily, "I must say that *The Galloway Gazette* is an excellent publication – it's such a pity that the authorities never read it. Had they done so, they would have discovered that at least three significant burglaries have taken place in the last four months, as far east as Dumfries, as far west as Stranraer and as far north as Ayr.

"What they all have in common of course, is that they are all less than three hours train journey from Kirkcudbright, which may well be a little unassuming town which attracts little attention but is also the busiest harbour in the area."

"So, it is from Kirkcudbright that the thieves have been shipping their booty?"

"I believe so, it is the perfect, inconspicuous location."

"But where are they shipping it to?" I asked.

"To the Continent, or France to be more precise."

"How do you know that?"

"If my theory was correct that the little town was used as a distribution point, shipment could only be made by either rail or sea. Given that towns like Dumfries and Ayr have mainline rail links, I worked on the hypothesis that sea travel would be the more likely option.

"I didn't know the destination however, until I visited the harbour. Among the many boats that were quite obviously local fishing vessels, was moored a slightly larger boat – the *SS Alsace*. Beside the name on the rear of the boat, someone had crudely tried to erase the French tricolour, without much success, I might add. There was no sign of life on the vessel. I looked across at the shabby little building on the dockside, over which hung a sign that stated rather optimistically that it was the Harbour Master's Office."

I chuckled at Holmes's disparaging remark. He failed to see the humour and continued his narrative.

"The occupant of the office was standing in the doorway, enjoying a pipe.

"'Good morning,' I said, indicating towards the dozen or so vessels bobbing gently and at the glinting sea beyond, 'A beautiful sight.'

"'Aye,' he replied, 'I never get tired of it.'

"'You've been here quite some time then?'

"'Ye could say that – thirty years next year.'

"'Good heavens, thirty years. No doubt most of these boats have a similar length of service.'

"'Aye, one or two but ye always get the odd one who turns up,' he said nodding towards the *Alsace*."

"'Really? I must say I was admiring that boat earlier. In fact, I am just visiting the area and was thinking about hiring a boat for the day to explore the coast a little more. You don't know if she's for hire, do you?'

"'I would'nea think so. She's docked a few times over the past couple of months but is just normally moored for the night. It was supposed to be the same this week but apparently there's been a change of plan.'

"'Oh dear,' I feigned disinterest and much to my satisfaction, the garrulous Harbour Master continued with his indiscretion.

"'Aye, she was supposed to sail yesterday morning, first thing, but now y'r man came in only this morning and told me she will set sail on Wednesday.'

"'Wednesday? That means it would be free tomorrow. I wonder if Mr...?'

"'Ross, Duncan Ross.'

"'Yes, Mr. Ross, I wonder if he would be receptive to taking me out tomorrow?'

"'Ye can always ask I suppose, he's staying at *The Selkirk Arms* with his two crew.'

"It was at that very moment that all the links fitted together and the matter appeared as clear as crystal. The name the man gave me took a little while to register but I suddenly realised what – or should I say, who – we had stumbled upon."

The name sounded familiar to me as well, but I couldn't quite place it.

"'Ah, Mr. Ross,' I said to the Harbour Master,'" Holmes continued, "'I think I have seen him, as I, myself am staying at *The Selkirk Arms*. He is the tall chap with an olive complexion.'

"The Harbour Master took the pipe from his mouth and looked at me, "No, no, y've got the wrong man, sir. He's a wee fella with bright ginger hair. There's no mistaking his nationality,' he said with a chuckle to himself, 'has a very well-spoken Edinburgh accent.'"

"'Ah, I must be mistaken,' I said, 'not to worry, no doubt I can make other arrangements.'

"With that, I bid the man a good morning and found the local police station."

"What did you do there I asked?"

"There are no official detective policemen in the area so I asked the uniformed officer to contact with the nearest force. The man was a complete imbecile but he got finally through to the Chief Constable at Dumfries who said he was would send a man through to help."

"Help with what?" I asked.

"With preventing the attempted burglary that will take place at Barstobrick House tomorrow night."

Before I could question Holmes further, William and Jeannie came over and we all returned to the farmhouse. Along the way, Holmes asked if Mr. and Mrs. Wallace, the cook and her daughter from the big house could join us. When they were all assembled, he repeated his story to his spellbound audience.

"Well, I never," exclaimed William, "who would have thought something like this could happen here."

"You said yourself Mr. McFadden – everyone knows each other's business in a small community like this, and when the thief learned that Mr. Neilson had purchased the valuable artwork of ..." Holmes gestured, trying to recall the artist's name.

"Hornel," I prompted.

"Indeed; and then learning that the Neilsons were out of the country, he saw it as the perfect opportunity for his next job."

"Little did he know that the owners were having their house decorated in their absence," I said. "Had he not caused the fire, he would most likely have got away with the painting from under our noses."

"But now he thinks he has a second chance. The incident was reported in this morning's local newspaper. It stated that Barstobrick House was undamaged and there was no suspicion of any wrongdoing. The thief therefore knows that the valuable painting is still intact and I believe that temptation has gotten the better of him. He has held the French vessel back from sailing and it can only be with the intention of making a further attempt, believing that his failure has been undetected and knowing that the house is still empty."

"Why would the thief go to the trouble of sailing to France, Mr. Holmes?" asked Jeannie.

"It is much easier to dispose of valuables on the Continent than it is here, Miss McFadden. The other burglaries I referred to include pieces of diamond jewellery, a coin collection apparently worth thousands and an ancient artifact initially owned by one of the Mughal Emperors. All small enough to carry and make off with; all valuable enough to profit from if a buyer can be found. Sadly, the Continent is full of such unscrupulous characters."

"What can we do in the meantime?" asked Mr. Neilson's man.

"Other than wait, Mr. Wallace, not very much I'm afraid. The policeman is arriving from Dumfries at noon tomorrow," – he turned to the cook – "Madam, I think it would be wise if you vacated your rooms and stayed here with Mrs. McFadden for the next two nights."

Elen put her arm around the elderly lady who was obviously shaken by what she had just heard, "I'll come and help you pack some things."

Chapter IV

The policeman who arrived from Dumfries the following afternoon was a large, gruff individual with a shock of auburn hair and matching full beard. He identified himself as Malcolm Fraser, a sergeant in the local detective force:

"The Chief Constable asked me to come down and help you capture this baddie," he said with great enthusiasm. "The Chief had spoken with Inspector Lestrade of Scotland Yard who said you'd helped him on a couple of occasions."

Typical of Lestrade I thought to myself. Holmes saw my expression and smiled.

"Yes, one or two," he said to Fraser.

Holmes, Fraser and I, joined by the two local constables, took up our positions in the big house shortly after six o'clock. While four of us secreted ourselves in various places in Neilson's large study, one of the uniformed officers remained hidden in the hallway – Holmes's theory being that if the thief somehow evaded capture in the act of the theft, the constable outside would be able to apprehend him on the way out. Knowing it would be after midnight – if at all – that the thief would appear, I settled down for a long wait.

"We must sit without light," said Holmes turning down the lamp. Then he added, "and try not to fall asleep, Watson."

The grandfather clock in the hall outside signalled each excruciating hour. Although I would never admit it to Holmes, I felt my eyelids drooping when I was awakened by the clock striking two. Shortly afterwards I heard a noise, distinct from anything else inside the house. It was the sound of the door to the glass annex opening and shutting. When it was shortly followed by the noise of the small window beside the door leading into the house being jemmied open, there was no doubt that this was it. I instinctively looked across at Holmes but couldn't make out his features in the pitch darkness. The sound of slow, soft footsteps could be heard in the hall outside and I hoped that the constable stationed there didn't get too enthusiastic in his duty to arrest. I heard the sound of the doorknob to the study turn and sensed the large door opening. My heart pounded in my chest with excitement and anticipation.

Peering through the darkness, my pupils struggling to focus, I saw the vague outline of a diminutive figure. He seemed to stand for a moment, as if sensing something was wrong, but then moved forward towards the desk. I dare not breathe.

"*NOW!*" cried Holmes, turning up the lamp and almost causing me to jump out of my skin.

Within an instant Fraser and the uniformed constable had hold of the little man who was literally in the act of reaching up towards the painting. The look of horror and surprise on his face was something to behold. The other uniformed officer rushed into the room and took the arm of the prisoner held by Sergeant Fraser.

"Alexander Murray, I presume?" said Holmes, "Occasionally Duncan Ross, William Morrison and no doubt several other aliases as and when required?"

The man was now being held by the two uniformed officers but neither prevented him for drawing himself up straight and assuming a haughty, authoritative air, "And who the devil are you?"

"My name is Sherlock Holmes."

Even the dim light of the study could not conceal the colour from the prisoner's face draining away, as he slunk down again and adopted a demeanour of abject defeat.

"Ah, I see my name is familiar to you," added my friend. "No doubt your erstwhile partner in crime alerted you to me, following his apprehension – in not so dissimilar circumstances if I recall – some years ago. His detention did not stop you from carrying on your career in thievery however, I see. The only difference being is that you have replaced the rich pickings of the big city banks with the rather easier pickings of your rural homeland.

"The game is up, Murray." Holmes's tone was cold and unforgiving, "This particular crime route, leading to your unscrupulous foreign market is well and truly closed. And no doubt will be for some time as with any luck, you will find yourself under lock and key for some time to come."

Murray looked up, "I hope you rot in hell, *Mister* Holmes."

"No doubt I shall see you there," said Holmes, casually, and with a clipped nod to the policemen, Murray was yanked away and led to the police wagon which had been secretly parked in one of the cow sheds.

"It's been a pleasure working with you Mr. Holmes," said Fraser.

"The pleasure was all mine, Sergeant. If you go down to the harbour in town in a couple of hours' time, I'm sure you will also be able to apprehend Mr. Murray's accomplices aboard the *SS Alsace*."

"Will do, sir." With that, the policeman followed in the direction of his colleagues.

As we watched the wagon disappear into what was left of the night, I turned to Holmes:

"How on earth did you know who this man was?"

"Later, my dear fellow," was his infuriating reply, "I think it's time we got some sleep before our own long journey."

With the blood coursing through my veins following all the excitement, I slept only fitfully in the few hours before what could be decently described as morning. We breakfasted before Jeannie accompanied us back to the station for our return journey.

191

"It's been wonderful to see you again, John" she said with a warm embrace on the platform. "And you too Mr. Holmes," she added, offering a hand.

"Thank you for hospitality, Miss McFadden. It has been a most enjoyable stay."

I promised to keep in better touch with my childhood friend and made tentative arrangements for a return visit the following year. With that, our train pulled away and it was off back to the capital once again. As there were several hours to pass, I broached the subject again of the unexpected events of the previous night.

"I don't understand who Murray is – and what on earth put you on to him?"

"You may remember, Watson, our adventure some years ago that was brought to our door by Mr. Jabez Wilson."

"Certainly. What started off as an amusing practical joke, ended with a serious attempted robbery."

"Precisely. We apprehended John Clay in the cellar of one of the principal London banks. His 'pal' as he described him – Archie Nichols if my memory serves me – was also arrested as he tried to escape through Mr. Wilson's shop next door. There was a third man in Clay's gang however, and he got away: our friend from last night.

"If you recall, the villains had hired offices at Pope's Court, to get Wilson away from his shop where they spent time in the cellar digging a tunnel into the bowels of the bank. The man Wilson met at Pope's Court was Murray, or as he called himself, Duncan Ross, also a beneficiary of the so-called Red Headed League."

"Of course," I said, "I thought the name sounded familiar, but that was nearly seven years ago."

Holmes nodded. "Upon learning that Clay had been arrested, Murray fled back to his homeland, where he has spent the last few years perpetrating low-risk burglaries for high rewards. I had noticed various stories in the newspapers over the months and years reporting periodic burglaries of valuable artefacts from remote areas of Scotland – the Highlands, the Borders, even the Isles of Skye and Arran were victims at various times. What they all have in common is that they are rural locations with minimum policing; why risk capture in the big cities of Edinburgh and Glasgow when there are such rich, unguarded pickings elsewhere?"

"And the remote areas of the Southwest also fitted the bill perfectly," I added.

"Precisely. Murray and Clay were from well-to-do stock and had contacts in high places, both at home and abroad. Murray therefore had developed the perfect scheme of perpetrating these robberies and shipping the spoils over to the Continent, where they would be sold on, while he disappeared back to Edinburgh to lay low for a few months before selecting his next location."

"John Clay is from the other end of the country," I said, perhaps naively, "they seem an unlikely pair."

"Not particularly, Watson," explained my friend, "the two met at Eton. I have a theory that like-minded people tend to gravitate to one another, whether they be good or bad. Moving in mutual circles, it was almost inevitable that the two would end up collaborating."

"And when Clay was captured," I concluded, "Murray decided to continue alone."

"Yes. I was a little chagrined that he slipped through our net that night and thought we would never see him again. Reading the newspapers all these years, I often suspected it would be Murray who would be perpetrating these thefts; little did I know that I would encounter him personally, four hundred miles away from my own hearth!" Holmes chuckled and wriggled in his seat, as was his habit when in high spirits.

Our train arrived on time under the darkening September skies. We took a cab from Euston Station back to our lodgings. As it turned onto Baker Street, I had an overwhelming feeling of being home. I'm not sure, when I left a few days earlier, that I had been looking for the answer of where *home* was, but as Mrs. Hudson welcomed us at the door, I assuredly found it.

Our ever-obliging landlady had prepared a blazing fire on what was now a sharp autumn evening and on the table was a steaming pot of coffee and a plate of buttered crumpets. I smiled at her thoughtfulness and the squeaking of my chair as I sank into it gave me a further feeling of comfort. I sat staring into the flames thinking about the events of the previous few days.

"I am completely worn out," said Holmes, "I feel as though I could sleep for a week!" He paused, as he headed towards his bedroom and put his hand on my shoulder, as if reading my thoughts, "You are not only a gentleman, Watson – you are a gentle man. Don't torture yourself unnecessarily, my dear fellow. I know something of elder brothers choosing their own path; one must let them decide for themselves which one they should tread."

He left me to stare into the fire and contemplate family and friends, past and present.

The Tyburn Mystery

Chapter I

As I have written many times, Sherlock Holmes lived for his work. Everything else was considered at best mundane, at worst an inconvenience. Even joyous events like Christmas and his own birthday held little interest for him. There was one year however, when the latter event brought great happiness, even excitement to my friend; not because he himself had some great epiphany on the day after twelfth night, but because the day itself brought a case to our door that was to prove one of the most gruesome and disturbing, we would ever encounter.

January was probably my least favourite month of the year during my days in Baker Street. The holidays were over and with it, the general feeling of good will to all men; the temperature was hard and bitter; and my slight feelings of melancholy always had a psychological effect on me, which inevitably led to a physical discomfort in my shoulder. The only positive throughout the month was the nights that drew out, making the days slightly longer and acting as a reminder that spring was only a couple of months away.

As I awoke on the particular January day I am referring to in this case, I had no reason to believe that it would be any different from most of the others. I had helped Mrs. Hudson take down our Christmas decorations the previous evening, so as I descended the stairs and entered our sitting room, I found our apartment had a bareness that did little to raise my spirits. I walked over to the window and looked down onto Baker Street and it seemed even the Christmas card scene of a few days earlier – excited revellers in virgin white snow – had turned into a dreary everydayness, as people now picked their way uncertainly through the frozen, brownish, crumbly sludge.

I turned my attention to the breakfast table. Our ever-accommodating landlady had already placed our breakfast plates on the table and – never sure when either Holmes or I would appear – had covered them with two silver domes. In the centre of the table sat a smaller dome which covered a plate of toast; alongside it was a selection of jams and a steaming pot of coffee acted as the centre piece. It was at that moment that I realised that many people in the world were not as fortunate as myself – I inwardly gave thanks for the life I had and resolved to snap out of my childish sulk.

I had just taken the first mouthful of my ham and eggs when I heard Holmes stirring in his room. A few minutes later he came rushing into the sitting room, levering himself into his dressing gown and heading for the mantle where he started sifting along until he found a match that satisfied the unlit cigarette he held in his hand.

"Good morning, Holmes. And a very Happy Birthday!" I said, as he drew long on his early morning stimulant.

He spun round, as if startled, "Oh, good morning, Watson." Before he could sneer at my congratulatory salutation, his eye fell upon two envelopes that sat on the mantle – cards from myself and Mrs. Hudson. He opened them and offered a simple, "Thank you."

"Come and have some breakfast, old man. Mrs. Hudson has excelled herself yet again."

Holmes quickly drew on his cigarette a couple of times before tossing what remained into the fire and joining me at the table. We spoke little, Holmes probably reflecting the mood I found myself in earlier. That was until an unexpected visitor changed my friend's mood dramatically. We had just finished our breakfast and were still sitting at the table when we heard someone hurrying up the stairs.

"Someone light," said Holmes, "not a man, yet a woman would not move so quickly. It can only be…"

"Mr. 'olmes! Mr. 'olmes, sir," the little urchin burst into our sitting room in a state of some excitement.

"…Wiggins! I never called for you Wiggins, what brings you here?"

"A body, sir!" – the child immediately had our full attention – "Me and a few of the lads was mud-larking at low tide, down where the Tyburn meets the Thames. All of a sudden, Albie spots something lying on one o' the mudflats. We goes over and sees that it's a man lying dead."

"Are you sure he was dead?" asked Holmes.

"Well, he 'ad his 'ead off, so I would think so!"

Holmes and I looked at one another and couldn't help but burst into laughter at the boy's impudence.

"In that case, we must move quickly," said Holmes rising from the table and moving towards his room. "Watson, have a cab ready and I'll meet you downstairs in five minutes!"

Wiggins and I followed Holmes's instruction. The temperature was bitter and while the pavements had been cleaned and scraped, they were still dangerously slippery. I looked down at Wiggins and wondered how the boy managed in clothing that was wholly inappropriate for the conditions.

He must have read my thoughts as he said, "Don't worry, sir, I'm used to it by now."

No sooner had the hansom pulled up, when Holmes appeared attired, like myself, in ulster and cravat wrapped tightly round his neck to ward out the winter chill. He appeared as ambivalent as Wiggins himself to the boy's meagre clothing as we crammed into the cab.

"Will the other Irregulars still be with the body, Wiggins?" asked Holmes as our cab rattled along Baker Street.

"Not likely, sir. We don't like hanging about when there's trouble."

"Then I fear we will be too late."

"Too late?" I asked.

"Someone else is bound to have spotted the body by now and will have reported it to the police. No doubt Scotland Yard's special herd of buffalo will be on the scene as we speak."

Holmes's speculation proved accurate, as did his analogy of the buffalo. Any doubts our cabbie may have had as to our preferred drop-off point was quickly dispelled, as a large crowd that had gathered on the edge of the mud-flat could be seen from many hundreds of yards away. The vapour from their collective breath partially obscured them and somewhat resembled a gathering of large animals on the plains of Africa or North America.

The unmistakable figure of Inspector Lestrade could be seen with his back to the crowd, who were being kept in order by two uniformed policemen. As our hansom drew to a halt, the onlookers were all straining their necks, trying to follow Lestrade's gaze as he supervised from afar, a group of four mud-caked police officers who were preparing to retrieve the body. We saw from a distance that one of the uniformed officers broke away from his task and was doubled over clutching his stomach.

"Get a grip of yourself, McKenzie!" shouted Lestrade at the young man.

As Constable McKenzie re-joined his colleagues and completed his mission, the reason for his emesis became apparent. The whole crowd gasped in horror and many turned away as the mud-caked body – or what was left of it – was hauled onto the wharf.

It was difficult to make out any details under the coating of brown slime, other than to note it was the remains of a barrel-chested male. The cause of everyone's astonishment however was the condition of the remains. It had not only been decapitated, but the body had also been diagonally sliced in two from the left shoulder to the underside of the right armpit. The head and right arm were missing. Muscle sinews and bone fragments protruded from the gaping, sickening wound, while fragments of skin tissue hung raggedly at all angles.

"This is a pretty little problem, Lestrade," said Holmes.

The policeman looked up in surprise from the body, "Mr. Holmes! Doctor Watson! I should have known it wouldn't be long before you showed up. How did you find out about this?"

I looked round but there was no sign of Wiggins. "It came to our notice," was Holmes's simple reply.

Lestrade returned his attention to the grisly sight that now lay at his feet, "Probably had too much to drink – possibly a vagrant – wandering along, slipped and fell in. Or perhaps a robbery – clonked on the head and thrown in the river. Either way, drowned most probably, before being mangled in one of the large dredger's equipment. There's nothing that can be done for this poor chap now." He scratched his forehead under his bowler, "I suggest we get him down to the mortuary where we can have a closer look at him."

"Just a moment, Lestrade, if I may."

Holmes reached down with his cane towards the supine figure and turned back what was left of the man's topcoat; he then flipped open the sodden frockcoat. Again, with the tip of his cane, he scratched the loose mud away from the label sewn onto the inside pocket. Peering down, I could just about make out the label for John Henry and Co. one of the most elite tailors on Savile Row.

"Not just your average vagrant, I would suggest," said Holmes.

"No, no, that's quite right Mr. Holmes," replied Lestrade, "I was just about to do that myself."

Holmes flashed a knowing glance at me.

In an effort to regain some credibility in front of his men, Lestrade asked, mischievously, "I suppose you will want to inspect the mud-flat for yourself, Mr. Holmes?"

"No that won't be necessary, Inspector. He's clearly been in the water some time and other than the midden created by your floundering men – not to mention the contents of Constable McKenzie's stomach – I don't think there will be much to see out there. I would however be interested in any developments."

"I'll keep that in mind," said the detective and then turning to his subordinates, "now get this loaded onto the wagon and you lot go and get yourselves cleaned up."

I had read of more than one incident where a mangled corpse had been fished from the Thames after being caught in the underwater equipment of one of the large dredgers. The stories I had read suggested on each occasion the corpse was intact and, in some cases, the ship's crew were not even aware of the happening. In each case, the poor unfortunate, turned out to be a gentleman of the road, who had drunk too much and slipped into the river after dark. There was some credibility to Lestrade's hypothesis, therefore.

"What are your thoughts, Holmes?" I asked as we wandered back towards our lodgings.

"Without sufficient data, it's too early to tell. It's a capital mistake to theorize before we have more evidence. However, my instincts tell me this is more than a vagrant being accosted on the street."

We were back in Baker Street that afternoon and with all the wintry morning air, I found myself nodding over a novel in front of the warm fire, unable to keep my eyes open. Holmes sat opposite as usual with his legs outstretched and his pipe tobacco within easy reach. Suddenly, I was alerted with a start for the second time that day, as hurried footfall could be heard on the stair. This time, it was clear it wasn't a child who was hurrying towards us. Moments later, the door burst open.

"Mr. Holmes! Mr. Holmes!" panted Lestrade, as he stood holding the door with one hand and the casing with the other to save himself from falling in. "It's the body we found this morning!"

"Well, what *of* it, man? Has it leapt from the table and run off?"

I couldn't help laughing aloud at the comical thought.

"No," replied Lestrade, "we have found the head!"

Holmes whistled, his eyes sparkling like jewels in excitement. "Where?"

"As the tide brought the river back in, it was washed up near Westminster Bridge. It was in the same state as the body so we moved it to the mortuary where Dr. James is conducting the *postmortem*."

"Watson, back into our coats! Lead on Lestrade!"

Within twenty minutes we were in the mortuary staring down once more at the wretched creature we had first encountered that morning. The body had been washed clean and the lower half was covered with a white sheet. It was the other end of the table however that attracted our attention. The head and partially severed right arm had been placed roughly where they should have been joined to the rest of the body. It lay there like an ill-fitting puzzle and somehow it reminded me of the Highland Boundary Fault in Scotland.

If it were possible, the recent discovery was even more horrific than the original. Approximately half an inch of the head on the left side had been sliced away, taking with it the ear and a good portion of the scalp, leaving brain tissue clearly visible. The left eye had been gouged out and a hollow black socket stared up in its place. But it was another injury that Holmes focused his attention on.

"With your permission?" he asked of Dr. James, the police pathologist. With a nod of assent, Holmes took out his lens and bent over the cadaver. "This man has had his throat cut," he said softly.

"What?" exclaimed Lestrade.

"I concur," said James, handing the inspector his written report. "It's all in here. You are probably right about the dredger theory, Inspector, but as Mr. Holmes points out, among the obvious catastrophic wounds suffered by this man there are obvious signs that there has been slashing of the throat severing the common carotid artery. As there was little water in the victim's lungs, it suggests that this was the cause of death."

"In conclusion," added Holmes, "the man was dead already before he was thrown into the river."

"That is highly likely," said James.

The four of us stood in silence for some time. "Well, I never!" said Lestrade.

"Tell me," asked Holmes, "where are his clothes?"

"I had them cleaned up and they are drying off in a room down the corridor," said Lestrade.

He took us along the cold passageway and showed us into a room where the sodden garments – cut from their owner – hung dripping. Holmes inspected them closely.

"They are of the finest quality," he mumbled. "Was there anything in the pockets?"

"No, completely empty," said the policeman, "I'm still working on the assumption that the poor man was robbed and thrown into the Thames."

Holmes thought for a few moments before bringing our visit to an end. "Well, thank you for keeping us informed, Lestrade. I will look into the matter myself, if you don't mind and will of course, share my own findings with you in due course."

"Very well, Mr. Holmes. Doctor."

"What do you make of it, Holmes?" I asked as we stepped into a hansom outside Scotland Yard.

"I think we should first test a hypothesis," was his enigmatic reply.

Chapter II

Holmes rapped on the roof of the hansom with his cane as we drove along Millbank and drew up near the junction with Thorney Street, not very far from where the body had been discovered that morning. It was now late afternoon and the light was fading quickly. As it was so often at this time of year, a freezing fog emanating from the river was beginning to whisper through the streets and lanes of London.

"Surely we can't see anything at this time?" I asked, assuming Holmes wanted to revisit the discovery site.

"We are not here to scour the river, Watson. I am interested in visiting our friend Wiggins. As soon as he saw the police this morning, he scampered off before anyone could ask any questions."

"Yes, I thought he became rather conspicuous by his absence."

Holmes paid the cabbie and we stepped out into the thickening murk. I followed my friend into a narrow passageway between a tobacconist and a laundry that opened out into a wider lane, which appeared as a kind of hub into which a labyrinth of tiny yards and alleys were connected. The general chatter and hubbub that could be heard at the exchange on the wharfs and in the taverns all along the river died away to create an eery silence.

It was slippery underfoot as we picked our way along the dark lane, around tar barrels and crates; ropes, pullies and hoists, presumably used by boatmen and river workers. After walking carefully for a few minutes, Holmes turned into one of the passages that now simply appeared as black holes that would baffle the most experienced astronomer. Holmes had the air of a man who knew exactly where he was going however, and I had no hesitation in following him.

I took care to remain no more than two paces behind him at all times, such was the lack of visibility. This almost resulted in me banging into him when he stopped abruptly in front of a shabby door. He wrapped on the door with the silver crook of his cane, which prompted a scuttling sound from inside. Hissed whispers were preceded by the door being unbolted and a tiny face appearing as it cracked open.

"Good evening, Wiggins, may we come in?"

"Mr. 'olmes, sir!" said the urchin, opening the door wide, "what brings you down this neck of the woods?"

"It's about this morning's discovery," said Holmes as we crossed the threshold.

It proved to be an assault on the senses. I was immediately struck by the odour of decay which created a miasma of dreadful air. Sadly, that was nothing to the sight that I beheld. The one large room resembled that of a dungeon. There must have been as many as twenty boys – children – huddled together in groups of five or six on the rushes of the floor. Each group had a makeshift brazier providing a totally insufficient amount of warmth for the ragged youngsters. With no natural light, what little artificial illumination that was generated by the open flames, revealed the damp brick walls, dripping with condensation and home for all kinds of gastropods. As I had observed in Wiggins that morning, all his friends were dressed inadequately for the conditions, some even barefoot. As they looked up at their visitors, I could see not the sparkling, excited eyes of curious children, but brittle, lined eyes, that spoke of hunger and injustice. Had I not been wrapped tightly in my ulster and cravat, I am not sure I would have been able to stand the environment myself.

As some of the boys cowered at the sight of official looking men, Wiggins moved to reassure his friends, "Don't worry lads, it's not the police."

As our eyes adjusted to the dimness, Holmes saw what he had come to see, "Ah, I see your friend Albie got more than he bargained for with his mud-larking this morning, eh Wiggins?"

On the floor, placed on a dirty sheet of tarpaulin, was a wallet, a pocketbook, a fob watch and six five-pound notes. They were all wet and had been laid out to dry, although how long that would have taken in such a damp, cold room could only be guessed at.

Wiggins looked chagrined and one of the boys – presumably, Albie – slunk away into the shadows.

"It's all right, boys," said Holmes, "I will not be reporting anything to the police. I am simply interested in this morning's events. It is clear that you relieved the man of his belongings before reporting the discovery?"

"Well, we figured he wouldn't be needing them, sir," was Wiggins's cheeky reply, which brought a chuckle from Holmes.

"Be that as it may, these items are evidence in the matter. The man, you see, was murdered."

There was an audible gasp among the boys.

"I didn't do anything, sir!" said Albie as he emerged from his hiding place.

"I know you didn't," said Holmes, scooping the contents into a small bag he produced from his pocket, "I simply want to get to the bottom of the matter. I must take these items away with me for the time being. Wiggins, I want you and your colleagues to keep your collective ear to the ground, regarding this matter. If you hear anything in and around the area, I want you to let me know immediately. Do you understand?"

"Yes, sir, will do."

"Good man. Good evening boys."

There was a collective mumbling from the street urchins which appeared to me to be a mixture of disappointment at being relieved of their booty, whilst being grateful that it wasn't the official police force who had discovered their wrongdoing. We retraced our steps back out into what I considered civilisation. Despite the fog having thickened and the night having darkened, I somehow felt a greater sense of comfort, having been released from that dreadful claustrophobic hovel.

There was a line of cabs on Millbank that had been almost totally enveloped by the fog. Their soft, ghostly headlights were all that indicated their presence and I was pleased when we climbed aboard, knowing that it wouldn't be long before we would be back in Baker Street.

We travelled in silence. No doubt, Holmes was contemplating the case at hand while my own mind was occupied by the living conditions endured by those poor unfortunate boys, we had left just a few minutes earlier. How such a situation could be allowed to pervade within half a mile of Westminster – the heart of the Empire – was quite beyond me.

Back in our rooms, Holmes unwrapped the soggy package and went to lay the contents on the hearthrug, where they would stand a far greater chance of drying than when they were held in their previous location. Before my friend could deposit the items however – in deference to Mrs. Hudson – I managed to lay some old newspaper down to protect the rug, much to his annoyance. All we could then do was wait.

As the evening wore on, the five-pound notes gradually dried, although the once crisp white sheets now resembled crackly parchment. The leather wallet in which they were once housed had the initials O.V. embossed on the inner flap. The fob watch was still caked in a dry film of dirt but the makers inscription could be made out on the back: *Scotts of London*. A fine item and yet another sign that its owner was a wealthy man. Frustratingly however, there was no dedication on the inside of the lid as there often is with such an item. Other than the O.V. therefore, his identity was still unclear. The only clue I could take from the timepiece was the time at which it had stopped.

"Twenty-past eight," I muttered, "at least we know the time the man was killed."

"Probably," replied Holmes, as he reached across and took it back from me, "it is certainly the time the body entered the water and that is not without significance as I believe that was the time of the high tide. The question remains not only the man's identity, but what was the motive for the crime? Clearly not theft."

We both looked at the pocketbook that was still wet and dirty – its small compact pages taking longer to dry out. Intermittently, Holmes would delicately inspect the item before sinking back into his chair with a snort of frustration. He knew that the book had to dry out completely and then hope that once the dried soil had been carefully brushed away from each of the small pages, the ink would still be legible to give up some of the victim's secrets.

It got to such an hour that I was almost ready to turn in. Before doing so however, I suggested that we had a nightcap, "In celebration of your birthday – one you are unlikely to forget!"

It was apparent that Holmes already had forgotten but agreed to a brandy anyway. I sat with him for another twenty minutes or so before bidding him goodnight and going up to my room, knowing full well that he would be sitting as long as it took before he could inspect the notebook.

When I came down the following morning there was clear evidence to suggest that Holmes had been up for most of the night. The embers of the fire still glowed, while his desk was littered with pieces of paper that lay in his own scribbled hand; among them were grains of brown odorous dirt that had obviously been dusted from the – now dry and shrivelled – pocketbook which was the centre piece of the clutter.

By flicking over the pages of the book with the tips of my fingers, I could see that most of the ink had run and transformed into an almost illegible blur. This obviously hadn't stopped Holmes from poring over the contents and picking out words, numbers and parts of sentences that *could* be read. I referred to some of his various facsimilia and saw one in particular that lay immediately beside the dried-out pocketbook. He appeared to have spent more time on this one transcript as he had written notes in brackets under each entry:

- ..hn Hen.. Th...ay 3 ...ck
  (John Henry, 3 o'clock Thursday. Tailor?)
- *indecipherable* James
  (name of associate?)
- Sa.. ...wer, Cur.... ...reet
  (Sam Brewer, Curzon Street?)
- Molly *indecipherable,* 4 Wa..... ...rd, Tyburn
  (Female acquaintance? 4 Walcott's Yard, Tyburn?)
- Seamstress
  (Profession of Molly?)
- Machin...y rep...
  (Machinery? Owning? Access to? Responsible for?)

"What do you make of it, Watson?" I turned to find my friend standing in the frame of his bedroom door.

"You have been busy," I said by way of reply, "up all night, I suppose?"

Holmes ignored my question, wrapped his dressing gown tightly round himself and came over to join me at the desk. Lighting his cherrywood he resumed his analysis of the information that lay before us. "It is certainly an interesting little problem," he said indicating the paper immediately adjacent to the pocketbook. "The mysterious Mr. O.V. appears to have an eclectic mix of associates."

"Indeed," I agreed, following Holmes's indication, "from the opulence of Savile Row to the poverty of Walcott's Yard. And then the reference to Brewer, that wretched moneylender of Curzon Street."

"I think Savile Row should be our first port of call."

"Why is that?" I asked.

Holmes tapped the paper with the long stem of his pipe, "These are all the most recent entries and see this one here?" – he pointed to the item referring to John Henry – "Today is Thursday and if my decoding is accurate, it would appear that our man has an appointment with his tailor this afternoon at three o'clock. He clearly will not be able to attend but I wonder what we can find out in his place."

Chapter III

Savile Row wasn't as busy as some of the London streets, due mainly to the amount of luxury goods that were sold there – items that were way beyond the means of the average worker. Holmes and I ambled along, among the few window shoppers that were around, until around five minutes to three, when we found ourselves standing opposite the fashionable premises occupied by John Henry & Co. one of the most influential exponents of their profession for over fifty years.

"Let us cross, but don't enter," instructed my friend, who was watching one of the tailors carefully through the front window.

The man was busying himself, laying out a roll of cloth on the long counter. Apparently in need of another piece of equipment to help him with his task, he momentarily disappeared through a curtain to the rear of the shop.

"Now!" said Holmes, reaching for the door and in the process, disturbing the bell that hung above it, which in turn announced our entrance.

"I shall be with you in an instant, Mr. Vincent!" came a voice from behind the curtain.

We looked at each other and supressed a smile. The man we had observed some minutes earlier appeared carrying an opened ledger. Upon looking up he stopped in his tracks, "Oh, I was expecting someone else," he said, looking past us, seemingly a little put out by our presence.

"I am sorry," replied Holmes, "but I was hoping you could help my friend here. He's just arrived from abroad – doesn't speak a word of English – and as you can see, is in desperate need of some respectable attire."

I looked at Holmes, aghast at his effrontery. Fortunately, the man behind the counter must have taken my expression as one of bewilderment, as I listened to their conversation in a 'foreign' tongue.

"It is by appointment only," he said, haughtily.

"Oh, again, I'm so dreadfully sorry. In that case, perhaps I could make an appointment?"

The man exhaled impatiently, "Very well, I'll just go and get the book."

He put down the ledger he was carrying and disappeared once more behind the curtain. Holmes quickly spun the ledger round and pointed to the header on the page: Mr. Oswald Vincent, Cedar Villas, SW1. He indicated that we should leave and stealthily muffled the bell, whilst opening the shop door. We hurried across the street and concealed ourselves in a shop doorway opposite. A moment later, the poor man we had just deceived appeared on the street outside his shop looking agitatedly up and down, obviously trying to spot the two strange characters he had just encountered. Shaking his head after a few seconds, he checked his watch and re-entered his shop, obviously waiting for his expected customer who, we knew, was destined never to arrive.

Holmes chuckled mischievously at his charade. My expression must have betrayed my thoughts. "Oh, don't be so offended, Watson. Our ruse worked perfectly!"

I couldn't help but agree with his observation and reluctantly, found myself joining in with his mirth. "I just wish you had forewarned me about your intention that's all."

"It was rather improvised," was his reply. "Besides, your reaction enhanced our performance considerably!"

"Where to now then?" I asked as we re-emerged from our hiding place.

"Let's not waste the afternoon," replied Holmes, producing the piece of paper which he had used to decode some of the entries made by the man we now knew to be

Oswald Vincent. "I am intrigued by this reference to Sam Brewer, the moneylender. Curzon Street is not far, I think we should pay Mr. Brewer a visit."

Sam Brewer was an odious character who effortlessly flitted between his dealings with the landed gentry and the most destitute – those who lived cheek by jowl in the backstreets of the capital. He had a reputation for being merciless with his 'clients,' as he called them. It all meant that he was feared and hated in equal measure. The only satisfaction many of his creditors got was when they heard he had once been horsewhipped by Sir Robert Norberton on Newmarket Heath.

"Mr. Sherlock Holmes!" he cried, as we turned up at his premises. He leaned his portly frame back in his large leather chair, "to what do I owe the pleasure?"

"Brewer," said Holmes, coolly, "I am interested in a man called Oswald Vincent, I wondered if he was a client of yours."

"Mr. Vincent!" announced Brewer with a flourish. "How peculiar that you should mention him. Honoured me with a visit only a couple of weeks ago, just before Christmas."

"To…" – Holmes hesitated for effect – "…take advantage of your generosity no doubt?"

"Oh, you're a flatterer and no mistake, Mr. Holmes! No, no, not him." Brewer scratched his side whiskers, "Although I wouldn't mind being involved in some of his business. I've dealt with a few of his employees mind you."

"His employees?"

"Yes, that's what he came to see me about – asking if I was helping any of his staff. He owns Binnings' Textiles on Willesden Lane, you see. Right rascal he is by all accounts – they're always complaining about him when they come and see me for help."

Help? I couldn't help but be repulsed at the hypocrisy of the man who clearly made a good living from the misery of others – the heartless braggard. Holmes must have read my mind and flashed me a glance encouraging me to keep my feelings in check.

"And do you have the names of his staff who you...*help?*"

"Oh, I couldn't tell you that Mr. Holmes," said Brewer through a malevolent smirk, "there are certain ethical standards of confidentiality that need to be upheld when dealing with clients. The only reason I confirmed Mr. Vincent's visit is that he never took me up on my offer of assistance, despite me pointing out the mutual benefits. I don't suppose, you or your friend here would like a small advance?" concluded the moneylender impertinently.

"Thank you for your assistance, Brewer," replied Holmes before I could respond, "I think that will be all."

"Horrible man," I said to Holmes as we left Brewer's premises.

"Indeed, but nevertheless, he did assist us in developing our picture of the dead man. I think we should visit this Binnings' establishment," – he flipped open his watch – "but we will have to be quick if we are to catch them before they close for the day."

It was on the stroke of five o'clock and almost dark when we turned onto Willesden Lane, a gloomy thoroughfare that housed numerous blackened factories and various other industrial buildings. As we climbed down from our hansom, in front of a tattered sign which read, '*Binnings' Textiles est. 1849*', claxons sounded up and down the street to signal the end of another working day for the hundreds of flat capped and shawled figures, who proceeded to pour out of every conceivable nook and cranny of every building.

We struggled past the throng of Binnings' workers and addressed a man who was standing holding the door, as if waiting for his final colleagues to depart.

"Good evening," said Holmes to the man, "might I have a word?"

The man was taken aback by our sudden appearance and eyed us suspiciously.

"What about?" he asked.

"I believe it is concerning your employer...Mr. Vincent?"

"He's not here, right now."

Holmes and I exchanged glances – it was becoming increasingly likely that the man found the previous morning was Vincent.

"That is what we wish to speak to you about," said Holmes.

"Who are you?"

"My name is Sherlock Holmes and this is my friend and colleague Dr. Watson. May we come in?"

It was clear that our names meant nothing to the man and he looked over his shoulder at the large clock that hung above the looms and benches of the factory floor.

"We won't take much of your time, Mr...?"

"...Ball," replied the man, turning back and allowing us into the establishment, "Eric Ball. I'm not sure if Mr. Vincent would be happy mind you, if he knew strangers were coming round asking about his business."

"We're not asking about his business, Mr. Hall, we are asking about him personally. May I ask what your role is?"

"I'm the senior supervisor here. Been here since I was a lad – started as an apprentice in the weaving sheds, when old Mr. Binning himself owned the factory."

"Was Mr. Vincent related to Mr. Binning?"

"Yes, he was his nephew. Mr. Binning had no family of his own and when he died, the business went to his sister's son, Mr. Vincent."

"When was this?"

"About five years ago, I suppose."

"Are there any other relatives?"

"No, I don't think so. His mother was a widow herself and she died not long after her brother."

"When was the last time you saw Mr. Vincent?"

Ball thought for a while, "It was the day before yesterday. He said he had some business to attend to last night and he might be late in today. Truth was he never turned up at all."

"Is that unusual?"

"Not particularly," – Ball adopted a strangely, knowing look – "it seems he regularly has...*business* to attend to of an evening."

I took his emphasis of the word 'business' as a substitute for a more vulgar inference.

Holmes looked earnestly at the man, "Mr. Ball, I think you should prepare yourself for a shock. I believe that Mr. Vincent died the night before last. A body was found in the Thames yesterday morning and our initial findings appear to indicate that it is your employer."

"Good heavens!" said the supervisor, "what's going to happen to the factory now?"

"We are helping the police with their investigation. I wonder if you would mind identifying the body?"

Ball snapped out of his reverie at Holmes's question, "What? Er, yes, I suppose so if you think it would help."

"I think it would," replied my friend as he indicated that we should leave. "Perhaps we could arrange to meet at Scotland Yard at nine o'clock tomorrow morning? Oh, and I suggest you keep this from your colleagues for the time being, just until we are sure it is your employer."

We left the poor bemused man alone in the large factory as we made our way back to Baker Street, stopping along the way as Holmes sent a telegram to Lestrade. Once in our chambers – and after Mrs. Hudson's delicious supper – I poured us both a brandy.

"This is an interesting case that has fallen into our lap, Watson. Our headless friend is becoming less of a mystery."

"Yes," I agreed "I got the impression that Mr. Ball didn't have a great affection for his employer."

"Indeed, his first reaction was concern for the factory rather than for Vincent. I think that is the thread we should pick at Watson, and I believe in so doing – assuming that the deceased is Oswald Vincent – we will get to the truth of this man's demise."

I drained my glass, "Well that's for tomorrow my dear fellow. In the meantime, I shall wish you goodnight.

Chapter IV

"I received your telegram, Mr. Holmes!" announced Inspector Lestrade from the steps of Scotland Yard, as we stepped out of our hansom. How on earth did you find out who this man was?"

"Good morning, Lestrade," was Holmes's evasive reply, "all in good time. Ah! Here is Mr. Ball from Binnings' Textile factory now. He may be able to help us still further."

The supervisor whom we had met the previous afternoon rounded the corner and greeted us. After being introduced to the inspector, we followed Lestrade into the building and down into the basement mortuary. We entered the cold, stark room, where Lestrade had obviously organised the laying out of the body on the slab. It was covered by a white sheet.

"I suggest you prepare yourself for an unpleasant sight, Mr. Ball," said the inspector, "regardless of whether you know the man or not."

He peeled back the sheet and we stared down at the ghoulish, mutilated cadaver.

"That's him all right," said Ball, simply.

"Are you sure?" asked the policeman.

"I'm sure."

Lestrade covered the body once more, "Well I never," he said, "I didn't think we would discover the man's identity when we found him a couple of days ago."

I wanted to point out that he neither found the body, nor identified him but it didn't seem appropriate. It was clear that Holmes simply wanted to confirm the man's identity.

"Well, there is nothing much more we can do Lestrade," he announced, "I suggest we leave you to your further investigation."

The inspector addressed the Binnings' supervisor, "Thank you for coming down and helping us with our enquiries Mr. Ball. We will need to visit the factory."

"I understand, although I don't know what's going to happen to us all now." Again, Ball showed little interest in the demise of his employer on a human level.

"Perhaps we should leave now," said Holmes, "and you can pass this news on to your colleagues."

"Yes, perhaps I should send them home today, as there is little chance of any work getting done."

"That is probably the correct course of action," Holmes went to usher Ball away, "and then the inspector can come to the factory later this morning."

"Yes, I was just about to suggest that," said Lestrade, trying to regain some authority.

As we left the building Holmes asked Ball, "Tell me, are there any female workers at the factory by the name of Molly?"

Again, Ball showed little surprise, "Yes, we have a couple. Molly Aitken is a seamstress and Molly Atkins works in the dying room – has done for years."

"It must be quite confusing, given that their names are so similar."

"Not really. You couldn't mistake the two. Aitken is a fine-looking woman – only about forty I would say. Old Molly Atkins has been there longer than any of us – Lord knows how old she is."

"And are these ladies married?"

"Aitken is. Old Molly has been widowed for a few years now. Her old man also worked at Binnings – it's a real family business."

"Thank you, Mr. Ball."

We watched as the supervisor left to perform his unenviable duty.

"I suspect we are now to go in search of these women called Molly?" I asked.

"Just one, I think, Watson. We shall give Mr. Ball enough time to send the staff home and then visit Mrs. Aitken. If my code-breaking skills are accurate, I believe we should find her at number 4 Walcott's Yard, Tyburn.

The alleys and yards of Tyburn mirrored those which we had visited a couple of days earlier, to see Wiggins and his companions. The paradox of such abject poverty juxtaposed with such power and wealth was almost too much to comprehend. The only thing to distinguish this wretched area from the many others around the capital was the stream – known locally as the river – that ran into the Thames.

As always, Holmes appeared to know exactly where he was going and it wasn't long before we entered Walcott's Yard. The doors leading to the four tenements in the yard were in various stages of decay, while the foul odours emanating from the communal structure opposite added to the gloomy atmosphere. Holmes went to the last door along the yard and rapped on it with his cane.

There was a distinct sound of people scurrying around inside before a crack in the door tentatively appeared, revealing the eyes of a woman.

"Are you the police?" she asked fearfully.

"No, madam, we are not," replied Holmes. "But it seems you know what we are here to talk to you about. May we come in?"

The woman hesitated, unsure of what to do, before opening the door. We entered the melancholy room that served as living accommodation for a whole family. A kettle whistled on the fire but it was to the kitchen table that our attention was drawn. Sitting there was a man with his head in his hands. Touchingly, the woman offered us a cup of tea.

"That would be most welcoming on this bitter afternoon," said my friend with a smile, in an attempt to ease the tension that pervaded the premises. "I assume you are Mrs. Molly Aitken?"

"Yes sir, this is my husband, Bill."

For the first time, the man looked up from the table. His tired, bloodshot eyes suggested he was heavily deprived of sleep.

"My name is Sherlock Holmes and this is my friend Dr. Watson. We are not employed by the police but we are aware that they are working to solve the death of one Oswald Vincent, who I believe is your employer at the Binnings' Textiles factory."

Mrs. Aitken's shaking hand resulted in her spilling some of the tea on the table as she placed the mugs in front of us. "Oh, I'm sorry sir!" she cried, hurrying to fetch a cloth. She also poured herself and her husband a mug before sitting down. "Mr. Ball told us about it this morning," she said tentatively.

"If you tell us the whole truth, Mrs. Aitken, we may be able to help you. But if you fail to do so, I won't be able to protect you from the police."

The woman exchanged glances with her husband before speaking.

"Mr. Vincent was a horrible man! I've worked at the factory for twenty years now, since I was a girl. Old Mr. Binning was a lovely man who cared about his staff and his customers. When he died and it passed to Mr. Vincent, things changed. Standards dropped, along with the morale of the staff. Beforehand, everyone got on well together, but gradually, people started to fall out and withdraw from one another."

"Forgive me for being indiscrete, madam, but would I be correct in suggesting that this attitude was more prevalent among the female members of the factory?"

Again, Mrs. Aitken glance at her husband before answering, "Yes sir, it was." She dropped her head, "That horrible man abused his position. He used his power over people…especially the girls. The more vulnerable you were, the more pleasure he took."

I couldn't believe the poor woman's narrative. How anyone could behave in such a manner was beyond me. Mrs. Aitken looked up from the table and stared into the room, as if seeking some catharsis.

"Many of the girls had money troubles," – she laughed a hollow laugh – "we've all got money troubles I suppose but some more than others. Once he found out about that, he would prey on you…" her voice tailed off.

"That's enough, Molly." It was the first time her husband had spoken, his voice soft but firm. He stood up – a giant of a man. What he said next came like a pistol shot: "I killed him, Mr. Holmes. It's nothing to do with Molly or our Lucy."

Unlike myself, Holmes appeared completely unsurprised by the revelation but – again, like me – was surprised by the reference to a third person. "Lucy?"

Mrs. Aitken, rose from the table and linked the arm of her husband. "Lucy is our daughter," she said.

"Please," said Holmes, "sit back down and tell us what happened.

It was Bill Aitken who spoke. "I worked as a slaughterman at Murray's in Camden Town. Times have been hard these last twelve months and they had to lay people off – unfortunately, I was one of them. I've been out of work since November and things don't get any easier as far as money is concerned."

Mrs. Aitken then interrupted her husband's narrative. "I went to Mr. Vincent asking him for some extra hours," – she paused and bowed her head – "that's when all this trouble started."

Holmes and I both remained silent, allowing the two to continue. I think my friend shared my sense of where this horrible tale was leading.

Mrs. Aitkin continued, "Mr. Vincent had a reputation throughout the factory for...fraternising with some of the women and girls. I was to find out for myself what sort of a creature he was. He said in return for some extra hours perhaps I could help him in some way." She looked up at us – from one to the other – her eyes begging us not to judge her.

"Calm yourself, Mrs. Aitken," reassured Holmes, "what is said here will remain here."

"I...went...with him," she sobbed into a handkerchief. "Bill didn't know anything about it. I knew it would break his heart. I only did it because we were so short and what with Christmas coming and all.

"But of course, it didn't stop there. I was so naïve to trust such a man. He came back pestering me and threatening to tell Bill and everyone else in the factory. He then suggested there was an alternative – our daughter Lucy. She's only sixteen and she started as a trainee in the weaving room last year. If I didn't feel dirty enough, it made me physically sick thinking about what he was suggesting. I had no choice but to come home and tell Bill everything."

"I can't express how hurt and angry I was gentlemen," said Mr. Aitken, "but how could I blame my darling Molly, for what she had tried to do. We talked things through and sorted out what we could between us. Then I thought our luck was turning when I found a position in the coal yards at the back of Holloway Road."

But then Mrs. Aitken, added, "When the factory re-opened after Christmas, Mr. Vincent came after me again. And then Lucy told me that he had spoken to her in the weaving room. He had never been there before and she couldn't understand why he had gone to speak with her. The poor thing didn't know anything about what was going on, but I knew the game he was playing."

"When Molly told me this," said Mr. Aitken, "I knew I had to do something. I told her to ask him to come here so that I could talk to him, man to man, but not in his own surroundings. I am the first to tell you gentlemen that I was all ready to confront him, but I can't confess that I intended to kill him." It was Mr. Aitken's turn to stare into the middle distance, "He came all right, as arrogant and disrespectful as could be imagined."

Just then, the door opened and in walked a young girl, "Did you hear about Mr. Vi…" she stopped when she saw us sitting at the kitchen table.

"Hello, Lucy love," said Mrs. Aitken, "these gentlemen have just come to discuss some business with your father. Let's get you upstairs and we'll have a chat about what's going to happen in the factory."

The young girl was the picture of beauty and innocence. There is no doubt that as she grew into full womanhood, she would be just as striking as her mother. As Mrs. Aitken led her away, her husband resumed his narrative.

"You can see for yourselves, gentlemen. What man, blessed with two angels like that wouldn't act to protect them?

"I had made Molly and Lucy leave before he arrived the other night, to keep them out of the way. Lucy didn't know anything about what was going on and we wanted it to stay that way. When Vincent arrived, he was none too pleased to find me here on my own. I think he must have been expecting some other welcome. I tried to reason with the man but how can you reason with an animal like that? He started yelling and calling my wife and daughter all the vilest names under the sun. How a man could say such things about any women is beyond me. My blood was boiling by this point but I knew I had to control myself, for the sake of Molly and Lucy. He told me they would regret the day we had all tricked him like this and stormed out. I followed him out trying to appeal to his better nature, but what better nature does a man like that have?

"We got as far as the river at Primrose Hills when he turned on me and raised his cane to hit me. This was a mistake which we both now regret. Out of habit, I always carry a knife in my belt – ever since I started at the slaughterhouse. I've sliced better creatures than him in my time and when he raised his cane, I reached for the knife and had his throat open before he had the chance to wield it. I don't think I will ever forget the look of shock on his face. He just stood there for a moment or two before he slumped into the river – it was high tide meaning the body would just be washed down into the Thames, although I wasn't thinking about that at the time."

The man's gaze finally returned to us, "I've regretted my actions in the couple of days since then, gentlemen, but I can't say I was sorry at the time. I looked around me when I came to my senses but fortunately, no one was around to witness what had occurred. He was an evil man and I will have to take whatever consequences are brought against me, even if it's the gallows, I can go there believing that I did what I did to protect my wife and daughter."

We sat in silence for some time before Holmes, spoke, "Mr. Aitken, I wonder if you would ask your wife to join us." The man did as he was asked. "Mrs. Aitken, your husband has told us everything that has happened and I believe he has spoken honestly. Although it is the most serious of matters – a man has lost his life after all – I believe you both acted under the most extreme provocation. I am not sure if any other man in your position, Mr. Aitken, would have acted differently.

"I told you when we entered that we are not the police, nor are we retained by them to do their investigation for them. So, what has been said this afternoon shall remain between the four of us. The police believe Mr. Vincent was the victim of a random attack by drunken louts further up the river, so I do not believe they have the capacity or the imagination to establish what really happened. Therefore, Mr. Aitken, I am confident your liberty is not under threat."

"You have been quiet since we left Tyburn, Watson." It was true that I had been deep in thought during the cab ride and back at Baker Street I found myself staring into the roaring fire when Holmes broke my reverie. "Do you disapprove of my actions?"

"No, I can't say that I do. The Aitkens appear to be good people and, whereas I can never condone the killing of someone, I can't criticise Aitken for wanting to protect his wife and child from such a brute of a man as Vincent appears to have been."

"*Sic Semper Tyrannis!*"

I racked my memory, searching the vaults for my schoolboy Latin, "Thus always to tyrants!"

"Precisely!" At that moment, the doorbell rang. "Ah, we have a visitor, following my invitation, coming to collect his reward." Holmes reached for the wallet – still burgeoning with five-pound notes – and the pocket watch both belonged to the aforementioned tyrant in life. "I'm sure the Irregulars will find a good use for these."

And so, the disturbing case involving the death of Oswald Vincent ended as it had begun – with the sound of Wiggins's scampering step on our landing.

The Invaluable Assistant

Chapter I

My friend Sherlock Holmes was neither modest, nor boastful; he once told me that to underestimate oneself is as much a departure from the truth as to exaggerate one's own powers. There have been times when my companion has spoken quite candidly about his failures and I, myself, have witnessed on more than one occasion, an investigation ending inconclusively. As I pondered over the cases referred to in the foreword to this volume, it occurred to me that the one I am about to relate, is virtually unique, as I believe that it was none other than me who provided Holmes with the missing clue that allowed him to solve an investigation that had lain dormant for over fifteen years. What made the matter even more unusual is that there was no actual client involved to commission Holmes's services, proving yet again that it was the work itself – the pleasure of finding a field for his peculiar powers – that gave him his highest reward.

The delayed resolution to the matter involving the unfortunate Robert Barnet began one winter's morning when I came down to our sitting room to find the large tin box Holmes had dragged from his room the previous evening, still sitting in the middle of the floor. On the evening in question, I had suggested that he make our communal area a little more habitable by tidying away some of his papers. But it was then *I* who delayed this task when Holmes appeared with the chest and I discovered that it contained notes of his cases before we became acquainted. He then proceeded to tell me of his adventure involving his old college friend Reginald Musgrave and his unfortunate butler, Brunton. I had been so engrossed in his narrative, that time and inclination defeated us both and we went to bed, leaving the room in an untidier condition than it was at the start of the evening.

On the table sat around half a dozen bundles tied with red tape. Holmes had removed them from the chest before producing his record of the Musgrave case. I began to remove the bundles from the table with a view to replacing them, when I noticed that on one of them was written the name *Sir James Sydney*. Just then, Holmes appeared from his room.

"Holmes, what is this reference to Sir James Sydney?"

"Ah yes," – Holmes looked ruefully at the bundle which I held in my hand – "one of my unsatisfactory cases I'm afraid. As with Musgrave, it was one of my earliest."

"Forgive me for being excessively dull, old fellow, but is this the Sir James Sydney from Bart's?"

"The very same. I first became acquainted with him when I attended some of his lectures."

"*You* attended his lectures?" – he nodded matter-of-factly – "At Bart's?" – he nodded again – "St Bartholomew's Hospital? So did I!" I was incredulous.

"Yes, it had occurred to me before now but had never come up in our conversation."

"All these years we have shared rooms and you never thought to mention it?"

Holmes simply shrugged, as was his wont.

I turned my attention back to the bundle with Sir James's name marked on it. "May I ask what these notes refer to?"

"Not my finest hour I'm afraid, Watson," said he, lighting a pipe and settling into his chair. "As I told you last night, I was staying in Montague Street. While there, I enrolled on the Anatomy and Chemistry courses run at that hospital, the former of which involved attending lectures given by Sir James. In my final year of studying with him, he became aware of my chosen profession and took me to one side following one of his sessions. He informed me that several of his unpublished papers had been plagiarised before appearing in the *Lancet* and the *British Medical Journal* under different names."

"That's outrageous!" I cried.

"Yes, I know how precious you medical men are when it comes to your profession."

I ignored Holmes's gibe, "So he asked you to investigate the matter?"

"He did."

"And what did you find?"

"I found out that our great institutions are more concerned about their reputation than in truth and integrity." The look of bewilderment on my face prompted Holmes to elaborate.

"It was obvious that the perpetrators were attempting to further their own careers and – as the series of articles had previously gone unpublished – the likelihood was that it was someone close to Sir James. It was Sir James himself who asked me to investigate the matter discreetly but when the journal itself wrote to the hospital asking for Sir James's opinion on one of the articles, the issue was in danger of entering the domain of the public."

"I found him to be not only a brilliant surgeon and pathologist in my brief encounters with him," said I, "but an extremely modest man."

"Indeed," agreed Holmes, blowing blue rings into the air, "which is what raises him above many of his peers still further.

"When the board of governors approached Sir James for comment, he revealed that it was his own article and that he had commissioned my services to find out who was behind the plagiarism. They acted quickly to avoid a scandal. Summoning me directly, I was informed that an internal enquiry would be carried out and my services would no longer be required. As the incident coincided with the latter stages of my studies, I left them to it."

"Now you mention it," I said snapping my finger, "I vaguely recall rumours going round at one point about some dispute with *The Lancet*. The rumourmongers must have mixed the story up – it wouldn't have been a dispute with the journal, it would have been an internal issue. But who were the articles attributed to if not Sir James?"

"That was the confusing point. They were not attributed to any one person but different individuals from the medical profession." Holmes took the bundle from me, undid the red tape and started leafing through the papers. "Ah, yes, here we are – Royle…Stevens...Robertson… Coxon..."

The names strangely created a spark of recognition. I shook off the feeling wondering if I had actually read some of the articles in *The Lancet* myself. "Were they all from home or were there some from abroad?"

"When I made my enquiries to the journal, I was told that the authors were from all around the country and all had their articles submitted through a literary agent."

"A literary agent? What medical man has a-," I was stopped by Holmes's raised eyebrows and creased forehead.

We both simultaneously burst out into a roar of laughter at my stupidity, at which point Mrs. Hudson appeared, with view to clearing away our breakfast dishes. With a look of admonishment at the state of our quarters and then at our two selves, we resolved to tidy our room.

Holmes was between cases and the previous evening I had asked him to recite his adventure at Hurlstone involving his old college friend. By doing so, I was pleased that I had kept him from sinking into one of the morose crevasses I have often witnessed when his great mind is without stimulus. And again, that morning, our light-heartedness had created a suitable distraction. But by lunchtime, my companion appeared to retreat further into himself and I feared I could do nothing but wait for his next case to provide a remedy for his melancholic stagnation.

I decided to leave our cheery fire and go out for a walk. The sharpness of the morning had transformed into a beautiful, crisp early afternoon and I returned to Baker Street around three o'clock, feeling greatly invigorated. Upon entering our sitting room, I found Holmes sitting in his chair, where I left him, seemingly oblivious to his scraping away on the violin that sat on his knee. Pleased at least that he had not resorted to the syringe, I decided to leave him to it and went up to my bedroom to resume my escapism in one of Clark Russell's nautical adventures.

After an hour of reading about the second mate Mr. Royle and Captain Coxon, it suddenly occurred to me that those were the names that I had recognised that morning, when Holmes was telling me about the plagiarised articles in *The Lancet*. What a strange coincidence. I initially considered returning to our sitting room to share my discovery with Holmes but then thought better of it, as it was more likely that I would be ridiculed for succumbing to my adventurous imagination. Settling back into my novel, I read on for a further few minutes, only to discover a character called Robertson – wasn't that one of the other names in Holmes's notes? If it was, it was surely too much of a coincidence and if *that* were the case, it may lead to a further avenue of enquiry in the dormant investigation. I decided to risk the ridicule of my companion and descended the stairs, from where the sound of the bow scraping on the violin could still be heard.

"Holmes, do you mind if I take another look at those papers regarding Sir James Sydney?"

Holmes broke from his reverie and looked at me for a moment as if I were a stranger. "Not at all," he said at last with a disinterested gesture.

I brought the chest containing Holmes's previous cases, from his room once more and retrieved the bundle of notes on the aborted investigation that had been the subject of our conversation that morning. Settling into my chair opposite Holmes, I leafed through the scraps of notes and intermittently cross-referenced with the Clark Russell novel I had been reading a few minutes earlier.

My strange actions appeared to provoke Holmes's curiosity, as his drooping eyelids gradually opened, "What are you doing?" He reached for a match and encouraged his pipe to life by inhaling heavily and sending slow wreaths of smoke curling towards the ceiling.

"Testing a theory about this case involving our former lecturer," I replied. I suppressed a smirk, as I was suddenly aware that it was the kind of cryptic answer, I had been subjected to on many an occasion.

His sharp grey eyes pierced through the haze and transfixed me with their examining stare, "What sort of theory?" He was fully attentive now.

"Hah, Stevens! They're all here!" I cried, ignoring his question. I was beginning to enjoy this role reversal immensely.

I had never previously seen the expression on Holmes's face until that moment and felt obliged to explain my outburst.

"The names you quoted this morning, regarding the plagiarising of Sir James's work. They all seem to be taken from this seafaring adventure." I held up the novel I was reading, while continuing to sift through the notes on my lap, "And here! Look at this! The literary agent who provided the articles on behalf of his fantom clients was none other than a Mr. H. Nelson of Trafalgar Street,

Liverpool. Mr. H. Nelson – Horatio perhaps? They all have maritime connotations. Surely this is too much of a coincidence. My theory is that this man is a nautical enthusiast who was not only stealing Sir James's work, but he was also amusing himself by combining his misdemeanours with his own private interest."

"Watson my boy!" cried Holmes, "not for the first time, you have shown yourself to be a stormy petrel! Although this particular horse has long since left its stable – or perhaps the ship has sailed would be a more appropriate analogy – it may be worth exploring further."

I was flattered by Holmes's compliment but even happier to see that he had completely escaped the cursed lassitude of inactivity and assumed the sharpness of the eager detective once more. He continued:

"It would be extremely difficult to pick up a meaningful thread after so long, but there may be someone who could help us. What say we seek out our former mutual acquaintance Stamford, to see if he could shed any light on the matter."

"Young Stamford!" I cried, remembering the morning he introduced me to Holmes in the chemical laboratory at the hospital several years earlier, "now *there* is a name from the past."

Chapter II

Making some enquiries at Bart's the following day, we discovered that young Stamford had left the hospital five years ago to take up a teaching post at St Thomas's.

"If you don't find him there," said the elderly medic, in a white coat which looked as tired as its owner, "you may see him at the Criterion Bar."

I smiled as I recalled my chance meeting with Stamford in the very same bar prior to him taking me to meet Holmes.

As it was late morning, I suggested we have some lunch at the Holborn and then visit the Criterion before the hospital. If we didn't see Stamford there, at least we would have had some refreshment before going on to St Thomas's. Holmes shrugged, muttering something about my stomach, which I took as a somewhat grudging acquiescence.

By one o'clock, we found ourselves among the noisy, smoky fug of the Criterion. City types, haggling over deals, mixed with hardened drinkers, who spent most of their time – not to mention their income – in the establishment. Fortunately, I spotted Stamford from afar. He was standing by the bar on the very spot where I stood prior to our last encounter. I gestured to Holmes who followed me as I picked my way through the crowd. I tapped our man on the shoulder.

"I thought after all these years," I said as he turned, "I would try a little role reversal."

A merest hint of grey around the temples was the only discernible change to my former dresser as he turned and paused for the briefest of moments before my face registered with him.

"Watson! After so long! To meet-" he interrupted himself as he saw Holmes at my shoulder – "and Sherlock Holmes!

As I live and breathe – surely you two are not still lodging together?"

"We are," I shouted over the hubbub, "although much has gone on since we last met."

"Stamford," said Holmes with a nod, as though he had just been speaking to him earlier that morning.

"Good heavens, how long could it have been?"

"As long as it has been since the very morning you introduced us," I replied, vigorously shaking his hand, "it's marvellous to see you again."

"What brings you here?" asked Stamford, full of wonderment at the sight of the two of us.

"We were hoping you could help us with a matter we are looking into," said Holmes, "could we perhaps find a rather quieter spot.

Just then, I saw three men in business attire vacate a table in the far corner of the bar. Indicating to my two companions, we quickly made our way across before someone else could sit down.

"So how have you both been?" asked Stamford.

"Such a lot has happened over the years," I replied, "too much to recite here but here we are, having come through it. And you – I believe you are teaching now?"

"Yes, at St Thomas's," he thought for a while, "must be five or six years now."

"It is on the subject of teaching that we would like to speak with you." Holmes characteristically wanted to get to the business at hand.

"Oh?"

"You will remember that shortly before Watson here started working at Bart's, you and I became acquainted when I attended lectures given by Doctors Russell, Whitelaw and Sir James Sydney?"

Stamford paused in thought briefly, "Yes, I remember you were studying…no, don't tell me…anatomy and chemistry for quite some time."

"Do you recall the plagiarism affair involving some of Sir James's writing?"

The light went out of Stamford's eyes for the first time and his head dropped. "Yes, a terrible business. It cast a gloomy shadow over the whole place for quite some time."

"Yes," I agreed, "I remember hearing something at the time but as I hadn't been there very long, I didn't know the details and as I was still finding my feet, I didn't take much notice."

"It was a sad business," continued Stamford, "and resulted in Sir James's assistant Robert Barnet having to leave. I started at Bart's with him in '75 – I thought he was a good chap."

"He was the supposed perpetrator of the plagiarism following the internal investigation?" asked Holmes.

"Yes. I thought it was odd that such a diligent chap would suddenly decide to do such a thing after working with Sir James for quite a few years."

"Do you know what happened to him?"

"He lost everything – became disowned by the family he had; was made destitute and died in the workhouse in Lewisham." He reflected for a while, "Why do you ask?"

Holmes allowed me to answer, but before I did, I asked, "Tell me Stamford, was this young Barnet a nautical man?"

"Excellent, Watson," said Holmes.

"Not to my knowledge," answered Stamford.

"We are testing a hypothesis that the perpetrator of the misdemeanour had some sort of seafaring background or interest. If we find that Barnet was innocent of the wrongdoings he was accused of, it will be too late to save the poor lad's soul, but we may be successful in restoring his reputation and bringing to justice the real perpetrator."

Stamford turned back to Holmes, "From memory, didn't Sir James ask you to look into the matter?"

"He did."

"What have you discovered now after all these years?"

It was now Holmes's turn to look slightly crestfallen, "I have discovered that I should have been more forceful in my investigations at the time. I had the impression that I found out too much and was asked to stand down from my enquiries. I now deeply regret my agreeing to do so."

"What did you find out?"

"It became clear to me at a very early stage that the thieves must have been close to Sir James and therefore, the likelihood was that it was someone from within the hospital. Once I disclosed this to the governors, I suspected that the hospital was more concerned about protecting its own reputation, rather than uncovering any wrongdoing. It seems it has been convenient to blame the young, unqualified assistant."

"You said thieves – do you suspect more than one person?"

"It was my line of enquiry at the time, because the articles were apparently submitted by different people." Holmes turned to me, "but the imagination of our friend Watson here has proved invaluable and re-ignited my interest in the matter."

"So, who do you suspect? And how can you expose them after all this time?"

Holmes's answer was as much to myself as to Stamford, "It is too early to say but I suggest we go back to the beginning once more by making an appointment to see Sir James."

Frustratingly, it would be a further two days before we could see the eminent surgeon. Holmes's reaction was uncharacteristically phlegmatic, "I suppose the investigation has lain untouched for many years, another couple of days is neither here nor there."

We returned to Bart's and were directed to Sir James's office.

"It is!" he cried, as we entered, "it's young Holmes! I thought I recognised the name."

"Good morning, Sir James, thank you for taking the time to see us."

Sir James Sydney was a man in his late sixties; he had been at the top of his profession for over four decades and was still without peer. Although I never worked with him personally, I had the privilege of attending some of his lectures in my time at Bart's, and I referred to his work on numerous occasions before and after my time there.

"You may remember my friend, Doctor John Watson?" said Holmes stepping aside.

Sir James looked at me earnestly and thought for a while, "Of course, Watson. I have read some of your accounts involving our friend here in *The Strand.*" He turned back to Holmes, "You've come a long way since you sat up there in the lecture theatre," – and then again to me – "You were here for a while yourself if I recall?"

"I was indeed."

"So, what can I do for you both after all these years?"

"You will recall, Sir James, that you asked me to look into an issue during my studies?"

"Yes, I do. It was that silly business about my articles being plagiarised if I recall."

"That is correct. The governors asked me to stand down from the case – do you recall what happened?"

"Well, yes, I do as a matter of fact. They had an internal enquiry and my young assistant – a lad called Barton – was found to be the guilty party. He had to leave the hospital."

"May I ask what your reaction was to this?"

Sir James looked questioningly at my companion, "I was extremely disappointed if I am honest. I trusted the lad implicitly – he was diligent in his work, the model pupil, invaluable at times. I never thought him capable of such a contemptable act. He was always willing to learn. He protested his innocence but the evidence was quite compelling by all accounts."

"By all accounts?" repeated Holmes, "did you yourself see the evidence against him."

"No, I didn't. I did ask but was told that it wasn't necessary for me to study the information. The governors were keen that the matter should be hastened to a conclusion as quickly as possible, for the sake of everyone."

"I'm sure they were," mumbled Holmes. "May I ask Sir James, if you were questioned as part of this enquiry?"

The surgeon looked ever-more puzzled at the man he viewed as one of his former students. "I don't think I was, as a matter of fact."

"And who carried out this internal enquiry?"

"From memory I think it was Lord Farquharson, one of the governors."

"Is he still a governor?"

"No, he died quite a few years ago now. Why do you ask?"

Holmes ignored Sir James's question, "And do you know what happened to your former assistant, Barton?"

"No, I'm afraid I don't. You tend to lose touch with former colleagues in this line of work. Do you have news of him?"

"I'm afraid – we learned only this week – that the poor lad died some years ago following his being dismissed from the hospital in disgrace."

"Goodness!" Sir James sat for a few moments staring at his desk, "I had no idea. He was such a bright young man. What a tragedy."

"Sir James, may I ask if any of your colleagues – or perhaps former colleagues – had any interest in nautical matters?"

The seemingly odd question raised the surgeon from his reverie, "Erm…I'm not sure. What a strange thing to ask."

"We are simply testing a theory, that is all."

"And what exactly is this theory, Holmes?" Sir James was now regaining some of his authority.

"That this young Barton was not the culprit all those years ago. It doesn't make sense for a junior apprentice to try and pass himself off as being an authority on any matter."

"Whitelaw!" cried Sir James, suddenly. "You asked about a colleague with a nautical background. "I'm sure Whitelaw was in the navy before he came to Bart's." He thought for a while longer, "That's right, because he had a friend that used to visit him regularly at the hospital called Collingwood. It always amused me that a navy man made a point of mixing with people who had nautical names."

Holmes and I briefly exchanged a glance.

"I remember Dr. Whitelaw," said Holmes, "I attended one or two of his lectures. Does he still work at the hospital?"

"No, he left a few years ago. From memory, I think someone said that he went to France but I couldn't swear to it."

"That is very interesting and most informative Sir James, thank you for your time. We won't keep you any longer."

"Not at all," said the surgeon, "it was lovely to see you both again, even if it was under such unusual circumstances. I would be interested to know the outcome of your enquiries."

"It may come to nothing, Sir James," said Holmes, "as my first effort did, but we will be sure to keep you abreast of any significant developments."

The name of Whitelaw was the only line we could follow after leaving Sir James, and I suggested that we check his whereabouts on the register at the Royal College of Surgeons at Lincoln's Inn Fields.

"An excellent idea, Watson. Why not muster our resources? I believe the Royal College also holds records of navy and army surgeons. Perhaps we could kill two birds with one stone, when looking into the movements of Dr. Whitelaw."

Chapter III

We arrived at the Royal College shortly after lunch and went our separate ways, Holmes to see what he could find out about Dr. Whitelaw's naval service, while I was to look into the man's civilian career. We reconvened later that day in the foyer to share our findings; Holmes had the familiar glint in his eye when on a case, like the eager bloodhound once more on the trail of its quarry. Outside was a row of stationary hansom cabs; horses pulled impatiently at their bridles while the cabbies lounged, chatting to one another. When the first saw a fare approaching, he resumed his station and touched the brim of his hat.

"Baker Street," ordered Holmes as we climbed aboard and my friend leaned back in his seat, smiling. "Well Watson, what did you find?"

"An interesting career," I announced. "I couldn't find anything before '76 – presumably, that was his navy career – but then he appears at The Hampshire County Hospital in October of that year. A swift career path then followed with spells at The Royal Victoria, in Folkstone; the University Hospital, in Lewisham; then the period at Bart's that we know about, before moving on to St Thomas's. His latest position is marked as being in Edinburgh, although that could only be confirmed through the Royal College there."

"Edinburgh!" repeated Holmes, "the moving target is obviously moving further afield. But to Scotland and not to France as Sir James believed."

"What did you find out about his naval career?" I asked.

Holmes turned and looked directly at me before announcing, "Precisely nothing!"

"Nothing?"

"Our friend here has an effrontery to claim he was ever *in* the navy! It seems his early career was not dissimilar to your own, Doctor. He took his degree at the University of London and barely scraped a pass from the documents available. He then enrolled on the course prescribed for surgeons in the navy and again, got through the course but with extremely modest marks. It was at that point that his naval career ended. He bought himself out of the service in early '76 and seemingly at that point travelled to Hampshire to begin his civilian career."

"How very strange," I said, almost to myself.

"And potentially very revealing," said my companion staring directly ahead. "I believe there is enough interest in this individual for us to follow the trail north and see what else we can find out. Are you game, Watson?"

"Of course," I said eagerly.

"Excellent. I suggest we take the overnight train this evening from King's Cross and pick up the scent tomorrow morning."

No sooner had we made arrangements with tickets and a hotel booking at *The Imperial* when Holmes received a telegram. He ripped it open and snorted his derision.

"Mycroft!"

"What is it?" I asked.

"Brother mine has summoned me to Whitehall on an *urgent* matter." He emphasised the word 'urgent' as if to mimic his brother, before rhetorically asking, "isn't everything urgent in the corridors of power?"

"What will you do?"

"Knowing Mycroft, I have little choice but to go and see what the problem is. But there is no need for you to stay, my dear fellow. How do you feel about making the trip north yourself and I will join you in a day or two?"

As I had nothing else to occupy my time and believing that Holmes would now be otherwise engaged, I had no objection. "If you think that would be of use."

"Of course I do, my dear fellow. I might suggest repeating our visit to the Royal College *there* to view their registers and see if we can locate our man. See what you can find out and I will join you as soon as I can."

Holmes had sent me on a similar mission of reconnaissance a few months earlier and, much to my chagrin, told me upon my return that I had done remarkably badly. I was therefore determined to perform my duty diligently and regain some credibility in the eyes of my friend on this occasion.

So, I took the overnight sleeper train from King's Cross alone and awoke the next morning to find the greenery and heather of the Scottish countryside was giving way to the thickening stone and granite of the nation's capital. Having enjoyed a hearty Scottish breakfast on the train, I took a hansom from Waverley to my lodgings.

Once I was settled in, I wasted no time in visiting the Royal College of Surgeons to view their registers. Knowing exactly who I was looking for, it took me no time to find a Doctor Daniel Whitelaw, who did indeed work at The Royal Infirmary and was formally of St Thomas's in London. It also listed his address, which – given that I had never actually seen Whitelaw and therefore would not recognise him – I decided to make my next port of call.

The address listed turned out to be an elegant town house one in a row on the quiet Glengyle Terrace. Opposite was a large park with shrubbery and railings from behind which I could discretely view the house.

After a few hours of tedious observation of the street, with nothing more than a hansom cab and a nanny wheeling a pram to note, a man finally came walking along the street on the opposite side. My instinct told me that this was the man who was the purpose of my visit. He was a tall, well-dressed man of around fifty, who walked with a confident air. Sure enough, as he approached the house I was observing, he took out a set of keys, climbed the few steps to the front door and let himself in. So, "Daniel Whitelaw, I presume," I mumbled to myself. I made my way on foot back to my hotel and sent a telegram to Holmes informing him that I had located our man. In truth I was unsure as to how I should proceed but my spirits were raised over dinner when I received a telegram of my own from Baker Street:

EXCELLENT WORK STOP
DISCOVERED WHITELAW WAS ASKED TO
LEAVE ST THOMAS'S STOP
HOPE TO JOIN YOU TOMORROW END

The following morning, I decided to get up early, make my way to Glengyle Terrace and – assuming it *was* Whitelaw who I saw the previous day – follow him to the hospital to confirm he was indeed the person in whom we were interested. As I left the hotel, my stomach growled its displeasure as I caught a waft of the delicious Scottish kippers on offer in the dining room. I was determined however, to be as efficient as possible in my task and I took my position in the park on Glengyle Terrace shortly after seven-thirty, although the sharp Edinburgh morning had me questioning not only my course of action, but also my inadequate London attire.

At around eight-fifteen, the man in question appeared from the house and began to retrace his steps from the previous evening. I left my hiding place in the park opposite and followed at a discreet distance. As we emerged from the quiet streets around Glengyle Terrace into the hustle and bustle of the city, I quickened my pace and narrowed the gap between myself and my quarry, save that I lost sight of him. I was delighted when I saw him turn onto Lauriston Place and enter the grounds of The Royal

Infirmary and, as staff came and went, going about their business, I hurried still further to enter the building just a few paces behind him. My mission was rewarded when one of the nurses said, "Good morning, Doctor Whitelaw." I decided that was all I needed at this stage and took a seat in the entrance hall to plan my next move.

My reverie was disturbed by my stomach which growled again, reminding me that I hadn't yet had anything to eat. I therefore stirred myself and found a small coffee house close by where I could have some breakfast. What would Holmes do, I asked myself, as I had my ham and eggs. I smiled as, in my mind's eye, I could hear him say, *'You know my methods. Apply them!'* The truth was that I wasn't sure what the best course of action was now that I had identified Whitelaw. Should I confront him? If so, what would I accuse him of: plagiarising Sir James's work? Not being in the navy? It all suddenly seemed a little tenuous.

Without a meaningful plan of action, I wandered back to the hospital, wondering what to do next. As lunchtime approached, I decided to up the stakes and play a slightly more dangerous game. I waited outside near the entrance, hoping to see Whitelaw emerge once more and safe in the knowledge that, amongst the scores of people that were constantly entering and leaving the building, he wouldn't notice me.

Shortly after mid-day, Whitelaw appeared and I followed him to a restaurant. Standing across the street, I saw him take a seat inside and satisfied myself that he would be there for some time. It was then that I hurried back to the hospital and approached a young man who had his head buried in some paperwork on the front desk.

"Excuse me, I wonder if it would be possible to see Doctor Whitelaw?"

The man looked up, as if annoyed by the disturbance, "May I ask what it is in connection with?"

"Oh, it is just a social call really. My name is Dr. John Watson and I knew Dr. Whitelaw at St. Bartholomew's in London. I just happened to be in Edinburgh and thought I might call to pay my respects."

"If you would just wait there, Doctor, I will see if he is available."

The man disappeared for a few minutes before returning to his station. "I'm afraid Dr. Whitelaw is out on his lunch at the moment, Doctor Watson. Can I arrange to take a message for you?"

"Ah, not to worry. Perhaps you could simply tell him that I called in to say hello and I will try and call back again tomorrow."

As the man wrote the message down, he said, "I am just about to go out myself, but I will make sure my colleague passes this on for you."

"Thank you."

I went outside once more and stood behind one of the columns, anticipating the young man's departure. After ten minutes, I saw him leave and felt safe enough to go back inside without being recognised by anyone. After a further half hour or so, Whitelaw appeared once more. As he walked through the entrance area, a heavy-set matron called out from behind the front desk:

"Doctor Whitelaw, there is a message for you here."

I was seated about twenty paces from the desk, close enough to see and hear the exchange but hopefully far enough away as not to arouse suspicion.

Whitelaw took the piece of paper hesitantly and read it. "What did this man look like?" I heard him ask.

"I have no idea, Doctor, I wasn't here when he called. I was just asked to pass the message to you upon your return."

Whitelaw paused for a moment in thought, before turning on his heels and heading out of the hospital once more. As he did so, he seemed to catch sight of me and I quickly buried my head in the newspaper I had bought earlier. Satisfied that the glance was one of the meaningless hundred we all make each day, I moved to follow him. Through the crowd, he hurried to a telegram office on Chalmers Street, before thoughtfully wandering back to the hospital, presumably to resume his duties.

"What an interesting reaction," I thought to myself. *"Who could he be sending a telegram to?"*

I settled down with my newspaper for another long afternoon of waiting in and around the hospital, interrupting my duties only briefly to visit the coffee shop where I had enjoyed my breakfast that morning. It was shortly after three o'clock when I retook my position on a bench in the hospital grounds. The previous day, Whitelaw appeared to have completed his duties at five o'clock, but as that hour now passed, I feared that I had been sloppy in leaving my post, thus allowing my quarry to slip through the net.

It was as I was inwardly castigating myself for my negligence when Whitelaw finally appeared at ten minutes to six. With a sigh of relief, I fell in line behind him, assuming that he would be making his way home. To my surprise however, instead of walking in the direction of Glengyle Crescent, he continued along Gilmour Place, where my hotel was situated. My surprise turned to horror when he slowed and entered *The Imperial.* He must have somehow discovered who I was! But how could he know where I was staying?

I was crestfallen, believing that I had failed in my task. The watcher had been found out! Reluctantly – at least knowing that Whitelaw did not know what I looked like – I entered the hotel a few moments later. He was standing at the reception counter waiting for some assistance.

"Good evening," he said as the clerk appeared, "I am here to meet a friend of mine, "A Mr. George Campbell. My name is Whitelaw."

The man referred to the large book in front of him, "Ah, yes, Doctor Whitelaw. Mr. Campbell arrived just a few minutes ago. He left a note here to inform you that he will meet with you in the dining room at a quarter past six."

He indicated the dining room to Whitelaw, who followed his directions without a backward glance. My relief was palpable. I checked my watch; it was ten minutes after six. As I looked up a man descended the stairs and headed in the direction of the dining room. I assumed him to be Campbell, the subject of Whitelaw's assignation. I wanted to immediately follow but felt it was too much of a risk – I would surely look too conspicuous walking in on my own and taking a table beside them. A better option would be to wait for another party and follow them in, making conversation with them as cover for my subterfuge. Within moments, I was in luck, as two elderly ladies descended the stairs and turned in the direction of the dining room.

"Good evening, ladies," I said falling in beside them, "a lovely evening."

"Oh yes," said one, full of excitement, "we come here every year, don't we, sister?"

"Yes, that's right, sister," said the other, "every year."

"It's my first time, here at The Imperial" I said, as we walked slowly towards the dining room, "I must say I am very impressed."

Looking through the door, I saw Whitelaw stand up to greet the man I had seen in the foyer some moments earlier, someone I now knew to be a Mr. Campbell. So engrossed were they in their own company, it was unlikely they even noticed me and my two companions, as we appeared to the outside observer to be deep in conversation.

As I steered the sisters past the two men, I heard Whitelaw say, "Thank you for coming at such short notice."

"Your telegram sounded urgent," replied Campbell, as the two sat down.

I guided my two companions to a table and held their chairs as they seated, "Do enjoy your dinner, ladies," I said quietly, "it was a pleasure to meet you."

I took a table myself between my fellow visitors to Edinburgh, and the two men whom I was particularly interested in, hoping it would be a position from where I could overhear their conversation. By this point in the day, the newspaper I carried held absolutely no news for me but I had little option but to open it once more and use it as a stage prop. I was about ten feet away from the two men and as the dining room started to fill up, I found it increasingly difficult to pick up what they were saying.

I did hear the word "Bart's" hissed by Whitelaw, which confirmed to me that it was my note from earlier in the day that had set these particular wheels in motion.

"Calm yourself," replied Campbell, "what is there to know after all these years?"

Whatever Whitelaw replied was drowned out by a party of two couples who noisily took their seats diagonally opposite to where I was positioned. Thereafter, the clattering of cutlery and idle chatter of guests made it difficult to hear much of what was being said. I had the impression that Campbell was continually seeking to reassure Whitelaw that there was nothing to worry about.

I had been sitting for the best part of an hour, moving my food around and intermittently looking at the now completely redundant newspaper. I couldn't help myself from glancing up every now and then at my subjects, to see if I could glean anything further. Suddenly, I saw an old man appear on the far side of the dining room. I hadn't seen him enter and he was sitting there quietly by himself. With white side whiskers that looped round his large ears, a hooked nose and crooked posture, he looked somewhat incongruous with this elaborate setting.

And then it dawned on me. Holmes! He had come to Edinburgh and appeared incognito. I was inwardly furious. He didn't trust me to follow Whitelaw after all and used a bogus telegram from Mycroft to trick and test me. I wondered how long he had been here – perhaps he was even on the same train without me ever knowing.

As angry as I was, I refrained from confronting him, as such an action would not only draw a scene, but it would also completely compromise the surveillance of Whitelaw and his companion. Before another thought, the two men rose and shook hands once more.

"I will come and see you tomorrow in your office," I heard Campbell say. "Let's see if this doctor turns up."

This appeared to placate Whitelaw and he turned to leave. I knew where he lived so felt there was little point in following him. Instead, I decided to follow Campbell to discover in which room he was staying. As luck would have it, the two couples also rose from their tables and I discreetly followed behind them as they climbed the stairs, between myself and Campbell. As they continued to the third floor, Campbell continued along the second. I held back at the end of the corridor and watched him enter his room before quickly hurrying along behind him to note down the room number. I now knew his name, his link to Whitelaw and the room he was staying in. It was time to return to the dining room to share this information with Holmes, while expressing my displeasure at his own behaviour.

I was disappointed to find the dining room empty upon my return, so I decided to go for a walk before turning in. The cold temperature of the morning had gradually altered as the day progressed and by the time I was out on the street, it had turned into a bleak night. It wasn't long before a squalling wind heralded rain, which had threatened all afternoon. It rather summed up my unhappy mood, despite what should have been considered a successful day. I returned to my hotel and faced with a choice between a drink in the bar or an early night, I chose the latter.

Chapter IV

I was seated in the dining room the following morning having breakfast wondering if all my work the previous day had been a waste of time, given Holmes's appearance. Guests gradually appeared: the two sisters I had met the previous evening; one of the two couples who I followed up the stairs – but there was no sign of Campbell.

It was as the waitress was clearing away my plate that Holmes appeared in his normal guise.

"Good morning, Watson," he said, cheerily.

"Good morning, Holmes," my response being rather brusquer.

"A fine morning for the chase!"

He sat down and ordered another pot of coffee. As he did so, I glanced past him and saw the elderly man from the previous evening shuffling in and taking a seat near the door.

"What is it, my dear fellow?" asked Holmes, "you look as though you've seen a ghost?"

"But I thought…surely…when did you arrive?"

"I've come straight from the station. I took the sleeper from King's Cross last night. Did you not receive my telegram?"

"Erm…yes," I spluttered still looking from Holmes to the old man and back again.

"I must say, my dear fellow, I have found you in a very strange mood this morning. Judging by your telegram, I thought you would have been pleased with your efforts in tracking down this scoundrel, Whitelaw."

"Yes, of course," I said, as my mood instantly changed, despite my feeling a little foolish. "I wasn't altogether sure how to proceed, so I relayed a message to him suggesting that I would call on him at the hospital today."

"Really? And what do you intend to do when you meet him?"

I looked squarely at Holmes and decided that honesty was the best policy. "I've absolutely no idea," I said, rather awkwardly.

We looked at each other before bursting into laughter at my crude, unthinking method. I was pleased to see my friend in such jovial spirits and he was generous in his assessment:

"It's perhaps not the worst approach to this little problem, I suppose. I have also arranged to visit the hospital."

"To see whom?"

"Two of the governors. I informed you in my telegram that Whitelaw had been asked to leave St Thomas's after a very brief period there. Between meetings with Mycroft, I managed to perform a little investigating of my own. Apparently, a senior surgeon questioned his teaching methods and when the matter was investigated further, it transpired that his application to the hospital had been somewhat exaggerated. Much like Bart's, he left rather than cause a scandal for the hospital. Having exhausted his luck in the south of England, I'll wager that he decided to move north; and if that meant re-registering with another College of Surgeons in another country, then all the better.

"I had a telephone conversation with one of the governors yesterday and expressed my concerns. Although he was sceptical of my suggestions, he acknowledged my willingness to travel from London to Edinburgh to discuss the matter further and agreed to meet me with one of his colleagues."

"If we can prove Whitelaw's guilt, how can we go about having the man apprehended?"

"This is where the famous Mr. Mac's influence takes hold. Since he shot to national prominence, the Chief Inspector is revered in his homeland; I met with him at Scotland Yard yesterday and he alerted an Inspector Ernespie of the Edinburgh City Police and asked him to meet us at the hospital shortly before noon."

"And when is your meeting with the governors?"

"Eleven o'clock."

As we were speaking, I saw Whitelaw's confederate, Campbell, enter the dining room. Fortunately, oblivious as he was to the reason for our presence there, he took no notice of us and sat down at a table on the other side of the room, which allowed me to complete my report concerning my surveillance from the previous day, unhindered.

"I must say," said my friend in similar hushed tones to my own, "I have to congratulate you on some excellent work, Watson." He continued, "It would appear our enquiries have been running on parallel tracks. Yesterday, when I spoke to good old Mr. Mac about our little problem, he not only contacted his colleagues in Edinburgh, but he also made some enquiries in Liverpool with regards to the so-called literary agent who submitted the various articles to *The Lancet* all those years ago. He came to Baker Street last night before I left to share his findings.

"You won't be surprised to learn that Mr. Nelson of Trafalgar Street, Liverpool was not in fact a literary agent but a pawn broker. When questioned – such were the unusual circumstances – he revealed that he had been contacted and commissioned by a man in Glasgow to submit the articles on behalf of the man's clients."

I wanted to announce the man's name triumphantly but refrained from crying out. "Campbell," I whispered, stealing a glance across the room at our subject who had his head buried in the morning newspaper.

"The very same," confirmed Holmes. "It was good income for the small pawn shop, so the owner wasn't concerned about the background to the commission. As for Campbell, the tiny establishment in Liverpool was a sufficient distance from both Glasgow and London as not to arouse suspicion or connection with either Campbell or Whitelaw.

"With a little luck, we will not only succeed in exposing Whitelaw for the fraudster, swindler and imposter that he is, but we may well snare this Campbell character as well."

As one of the waiting staff served Campbell his breakfast, it acted sufficiently as a distraction to allow us to make our exit from the dining room without attracting any undue attention.

We entered The Royal Infirmary at five minutes to eleven and were shown into the library, where two elderly men sat, clearly agitated and inconvenienced by the meeting.

"Good morning, gentlemen," said my companion, ignoring their disposition, "my name is Sherlock Holmes and this is my friend and colleague, Doctor John Watson."

"A doctor?" said one in surprise.

"Yes," I replied, "former army surgeon and late of St. Bartholomew's in London."

My announcement appeared to placate the two men somewhat and their mood visibly softened.

"I'm a former army man myself," said the man, rising and offering a hand, "Lieutenant Colonel Fraser Carmichael, of The Royal Scots, retired. This is Sir Alexander Hamilton."

The second man rose and shook both our hands before addressing Holmes, "So, what is this business concerning Dr. Whitelaw?"

"Gentlemen, I'm afraid this man is not all he appears. I believe he is a man quite unworthy of your trust and, if left to his own devices, someone who may do considerable damage to the reputation of this fine establishment."

This final comment certainly captured the attention of the two governors, who both stood in silence for a few moments.

"I don't understand," said Sir Alexander, "what is he accused of? He came with an excellent reference, I have it here."

"May I see it?" asked Holmes, and then, after receiving it, "signed by Lord Farquharson of St Bartholomew's.

As I had been involved in the investigation since our meeting with Sir James at Bart's some days earlier and I appeared to have some credibility as a doctor and an army man in the eyes of the two governors, I felt confident in stating, "Lord Farquharson died several years ago."

Holmes clearly had no objection to my interruption and added, "This is a forgery, I'm afraid. It is in keeping with the rest of this man's career."

"But he is also an ex-military man," protested Carmichael, "a navy surgeon."

"He may have briefly enrolled in the service, but once he completed the surgeon's course, he promptly left. Spells in various hospitals in the South of England then followed – all of which resulted in him leaving in unusual circumstances – before he travelled north of the border to start a new chapter. Can I ask, has he performed any surgery since he has been employed?"

"Not to our knowledge," said Carmichael, "I think he has just lectured."

"That is extremely fortunate, not only for the hospital, but for any potential patient who may have been laid out before him."

"Again, I don't understand."

"I can only find one record of Whitelaw ever performing surgery in a career that spans almost fifteen years. That came when he worked at a hospital in Folkstone in Kent. The senior surgeon was called away an hour before a patient was due to receive an appendectomy. As Whitelaw was the only supposedly qualified practitioner on the wing at the time, he was asked to step in, no doubt much to his horror. The patient barely survived the operation and Whitelaw was asked to leave the hospital, no doubt as much to his own relief as to theirs."

The two governors sat in stunned silence for a while before a knock on the door interrupted the stillness and a young man's head appeared.

"There is an Inspector Ernespie here, gentlemen."

"That is at my request," said Holmes, addressing the governors, "with your permission perhaps we could ask him to join us?"

Both men wore the same expression: a combination of confusion and uncertainty on how to proceed. They assented to Holmes's request without speaking. Moments later, a large fair-headed man was shown into the library.

"Good morning, gentlemen. Finlay Ernespie at your service. Chief Inspector MacDonald has filled me in on this Whitelaw character. I'm pretty sure we have enough to arrest the laddie."

"We need to bring him here." It was the ex-army man who suddenly took charge of the situation.

He left the room momentarily to speak with the young man who had shown the inspector in a few minutes earlier. After a further ten minutes, there was a second knock at the door and the young man announced the arrival of Dr. Whitelaw.

Whitelaw entered and was immediately clearly taken aback by the tableau that beheld him. His eyes narrowed and darted from one to the other, until he had surveyed each of us. His composure quickly regained; he spoke at last:

"I believe you asked to see me, Colonel Carmichael? I do have another appointment with an old colleague from St Bartholomew's shortly."

"That would be with me," I said, without offering a hand, "Doctor John Watson."

258

Whitelaw looked perplexed, "Forgive me Doctor, I can't remember meeting you."

"And you must find that troubling," interrupted Holmes, "after all…*Doctor* Whitelaw, a good liar must have a good memory."

Whitelaw paused and looked at Holmes, a fleeting expression of recognition passed over his face before raising his voice, "How dare you, sir, whoever you are!"

Holmes calmly lifted the bogus reference, "Forged!" he announced.

The one word appeared to disarm Whitelaw immediately and it was as if his racing mind prevented him from speaking. Holmes continued:

"You are a fraudster, an imposter, a swindler. It can only be guessed at how many people you have wronged in your time. I know of one such unfortunate – Sir James Sydney's assistant who was wrongly accused of plagiarising his mentor's articles. It was you who sought to advance your career and make money at the expense of others' hard work."

Whitelaw initially said nothing, unable to contradict. Finally, in pathetic tones, "That matter was investigated."

"By this Lord Fortescue," Holmes retorted, holding up the forged document once more, "he is not here to defend himself, so we will never know what was in his heart and mind when he was conducting whatever enquiries he undertook. What I do know is that those enquiries were inadequate and the conclusions were erroneous."

It was at that point that Whitelaw appeared to place Holmes as the student who initially asked about the affair. "I remember you now," he said, almost oblivious to his predicament.

"Yes, and now I am free from the shackles of the people who should have known better, I am able to look, unhindered, into the misdemeanours throughout your counterfeit career. Not only the plagiarising of Sir James's work, but also the fraudulent application to Bart's in the first place, where you claimed to have been a ship's surgeon for five years, whereas in fact you never served in the navy. There followed a similar fraudulent application to St. Thomas's, not to mention the near fatality at the Royal Victoria, or the missing funds from the Hampshire County Hospital, something that came to light shortly after you left."

"Apart from that letter you hold," said Whitelaw in brazen tones, "most of what you claim is hearsay,"

"There's enough there for us to look into, laddie," said Inspector Ernespie, speaking for the first time, "I think we'll take it from here."

As if on cue, two uniformed officers entered and clattered a pair of handcuffs on Whitelaw's wrists before leading him away.

"Inspector?" called Holmes, "we believe this man has a confederate who should be arriving at the hospital any time now, "a man called Campbell."

The young man who had in effect, acted as a butler for the last hour, and who was now standing in the doorway, said, "I'm sorry, sir, but a gentleman of that name was here earlier asking for Dr. Whitelaw. When I told him he was in with the governors and some other gentleman, he became quite agitated and left in a hurry."

"He will be heading back to Glasgow," said Holmes.

"I'll get some men to Waverley right away," replied Ernespie, hurrying off.

Our work done, we collected our belongings from the hotel and took a leisurely train back to London, arriving later that night.

The days and the weeks that followed saw various internal investigations carried out at the establishments where

Whitelaw and his associate Campbell – who had duly been arrested at Waverly station – had practiced and advanced their dishonest careers.

It has always been a philosophy of mine that like-minded people, whether good or bad, invariably gravitate towards each other. So it was with these two villains. They had met at public school, their families being wealthy enough to pay for a privileged education but not wealthy enough to provide for them following it. They were forced to make their own way in the world therefore and, although reasonably intelligent, their natural idleness and lack of dedication to anything of value would always prove an obstacle. They therefore turned to nefarious activity almost immediately.

Under questioning, Whitelaw admitted that he had aided Campbell during their exams by passing him some of the answers. This allowed them both to pass – all be it with extremely modest marks – and advance their respective careers in medicine and law. Whitelaw was always interested in the navy but as we have seen, had neither the dedication nor discipline to forge such a noble career. Instead, he began his journey around various teaching hospitals, exaggerating his achievements and impersonating a skilled practitioner. Whenever a scandal or an investigation seemed likely, he would move on.

Campbell's career in law was a mirror image, with sophistry and heartlessness his main weapons in advancing his career from London to Glasgow, to Birmingham, to Liverpool and finally back to Glasgow. Their schoolboy pact of assisting each other whenever one was in trouble remained steadfast throughout adulthood. That was until we caught up with them in Edinburgh, when they had little choice but to subsequently admit to their crimes. We left the authorities to their duties.

We did however, re-visit Sir James Sydney at Bart's to inform him of the delayed resolution of his case almost two decades earlier. He was staggered by our account and told us he felt desperately guilty about the demise of his assistant Robert Barnet. Sir James said he would write to the boy's mother and insisted on re-imbursing us for our expenses in solving the matter.

Back at Baker Street, we resumed our usual stations by the fire. Both of us sat in silence for an hour or so, pondering the case and the sadness it had brought to many. Finally, Holmes broke the stillness:

"Do you intend to publish this account, Watson?"

"I may do," I replied, "it has had quite an effect on me I must say. I am struggling to get the unfortunate Robert Barnet out of my mind. The injustice of it all."

"Indeed. If you do decide to seek out your literary agent once more, could I suggest a title for your adventure?" He looked at me affectionately through the blue smoke that curled up from his pipe and partially covered his face, "I think it is worthy of the title, 'The Invaluable Assistant.'"

The New Forest Gamekeeper

Chapter I

Not for the first time, I resolved recently to finally produce a definitive catalogue of the innumerable cases involving my friend Sherlock Holmes. Previous efforts had seen me try to categorise them by year or put them in the chronological order in which they occurred. There was then an attempt to divide the cases between Holmes's earlier, unaccompanied investigations and then those directly involving myself. And even an effort to split his career into two distinct halves – the period before his three-year hiatus and those following his return and his appearance in my surgery on that remarkable day in April 1894.

As I had failed miserably with each effort, I decided on this occasion to simply list the cases in alphabetical order. Alas, this too was doomed to failure. I no sooner picked up my notes regarding the strange events at Abbey Grange when I was reminded of another, previous unrecorded, investigation, which admittedly hardly stretched the analytical skills of my friend, but nevertheless I believe had a profound effect on him.

I have recorded elsewhere that it was Inspector Stanley Hopkins who had called for Holmes's assistance following the killing of Sir Eustace Brackenstall on that fateful morning and my friend commented to me that it was one of seven occasions on which Hopkins had called for his help.

In glancing through the notes of the Abbey Grange, my mind naturally wandered to the other six cases and settled on the one that took us into the New Forest during the final decade of the last century. I cannot be sure of the exact year of the case as for some reason, I never noted the date but it must have been during the three-year period between my re-joining Holmes at our Baker Street chambers in '94 and the Abbey Grange case in '97.

I had been away from Baker Street for a couple of days, on one of the many reunions I enjoyed with my old teammates from Blackheath, and I returned to find our rooms empty and a note sitting on the mantle:

The Black Lion Inn, Beaulieu, Hampshire

My Dear Watson,

I have been called away by our friend Stanley Hopkins to investigate an interesting little problem. I should be delighted if you could join me at your earliest convenience.

Yours,
SH

"Beaulieu?" I mumbled to myself – I had visited that pretty little village several times whilst convalescing at Netley – "I wonder what took Holmes down there?" I wired ahead to inform him that I would travel down to Hampshire the following day, before making the appropriate arrangements.

The morning of my journey had the merest sharpness to it as the last vestiges of summer teetered on the cusp of autumn. Although my hansom delivered me to Waterloo on time, I found myself among a throng of frustrated passengers, all delayed by an apparent accident somewhere around Stevenage. Rumours were spreading of several casualties due to a collision and any scheduled northbound trains had all been cancelled as a result. It was a great relief therefore when my *south*bound train rumbled out of the station, all be it an hour late.

As the grey, urban sprawl of the capital gave way to the greenery of the fields, and eventually the ancient woodlands and open heathlands of the New Forest, I was reminded of what Holmes once told me: 'the lowest and vilest alleys in London do not present a more dreadful record of sin than does the smiling and beautiful countryside.' I smiled at his cynicism but then felt it best to reserve my own judgement until I discovered what I was heading towards. Arriving shortly after eleven o'clock, the picture-perfect village was just as I remembered it from my time at Netley.

I walked along the little cobbled high street until I reached the Black Lion Inn. Entering the bar, I saw my friend at a table in the corner; he was deep in conversation with a man I recognised as Inspector Stanley Hopkins from Scotland Yard. The young detective appeared to be listening intently to the methodical approach of my friend as a pupil would, learning from his master. The two looked up as I approached.

"My dear Watson, how wonderful to see you! You remember Hopkins."

"Doctor," greeted the young man, standing and offering a hand.

"Gentlemen," I said, removing my coat and joining them at the table, "what brings us down to this idyllic setting?"

It was Hopkins who replied, "We were called in by Lord and Lady Gelston of the Castle Fleet Estate. They believe their daughter has been kidnapped."

"Kidnapped? How terrible. I would have thought such an incident would have found its way into the national press – surely it is a sordid gossip columnists' delight?"

"His Lordship is keen to keep it as discreet as possible for that very reason. That is why he moved quickly to involve the local police, who in turn called Scotland Yard in and I, in turn, imposed on Mr. Holmes."

"When did this happen?"

"Three days ago. Lady Alexandra was last seen on Saturday night. When her parents were getting ready for church the following day, it was found that she was not in her room."

"Had her bed been slept in?"

"Excellent, Watson!" interrupted Holmes.

"No," replied Hopkins, in answer to my question.

"So, what do you propose now?"

It was Holmes who answered, "I only arrived myself yesterday and Hopkins here has been apprising me of the facts."

I was surprised that Holmes had not inspected the scene of the suspected abduction, knowing his eagerness to progress a case. It was as though Hopkins read my thoughts:

"His Lordship is a very private person. He reluctantly gave his permission for the local man, Eastman, to contact the Yard – when he found out I had also asked Mr. Holmes to accompany me, he banned us from entering. I've told Eastman that time is of the essence and it is essential that we attend. We are waiting for him to provide us with an update."

No sooner had Hopkins finished speaking when the update duly arrived. But it was to be as far from the everyday sharing of information as could be imagined: a ruddy-faced man burst through the door and quickly scanned the room before his eyes fell on our companion.

"Inspector Hopkins! Inspector Hopkins!" he gasped, rushing over to our table.

"Eastman, what is it?"

"It's Lord Gelston," said the man Hopkins had identified to us, "he's dead!"

The three of us barely waited for an explanation, as we hurried into our coats and followed the local policeman outside, where he had a brougham waiting.

"It's Lord Gelston's" explained Eastman, "Lady Margaret gave us permission to use it."

As we climbed aboard, Eastman indicated for the liveried coachman to slap the pair of beautiful chestnut horses into action.

"I informed you of Mr. Sherlock Holmes yesterday," Hopkins said to Eastman, "this is his colleague, Dr. Watson."

"Gentlemen," acknowledged the Hampshire man with a nod, before explaining, "Lord Gelston was found this morning in his study. The poor man just seems to have collapsed and died on the spot sometime during the night. There is a pathologist there now."

Within twenty minutes, we were faced with the two large stone lions that sat upon the gateposts of Castle Fleet Manor. The house itself could not be seen from the road, such was the density of the woodland that dominated the estate. The long driveway meandered through the trees until the manor-house itself appeared in all its grandeur.

Our brougham pulled up behind a hospital carriage, the rear door of which was open and apparently awaiting the removal of the deceased from the house. We disembarked and were met at the door by a member of staff who – understandably, in the circumstances – wore a saturnine expression.

"Good morning, gentlemen, my name is Parton. I am Lord and Lady Gelston's butler. If you would like to follow me."

He showed us along the wood panelled hallway that was adorned with family portraits – ermine-clad, elderly men who could only have been the ancestors of the now, late Earl. We entered the library, which clearly held several

267

hundred volumes. I sensed Holmes's frustration at the further delay of being led into, what was in effect, a waiting room, but out of respect for the shocked household, he reluctantly accepted the protocol.

"I'll be with you presently, gentlemen," said Parton as he left. Some moments later, he returned and announced, "Lady Gelston is in the drawing room and can see you now."

"Would it be possible to see the Earl's body and the room in which he died first?" Holmes's directness took the man back somewhat.

"I…I suppose so," he said, "although the doctor is preparing to have His Lordship's body removed."

"All the more reason to see it quickly then," said Holmes motioning towards the door.

The flustered butler led us further down the hall towards the Earl's study. Outside lay a beautiful golden retriever, with his ears down, as if sensing his master's demise. The room itself was as impressive as the rest of the house: a large stone fireplace had an ornate mantle on which stood a large brass clock and candles that had evidently burned down during the night. A round table of dark wood and several chairs occupied the centre of the room and there were more candles still smouldering there. Two long, heavily curtained windows flanked either side of the large desk and a thick rug was draped on an otherwise bare wooden floor.

Behind the desk lay the supine body of Lord Gelston. Two attendants waited patiently for their instruction from the doctor who was concluding his initial examinations. Holmes carefully picked his way through the shards of crystal glass and liquid that had shattered and spread across the floor; debris from a tumbler of brandy the Earl was presumably holding when he fell.

The doctor looked up as we entered and Inspector Eastman spoke quickly to prevent any confusion or feelings of intrusion:

"This is Mr. Sherlock Holmes and Inspector Hopkins from London. They have come to help with the mystery. This is Dr. Goring-Boyce, the pathologist from Lymington."

The doctor looked suitably non-plussed and irritated that strangers were interfering with his work. "There is little mystery with the matter. It is obvious that Lord Gelston died suddenly: a heart attack, a stroke, an aneurysm perhaps. I will conduct an autopsy this afternoon to establish which it is."

"It is the disappearance of young Lady Alexandra that they have come to help me with," clarified Eastman. "His Lordship asked me to use whatever resource was necessary to find his daughter and I contacted Scotland Yard. Inspector Hopkins here, in turn contacted Mr. Holmes."

"And you are?" Goring-Boyce asked, turning to me.

"I am Dr. John Watson, an associate of Mr. Holmes."

He eyed me up and down with a commingled look of suspicion and contempt, clearly unimpressed by outsiders being asked to assist, whatever the justification. He shrugged and was about to motion for the two attendants to step forward when Holmes stopped him and indicated towards the body.

"With your permission, Doctor. Could I just have a moment?"

Reluctantly, Goring-Boyce moved out of the way and Holmes leaned over the body and touched the rigid arm. "Been dead at least twelve hours, judging by the rigidity of the muscles."

"I agree," said the pathologist.

Holmes then glanced at the guttered candles around the room and nodded. Something then caught his eye; he eased up the body and retrieved a burned-out cigar stub; again, presumably dropped by Lord Gelston as he collapsed. Holmes smelled what remained of the cigar, "Hum, the finest Havana. Expensive, imported from the East Indian colonies."

"In keeping with the rest of His Grace's lifestyle, if I may say." Goring-Boyce shot a look of admonishment across to Eastman who had made the comment. "No offence intended, I should add," added the policeman.

Holmes got to his feet and nodded to the pathologist who, in turn, signalled to his two assistants to remove the body. Once the task had been completed, Holmes studied the area covered by the corpse and then turned to Parton, the butler, "Perhaps we could speak with Lady Gelston now?"

"Certainly, sir."

He led us back into the corridor and across to an even bigger room on the opposite side of the house. I was immediately struck by the large portrait of the 7th Earl of Gelston that hung above the huge fireplace. My eye then shifted to the solitary figure, seated beside one of the long, elegant windows; she was staring idly onto the lawn outside.

"Lady Gelston," announced Parton, "these are the gentlemen from London who have come to help Inspector Eastman."

"Gentlemen," said the graceful lady as she rose, "thank you for coming."

"Please don't get up, My Lady," said Holmes before deferring to our police colleagues to formally introduce us.

"I am Inspector Stanley Hopkins from Scotland Yard, My Lady, and this is Mr. Sherlock Holmes and his colleague Dr. Watson."

"Please accept our deepest condolences for your loss," added Holmes.

"Thank you, and thank you all for coming to see us," said Lady Gelston. She looked up at the portrait of her husband in a strange manner and I found it hard to fathom her emotions at that point.

"It was Lord Gelston who asked me to get some assistance in the search for Lady Alexandra," reminded Inspector Eastman, who appeared to be increasingly relieved with the support he was receiving from Hopkins and Holmes, "but when he learned that Inspector Hopkins here had also invited an amateur, he told us to keep away."

"Yes," she said simply, "Well, John is no longer here but you are and I appreciate your help." She then admonished herself, "Where are my manners? Parton, please arrange for some tea to be brought in."

Like the butler, it was inappropriate for any of us to object to the instruction. Lady Gelston indicated that we should sit down and, as Parton left the room, Holmes addressed our host.

"My Lady, I understand this must be incredibly painful for you but I must ask about the disappearance of your daughter."

"Yes, of course."

"I believe she disappeared on Saturday night?"

"That is what we assume. She did not come down for breakfast on Sunday and as we were preparing for church, I went up to see her and found her room empty."

"Were you aware of any strangers on the estate who may have been involved?"

"No, everything appeared as normal."

"It is certainly a large estate with a long drive up to the house; it would not have been easy for someone to approach unseen, abduct Lady Alexandra and make off without disturbing the household."

"I agree, Mr. Holmes, as did my husband. He suspected our gamekeeper of being involved."

"Your gamekeeper?"

"Yes, a man called Rice. He has also gone missing; nowhere to be found apparently."

The room was silent for a few moments before it was disturbed by Parton returning with some refreshment. After he had poured the tea and left, Holmes resumed his questioning.

"How long has this Rice been with you?"

"Quite some time I believe. I leave the outside staff to my husband but I would estimate he is a man of approaching forty and has been with us since he was a young boy."

"Do you know if your husband has ever had problems with him in the past?"

"I'm not sure if he had any more problems with Rice as with any other member of staff." Lady Gelston gave a weak smile to herself, "John would regularly complain about the staff – how they were always out to disobey him and sully the family name. When he discovered that Rice had gone missing, he exploded in a fit of rage, convinced it was a 'crime from within!' as he termed it."

It seemed an odd theory to me and I'm sure the others in the room shared my view.

"Has there been any contact from anyone regarding your daughter's whereabouts?" asked Holmes.

"None."

"Then I think it would be wise to announce your husband's passing in the national press, immediately. Let us see if that produces any reaction from anyone."

"Certainly," agreed Lady Gelston, "if you think it will help."

"I do. Now, I wonder if I could inspect your daughter's bedroom?"

"Of course." She tugged the bellpull by the fireplace and Parton appeared momentarily. "Show these gentlemen up to Alexandra's room, Parton. And then, notify *The Times,*

Telegraph, Observer and *Guardian* of Lord Gelston's death."

"Very good, My Lady," said the butler with a nod.

"Just one more question Lady Gelston if I may," said Holmes, "how many staff do you employ?"

"There is just Parton here, our cook and a housekeeper. We then have the outside staff – gamekeeper and assistant, the gardening staff, a groom and stable lad."

"And do the outside staff all report to the gamekeeper?"

"Yes, he lives in the gatehouse at the end of the drive."

"Ah yes, we passed it on the way. I may need to inspect that as well and interview the staff if that is possible."

"Certainly, anything you need just ask. Although, I am aware that not all the staff are here today. Perhaps I could make arrangements for them all to attend tomorrow morning."

Holmes nodded and smiled, "That would be most helpful, Lady Gelston, thank you again."

We followed the butler out and up a sweeping staircase to a landing along which were positioned occasional Queen Ann chairs of the finest quality. Parton opened one of the doors and stood back, allowing us to enter.

"This is how the room was found on Sunday morning, gentlemen," he said, "nothing has been disturbed. Would you like me to remain?"

"No, that won't be necessary, Parton," said Holmes before either of the policemen could reply, "we shall meet you downstairs when we are finished."

"Very good, sir," he said, with his usual nod.

The bedroom was in keeping with the style and grace of the rest of the house. Two sash windows were framed with dark green velvet curtains, secured with a heavy silken rope, which created an elegant swirl of the material. Similarly, the carpet and bed linen were of the finest quality; the two large teak wardrobes were full of beautiful clothes; and the free-standing furniture – full length mirror, chaise longue and dressing table – gave the room a stylish appearance.

Holmes began to pick his way carefully round the room. He mumbled an obvious point, even to those of us who did not possess his talents: "No sign of a struggle."

On the dressing table was an assortment of items: circular baskets that overflowed with ribbons and hairpins, bottles of perfume, a jewellery box that sat open, a few family photographs and a hairbrush, the white bristles of which were intertwined with long chestnut-coloured hairs.

A gauzy nightgown was draped over the full- length mirror and a camisole had been laid out on the chair beside one of the windows. Holmes dropped to his knees and looked under the bed; he then spotted something under the chair and reached out a long arm to see what it was. He pulled out what looked like a child's toy – a tiny ballerina that had been broken at its feet. Holmes glanced back to the dressing table and to the jewelry box in particular. Upon closer inspection we could see the legs of the little figure protruding from a small plinth on the base of the box. The main body of the figurine had been broken off and cast aside.

Holmes went across to the window and unsnibbed the latch; raising the sash he took out his pocket-lens and began to inspect the sill. Leaning out to inspect the outside of the window, he quickly turned his attention to its twin. Following the same process as a moment earlier, he leaned out of the first-floor window and looked down. Coming back into the room, as it were, he delivered his summary.

"There is little doubt that Lady Alexandra left of her own free will. You see here that this chair is out of place," – he indicated with his cane – "Look closely three feet to the right and you will see the indentations of the carpet, indicating its usual resting place. You can then follow the marks where it has been dragged to this window, where the young woman has used it to climb on and exit the room – there are almost imperceptible scuff marks on the sill."

He handed me his lens and I peered down, "Indeed there are," I confirmed.

"Why that window and not the one closer to it?" asked Eastman.

In following Holmes's methods, I looked out of the window and answered the policeman's question on Holmes's behalf, "Because there is a drainpipe adjacent to it."

"Excellent, Watson! She has climbed out of the window and clambered down the pipe. Let us go downstairs, gentlemen and see what we can see outside." We followed Holmes out onto the gravel curtilage and stood directly under the bedroom we had just left. "There you see – footmarks and displaced gravel where the young woman has leapt the final few feet. And beside it, signs of a larger object – presumably, a bag thrown from the window before she began her descent."

"Well, I never!" said Eastman.

"You've shed a little light on a gloomy situation, yet again, Mr. Holmes," agreed Hopkins, "but the question remains, why did the young woman abscond?"

"We perhaps need to visit the gamekeeper's residence to find out a little bit more," was his reply.

We climbed aboard the brougham that had remained outside the front entrance and the coachman took us back down the drive to the pretty lodge that was nestled beneath two enormous oak trees by the gates. Parton had provided us with a key to the building and the three of us followed Holmes inside. The interior of the building was tidy but did not come close to reflecting the beautiful appearance of the exterior. It simply gave the impression of being an expedient for a single man who worked on the estate.

It was to the small living room that Holmes focussed his attention. Creeping slowly around the room, he was drawn to a chair that was positioned to one side of the fire, beside which was an occasional table. On the table was a discarded piece of paper which Holmes studied for a while. He then withdrew a small envelope from the inside of his jacket and, dropping to his knees, gently eased something on the floor into the tiny packet with his pocketknife. Looking behind into the grate of the fire, he smiled and mumbled to himself. He retrieved the stub of a cigar and placed it in the envelope. He then turned his attention to the other side of the chair and chuckled.

"He has been here gentlemen!" he announced. Before we could question him, he elaborated, "Lord Gelston was here, probably last night. In this envelope is the same finest Havana we found under his body. And here," – he indicated to the side of the chair furthest from the fire – "long dog hairs, no doubt matching those of his faithful Retriever."

"What was he doing here?" asked Eastman.

"That is what we need to find out," replied Holmes. "He could not have been here to confront the man, as he knew Rice had gone missing. He must have been looking for something, therefore. Perhaps this note holds a clue."

He handed me the paper, " '20, 25, 30, 40. All good.' What can this mean?"

"Without any further data, I cannot be sure at this stage and it would be folly to speculate. The mere fact that it is a woman's hand makes it interesting."

"How can you tell?" asked Eastman.

"The quality of the paper, the gentle swirl of the handwriting – it is not the hurried, course scribble of a working man. Still, there are many loose ends in this case gentlemen and given that the main protagonists cannot help us, it may take some time to fathom."

"Oh, I don't know, Mr. Holmes," said the Hampshire man, "you've made more progress in a few hours as we have in as many days."

"Quite." Holmes flashed me a glance. "Let us return tomorrow and see if we can make a little *more* progress.

Chapter II

Holmes chose to remain in his room at the Black Lion that evening, leaving Inspector Hopkins and I to enjoy each other's company over a hearty evening meal. As it had been a long, wearisome day and neither of us could hope to compare our deductive powers to Holmes, we spent little time discussing the case.

"Should we not check on Mr. Holmes, Doctor?" asked Hopkins at one point.

"No, that won't be necessary, Inspector. I can picture him now perched by his window in a cloud of smoke from his strongest shag tobacco, analysing the day's events. He is best left alone when in such a state."

"He's quite a character," said the policeman with a philosophical air, "I'll give you that."

The following morning, it was no surprise to find Holmes had beaten us both to the breakfast table, eager as he was to advance his investigation.

"Good morning, gentlemen!" he cried, looking up from his ham and eggs, "you really must try the food in this establishment, it is excellent!"

I exchanged a wry smile with Hopkins before sitting down.

"A successful evening, Holmes?"

"Not enough data," was his frustrated reply. "However, I am confident by the end of today, the fog will have cleared somewhat."

On the chair beside him was a pile of newspapers.

"Ah, the notification of Lord Gelston's death?" I said, reminding myself of Holmes's suggestion the previous day. I picked up the copy of *The Times*, "Does it appear?"

"Yes – page 5. Let us now see if it provokes any reaction."

"Good heavens!" I cried, after reading the short announcement and turning back to the headline on the front page, "what a dreadful tragedy! This is what delayed me yesterday."

I read with horror about the railway accident that I assumed had been an inconvenient incident; I now discovered that it was in fact, an awful collision that had resulted in over thirty fatalities and dozens of injuries. A troop train, carrying soldiers to their training camp at Shoeburyness, collided with a passenger locomotive between Bedford and Stevenage because of a signal failure.

I had to tear myself away from the report when Inspector Eastman arrived at nine o'clock sharp and we made to retrace our drive to the Castle Fleet Estate. As our journey took us through the beautiful hinterlands of the New Forest, Holmes sat with his eyes closed, no doubt preparing himself for what obstacles the day would offer. With little else to do, the rest of us looked idly out of the window admiring the tranquil sights and sounds of this beautiful idyll.

"Look at that wonderful herd of deer," said Hopkins, pointing.

"It's actually a *rangale*, Inspector, if you don't mind me correcting you," said the local man. "A rangale of deer. Wildlife is my passion when I'm not working you see."

"I stand corrected. You certainly have plenty of opportunities in this part of the world to practice that passion."

"Indeed. *Parliaments* of owls, *strings* of ponies, *ostentations* of peacocks, *t-*"

"And what is the collective noun for crows, Inspector?" interrupted Holmes.

"Oh..err...a murder, I believe."

"Quite; Well, let us hope that is the last time we hear that word during our trip."

"Yes," agreed Eastman, a little chagrined.

Upon our arrival, we were greeted again by Parton who informed us that Doctor Goring-Boyd had completed his *postmortem* examination of Lord Gelston and had delivered his report. "With Lady Gelston's permission, I have left it for you to read in the library. If you would like to follow me, gentlemen."

He further informed us that once we were ready, the staff could be spoken to in the kitchen.

Once in the library, Holmes took the report and snorted, "*Hieroglyphics!* Watson, perhaps you could assist," – he handed me the report – "why doctors cannot write like normal human beings is beyond me!"

I took the report and read the pathologist's findings aloud:

"*Examination of the auditory nerves found them to be shrivelled and lacking nerve impulses. Arteries dilated, liver shrunk to half its proper size and of a greenish-blue leathery consistency; surrounding vessels much narrowed and bloodless. The stomach and bowels greatly distended with air and both kidneys contain a thick brown fluid. Probable cause of death: alcohol induced cardiac exhaustion leading to catastrophic organ failure.*"

Holmes and the two policemen sat in silence for a few moments, taking in the contents of the report. Parton broke the quietness: "Would you like to see the staff now gentlemen?"

"Yes, thank you," replied Holmes, "perhaps we could start with yourself?"

I had the impression that the butler hoped to avoid an interrogation but – probably knowing it was inevitable – he acquiesced and sat down.

"How long have you worked for Lord and Lady Gelston?"

"For almost three years now, sir."

"That doesn't seem very long for a man of your experience."

"Lord Gelston made an extremely attractive offer that tempted me from my last position, sir. I hope that doesn't reflect poorly on me?"

"Not in the least, Parton. I would never criticise anyone for trying to better themselves. And are you happy here?" Holmes's question was an interesting one as Parton seemed to wear a permanent mask of ambiguity.

The butler expressed his surprise, "Happy sir? I'm neither happy nor unhappy, I suppose. I just perform my tasks to the best of my ability."

"How well do you know this man Rice, who Lord Gelston suspected of kidnapping his daughter?"

"Not terribly well, sir. I don't have much to do with the outdoor staff. From the little I have dealt with him, I must say he always struck me as a reasonable fellow."

"Do you know how long he has been employed on the estate?"

"I am aware he is the longest serving member of staff; around twenty-five years or so I would estimate."

With apparently little more to glean from the man, Holmes asked to see the rest of the staff. Parton took us into the kitchen to meet with each member individually. We entered the kitchen and were introduced to Mrs. Arnott, the cook, who was supervising a young lad to crate up dozens of jars full of honey. She broke off from her task as we entered and asked the lad to come back later.

"I'm not sure I can help you, gentlemen," she said, shaking her head, "terrible business, terrible business."

She was correct in her prediction – she could throw no light on the events at Castle Fleet over the previous few days. As with the butler's interview, Mrs. Arnott's – and each of the other members of staff – lasted only a few minutes. No one appeared to know very much and I was struck by the fact that each one of them had not been in the household's employment for very long: Mrs. Arnott, herself – less than two years; Mrs. Gallagher, the housekeeper – nine months; young Eddie, the gamekeeper's assistant, who we had seen helping Mrs. Arnott before being introduced – only six months. Similarly, the gardening staff, the groom and the stable lad all had less than five years' service between them. None spoke in any derogatory terms about William Rice and yet all appeared reticent and evasive when Holmes asked about their employer.

"What do you make of it, Mr. Holmes?" asked Hopkins as he completed his last interview.

"An interesting pattern, don't you think? Very few staff employed in such a vast edifice – and those that are, only for such a brief period of time. It would appear that the late Earl had to pay a hansom salary for *anyone* to come and work for him."

"I was thinking the same thing myself."

"And yet, this man Rice appears to be the exception," Holmes mused to himself. "I suggest we go and speak to Lady Gelston once more."

Parton again escorted us to the same drawing room as the previous day. Lady Gelston stood up as we entered.

"Gentlemen, is there any news?"

"I'm afraid not, My Lady," said Holmes, "although the last few hours have proved quite informative. This, I'm afraid, must force me to ask some difficult questions."

The lady sat back down, with an expression suggesting she was expecting such an eventuality.

"Have you seen the pathologist's report, concerning your husband's *postmortem*?"

"Yes," she said, almost in a whisper.

"And may I ask what you made of it?"

She looked at her questioner, "I can't say I was terribly surprised, Mr. Holmes."

"Lady Gelston, forgive me but I must ask – did the late Earl suffer with any mental excitement? I must ask you to be perfectly frank with me."

Lady Gelston looked out through the window at nothing in particular, "My husband neglected himself for many years. When we were first married, he was such a handsome man; gay, carefree and generous. But he gradually changed as the years went by, becoming distant, morose and possessive. I cannot claim to have enjoyed a happy marriage in the last ten years."

"There appears to have been a large number of staff coming and going over those years."

"That's an example of John's behaviour. Whereas we once had a house full of happy staff, they were all gradually whittled down to the handful you have met this morning. And even they had to be enticed with an excessive salary offer. John descended into a state where he continually suspected disloyalty and betrayal from the staff. And of course, in time, if one treats people like that, it is the very thing that one can be assured of.

"As he got older, his hearing became more defective, which in turn led to him being more irascible. He would then drink more and more until it was impossible for him to get off the descending spiral of despair he had created for himself."

What a remarkable woman, I thought to myself. I had seen a lot of such cases in my professional career and couldn't help but sympathise with those close to the person suffering.

"And what was his relationship like with his daughter?"

Lady Gelston looked at Holmes and gave a thin smile, suggesting she was impressed by his perceptive powers, "Not particularly good, if we're honest. Alexandra was not the young girl John wanted her to be. Even as a child, she was happier climbing trees, running, scraping her knees and learning practical skills. She was never a little girl who would play inside with pretty dolls. As she grew into womanhood, the two argued frequently."

Holmes returned to the question of the staff, "William Rice appears to be the one exception to the frequent coming and going of employees. He has been here for twenty-five years."

"Yes, I think his love of the estate and the wildlife we have here has kept him."

"So why then would Lord Gelston believe he had kidnapped your daughter?"

"Again, since she was a young girl, Alexandra developed a love for the wildlife and this drew her towards Rice, who appeared to enjoy teaching her about the ways of the animals and insects. The two have always been close. John thought that Rice's instincts had developed into a," – she hesitated, embarrassed at the thought – "more vulgar attitude."

"Lady Gelston, I must inform you that after inspecting your daughter's bedroom, I cannot concur with the idea of an abduction. It appears to me that she left of her own free will."

"Then they have eloped together?"

"I do not say that, but I am reluctant to accuse Rice of anything at this stage. If your daughter did leave of her own accord, have you any idea as to where she may have gone?"

"No, we don't have any family elsewhere and I know the governesses she had as a child all moved away – abroad in fact."

Listening intently to the exchange, Inspector Eastman spoke for the first time since Holmes's rebuke during our journey that morning, "It seems there is very little I can do at this stage." By this point, he must have felt like an intruder, such was his lack of activity in the investigation. It was a feeling Inspector Hopkins must also have share as he announced:

"I agree, Inspector. I think it would be best if I returned to Scotland Yard."

"Thank you for coming, gentlemen," accepted Lady Gelston, "I'm sorry if your visit has been a waste of your valuable time."

"Not at all, My Lady," replied Hopkins, "I know I am leaving you in the capable hands of Mr. Holmes and Doctor Watson here. I shall remain available if you need me to return at any point."

We all turned to leave, but Holmes had one last question. He produced the piece of paper he found in the gatehouse the previous evening and showed it to Lady Gelston.

"May I ask if you recognise this handwriting, My Lady?"

"Why yes, it is Alexandra's, where did you find it?"

"It was in the gatehouse. I believe your husband was also there last night."

"John? What would he be doing there?"

"Perhaps like me, he was looking for clues as to the whereabouts of your daughter. I doubt we will ever know."

"What do you think it means?" she asked, referring to the note.

"It must have been left for Rice by your daughter if she left alone; or left behind *by* Rice if they left together. As to the contents, we cannot say at this stage."

"I don't see there is anything further we can do, therefore. I suppose you must follow your police colleagues?"

There was almost a pleading tone to the lady's comment and yet it was as obvious to us as it was to her that the case had reached a complete impasse. We had no idea as to where the young woman may have gone; the movements and motives of the gamekeeper remained a mystery; and

285

the 7th Earl of Gelston had taken his thoughts and suspicions to the grave. Had we been back in Baker Street, this interminable period of waiting without knowing would have been almost unbearable for my friend. I have witnessed him on too many occasions biting his nails, drumming his fingers or smoking incessantly, as he waits in frustration for a significant discovery.

In an effort to avoid a repeat of such an episode, I suggested, "We might delay our departure for London on the chance that the newspaper notices might turn something up?"

"I would appreciate such a level of support if you don't mind, Doctor; Mr. Holmes."

"In that case, we shall remain a further day," agreed my friend, with a smile.

"Please avail yourself of the estate, you're more than welcome to roam around as you see fit."

"That's very kind, Lady Gelston," I said, "perhaps we could enjoy a walk around and if nothing is forthcoming this afternoon, we can return tomorrow – we have lodgings at the Black Lion Inn, in Beaulieu."

Chapter III

I articulated my thoughts to Holmes when we were outside, "What a remarkable woman."

"Yes, and yet there is a vulnerability about her. She has clearly suffered in a difficult marriage for some years and if her daughter remains lost, it will be a challenge for her to continue without the controlling hand of her husband. Even if there was an element of resentment during the latter ten years, Lady Gelston has long since learned that subservience was her best ally. She has therefore grown accustomed to a level of acquiescence that will be difficult to free herself from, as she prepares for old age alone."

I was struck by the rare feeling of concern Holmes expressed for the poor woman. We wandered aimlessly for a while contemplating the sequence of events that brought us to this point, when we came to a clearing with a stunning meadowland, beside which was built rows and rows of beehives. In the middle of the hives was the gamekeeper's assistant, Eddie, who was removing wax from some of the frames. We had seen him earlier, in the kitchen, stacking the jars of honey, now here he was at what was obviously the start of the process. He saw us and broke off from his task to come over.

"Good afternoon, Eddie," said Holmes, "I see you are kept busy."

The young man removed his hood and gloves, "Yes sir, it's a slow process now that I am on my own. If we don't get all the honey, we will run out of space for the queen to lay her eggs – the colony will swarm and we'll lose most of our bees."

I looked at the dozens of rows of hives and asked, "How many are there?"

"There are a hundred, sir. William started them many years ago, I believe. I learned all I know about them from him and then Lady Alex."

"Lady Alexandra?" I asked, "how is she involved?"

"She works closely with William on the bees, sir. She loves them almost as much as he does. Now, with both of them gone, I am trying to harvest the rest on my own."

"What exactly are you doing?" asked Holmes.

"Once you take out the frames, you remove the wax and then strain the honey into the jars. We can then sell the jars."

"Fascinating," said Holmes. He thought for a while, before asking, "how long does it take to harvest the whole colony?"

"We've been working on it for three weeks now, sir. We just do *what* we can *when* we can. I'm not sure if I'm going to be able to do it on my own."

"Do you have a list of the hives that have been tended to?" asked Holmes.

"Me and Lady Alex did whatever we could and just let William know."

Holmes burst into a hearty laugh, much to the confusion of Eddie. He produced the piece of paper from his pocket, I recognised as being the note he had taken from the gamekeeper's lodge. "Could this be a note from Lady Alex to William regarding the hives she had attended to?"

Eddie took the note from Holmes and read it. "I'll go and have a look, sir," he said putting back on his hood and gloves, "each of the hives tended to have been marked."

He left us for a moment and walked back into the bee farm. I watched as he moved between the hives, studying the ones indicated by the paper. I turned to speak to Holmes but stopped myself as I observed my friend, with his eyes closed and a smile of contentment on his face. Standing in the meadow on that sunny afternoon, I sensed a tranquillity in him that I had rarely witnessed previously. It gave me pause to also take in the moment; the rapid beating of hundreds of thousands of tiny wings was the only gentle noise that could be heard.

After a few minutes, Eddie returned to us nodding enthusiastically, "Yes, sir, they've all been done. I know I didn't do those ones listed, so Lady Alex must have harvested them."

"Well, that is one little mystery solved," said Holmes with a smile.

Our conversation was disturbed by a distant voice shouting.

"Mr. Holmes! Mr. Holmes, sir?"

We turned to see one of the young gardeners we had met that morning.

"Mr. Holmes, sir," he called as he ran up to us, "Mr. Parton asked me to pass a message on from Lady Gelston, sir. She has just received a telegram from Lady Alexandra, sir." He handed the missive to Holmes.

"*'Just learned about* pa-*Pah,'*" he read, "*'We shall return tomorrow.'* Interesting, our little gamble appears to have paid off."

"And the '*We*' is also interesting," I commented.

"Indeed. Perhaps we will see the rest of the mystery solved after all."

We spent another night at the Black Lion before returning to Castle Fleet Manor for a third morning in succession. Lady Gelston was clearly on edge as she waited impatiently for the arrival of her daughter and the gamekeeper. There was no intimation from her that she intended to punish her daughter in any way; instead, I had the impression that she would be relieved to have her back, especially considering her husband's passing. Had the late

Earl still been alive upon Lady Alexandra's return, I had a feeling the atmosphere would have been far different.

It was shortly before twelve when Parton entered the drawing room and announced the arrival of Lady Gelston's daughter. Moments later, the young woman entered and the two women rushed into each other's arms.

"Oh, ma-*Mah*, I'm so sorry to have left you. I've couldn't believe it when I read about pa-*Pah*. I would never have left if I had known this was to happen."

"Don't distress yourself, Alexandra. You're home now and that is all that matters. It is no one's fault that your pa-*Pah* died – it is certainly not yours. What it *is*, is an opportunity for us to start afresh."

The two affectionately embraced again.

It was only then that I turned to look at the man who had accompanied Lady Alexandra. Much to my surprise he looked nothing like the forty-year-old gamekeeper I had expected. This man was well-dressed, clean shaven and appeared to be no more than twenty-five. He was looking down as I observed him, clearly as embarrassed as we were at our intrusive presence during this mother and daughter reunion.

Finally, Lady Gelston released herself from her daughter's embrace, "Alexandra, let me introduce you to Mr. Sherlock Holmes and his friend Dr. John Watson who have been helping me through these difficult few da-." She interrupted herself as she turned to see the other man present in her drawing room, for the first time.

"Ma-*Mah*, this is George Curran," – she went across and linked the young man's arm – "I'm sorry but I didn't know how to tell you and pa-*Pah*. As you probably know by now, George is the nephew of William."

Lady Gelston was clearly shocked, "But...how? How did you meet? How could I have known? Where have you been?"

Lady Alexandra seemed equally as surprised by her mother's lack of knowledge regarding the situation. "But didn't William tell you?"

"William Rice? The gamekeeper?"

"Yes of course. He followed me to Sheffield where I went to see George."

"Sheffield?" Lady Gelston closed her eyes and shook her head in confusion, "I don't understand any of this!"

"I asked William to explain."

"I haven't spoken with William," replied her mother irritably, "we thought he was with you!"

"He hasn't returned?" said Lady Alexandra, "So you don't know anything of this?" As her mother slumped to the sofa, she sunk to her knees and took her hand, "Oh, ma-*Mah*, I am so sorry! The worry I have put you through."

There were a few moments of confused silence before George Curren spoke:

"I'm so sorry for putting you through such worry Lady Gelston. It was never our intention to hurt you in any way. And now we are meeting in these unfortunate circumstances. I can't apologise enough."

Lady Alexandra then explained what brought them to this point: "I first met George last year when he came to visit William," – she looked at him affectionately – "he is as sweet and as kind as his uncle. We became friends instantly as he shares our love of nature and wildlife. We grew close and George returned on three occasions."

"As much to see Lady Alex, as to see my uncle, if I am honest," he added returning the young gaze.

"Why didn't you say anything to us?" asked Lady Gelston.

"What would pa-*Pah*'s reaction have been?" There was contempt in the young woman's tone. "He wouldn't let me do anything. The thought of becoming close to the gamekeeper's nephew – however true and honest he is –

would have been abhorrent to him. *'You would be marrying beneath you; you can't leave the estate; there are plenty of young men of our standing at my club.'"*

Lady Alexandra broke off from mimicking her father when she realised the inappropriateness of it in the current circumstances.

"I'm sorry ma-*Mah*, but you know what he was like. We had another row on Saturday night after you had retired."

"He never said anything."

"No, well, there were so many weren't there? It was as though he would pick a fight over the smallest thing. For no reason he started to admonish me over the type of jewellery I was wearing – told me I was flaunting myself unnecessarily. It was intolerable. I couldn't stand it anymore and decided to leave there and then.

"I had spoken to William about it," – she turned to Holmes and me to explain – "he is like an older brother to me. I can say anything to him. He had warned me about the trouble it would cause but I couldn't help myself, I was so angry.

"It was the early hours of the morning when I took a trap from the stable and made my way into Beaulieu. I was lucky enough to run into two farmers – one of whom had a cart of his own – who were coming out of an Inn, following their success in persuading the landlord to let them stay. Although they were a little worse for wear, I asked if they would return the trap to the stable for a small fee. The arrangement was mutually beneficial: they were appreciative of the chance to replace some of the money they had spent, and I was happy that my father wouldn't immediately be alerted to my leaving, if it were found that the trap was missing. I then persuaded the driver of the early-morning milk train to let me take the return journey with him to Southampton. From there I made my way up to London and then on to Sheffield to be with George.

"Little did I know that William would soon be following me. He had overheard George and I speaking during his last visit and realised how unhappy I was. I had told George that I would like to be with him all the time and William took me to one side later and cautioned me from doing anything I would regret – I think he knows how impetuous I am.

"He followed me to Sheffield and told me he had heard the trap leaving the estate and then returning an hour later. He then stopped the men who had returned it and as they left asked them what they were doing. When they told him about the young woman who had asked them to carry out their task, William knew immediately what had happened. He rushed through to Beaulieu but apparently missed the milk train by half an hour. As he had to wait until later that morning to catch a train, I had a head start. I had only joined up with George when William arrived later that night.

"Like everyone else, William has a difficult relationship with my father but unlike most of us, he can restrain himself and keep his emotions in check. He said that he would return to Castle Fleet and try and speak with pa-*Pah* on my behalf, although much good that would have done," – this last comment was spoken as much to herself as anyone in the room.

"When did William leave you?" asked Holmes.

It was then that Lady Alexandra remembered her mother telling her that the gamekeeper had not returned. "Oh…erm…yes…it would be Monday evening I suppose. I can't understand why he would not be back by n-."

She suddenly stopped as a horrible realisation dawned on her. Disbelief filled the room as she was clearly not the only one who had the same thought.

"The accident!" she cried, "Oh, please, surely not!"

The look of shock on the young woman's face mirrored that of both her mother and the gamekeeper's nephew. Holmes spoke in an effort to assuage them:

"Perhaps Watson and I could make some further enquiries on your behalf and we can report our findings if we discover anything."

By way of an epilogue to this strange case, it occurs to me that not only was no crime ever committed, but we were destined never to meet the man at the centre of our interest. For it is with a heavy heart, I must record that following our departure from Castle Fleet Manor, we discovered that tragically, William Rice was indeed one of the fatalities in the horrific train crash that had occurred some days earlier. When we reported our findings – as can be imagined – the news of the popular gamekeeper's death cast a heavy dark cloud of shock and despair over the whole estate. I learned that Eddie, William's assistant, broke down when he learned of the loss of his mentor and friend, while Lady Alexandra and George Curran blamed themselves for their rashness of youth, which prompted the honourable fellow to make his fateful journey in the first place.

In deciding to publish this case, I recently made some discrete enquiries as to how the main players in the matter turned out. Lady Gelston remained a widow and continues to enjoy the loyalty of her long-serving staff. Lady Alexandra and George Curran married and remained on the estate – they had a son they named William, while Eddie was made head game keeper.

As for Sherlock Holmes, I never did ask him how much this investigation had an influence on him and his decision to retire and keep his own bees on the South Downs. I must remember to broach the subject the next time I travel down to visit my friend.

The Rouen Scandal

Chapter I

In the years following the publication of my first account of an adventure involving Sherlock Holmes, his notoriety quickly grew, not only nationally but internationally. This was often to *his* annoyance and – I must confess – to my own embarrassment. Whenever I am now introduced to someone new by a friend or acquaintance, I am invariably asked to choose just one case among the thousands my friend has undertaken during his career. I always find it an impossible choice to make. Over the years I have often struggled to choose which cases to put forward for publication and which to leave out. After all, Holmes has been involved in uncovering almost every crime imaginable; there have been some investigations where our own lives have been put at risk, and even some others that have baffled those peculiar analytical qualities unique to my friend.

Although I usually bluster my way through some response before changing the subject, whenever I *am* asked the question, it invariably leads me to reflect on our friendship and some of the incredible things I have witnessed through my association with that remarkable man. If it was a case of the ridiculous, then surely the matter of the hapless Cumberland cartographers would be near the top of the list; if there was a light-hearted tale to be told, then the amusing denouement involving Mrs. May's egg-timer must surely merit mention. But if I were asked to concentrate my thoughts on the cruelty of mankind, then it would unquestionably be characters such as Baron Gruner or Jonas Oldacre who would no doubt be at the forefront.

That all notwithstanding, there does remain another case that I still find the most sickening of all whenever I recall it. For it was not only the slandering of an innocent woman that I found repellent, but the fact that members of my own profession could enter such an evil conspiracy was astonishing, as was the scale on which such despicable actions were perpetrated.

The case began as a seemingly trivial matter that gradually developed into something beyond imagining. I had left Holmes earlier on the morning in question and went out for a walk. Upon my return, I heard voices as I climbed the familiar stairs to our sitting room – clearly Holmes had a client. Upon knocking and entering I found my friend in his usual chair by the fire talking to a man opposite.

"Ah Watson, the very man!" cried my friend, "do come in as you may be of invaluable assistance. I don't believe you have met Inspector Merivale of the Yard before?"

Holmes's guest stood and offered a hand, "Good morning, Doctor, Mr. Holmes has told me a lot about you."

"Pleased to meet you, Inspector, Holmes has also mentioned your name in the past."

"Merivale has been telling me about an unusual little problem in Camberwell. I think it may be worthy of our interest."

Merivale responded to Holmes's gesture, indicating that he should repeat his story for my benefit.

"We had...not so much a complaint...more of an observation passed our way yesterday from a Mrs. Baxter of Grove Lane. She reported that she had seen her neighbour recently with a baby."

"What's so unusual about that – hardly a crime I would have thought?" I commented with a smile.

"Well, no, not really, but the thing is, Mrs. Baxter said there was no sign of this neighbour ever being pregnant. She is around thirty years of age, unmarried and lives alone; doesn't seem to have any gentleman callers, yet suddenly, she is seen walking out with an infant in a pram."

"It sounds more like a busybody neighbour to me. The woman could be looking after the child – a nephew or a niece perhaps?"

"That is what I thought initially, when it was brought to my attention by my desk sergeant, Hendricks. What prompted him to do so is that he remembered two other similar reports over the past twelve months. He didn't think any differently from you at first, Doctor, but each case followed the same pattern – young, unmarried woman suddenly being seen with a baby. In each case, the person reporting the matter has commented on how reluctant the 'mother' was to speak to them about the new-born when asked. Working on the principle that once is happenstance, twice is coincidence and third is suspicious, Hendricks brought it to my attention. As we are a little short-handed at the moment – what with Gregson on holiday and Jones laid up with a nasty bout of influenza – I wondered if Mr. Holmes would be interested in looking into the matter."

"Not within our usual purview eh, Watson?" interjected Holmes, "but anything to break the stagnation and monotony of the last few weeks."

He took the details of the three separate accounts from Merivale and informed him he would report any significant findings within a week.

"Probably nothing, gentlemen," said the policeman, as he made to leave, "but we appreciate your help as always."

The three reports Merivale referred to were at locations in Battersea and Brixton, as well as the case in Camberwell.

"Where should we start?" I asked.

"We shall start," announced Holmes, "with a note. *Billy!*" he cried.

Within seconds, the page came scampering up the stairs. "Yes, sir?"

Holmes was scribbling a message as Billy entered. "I want you to deliver this note to a Miss Sally Potts of 3 Mortimer Street, Lambeth."

"Right away, sir," said the lad darting away on his latest mission.

"Who is Miss Sally Potts?" I asked.

"Another vital member of my underworld network. It would be inaccurate to say we are embarking on women's work, but the assistance of the fairer sex in such delicate matters won't go amiss."

Three hours later, a young woman was announced by our landlady, "A Miss Sally Potts to see you Mr. Holmes."

"Thank you, Mrs. Hudson," replied Holmes, rising from his chair.

In the doorway stood a woman of about thirty: she wore her auburn hair under a blue bonnet; attractive but with a bearing that suggested that she was familiar with the hardship of the working classes.

"Good afternoon, Sally," said Holmes, welcoming our guest. "This is my friend and colleague, Dr. Watson, before whom we can speak freely."

"I came as quick as I could after I got your message Mr. Holmes. What can I do for you?"

Holmes informed our guest of the meeting which we had had that morning with Inspector Merivale. He gave her the three addresses passed to him by the Scotland Yard man.

"I would like you to find out what you can about these women and their babies," he concluded.

"Certainly, Mr. Holmes, give me a few days and I'll let you know." With that, she left.

"How on earth did you know that young woman?" I asked.

"Sally and her mother both worked in the service of a Duchess in Chelsea. They were both wrongly accused of stealing from their employer some years ago," said Holmes, as he worked on re-lighting his pipe with a glowing cinder, which he held between the tongs. "It was before your time I think Watson, but Sally was so grateful, she said she would be willing to help with my work if ever there was a need for a woman's touch. On occasion since then – when the use of the irregulars or my rather heavy-handed informants have been inappropriate – she has demonstrated herself to be extremely useful. I'm sure she will prove to be the perfect ally in this case."

"You never cease to amaze me," I said, shaking my head as I picked up my newspaper once more.

Unsurprisingly, Holmes's confidence in the abilities of Miss Potts proved to be well founded. She returned to Baker Street three days later with a summary of her findings.

"I've heard of middle-class women before, who are unable to have children seeking out people who can help them. From what you told me Mr. Holmes, it sounded to me as though this was the case here, and so it proved to be. I spoke to all three of them – gaining their trust and making as if I was wanting a baby myself. Rather than shoe me away and risk me going to the police, each of them took me in and told me their stories. And in each case, the same name came up. They referred to an Agnes Jakes and gave me an address in Kensington. She was the one who supplied the kiddies to these women, although they don't know where she got them from. As they were so desperate for a child, they didn't ask – they just paid her the money and took their new baby. I thought you would want to follow her up, Mr. Holmes so I took the liberty of going round there myself with the same story."

Holmes smiled at Miss Potts' initiative, but offered a mild rebuke, "I don't want to put you in any danger, Sally. In future, make sure you check with me first before taking on any extra task."

"Yes, sir," said the young woman with a slightly embarrassed smile. "Anyway, as soon as I told this Mrs. Jakes what my business was, she hurried me into her house and took me into a room at the back. I told her that I couldn't have children and I had been given her details by a friend. She accepted what I said and told me she could arrange something for me. It would take a month to organise and would cost £100."

Holmes whistled. "What did this woman look like?"

"She would be a bit older than me – in her forties? Attractive woman, black hair, green eyes. Spoke in a funny way – I couldn't quite put my finger on it but it sounded strange."

"Strange? What, like an accent?"

"Yes, it could be but it was difficult to say. If she was foreign, she was a very good speaker of English."

"Anything else?"

"I noticed there was a cross with Jesus on the wall."

"A crucifix?"

"Yes, that's the word I was looking for – a crucifix."

"Thank you, Sally, that's excellent work." Holmes handed the woman an envelope."

"Oh, thank you, sir, you needn't have bothered with this after all you did for us."

"Please pass my regards on to your mother," said my friend, drawing the meeting to a close. And then, once Miss Potts had left, "I have a strange feeling this case might be much bigger than it first appears, Watson."

"Are we now to visit this Agnes Jakes?" I asked.

"No, not yet." He opened the door to our sitting room once more – *Billy!*"

After he had sent the page to the telegraph office again, he explained that he was contacting the British Embassies in Madrid, Paris and Rome.

"Why?" I asked.

"Sally's observations may prove significant in this matter. She referred to the woman possibly having a foreign accent and referenced a crucifix. If this is true, then the likelihood is that the woman hails from a country heavily steeped in the Roman Catholic faith."

"Surely someone with any type of faith could not be involved in something as cruel as this?"

Holmes looked at me kindly, "The complexities and hypocrisies of humanity know no bounds, my friend. Some can go to any lengths to justify their actions to themselves and sadly, even the most pious are seldom exempt from cruelty and wrongdoing," – he paused before adding – "as the three most likely countries to follow that faith are Spain, France and Italy, I contacted the Embassies there to enquire with the respective police headquarters as to whether there is any record of such a woman involved in child abduction."

Much to his frustration, there were no replies to the telegrams for three days. Then all at once, they arrived together. It was Mrs. Hudson who brought them up and Holmes practically, snatched them from her tray in his haste. Our landlady – well used as she was to such unintentional rudeness – rolled her eyes and left him to it.

He ripped open the telegrams and snorted his contempt at the first two, tossing them behind him into the fire without a second glance. The third however, obviously gave him the answer he was looking for:

"*Ha!* Into our coats, Watson!" he cried, as he hastened to his room to change from his dressing gown.

I reached for my hat and coat and met him on the landing as he made to hurry downstairs. We almost bundled over

301

Mrs. Hudson who had only just reached the hallway from visiting our sitting room.

"*Billy!*" shouted Holmes once more, almost frightening the life out of the poor woman in the process. As ever, the lad appeared momentarily. "Go to Scotland Yard immediately and ask for Inspector Merivale. Tell him to meet me at this address urgently – he'll know what it is about." He scribbled down the address in Kensington.

"What if he's busy?" asked Billy, not unreasonably.

Holmes looked startled at the lad's question, "Tell him to come anyway!"

"Right away, sir," said the page with a salute.

We followed Billy outside and while he dashed off down Baker Street, we hailed a hansom. Once inside, I asked Holmes to explain the contents of the telegram.

"I asked if there were any unsolved cases involving child abduction or smuggling. The responses from Madrid and Rome were negative, but the third message from Paris informed me that there is a continuing investigation into a suspicious number of infant deaths in a clinic in the northern city of Rouen. While one of the suspects has been arrested for murder, the other one absconded three years ago. Her name is Agnès Jacques."

"Agnes Jacks!" I exclaimed in wonderment.

"Quite possibly. That is what we are going to find out."

Under Holmes's instruction, our cab pulled up a little further along the road from the address given to us by Sally Potts. Significantly, there was another hansom waiting outside number 32, the address in question.

"We'll walk the rest of the way," said Holmes descending onto the pavement. I paid our fare and hurried after him. "It seems we are just in time," he said over his shoulder as we climbed the steps to the front door that was ajar. He rang the bell.

"Yes, I'm coming!" shouted a woman's voice from inside.

The door swung open and the woman visibly stepped back in surprise at the sight of two strangers.

"Bonjour, Madame Jacques. Je m'appelle Sherlock Holmes et voici mon ami le docteur Watson."

Before the woman could respond to Holmes's flawless French, my friend had eased passed her into the entrance hall. I followed and observed two suitcases, waiting to be collected.

"What is the meaning of this?" cried the woman, trying to regain some composure.

"Ah, English it is, then," said Holmes casually, "I see you appear to be planning a little trip?"

"Who are you? What are you doing here? Do you have a warrant to enter my home?"

"We do not, but officials from Scotland Yard do and they will be here shortly."

The words appeared to deflate the woman, who gave the appearance of someone facing defeat. Holmes continued:

"You are Agnès Jacques, wanted in your home country for infanticide."

"That accusation is outrageous!" cried the suspect, "I have never murdered a child in my life."

"In that case, you are either party to such atrocities, or you are guilty of another crime – kidnapping or smuggling perhaps?"

Significantly, the woman never responded. Just then, the police wagon drew up outside and Inspector Merivale and two constables appeared at the door.

"I got your message, Mr. Holmes," said Merivale, "what's all this about then?"

"I think you need to take this woman away, Inspector and inform the Sûreté of her arrest. I wouldn't be surprised if one of your colleagues from across the Channel may wish to come and help you with your questioning. If my suspicions are correct, then this woman's crimes run far

303

deeper than her involvement in providing two babies to wealthy middle-class childless mothers in London."

"Very good, Mr. Holmes. Thank you as always for your help."

"If you need any further assistance Merivale, don't hesitate to ask. Oh, and by the way, I would draw your attention to the telegram she has carelessly left on the little bureau in the hall. This, coupled with her apparent imminent departure, suggests she had been alerted to your interest."

Merivale picked up the telegram, "It's in French!"

"Yes, it has been sent from Rouen, in Northern France, and is alerting Madame Jacques here to the exposure of their operation."

Jacques kept her head down as Holmes concluded his theory. The two constables led the woman away and we took advantage of the cab outside to return to our lodgings.

Chapter II

It wasn't long before Merivale had availed himself of Holmes's offer of further assistance. Within twenty-four hours, my friend received a note from the Scotland Yard man inviting him to attend the matter. Inspector Francois Le Villard from the Sûreté was travelling from Paris and had asked that Holmes continue his involvement in the case.

"Le Villard!" Holmes announced, "this must be a bigger case than first imagined. Since my last encounter with him, I had heard that the authorities were now using him all around the country. Now abroad!"

I had never met the French detective myself but had heard Holmes speak favourably about him in the past. I agreed with my friend that it must be a serious issue if the French authorities were sending over one of their best men to oversee the matter. It was with a sense of eagerness and anticipation that I accompanied Holmes the following morning to meet Le Villard and find out more about this mysterious Madame Jacques.

The Frenchman greeted my friend warmly, as is their custom, much to Holmes's discomfort and the amusement of Merivale and myself. Holmes introduced me and I thrust out a firm hand in greeting for the man I had looked forward to meeting for some time.

"Bonjour, Doctor, I am pleased to meet you."

He spoke only broken English but as Holmes was fluent in French, communication was of little problem. Le Villard explained that Agnès Jacques had fled the country three years earlier, upon the death of her brother Claude Carere. The two had been running refuges across Normandy for impoverished women and unmarried mothers, telling them they could find homes for their babies with wealthy couples in exchange for money. Far from being philanthropic, the establishments they were running became known as 'baby farms,' where any monies received found their way into the coffers of Carere and his sister. When the atrocity was uncovered, Carere had a sudden heart attack and died, while his sister fled.

"We finally now know where to," concluded Le Villard.

"So, it seems that this woman has commenced the same despicable practice here in London?" I asked.

"Not so, Doctor," Le Villard replied before his English failed him. Holmes translated: "It would appear that at least one of these refuges still exist as we now believe the babies that have appeared in London, originate from France."

"How do you know this?" asked Merivale.

"We had information passed to us from an anonymous source claiming that there is a clinic in Rouen that has seen several suspicious baby deaths. I have men there as we speak."

I noted the reference to Rouen, the city from whence the telegram received by Madame Jacques was sent.

"If the brother is dead," said the Scotland Yard man, "then who do you suspect of coordinating the wicked scheme."

"Based on the information we have, we suspect his widow, Madame Marguerite Montpensier. If the infrastructure of the villainous practice were in place during her husband's lifetime – and she was party to it – it would not be impossible to continue it in his absence."

The three of us looked at the Frenchman for further explanation.

"Madame Montpensier married Carere six years ago. When he died, the Republic seized most of his assets, therefore his widow inherited very little of his estate. She potentially therefore has the knowledge and the motive. She re-married two years ago and our information is that she has been running an even more sinister operation since – an operation that has seen babies being kidnapped from the clinic of St Marie in Rouen. Certificates of death would be forged and the infants would then be whisked abroad to be sold for money."

I was dumbfounded by the narrative. How anyone could be so cruel was quite beyond me.

It was Holmes that broke the silence, "I assume Madame Montpensier has been arrested – the note I received said someone had been arrested on a charge of murder?"

"Yes, but not for the murder of the children," replied Le Villard, "those individual cases are still being investigated. It is on the suspicion of murdering her stepdaughter Mademoiselle Lucille Carere."

"Her stepdaughter!" I repeated, involuntarily.

"What has she got to do with it?" asked Merivale.

"That is what we are trying to establish, Inspector. We have yet to find the body."

"Then how do you know she has been murdered?" asked Holmes.

"When we were alerted to the suspected practice, a separate source came forward and suggested that the stepdaughter had found out about Madame Montpensier's wrongdoing and was about to go to the police. As there appears to be some substance to the Rouen clinic, we have taken the woman in for questioning about both matters."

"And this second source was also anonymous, I assume?" Holmes's question garnered a nod from the policeman, "And what was her response to the charges?"

"She naturally denies all knowledge of both the child kidnappings and the disappearance of her stepdaughter. I didn't have an opportunity to fully question her myself when I got the call from London about Jacques."

"Yes, this woman is interesting," said Holmes, turning to Merivale, "what is her response since her arrest?"

"She has been evasive and non-cooperative. It'll be interesting to see her reaction when our French friend here walks in. Would you like to accompany us, Mr. Holmes?"

"No, I will follow my own line of investigation, gentlemen. But before I do, Merivale, could I trouble your man Hendricks once more for the actual dates of the suspicious child sightings you told us about."

"Certainly." The inspector returned a few minutes later and handed Holmes a piece of paper.

"Thank you. Perhaps we could all meet later tonight in Baker Street to share our findings?"

"Yes, certainly," agreed Merivale, a little confused.

"Excellent, we shall see you both at seven."

"Where are we going?" I asked as we left the two policemen to their questioning.

"To the offices of the Southwestern Railway Company on Pall Mall."

"Are we to book tickets for the continent?"

"Not yet Watson, but I think a trip to France may prove to be of interest in this case. For the moment however, we are interested in trying to identify the confederates of Madame Jacques. I believe this case involves more individuals than the one we encountered in Kensington.

"You will recall that we intercepted her during the act of her departure? The telegram on her bureau confirmed that she had been alerted to the authorities' pursuit of her. It was probably sent by the person – or more likely – persons who transported the infants from France."

"You think there will be more than one?"

"A woman on her own travelling with a child would be a slightly unusual sight and would attract a little attention; for a man to travel alone with an infant and remain inconspicuous would be impossible; but no one would ever suspect any wrongdoing involving a young couple travelling with their new baby. As we now have at least three dates when young children appeared in their new homes – and working on the hypothesis that Madame Jacques was recently expecting another visit – it will be interesting to examine the passenger lists of the Channel crossings run by the company, to see if we can identify any repeat travellers who were making the journey at the corresponding times."

As Holmes concluded his line of reasoning, our cabbie pulled up at our destination. We entered the offices of the Southwestern Railway Company and approached the official on the front desk. He had all the appearance of a railway devotee and therefore someone who loved working for one of the top companies in that industry. His bald dome protruded above a visor that shielded his eyes, while his slightly faded black waistcoat and matching oversleeves gave some indication of his length of service in the role. Sadly, his manner did not match his appearance of enthusiastic professionalism. His expression was one of being inconvenienced as we approached.

Naturally, Holmes was not put off by his demeanour, "Good morning, we would like to inspect the passenger lists for the Channel crossings from the Normandy ports over the past two years."

The man reluctantly removed the pince-nez that teetered on the end of his nose, "For what purpose? Such records are not easily obtained."

"My name is Sherlock Holmes and I am assisting Scotland Yard and the French Sûreté in a matter of extreme importance."

The demeanour of the man changed instantly. He clearly recognised Holmes's name and this, combined with the mention of Scotland Yard, made him leap from his seat.

"Certainly Mr. Holmes, I'll get those records for you right away!" He hurried off and returned within five minutes.

"Here you are Mr. Holmes. We have records here from the crossings from Caen, Cherbourg and Dieppe dating back the last two years. You can study them over here at this desk if you like. Just let me know if you require any other records – they are all readily available."

I smiled to myself as the man couldn't now be more helpful. Holmes paid little attention to the change in his conduct, concentrating instead on the ledgers with which he had been provided. He gave one to me and – armed as we were with the relevant dates – we sat down to study the list of names that travelled to and from the Continent around the times in question.

We had been examining the lists for about an hour when Holmes asked, "What have you found, Watson?"

"I think I have something," I replied with some enthusiasm. "On or around the dates in question, there is a Mr. and Mrs. Fox 'with child' – as it states – arriving at the various British ports from Normandy."

"Each journey being a one-way ticket." It was more of a statement than a question.

"Yes, now you mention it they are."

Holmes gave me one of the ledgers he had been studying, "Now examine the departures listed for the days following our dates and tell me if there is another pattern."

I followed Holmes's instruction and after about ten minutes announced, "Yes, there do appear to be regular entries for a French couple making repeated journeys in the opposite direction. A Monsieur and Madame-"

"Renard," interrupted Holmes.

"Yes," I said, looking up, "how did you know?"

"Because I had observed the exact same entries. Again, taking one-way journeys."

"Yes."

"And with no indication of a child?"

"No."

"I think we have our confederates, Watson."

"How can you be so sure?"

"Because, my dear fellow, the French for fox is *renard*. Let us do a little more digging of our own and see what addresses are associated with these two couples."

The official who had provided us with the ledgers earlier was only too pleased to help further and hurried off following Holmes's request. Upon his return some minutes later, Holmes immediately scoured the pages, placing markers in each one of interest. Finally, he announced his discoveries:

"As I suspected, the address attributed to 'Mr. and Mrs. Fox' is the same as Agnès Jacques in Kensington, while the address of 'Monsieur and Madame Renard' is a house in Rouen. These people are the next link in this chain of misery, Watson."

"That's remarkable Holmes, I must congratulate you."

"It is true we have advanced, but there is still a long way to go. We will meet with our Anglo-French friends tonight and decide on the next steps."

When the two police inspectors did meet with us in Baker Street at the appointed hour, they were both equally fulsome in their praise of my friend's remarkable deductive powers.

"C'est magnifique!" cried La Villard.

"Even I understood that," said Merivale, "and I couldn't agree more."

"Let's not get ahead of ourselves, gentlemen," said Holmes, characteristically dismissing the praise, "there is still much work to be done. We may have a plausible hypothesis regarding the process for moving the infants across the Channel, but we are no nearer to establishing the actual identity of those involved. What is more, it is highly unlikely that these people are the only ones involved in such heinous activity."

"I am aware of that," said the French detective in his broken English, "We must try to identify these people."

"And for us to do that," replied Holmes, "we must go to France!"

"That's a little beyond my jurisdiction, Mr. Holmes," said the Scotland Yard man, I'm afraid I'll have to leave you to it."

Holmes addressed the French detective, "You will no doubt be taking Madame Jacques back to France with you?"

"Yes."

"Then we shall come with you," – he turned to me almost as an afterthought – "if you are receptive to such a suggestion, Watson?"

"Why yes, of course," I said, excited by the prospect of a trip to the Continent, even if it was in such distasteful circumstances.

As it was one less matter for Merivale to trouble himself with, I had the impression that he was content enough to see a satisfactory conclusion to the London end of the nefarious operation. "Bon voyage, then!" he said in the worst French accent imaginable as he rose to leave.

We agreed to meet Le Villard at Scotland Yard the following day where we would accompany him and his prisoner to Newhaven, before crossing to Dieppe and then on to Rouen.

Chapter III

The Channel crossing was bleak and uncomfortable. We sat in a communal area with the other passengers while the wind howled and screamed outside. The visibility was virtually non-existent as oversized raindrops assaulted the windows of the boat, like a fusillade of bullets. The vessel bucked and swayed violently in the conditions, much to the distress of some of the passengers, but throughout Madame Jacques remained silent, refusing offers of food and staring directly ahead.

Although the subsequent two-hour rail journey to Rouen could hardly be described as comfortable, I was thankful to be on dry land again, knowing that we were on the final leg of our journey.

The Rouen police headquarters was a modest, rundown building in what seemed to be a quiet backwater town. From the villains' point of view, it was an ideal location from which to run such a despicable operation. Far from Paris, Lyon and Marseilles – not to mention it's close proximity to the northern ports – its geography combined with its anonymity provided the perfect setting.

Once again, I relied on Holmes to act as translator when speaking with and being party to conversations with the local officials.

I had the impression that the Rouen officers thought that such horrible activities as those that they were investigating had ended with the demise of Carere some years earlier. Perhaps a little complacency had set in during the subsequent duration but the presence of Inspector Le Villard from the capital was certainly now renewing a sense of urgency among them.

We were shown into an office that was stark and cramped. I could only guess at the last time it had been painted. I was surprised therefore when the Parisian detective commented to Holmes how much tidier the station was and how smarter the uniformed officers were, since his last visit a few days earlier.

The sergeant on the front desk took Madame Jacques into custody and showed her to a cell at the rear of the station. Le Villard informed us that Madame Montpensier was already held in one of the other cells.

"I have arranged for us to lodge at l'Hotel de Ville. I suggest we go there now, have something to eat and get some rest. We will then question the two women in the morning."

I sensed Holmes's frustration at the suggestion but he knew that after a full day of travelling, the proposal was a logical one. For my own part, I was delighted as it had escaped my memory that I had eaten nothing meaningful since breakfast."

Suitably refreshed, after a good night's sleep, we returned to the station to interview the two women at the heart of the case. Madame Montpensier was first and although I couldn't understand her first-hand, she struck me as being quite sincere in her protestations. Holmes appraised me of what was being said.

"Madame, you know the charges against you," said Le Villard, "and you must surely be aware that these are considered capital crimes. Not only your liberty, but your life is at stake here."

"I am well aware of that, Inspector. If I knew anything of significance, I assure you I would have told you when I was first arrested."

"Let us go back to the beginning. When did you first meet Monsieur Carere, your late husband?"

"It would be about seven years ago. A mutual friend introduced us. He was a charming man – a widower – and the two of us became close from there."

Le Villard referred to his notes, "And you married the following year?"

"That's correct. We were married for two years when he was arrested and passed away."

"What did Carere tell you about his business?"

"Very little. I believed he was a philanthropist who helped people. I was astounded and ashamed of my own naïveté when I found out the truth."

"You didn't inherit his estate?"

"I did not want it, gained as it was. It was seized by the Republic and they were welcome to it. I was questioned at the time about my involvement and the Sûreté were satisfied that I had nothing to do with the matter."

"It could be viewed that you were bitter about losing an estate worth tens of thousands of Francs, so you were motivated to keep the practice on."

"That is a despicable thought, Inspector. You can think what you like but I would never consider getting involved in anything so horrible as that. I met my husband Monsieur Montpensier two years ago. We run a little boulangerie together in Bois-Guillaume. This is hardly the lifestyle of people who are making fortunes from illegal activity."

The suspect was making a compelling case regarding her innocence. Le Villard clearly had little evidence to associate her with the removal and abduction of children from the clinic in the centre of the town. He therefore moved on to the matter of Carere's daughter, Montpensier's stepdaughter.

"When was the last time you saw Lucille Carere?"

The woman laughed, "This was put to me when I was brought in earlier this week and accused of her murder. It's ridiculous! I haven't seen Lucille since her father died. We

315

were never close and I think it suited both of us to start a new life apart."

"You say you were never close – how old was she when you married her father?"

Madame Montpensier thought for a while, "She would be in her early twenties – about twenty-two, I think. I believe she had not long returned from studying at university in America. Her father used to boast that she was amongst the first female students admitted to one of their so-called Ivy League universities."

"And what did she do upon her return?"

"Not very much from what I could see. She was close to her father who seemed to find her work at the hospitals from time to time."

At this point, Le Villard broke off from his questioning and glanced at Holmes who gave the merest shake of the head, indicating there was nothing further to be gained by pursuing the questioning. Almost as imperceptibly, the French detective nodded his agreement.

"I think that will be all for now, Madame, you are free to go. I would ask that you remain at home however as we may need to speak with you further regarding both the abductions from St Marie's and the disappearance of Lucille Carere. I will arrange to have you taken home."

The detective called for assistance and a uniformed officer entered and escorted the dignified woman from the room.

"What do you make of it, Mr. Holmes?" he asked after they had left.

"There is little or no evidence to associate her with either crime. It would appear on the face of it that Madame Jacques and her confederates have steered you towards the woman to divert attention away from themselves. I assume others from St Marie's have been detained?"

"Of course. A registrar, two midwives and a Catholic priest have all been arrested in connection with the practice."

"No doctors?"

"No. There are only two resident consultants at the clinic," – Le Villard referred to his notes – "Dr. Villeneuve from Brittany, and a Dr. Róka from Hungary. Villeneuve has been on a leave of absence for two months as his wife is suffering with cancer, and Róka had to leave urgently for Budapest as his mother has apparently been taken ill."

"How long has he been away?"

"Just a matter of days apparently. I have contacted the Budapest authorities to try and locate him but I haven't heard anything from them as yet. I also have a man speaking with Villeneuve – I will receive an update from him later today."

"How is the clinic being covered in their absence?" I asked.

"Locum consultants are covering the duties, Doctor. We have checked on them all and do not suspect any complicity."

"No doubt you are now going to speak with Madame Jacques?"

"That was my intention."

"Then with your permission, we will go to the clinic of St Marie and see what we can find out."

"Certainly, Mr. Holmes. Your help is most welcome."

"Until later, then."

Holmes and I made our way to the clinic. It appeared a soulless, dirty building from the outside but perhaps my assessment was influenced by the knowledge of what had happened at this place. Upon our entering, I was surprised at the cleanliness and seemingly professional environment. What came as no surprise, however, was the gloomy atmosphere that pervaded the interior. It was as though a heavy cloud was following the staff that remained around the building, as they tried to continue their duties, no doubt full in the knowledge that their place of work – and their association with it – would be tarnished forever.

Two uniformed officers were present in the entrance area and Holmes introduced us, explaining that we were helping Inspector Le Villard with his investigation. One of the two men saluted and turned to one of the hospital staff who appeared to be performing reception duties. Clearly the policemen were there to oversee the various activities within the facility, given the recent revelations.

Again, Holmes translated for me, the officer's instruction to the staff member. He informed the man that we should be treated with the same respect as if we were police officers. Holmes thanked the officer for his assistance and asked the man behind the desk if he could see the file of Dr. Róka. Within a few minutes, the man returned and handed the buff-coloured folder over.

"Been here for almost five years," Holmes mumbled into the folder, "first position as a qualified consultant…excellent qualifications…" He suddenly looked up from the page and stared into the middle distance with the merest hint of a smile.

"Tell me," he said, addressing the man once more, "do you have a telephone in the clinic?"

"Of course, sir, please come with me."

We followed him into an office at the end of the main corridor and the receptionist indicated the telephone on the desk before leaving us to resume his duties. Holmes picked up the receiver, spoke to the operator and asked to be connected to the Hungarian Embassy. I was amazed when he put the phone down a few seconds later after asking only one question. He spoke to the person on the other end in French but I recognised him mentioning the name of the Hungarian consultant, Róka.

"Very clever," he said with a laugh.

"What was the purpose of that?"

"All in good time, my dear fellow," was his infuriating reply, "we are not quite there yet."

"Well, where to now then?" I asked, more than a little chagrined.

He ignored my question and picked up the receiver again to speak with the operator. I heard him mention Cherbourg; again, there was a delay as he waited to be connected. Once a voice was heard on the other end, Holmes launched into his native-like fluency in his effort to solve another strand of the mystery. I couldn't possibly understand everything that was being said but I distinctly heard him mention, 'Monsieur et Madame Róka.' Although I could neither understand nor even hear exactly what the man on the other end was saying, his excited jabbering was clearly audible. I took this to be an objection to Holmes's request but as soon as my friend mentioned the name of Inspector Le Villard of the Sûreté, the man stopped immediately. When Holmes replaced the receiver, he said the man would be ringing him back shortly.

"Who were you speaking to then?" I asked in response.

"In a moment, Watson," he said as he rose to leave, "perhaps you could man the telephone while I clarify something with our friend at the reception desk."

He didn't wait for me to reply and I was left sitting there, staring in terror at the telephone in case it rang. Fortunately, Holmes returned within a few minutes.

"I have asked our friend if he could arrange some refreshment for us. Perhaps you could go and collect it from him while I wait for our telephone call?"

I did as I was asked, relieved that I didn't have to answer the telephone, which – with my ignorance of the language – could only have resulted in me infuriating the man on the other end still further. I collected two cups of what could barely be described as 'tea' from the man and returned to the office in which Holmes sat impatiently, drumming his fingers on the desk.

Finally, after around fifteen minutes, the telephone rang and Holmes snatched at the receiver. There was a momentary delay as the operator connected the two parties. I knew that Holmes had had his theory confirmed as he gave a clipped smile following the information conveyed by the Cherbourg man.

"Dare I ask what is next?" I asked, as he hurriedly replaced the receiver.

"Quickly, Watson, to the telegraph office – we are at the mercy of the winds of the north Atlantic!"

"The Atlantic?" I exclaimed, as I scurried after him.

"I am hoping that Mr. Leverton, of Pinkerton's American Agency may be able to assist us."

The comment left me even more confused but knowing that I was unlikely to get any further information out of Holmes, I simply followed him out of the clinic and down the street, at the end of which was the telegraph office. He did share with me that he had asked the man on reception where the nearest office was, when he left me to guard the telephone. I waited outside as Holmes dealt with the postmaster. When he reappeared, he must have sensed my frustration at being kept in the dark:

"I'm sorry, Watson, I fear I have used you unfairly."

"It would be nice to be a little more informed," I said, rather sulkily. "It's difficult enough being in a foreign country, unable to communicate, without my closest friend adding to my frustration."

"Quite right, my dear fellow, I must apologise. If you will just show a little more patience, all will be revealed when we return to Le Villard."

Within fifteen minutes we were back in the company of the French detective, who looked as frustrated as I felt.

"My dear Le Villard," said Holmes, "how was your interview with Madame Jacques?"

"Unsuccessful!" was the young man's reply. "She continues to say nothing."

"Then perhaps I will be able to help. I have just sent a telegram to an associate in New York who may be of some assistance. I gave him the address of this police station and asked him to reply urgently. In the meantime, perhaps we can visit your prisoner again and see if I can have a little more success."

Le Villard looked up with a confused expression but acquiesced without hesitation. We followed him into the room where Madame Jacques was being held.

"I will not waste my time asking you any questions," said Holmes as we entered, "I will simply inform you and my colleagues of what I know. It will then be your own decision as to whether you co-operate or not.

"You are Agnès Jacques, sister of Claude Carere. You, your brother and your respective late spouses made your despicable living by selling babies delivered at your illegal," – Holmes searched for an appropriate word – "*establishments*. When Carere's wife died, he remarried the unfortunate and perfectly innocent Marguerite – now Montpensier – someone whom you have recently had no hesitation in falsely implicating to save your own skin. When the authorities uncovered your activities, your brother died while you fled to London.

"Madame Montpensier may not have been involved in the dreadful operation during her marriage to Carere, but what the authorities overlooked was the fact that her stepdaughter – your niece Lucille Carere – certainly was.

She studied at the Cornell University in the state of New York where she met István Róka, a medical student from Budapest. They returned to France together following their studies and your late brother employed Róka at the facility here in Rouen. Once you had established yourself in London, following your brother's death, you reignited your foul practice, this time with your niece who had access to the clinic through her husband."

"Her *husband!*" cried Le Villard.

"Yes, her husband," repeated Holmes, turning back to Madame Jacques, "István Róka. He would steal the children from the clinic, informing the mother that her child had died; he and his midwife associate would then whisk the child away to Mademoiselle Carere, the name she still used, lest she attracted attention to herself and her husband. The two would then travel together to London, under the name of Reynard where they would hand the child over to you; you, in turn, would have your desperate client waiting.

"When your wretched scheme was discovered, your niece alerted you, before promptly fleeing. You then sought to confuse and distract the police by anonymously informing them that the perfectly innocent and unaware Madame Montpensier had murdered her stepdaughter. Dr. Róka then slipped away informing everyone that he was visiting his sick mother in Hungary, when in fact he was meeting his wife at Cherbourg, from where they boarded the SS St Paul bound for New York five days ago."

During Holmes's narrative, Madame Jacques' expression gradually changed from one of stoic resistance to one of complete incredulity at what she was hearing. I did not need to understand the language to see that Holmes had struck home and uncovered the whole unbelievable truth. There was silence for quite some considerable time before Inspector Le Villard addressed his prisoner.

"What is your response to Mr. Holmes's summary?"

It occurred to me how little I had heard the woman speak in the few days I had been in her company. I was almost surprised therefore when she responded to Le Villard.

"You cannot prove any of this," was her rather weak response.

"There are simply too many unanswered questions, Madame," said Holmes. "Where were you going in such a hurry when we stopped you? What evidence is there that Madame Montpensier murdered her stepdaughter? If she did, how could a baker's wife commit such a crime and dispose of a body without being seen or somehow alerting the authorities? How is it that Dr. Róka disappeared at exactly the same time as your niece, just as St Marie's was being raided by the police? And given that he can't be traced in Hungary – not to mention the fact that a Mr. and Mrs. Róka are listed as being on board a vessel bound for New York, a place where both Róka and your niece studied together – how can you explain his whereabouts?

"No-no, it simply will not do, Madame."

"How do you know that the passengers on board the ship are the people you say?"

"On the balance of probability," was Holmes's assured reply. "Although your confederates were wicked in their actions, thankfully, they were not very imaginative in covering their movements. The couple who delivered the children to your house travelled under the name of Fox in England, and Renard in France. As you know, renard is French for fox. In Hungarian, róka is the name of the same creature. They simply translated their name as and when required, as an expedient to avoid suspicion."

Just then there was a knock at the door and a young officer entered.

"I'm sorry to disturb you, sir, but you asked for news from America."

He handed Holmes the telegram reply he had been eagerly awaiting. He passed me the note but the expression on his face already informed me of the disappointing news:

SS ST PAUL DOCKED EARLY THIS MORNING
BEFORE I RECEIVED YOUR TELEGRAM
STOP
ALL PASSENGERS DISEMBARKED BEFORE I
COULD ATTEND STOP
ROKA WHERABOUTS UNKNOWN END

LEVERTON

The prisoner understood the wordless exchange and gave a slight smirk.

"The message may be disappointing," said Holmes but your expression confirms your guilt and my theory concerning your allies."

Le Villard also addressed the prisoner, "I will speak with the Prosecutor as I believe we have enough to charge you with the crimes you are accused of. You should be aware that these are capital offences."

Madame Jacques' expression changed immediately but before she could respond, Le Villard indicated that the interview was over by rising and leaving the room. Holmes and I followed; it would be the last time that we would see the woman.

Le Villard was levering himself into his coat outside when he announced that we were to visit the Prosecutor. I was impressed with how the detective was taking charge of the situation and it was clear to me that Holmes felt the same way. It was a short distance to the Prosecutor's office which was situated immediately beside the city's courts. Le Villard announced our arrival and we were shown straight in to see Monsieur Clément, a large, impressive man, who projected an air of authority commensurate with his position. Fortunately, from my point of view, he also spoke fluent English.

"Mr. Holmes!" he cried, thrusting out a hand of greeting, upon Le Villard's introduction, "it is an honour to meet you, sir. Since your detection of that treacherous Brossard and his accomplices, your name is revered throughout France."

Holmes was politely dismissive of Clément's comments, "Thank you, monsieur, but we have a more urgent matter to deal with."

Holmes introduced me and invited Le Villard to share with the senior official what we had discovered.

Clément sat quietly for a while shaking his head. "I have been in this line of work all of my adult life and I am still amazed at the evil some people have in their hearts." He snapped out of his reverie, "What about the two in New York?"

It was Holmes who answered, "I have a good understanding with an excellent detective from the Pinkerton Agency. I will ask him to continue the search for Monsieur and Madame Róka and report his findings to Inspector Le Villard."

"Excellent, thank you Mr. Holmes, we can ask no more."

"There is one last thing," added my friend. "It occurs to me that no one defended Madame Montpensier from the accusations against her during her detainment. I might suggest that the poor woman deserves an apology."

"Quite right," agreed the Prosecutor. He turned to the policeman, "We will question the members of staff we have under arrest and charge Jacques. Perhaps you could then arrange to have Madame Montpensier brought here and I will speak to her personally."

"Certainly, sir," replied Le Villard and we all took our leave.

We later learned that, of the people arrested in connection with the scandal, one of the midwives was released without charge. It transpired that the other one was the anonymous source, who alerted the police to the wrongdoing in the first place. Apparently, she had got into a dispute with Róka over how much she was owed for her part in the deception. His refusal to pay her what she felt she was owed proved to be the starting point for the whole extraordinary chain of events. Because of her co-operation with the authorities, her capital sentence was commuted to one of hard labour and she became one of the first female prisoners to be sent to the French penal colony on Devil's Island. She was joined by the registrar who had faked the death certificates and the ex-communicated Catholic priest who aided and abetted the criminals.

It was six months following our return from France when we heard from Leverton, who succeeded in finally tracking down and arresting the stepdaughter of Madame Montpensier, along with her husband-doctor in New York. The Pinkerton man had alerted hospitals throughout the state to the rogue consultant, anticipating that sooner or later, Róka would apply for a position. His working hypothesis proved well founded when the Hungarian submitted a résumé to a maternity hospital in New York. Had he been successful with his application, his horrifying long-term intentions could only be guessed at. He and his wife were arrested and transported back across the Atlantic. I should finally record that my conscience is perfectly clear when I state that I was delighted to hear that they both followed Agnès Jacques to the guillotine.

The Sebastopol Clasp

Chapter I

It was the second Tuesday in December 1886 when Sherlock Holmes and I were enjoying a pipe while relaxing upon our two favourite couches in the drying room of the Turkish Bath on Northumberland Avenue. As Holmes had just completed his investigation into the Dial Square mystery and neither of us had any pressing engagements – not to mention the fact that my shoulder had been troubling me lately – I suggested we indulge in one of our guilty pleasures.

The heat and oils from the exotic establishment were acting as the perfect antidote to our lassitude and our relaxing morning was approaching its conclusion when I heard a familiar voice ask through the heavy atmosphere.

"Is that you, Watson?"

I opened my eyes to see an older man with a discernible limp padding across the tiled floor, "My goodness," I cried, "Woodward! what a wonderful surprise!"

"I *thought* it was my old companion," he said offering a hand.

"Holmes," I said by way of introduction, "this is Simon Woodward from Afghanistan. We were on the *Orontes* which bought us back to England," – Holmes barely creased a forehead in acknowledgement – "Woodward, this is my friend Mr. Sherlock Holmes."

"Yes, I've heard of you," said my old colleague enthusiastically.

"What are you up to these days?" I asked, a little embarrassed having lost touch with him after leaving Netley.

"Well, like you, my soldiering days are over," he replied with some melancholy. "Being a career soldier with a debilitating hip, regular work is difficult to come by. I tend to get by on the meagre pension they gave us and the odd temporary job as a clerk or a courier. When I can afford it, I come here as I find it a good alternative medicine for this wretched thing." He patted his hip.

"Yes, I can relate to that," I agreed, rubbing my shoulder with a sympathetic smile.

We chatted for a few minutes as old soldiers do, balancing the strange paradox of being pleased to see one another but sharing a reluctance to recall in any great details the dreadful experiences of the battlefield. As Woodward turned to take his leave we agreed to meet again.

"In fact," he said, "it occurs to me that I am getting together with a few old comrades from the Crimea on Christmas Eve, why don't you come along?"

"I didn't realise you were in the Crimea?" With my question, I realised that – as well as we became acquainted on the long sea journey back home – we must have spoken little of our military experiences. Clearly, we were thankful to be alive and concentrated instead on what the future held for us both.

"Only briefly," said Woodward in answer to my question, "I arrived with the last deployment troops, just in time to see the fall of Sebastopol. I was a young Subaltern with the Lancashires. We were only there less than twelve months before returning home. When we left, a few of us vowed to get together for a reunion every ten years to commemorate our first campaign together. This year will be thirty years." Woodward's head dropped as he adopted another melancholic smile. "There are only half a dozen of us left. And on top of all that, I had my campaign medal stolen last year."

"I'm sorry to hear that."

"Never mind," said my old comrade, "what do you say about the invitation – a little celebratory dinner and a chinwag with a few old duffers?"

"I shall be delighted," I said.

"Excellent!" cried Woodward with genuine enthusiasm, "I shall send over the details to your lodgings."

"What a pleasant surprise," I said, half to myself as I watched him leave.

"Do you believe in fate or providence Watson?" asked Holmes who had been lounging with his eyes closed throughout the whole exchange.

I looked across at my friend, surprised by his enigmatic question.

"I can't say I've particularly thought deeply about it. I suppose things always happen for a reason, whatever that reason might be. Our own meeting for example, when I returned from Afghanistan. Why do you ask?"

"Your simplistic explanation is as good as any I suppose," replied Holmes, languidly, "chance meetings often act as a portent for what lies ahead."

That night, we welcomed Inspector Lestrade to our rooms. He often called during the winter evenings to enjoy a whiskey and soda, and a cigar. I had come to appreciate that his visits were mutually beneficial to both the official policeman and the private consulting detective: Lestrade could pick Holmes's brains about thorny issues he and his colleagues were wrestling with, while Holmes enjoyed keeping abreast of the latest cases which had landed at the doors of Scotland Yard.

"Anything of interest lately, Lestrade?" asked Holmes as we stared into the blazing hearth.

"Not particularly," replied the policeman, "it's always the quietest time of year. I think the London criminal seems to take a break in preparation for the holidays."

"Typical!" sneered Holmes, failing to see any humour in Lestrade's comment.

"Come to think of it, it has been a strange year all round. We've been troubled by the rise of anarchism more than anything else. It appears as though the troublemakers of Europe are finding London their preferred destination these days – rioting, fire-bombing of businesses, looting of shops; anything to disturb and disrupt."

"Can you not identify the culprits?" I asked.

"It's exceedingly difficult, Doctor. The usual tactic is to throw a bottle full of kerosene through an office window in the middle of the night without any warning; by the time we move into the East End to investigate the next morning, it seems no one speaks English."

"How many deaths have these attacks caused?" asked Holmes, who had been listening attentively.

"Thankfully not that many," replied Lestrade, "because the attacks are aimed mainly at businesses, the buildings are mostly uninhabited."

"Mostly?"

"Well, there have been a few tragic losses – the most heart-breaking were the elderly couple who were lodging in a room above their shop in Bethnal Green while their house was being redecorated further down the street."

"They hadn't been targeted then?"

"It wouldn't appear so. The only incident that has raised my suspicions was the killing of a retired army man in July. His home was attacked one night but fortunately he managed to escape, only to be shot and killed a few days later. He was sitting in a coffee shop on the Tottenham Court Road when a gunman burst in. He seemed to have known who his victim was, as he didn't disturb any of the other customers who were beside themselves with fear at what they had witnessed."

"Yes, I remember reading about that," I said, "terrible business. From memory, the poor chap had enjoyed a distinguished career: mentioned in dispatches in Balaclava, decorated for bravery in Lucknow and distinguished service on the Northwest Frontier. How ironic that such a decorated, much travelled veteran would meet such a sad end on a London street."

"We handed the matter over to the Special Branch section who are looking into the Fenian outrages – probably one of them."

At the end of the evening, Lestrade invited Holmes and me to a small gathering at the station.

"We regularly get together at Christmas," he said, "we would be delighted if you would both join us."

Knowing my friend's strong aversion to society and ceremonial gatherings, I knew he would not welcome such an invitation – however well intended – and made some non-committal gesture in response. It was therefore left to me to show our guest out. Before going up to my room, I looked in on my friend who was still in his chair with his chin sunk upon his breast, gazing intently at the smouldering fire.

"Good night, old fellow."

The following day I spent the morning Christmas shopping. I think the whole of London – undeterred by the bitter temperature and the whisps of snow in the air – had the same idea. The Strand and Oxford Street were packed with every form of humanity: pedestrians and street vendors jostled for room on the pavements, while carriages and omnibuses moved from side to side to avoid collisions on the roads. Notwithstanding such activity and the noise and confusion it generated, it proved to be a productive morning. I chose a new billiard cue for my friend Thurston, a nice set of cufflinks for Holmes and a fragrant basket of pampering products from Gamages' People's Emporium for our selfless landlady Mrs. Hudson. The one thing I had underestimated was the journey back to Baker Street unscathed, whilst wrestling with the awkwardly shaped fruits of my morning's work. At one point I came close to being run over by an omnibus as I scurried awkwardly across Charing Cross Road whilst hailing a cab. Moments later, I was relieved to be in the sanctuary of the hansom, trotting back towards our lodgings.

Managing to ascend the stairs without being seen by either Mrs. Hudson or my fellow-lodger, I deposited my treasures in my room before going down to our sitting room, where I found Holmes in his grey dressing gown, chuckling to himself at the agony column of the previous evening's *Pall Mall Gazette*.

"A successful morning's work, I take it judging by your step on the stair," he said as I entered.

"Yes, it was, thank you. You seem in a very jolly mood."

"There is nothing more amusing and informative than the agony columns of the popular press."

Before he could elaborate on his statement, Mrs. Hudson knocked and entered.

"Mr. Holmes, there is a Mr. Bateman downstairs who wishes to see you. Says he has come directly from the Paddington express and needs help with an urgent matter before he returns home."

Holmes interrupted his own amusement and acquiesced, "Very well Mrs. Hudson, show him up."

Moments later, a ruddy faced man of around sixty entered our room, apparently quite agitated judging by his manner. He snatched his cap from his head.

"Mr. Holmes?" he asked, his eyes darting from one of us to the other.

"I am Holmes, this is my friend and colleague Dr. Watson."

"I hope you can help me Mr. Holmes, I don't know what else to do."

"Pray calm yourself Mr. Bateman," my friend said, soothingly, "Please sit down and tell us what brings a lefthanded, widowed lamplighter from Reading to our tranquil abode."

Our visitor slowly lowered himself into a chair with such a look of incredulity it was almost comical.

"How do you know me, sir?" he asked.

"Our good landlady told me your name and informed me that you had just arrived at Paddington on the morning express. If I know my Bradshaw, the only non-stop train to arrive at Paddington during the week is from Reading. As for your profession and personal circumstances, I note by your complexion that you clearly work outdoors; beneath your sleeve I can see that the wrist and hand on your left side is bigger than those on the right, indicating that you are clearly left-handed. When I see no fewer than seven droplets of oil spattered on your sleeve, I deduce that you are either an oilman or a lamplighter, probably the latter, seeing that you must return immediately – presumably before it gets dark."

"Both, as a matter of fact," confirmed our visitor, inspecting his workman's coat.

"And as your jackets are open," added Holmes, "I see a wedding ring hanging from your watch-chain. Such a small item could never fit on those fingers, Mr. Bateman; I can only conclude that your dear wife is no longer with us."

"That is true Mr. Holmes, just around this time last year."

"We are sorry for your loss," I said.

"Now," asked my friend, "how can I help?"

"It's my son, Mr. Holmes. He was always a good lad. His best pal growing up was young Percy Armitage from Crane Water, near Reading; you helped young Percy's fiancée with that trouble with her father. When I contacted Percy to see if he had any idea where Edward was, he suggested I come and see you."

"So, your son has disappeared?"

"Yes, he's been gone for weeks without a word or a by-your-leave. After his mother died, he's gradually gone off the rails. First, he started drinking heavily; mind you he wasn't the only one," – Bateman lowered his head in his own embarrassment – "then he gradually got in with the wrong crowd. It ended up where he came here to London where he got a job at Pritchard's Brickworks in Stepney. I hoped he was trying to improve his life before coming home, but when I didn't hear from him for a while, I contacted Pritchard's who told me that he had left. They didn't know where he went and hadn't seen him since. I don't have much money Mr. Holmes but I was hoping you could help in the circumstances."

"Don't worry about my fee, Mr. Bateman. After all, we are approaching the season of good will. Now, give me Edward's last known address and we will see what we can do."

"Thank you, sir," said Bateman, as he wrote down whatever details he could think of.

"As I have nothing else to do at this time," said Holmes after our visitor left, "I may as well start my enquiries into this disappearance. Are you game?"

"Of course I am!" I replied reaching for my hat and coat once more.

Chapter II

The natural place to start our investigation was the large brickworks, where the young man had been employed. Holmes sought out Bateman's foreman who informed him that the young man from Reading had only been with them for a couple of months.

"He just disappeared," he said, "Didn't show up one day – never seen him since. Not a bad worker but seemed a troubled young lad if you ask me."

"Do you know where he was staying?" asked my friend.

"I think he was at old Annie Carver's place on the Old Kent Road."

We followed the workman's directions, traversing the blackened streets of London's East End – two incongruous figures, drawing suspicious glances from those we passed – until we came upon a shabby looking establishment not far from the junction with Albany Road. A faded sign reading *Carver's Hostel* hung above old weather-beaten double doors whose timbers had once been coloured green but now, with most of the paint flaked away, were now a drab silver grey. Holmes entered without a moment's hesitation and I followed, wondering how many waifs and strays had crossed this threshold over the years. The entrance hall was as modest as the building's exterior.

"Mrs. Carver I presume?" asked my friend upon seeing an elderly lady through the open door of a room on the right.

The lady looked up from her knitting, apparently surprised to see such well-dressed gentlemen in her home.

"Yes," she said, with a combined air of suspicion and concern.

"Please don't be alarmed, madam. My name is Sherlock Holmes and this is my colleague Dr. Watson. We are here because we believe an acquaintance of ours may be staying here. An Edward Bateman."

In the years in which I had been with Holmes, I had often observed him obtaining information in the most subtle and discreet manner. This was usually done without revealing his own identity and convincing the source that the information he was sharing was of little or no interest to the detective. On this occasion, he obviously felt there was no need for such subterfuge.

"Oh, yes, he was here a while ago," said the old lady, standing up and unnecessarily wiping her hands on her apron. "Had to ask him to leave."

"Really? Why was that may I ask?"

"I run a respectable house, Mr. Holmes. If anyone causes any trouble, they're out!"

"What sort of trouble was he causing?"

"Coming in late, not following the house rules; but it was mainly the company he was keeping, one fella in particular. Funny sort he was."

"In what way?"

"Foreign!"

Holmes and I exchanged an amused glance.

"Madam, there must have been something more than the man's nationality which you found unpleasant?"

"Had no respect," recalled Mrs. Carver pensively, "used to come in here as if he owned the place. He always seemed to have a hold on the younger man. It got to a point I could hear them in Mr. Bateman's room, shouting and scuffling. I had enough and told him to leave."

"When was this?"

"About a fortnight ago."

"Do you know where Bateman went?"

"He said he was going to stay with Mr. Gregory."

"Mr. Gregory?"

"Yes, this Gregory bloke I've been telling you about."

"I don't suppose you have an address for this Mr. Gregory?"

"No," said Mrs. Carver with contempt, "and I wouldn't want to know either!"

"Thank you for your help, madam," said Holmes courteously.

"What do you make of that, Watson?" he asked as we stepped back out onto the street.

"Well, he is clearly our man and Mrs. Carver's experience appears to support his father's suspicions that he has fallen in with the wrong crowd."

"Indeed."

"Where to now then?" I asked.

"We're not exactly dressed appropriately to make enquiries at the local hostelries without raising further suspicion. I suggest we return to Baker Street and ponder our next course of action."

It was now well after three o'clock and the skies were darkening on the December afternoon.

We returned to our rooms where I found a note sent by my old friend Woodward confirming his invitation to join him and his friends for dinner on Christmas Eve.

"The Café Royal!" I said, "very nice."

Holmes showed little interest and shrugged at my enthusiasm. He retook his seat at his desk amid the test-tubes and vials in which he had been distilling various chemicals over the previous few days and resumed with one of his malodorous experiments. Anticipating some of the toxic odours which were bound to shortly fill our sitting room, I left him to it and retired to my own room.

I wrote a brief response to Woodward, thanking him for the invitation and telling him how much I was looking forward to meeting up with him and his old comrades. Checking my watch, I decided I could just about make it to the Post Office on Marylebone Road. On my way out, Mrs.

Hudson met me in the hallway and asked if I would do her a favour the following morning.

"Doctor? I have ordered a tree from Carswell's in the Edgeware Market; I wonder if you would mind picking it up for me?"

"Of course, Mrs. Hudson, I'd be delighted. There is nothing that gets us in the mood for Christmas more than decorating the tree."

"Hmm," she murmured, indicating upstairs with her eyes, "well, most of us anyway!"

I ran my errand and, on the way back, happened to pass by a small corner pawnbroker's. This gave me an idea for a gift for my friend, Woodward. Although the shop itself didn't have what I was looking for, the owner Mr. Wiseman, told me that the larger pawnbroker, Etherington's, on Sussex Gardens was likely to carry such an item. Knowing I was going to Edgeware Market the following morning anyway, I decided I could make a detour and visit Etherington's at the same time.

Over dinner that night, I informed Holmes about Mrs. Hudson's request of me. I smiled as his sigh of derision reminded me of her anticipation of his response.

"I shall leave you both to it then," he said, without elaborating on what he had planned.

By the time I came down for breakfast the following morning, Holmes had gone. I *myself* left an hour or so later and found that the throng of humanity jostling for space of the streets of the capital I had experienced the previous day had barely dissipated. I made my way first to Etherington's.

I explained to the proprietor what I was looking for and was delighted when he reached into a draw below his counter and produced the very article. It was a Crimean campaign medal which even had the distinctive curled clasp with the word '*Sebastopol*' pinned to its ribbon.

"That's perfect!" I exclaimed. The man was taken aback by my enthusiasm and I felt obliged to explain, "I have a friend who recently had his campaign medal stolen. He was in Sebastopol with his regiment towards the end of the war and I thought it would make the perfect Christmas gift."

"Very good, sir," said the pawnbroker wrapping it in some brown paper.

I then walked to the market off Edgeware Road where the shoppers inadvertently bumped and barged into each other as they searched for produce beneath the patchwork of awnings. I found Carswell's stall and informed the large, ruddy-faced man that I was here to pick up the tree ordered by Mrs. Hudson of Baker Street. He had two or three dozen trees tied up and began to sift through the labels. As he was doing so, I looked over to the next stall where a woman was inadequately dressed in a woollen shawl, fingerless gloves and a straw boater. Beside her was a steaming ern.

"Nice bowl of soup, sir?" she shouted above the din of the crowd, when she observed me looking over.

As appetising as the invitation sounded on such a morning, I politely declined, knowing that in a few moments I would be wrestling with a Christmas tree which would be as tall as I was.

"*Mrs. Hudson of Baker Street,*" announced the stall holder at last as he found the right label, "here we go sir."

As with the previous morning, I underestimated the task involved in picking my way through crowds with awkwardly shaped festive items. My mission on this particular morning was made all the more difficult with the narrowness of the walkways between the stalls and the varying heights of the different awnings. Following several 'excuse me's' and having to suffer many an affronted stare, I managed to extricate myself from the canvassed labyrinth and hail a hansom. Upon our arrival at Baker Street, I felt obliged to add a generous tip to my fare as I was aware the driver – unknown to him – would find his cab littered with pine needles. I gave an embarrassed smile as he was fulsome with his gratitude and wished me compliments of the season.

"Mrs. Hudson!" I called as I struggled through the front door.

"Oh, Doctor that's wonderful!" said our landlady as she appeared from the kitchen.

"Where are you going to put it this year?" I asked.

"I thought this year I'd move the coat stand on the halfway landing and put it there where we could all enjoy it," she replied. I am sure I detected more than a mischievous glint in her eye as she said it.

"Very well," I agreed making to heave it up the first flight of stairs, "the halfway landing it is!"

I reached the landing and saw that our resourceful landlady had already position a large container in which the tree would stand in the place where our coat stand was usually positioned. The stand itself had been placed inside our sitting room; I stood the tree in the large bucket and removed my hat and coat. Remembering I had Woodward's medal in my inside pocket, I removed it and placed it on the table before removing my jacket and re-joining Mrs. Hudson, who had followed me up to the landing with a large box of Christmas decorations.

No sooner had the two of us started to dress the tree when we heard the key turn in the front door downstairs – something which prompted us both to look at one another in a mixture of amusement and trepidation. As Sherlock Holmes ascended the stairway landing, he stopped as he saw what we were doing.

"Good morning, Holmes," I said casually.

My friend gave a sigh of resignation. "Good morning," he said at last as he squeezed past us and entered our sitting room.

Mrs. Hudson and I continued our task and after a few seconds I saw out of the corner of my eye, Holmes was standing in the sitting room and looking at the table.

"Everything all right, old fellow?" I asked, crossing the threshold from the landing.

"What is this?" he asked.

I followed his gaze which was fixed on the medal I had bought earlier that morning for my army friend. The brown paper in which the pawnbroker had loosely wrapped the medal in had naturally unfolded as I lay it on the desk.

"It's a gift for Woodward. You may recall that he told us his own medal had been lost when we spoke to him in the drying room the other day."

"*Fool!*" cried Holmes.

The outburst caused Mrs. Hudson – who was obviously party to the exchange – to drop a red bauble which she was about to position, and it rolled through the doorway, fortunately not breaking.

"That is unworthy of you, Holmes," I protested, "I am making what I believe is a kind gesture to a former colleague who has had the misfortune of losing something which was extremely precious to him."

"Watson," replied Holmes kindly, finally tearing his gaze from the medal, "pray accept my apologies; I don't mean you my dear fellow – I am scolding myself. If short-sightedness were a crime, our friend Lestrade would have every right to clap me in irons!"

"I don't understand."

"I have to leave once more," Holmes was passing Mrs. Hudson on the landing as he made this latest announcement.

The two of us were left staring at one another bemused, as we heard the front door slam shut.

Chapter III

Mrs. Hudson did a wonderful job of decorating the whole house. Coloured ribbon and foliage adorned everywhere, from the entrance hallway to the staircase leading up to my bedroom. The centre piece was the tree that I had helped decorate. She had even cleaned up by late afternoon and by the time I went to close the curtains in our sitting room, snow had started to fall on Baker Street as if to acknowledge our efforts in preparing for the festivities ahead.

It would be another hour before Holmes returned.

"Where have you been?" I asked as he brushed the snow from his hat and coat.

"I went to see Lestrade," he said, without elaborating.

"Was it to give yourself up?" I ventured, referring to the comment he made as he left.

"It may well be the case in time," said he, with a smile, "but I hope to have an opportunity to redeem myself."

It would be twenty-four hours before Holmes said anything further on the matter. He was prompted by Billy, the page, who knocked and entered at his usual pace.

"Got a letter for you Mr. Holmes!" he announced with great enthusiasm.

Holmes took the missive and ripped it open. He glanced at the clock which showed that it was almost five o'clock.

"Too late to reply," he mumbled to himself; and then to the page, "that will be all Billy, thank you. Come back first thing tomorrow when I will ask you to post my reply."

"Very good, sir," said the boy before scampering off.

The detective tapped the note absentmindedly with the stem of his pipe and looked into the middle distance.

"Holmes?"

Breaking from his reverie, he retook his seat by the fire, "Watson, I fear that these may be much deeper waters than we first thought."

"Was the note to do with young Bateman?" I asked.

"Yes," replied my friend while staring at the flames.

"I don't understand your reaction when you saw the Crimean medal earlier," I said, unsure whether *that* was linked to Bateman or not.

"It wasn't the medal itself that caught my attention, Watson, it was the clasp attached to it. When I saw the word 'Sebastopol,' the casual conversations we have had over the past few days, first with your friend Woodward, then with Lestrade and then finally with Mrs. Carver, were suddenly linked by a thread. If my suspicions are proved accurate, that delicate thread will develop into a substantial chain, the events of which may culminate in an eventuality that I dare not contemplate."

He raised his eyes from the fire and looked across towards me, but I was at a loss to understand what he was driving at. Before I could question him further, he asked:

"Tell me, do you know who is attending this dinner your friend has invited you to on Christmas Eve?"

"Not exactly," I answered, a little taken aback, "I know they are a few of his old army colleagues but beyond that, I'm not entirely sure who they are. Surely you don't suspect some malevolent intention from them?"

"Not *from* them, Watson, but potentially *towards* them – and by association, towards my dearest friend."

I had seldom heard my friend speak with such intensity of feeling and I found myself touched by his words.

"I would like you to contact Woodward and find out exactly who his friends are," he resumed. "I have been carrying out my own enquiries today and together, I hope we can prevent any further tragedies."

"Tragedies? With regards to whom? Are we still talking about Bateman?"

"I made some discreet enquiries about Bateman this morning, based on what Mrs. Carver told us. I have an agent working on the matter as we speak."

"No doubt one of the children from what you've described as your '*Baker Street division of the detective police force!*'" I announced with some humour.

"No," replied Holmes gravely, "this is not a task for children. I am hoping young Bateman will provide the final piece in the puzzle that will send a dangerous man to the gallows and disrupt the activities of a much wider criminal enterprise."

"But listening to Bateman's father, the young man sounded like someone who had just come off the rails following the passing of his mother. Surely, he can't have turned into a hardened criminal in such a brief period of time?"

"I am not talking about Bateman; I am referring to the company I believe he is keeping. Does the name Grigory Yubkin mean anything to you?"

I cudgelled my brain, "The name does sound vaguely familiar."

"You may remember I brought his name up at the end of the Dial Square case."

"Of course!" I cried, snapping my fingers in recognition, "he was the man you suspected of receiving the stolen ammunition from the factory."

"That is just one of his many misdemeanours." Holmes re-lit his pipe and sat back in his chair before resuming his narrative.

"Yubkin was from Crimea where his father was a serving officer in the Russian army. He was killed during the siege of Sebastopol and young Grigory fled with his mother. She died a few years later while he was in his teens, he started a nomadic existence, gradually travelling west through Europe, invariably seeking out fellow dissidents. As you know, radical political activity has grown into anarchism across the Continent and if there were any bombings or assassinations to be organised, our friend Yubkin was never too far away."

"As shocking as this is," I said, "what has this Yubkin got to do with our case?"

"He has everything to do with our case, Watson. Far from this being a relatively minor enquiry involving a missing person, I believe we have the opportunity of apprehending one of the most dangerous men in London.

"You will recall Lestrade telling us the other night about the Crimean veteran who was shot and killed in the coffee shop. I went to see our erstwhile colleague today and together we visited his colleagues in the Special Branch section who are investigating the murder – lamentably I might add! I discovered that the soft-nosed bullet used in the killing was one of the many consignments stolen from Dial Square over the past twelve months."

"They are a horrible thing!" I said, with some disgust.

"Indeed, designed to mushroom upon entry causing instantaneous death. The assassin's ammunition of choice I would suggest. What the police haven't linked – until I pointed it out to them of course – is that this particular killing could be lined with two others in Paris and Lyon earlier this year."

"France?" I exclaimed, "Forgive me Holmes, but your narrative is getting cloudier by the minute!"

"At the turn of the year, Yubkin was in France. His visit there coincided with two high-profile assassinations: both senior army officials and both veterans of the Crimean campaign and particularly the taking of Sebastopol."

"Holmes, I now suddenly see what you are driving at."

My friend nodded slowly, "Yes. As well as fuelling the anarchy in others, I believe Yubkin is carrying out his own personal vendetta against those he feels are responsible for his father's death."

"That is why you want me to find out who is attending Woodward's dinner on Christmas Eve."

"It is. Your friend has already mentioned that he and his colleagues are veterans of Crimea. If my theory is correct, this puts them in danger of Yubkin who is now back in London."

I sat trying to digest my friend's staggering deduction and the dangers which potentially lay ahead. Before I could articulate the feelings and thoughts that were wrestling for attention inside my head, Holmes spoke again.

"When we visited Mrs. Carver, she spoke of a 'Mr. Gregory' with whom young Bateman had become involved with. If my suspicions are correct, she had misunderstood Bateman when he was talking about his friend. I think the young man has become embroiled not with a Mr. Gregory, but with Grigory Yubkin."

"Yes, it's certainly plausible. I remember she commented that he was a foreigner. But where can they be?"

"I think I already know," revealed Holmes, much to my further amazement.

"You know!"

"Well, at least my agent does. I went to see him yesterday and put him on the trail. The note he sent me earlier told me that he had found our man Bateman."

"Who is this man of yours?" I asked,

"Shinwell Johnson!" my friend announced, and then, in response to my puzzled expression, "He has enjoyed a checkered career himself, even enjoying more than one period at Her Majesty's pleasure."

Although this was the first time I had heard Holmes speak of Johnson, I was not surprised that he had allied himself to the character he had described, such was his determination to explore every avenue of enquiry when engrossed in a case.

"And this Johnson chap has found Bateman?" I asked.

"He has," said Holmes with a chuckle, "If anything is going on in the criminal underworld of this great city, Johnson invariably knows about it."

"So, what do you propose to do now?"

"I will reply to Johnson tomorrow and see if he can lure him to Baker Street."

"And then what?"

"Find out whether he knows about Yubkin's intentions or not." If it were possible, Holmes adopted a graver tone, "If Yubkin does not know about the dinner, we may have an opportunity to set a trap which will snare this dangerous character."

I sat for a few minutes coming to terms with what my friend was suggesting. "When you first told us about Yubkin at the conclusion of the Dial Square robberies, I remember you said he was a small part of a much larger criminal enterprise; if you do succeed in apprehending him, could that not allow the friends he has in higher places to evade capture?"

"That is a risk we will have to take. If Yubkin is intent on continuing with his murderous rampage, as I suspect, we are duty bound to stop him. If that means delaying the apprehending of bigger criminal fish, then so be it." Holmes looked directly at me. "You realise what I am suggesting, Watson? I am risking the lives of innocent men and my dearest friend in order to snare this villain."

"I do," I replied meeting Holmes's stare, "and if it is in a good cause, which this clearly is, then I am your man!"

Holmes smiled affectionately and returned his gaze to the fire.

Chapter IV

As Holmes had suspected, as well as my old friend Woodward, my dining companions were to include three senior officers, all of whom were decorated for services in the Crimea. It seemed too fanciful that this Russian chap would attempt to assassinate such a group of retired old soldiers, but knowing and trusting Holmes's instincts as I did, I was not prepared to ignore his concerns.

It was four days before Christmas Eve when we heard that my friend's contact in the East End had been successful in locating young Bateman. He intended to bring him to Baker Street that night after convincing him that he was also an ally of Yubkin and there was a task the Russian wanted the two to perform. At the appointed hour, we heard feet on the stairs and the two men entered our sitting room. One was a thick set man, with a ruddy complexion and various marks on his hard face that indicated a tough life. The other was a much younger man, thin with wispy fair hair and a saturnine expression.

"Gentlemen! Come in!" announced Holmes with a flourish, "thank you for joining us."

"Mr. Holmes, sir," said the rough looking character who took up his station with his back to the door, blocking any exit.

The younger man looked confused and darted a glance between Holmes and the man who had brought him here.

"Do not be alarmed, Mr. Bateman," said my friend, "My name is Sherlock Holmes and this is my friend and colleague Dr. Watson. I must confess, Johnson here has brought you to Baker Street under slightly false pretences. But don't worry. It has been done to help you."

"I don't understand," said Bateman, first to Holmes and then turning to Johnson, "you said it was something to do with Grigory."

"And so it is," said Holmes before Shinwell Johnson could say anything. "I am aware that you have allied yourself to Grigory Yubkin. Whether you know it or not, Yubkin is an extremely dangerous man, guilty as he is of, amongst other things, theft, anarchy and murder."

The fact the Bateman did not protest suggested he was at least aware of some of Yubkin's activities. "He is only fighting for what he believes in," he said at last, rather pathetically.

Holmes did not hold back, "Murder and destruction are not worthy causes!" He composed himself before continuing, "Your father visited us a few days ago and asked me to locate you. He is concerned about you, Bateman. He has already lost his wife, and you have lost your mother; you must return home to Reading to be with him. I suspect you haven't been associated with Yubkin long enough to perpetrate any serious crimes yourself, but you could certainly be viewed as an accessory, even by association."

Bateman lowered his head as Holmes raised the subject of his mother's passing.

"It isn't too late," resumed my friend, "if you work with me, I can help you and you will be back at your father's table enjoying a goose on Christmas Day. If you work against me, I'm afraid your own goose will be cooked, and you will find yourself eating whatever is being served in the cells."

"What do you want me to do?" asked Bateman, while looking into his lap.

"Has Yubkin said anything to you about an event on Christmas Eve?"

Bateman looked up, "Yes, he did mention something. He asked if I could help him. He mentioned something about 'having his revenge' but didn't really go into any details. I'm due to meet him tomorrow to get the details."

"Did he say anything about the Café Royal?"

"No, not that I can remember. Why?"

"There is a dinner taking place there on Christmas Eve involving old soldiers who served in the Crimean War. It is my suspicion that Yubkin wants to murder them to avenge the death of his father at Sebastopol."

"What do you propose that I do?" asked the young man.

"I would like you to go ahead with your meeting and confirm if my suspicions are correct. If they are, I will make arrangements to have your friend arrested in the act of attempting his crime."

"And if it isn't what he is planning?"

"Then my friend here can enjoy his dinner with his friends in peace and we will keep an eye on what else Yubkin is up to. Either way, I would like you to return to your father and give up on this life you seem so intent on."

Bateman knew he had no choice and finally nodded slowly, "Very well, I'll do it."

"Do you think he can be trusted?" I asked as I watched Bateman and Johnson make their way along Baker Street, was now thick with snow.

"I believe so," replied Holmes, lighting his pipe, "Bateman was clearly emotionally vulnerable following the loss of his mother. He is only guilty of making some poor decisions during this period. I don't see him as a hardened villain, unlike some of the company he is now keeping. If all goes to plan, we shall be removing one dangerous man from the streets of London, while saving the soul of another.

On the night of the 23rd, two days following his first visit, Bateman returned to Baker Street with news of his meeting with Yubkin. It was as though the events of the previous forty-eight hours had brought the young man to his senses and he now realised the perils of the path he had chosen by leaving his father; he was also clearly extremely nervous about betraying his friend.

"You are correct Mr. Holmes," he said after retaking his seat from earlier in the week, "Grigory is planning to be at the Café Royal tomorrow night. And I am afraid that I may have made matters worse."

"How so?" asked Holmes.

"He told me that he had been monitoring the movements of a Colonel Richards for some months and it was him who he was intended to kill. But then I told him that other veterans would be there and this prompted him to change his plans."

"What was his reaction when you knew about the other veterans?"

"I simply said that Colonel Richards had been a friend of my father. He seemed to accept that. But Mr. Holmes," he added, "instead of taking a handgun to shoot Richards, he now plans to take a handmade bomb and throw it into the dining room."

My blood ran cold at the thought, and it was my turn to fully comprehend the dangers that lay ahead.

"That is useful to know, Bateman," said Holmes, "at least we can now prepare properly."

"What do you intend?" asked the young man.

"I will inform Inspector Lestrade and have him position his men at key locations in and around the foyer of the restaurant. When Yubkin enters – before he can ignite the fuse of his bomb – we will have him arrested."

"I have a request of my own," said Bateman, and then responding to Holmes's questioning expression, "I would like the police to arrest me as well, so that it doesn't look as though I have betrayed him. For the first time last night,

I saw what a dangerous man he is, Mr. Holmes. I would hate to think there would be any retribution against myself or more importantly, my dear father."

"I'm sure we can stage something that will protect your secret. As for any reprisals concerning your actions, I think you can rest easy on that score – I have never known anyone succeed in any retribution as they hang from the end of a rope."

After Bateman had left, Holmes sensed my nervousness.

"I wouldn't ask you to do this Watson, if I didn't believe you were the man for the job."

"It's not my own safety I am concerned about, Holmes. At least I know the dangers I am facing. The others do not and this is what is making me nervous."

"I believe it is the best way my friend. The least people know about this the better. We want everyone to be completely natural on the night so Yubkin doesn't suspect anything is amiss. Any nerves he senses from young Bateman will be just that – first night nerves as it were."

I nodded silently, still feeling uneasy about my dining companions' ignorance of the matter.

I slept fitfully, my mind constantly going back to the horrors of my experiences in Afghanistan. The following day was not much better. Christmas Eve has always been one of my favourite days, with a sense of anticipation that was unrivalled throughout the year. But Christmas Eve of that year was different: I was quiet throughout the day and had to be reminded at one point by Mrs. Hudson that I had promised to collect our Christmas goose from the poultry seller who set up during that time of year in Covent Garden.

Holmes had been away for most of the morning, briefing Lestrade on what was about to take place that evening. It was his usual habit to keep me in the dark about his periods of absence but on this occasion – understanding my apprehension – he informed me that the Scotland Yard man was to have plain clothed officers outside the restaurant, as well as other men in the foyer posing at staff. Holmes himself would be there to assist if necessary.

"Our night's work will be a serious one," he concluded, as he reached in the drawer of his desk, "and I am afraid that your army revolver will ruin the cut of your tails. You must therefore rely on me."

He checked the chamber of his pistol, snapped it shut. It was five o'clock when Holmes buttoned up his pea-jacket and slipped the revolver in his pocket; reaching for his heavy hunting crop from the rack, he left once again to meet Lestrade and prepare for the evening's events. I remained in Baker Street for a further hour and a half. Such was my state of anxiety, I had three attempts before successfully knotting my white tie. There was part of me that felt ashamed about withholding the information about Yubkin from Woodward and his friends, but I knew that to betray Holmes's instructions would not only be a treacherous act in itself, but it would also jeopardise the whole mission and put us all in further danger. I hardened my heart and put on my hat and coat.

As my hansom travelled towards Regents Street, I sensed the excitement amongst the people of London. From my cab I saw boisterous passers-by moving to-and-fro in the gas-lit streets, muffled in their coats and cravats; there were fathers, who had finished work for the holiday, giddily playing with their children in the snow. A group of carol singers making their way along Wigmore Street, while a waft of roasting chestnuts permeated my nostrils as we passed a street vendor selling his produce by an open brazier. We arrived shortly before seven and as I climbed down from the cab and paid my fare, there was a quintet of Salvation Army bandsmen along the street softly playing

Silent Night, their faces lighted by the rays of a horn lantern carried by another uniformed member of the group.

The street was already busy as diners were arriving in their dozens. I thought how catastrophic it would be if Holmes were unsuccessful in his plan to stop Yubkin. I quickly dispelled the thought from my mind and made my way inside, trying to pick out the police officers Holmes and Lestrade had positioned.

There were two uniformed doormen to meet and greet guests as they arrived. One seemed quite natural, continually touching the brim of his top hat and wishing everyone a good evening, the other stood stock still, looking straight ahead. Inside there were staff taking diners' coats and hats; one of the staff was the picture of awkwardness as he wrestled with an armful of coats, much to the concerned expressions of their owners. My attention was then drawn to a clatter of cutlery, dropped from a tray by someone coming out of the kitchen.

"Probably temporary staff employed for the holidays," I heard one woman say to her husband as I followed them into the vast dining room.

It was decorated with four large Christmas trees in each corner, while ribbons and bunting had been strung across the room from the ceiling. I saw my old friend Woodward waving at me through the crowd of people who were starting to take their seats.

"Watson!" he called, "how lovely to see you, thank you so much for coming."

"My pleasure," I said, rather unconvincingly.

Woodward turned his attention to his seated companions, "These are my colleagues from the Crimea." Except for Colonel Richards, Yubkin's original target, their names barely registered, such was my distracted state of mind – "Gentlemen, this is Dr. John Watson, a dear companion of mine from Afghanistan."

After pleasantries were exchanged, I took my seat. As the old soldiers launched into their various reminisces and waiters appeared from the kitchen with the soup course, my mind was filled with what was happening elsewhere. It would be a further hour before I relaxed into the evening and it would be still later that night, over a cigar and brandy, before Sherlock Holmes could properly enlighten me as to the sequence of events, I was unable to witness first- hand.

As he related later, Holmes had left me in Baker Street and met Lestrade and his men. The uniformed officers were kept out of sight while three were placed in positions of a fake concierge, a cloakroom attended and a member of the waiting staff (I must confess to being delighted at this information and inwardly congratulated myself or my own observations).

"We waited in position for Bateman and Yubkin. All the guests were inside and seated when the two arrived just as the nearby church bells sounded eight o'clock. I must complement Yubkin on his sense of propriety – he was dressed immaculately and would certainly pass for a restaurant patron himself who had simply arrived late. Bateman was driving a small landau and waited discreetly along the street for his would-be confederate to exit the building before making their hasty escape. When Lestrade and I saw Yubkin get down from the landau, we quickly made our way into the foyer where we assumed positions out of sight, alongside four other uniformed officers. Moments later, Yubkin appeared and calm as you like, handed his coat to one of the cloakroom attendants. From our hiding place, I could see he was holding something in the back of his hand, concealed from the member of staff, who directed him towards the dining room.

"I must say Lestrade's men played their parts well, for as Yubkin made his way through the foyer, one of Lestrade's constables appeared from the dining room dressed as one of the waiting staff, carrying a tray of plates. He knocked into Yubkin as they passed, just as the Russian was reaching into his pocket, I suspected to light the fuse of the device he was carrying. It was just enough to distract him momentarily from his task.

"'*Now!*' I signalled and the rest of Lestrade's men appeared from their hiding place and overpowered the man with a minimal of struggle. As they wrestled him to the floor, he dropped an object he was carrying and the book of matches he was reaching for. The unlit device started to roll away before I trapped it under my foot. A pretty little thing I must say, it was a variation on the Orsini Bomb but with its own fuse – designed to cause the maximum of damage. Fortunately, none of the patrons heard a thing.

"When he was searched, Yubkin even had a seating plan in his pocket with your friend Woodward's table indicated, so he knew exactly what he was doing.

"The final act was to march him out of the restaurant and ensure that he saw Bateman being arrested also, so as to protect the young man's reputation in the eyes of his former friend. He will be back on his way to Reading as we speak, whereas our Russian friend will no doubt be on *his* way to the Old Bailey."

"Good heavens!" I replied after hearing my friend's narrative, "you were just in time to prevent the most horrible of crimes."

Of course, I never knew any of this as I was inside the dining room at the time of the action; whatever noise came from the scuffling in the foyer was drowned out by the clanking of cutlery and crockery, and the general hubbub of the diners. The first I knew of my friend's successful operation was when I was tapped on the shoulder by the maître d, who held a silver tray on which sat a bottle of champagne.

"Sir," he said, "the gentleman in the foyer sent this over with his compliments."

I looked over the crowd to the door leading to the foyer to see the figure of Sherlock Holmes standing with just the hint of a smile on his lips. He touched the brim of his hat with his crop and was gone. I knew then that his mission had been successful. I thanked the Maître D and took the bottle.

Turning back to my dining companions who had been engrossed in their own conversation all night and therefore completely oblivious to any potential dangers, I filled their glasses.

"Gentlemen, I would like to wish you all the complements of the season"– and then raising my own glass – "Merry Christmas everybody!"

WE CONTINUED TO CHAT DESULTORILY FOR SOME TIME,
AS OLD SOLDIERS ARE BOUND TO DO...

ISAAC SCOTT (1834-1908)
PRIVATE 1622 17TH LANCERS

Literary Agent's Note

The inspiration for 'The Sebastopol Clasp' (and 'The Baroda Silver' for that matter) comes from my great, great grandfather, Isaac Scott, to whom this volume is dedicated. It is no exaggeration to say that this old boy changed my life, almost a hundred years after his death. He was a soldier in the nineteenth century with the 17th Lancers and served in the Crimean and Indian Mutiny campaigns (charging with the regiment at Baroda where the actual treasures were won). Sadly, his medals had been lost from the family some years ago. That notwithstanding, during my research into his life, I found out so much information about him that I decided to write a summary of his life and times. With that, I was well and truly bitten by the writing bug and over thirty years on, I'm still loving it.

As far as fiction was concerned, my favourite literary characters had always been Holmes and Watson (still are of course), so I decided to set an adventure involving our two heroes in my home city of Carlisle. I even gave Isaac a walk-on part in the book. To commemorate its publication, my wife – unbeknownst to me – commissioned an artist friend of ours to produce a Paget*esque* drawing of the scene where Isaac meets Doctor Watson in a local park.

Imagine my delight when a medal collector in America tracked me down a few years ago and informed me he had recently bought Isaac's medals at auction. He offered to return them to me and we came to an agreement. I had the medals cleaned, mounted and framed alongside the wonderful photograph I have of the great man. If you look closely at the medal on the left, this is his Crimean War campaign medal, attached to which is a curly bar. That curly bar is... (yes, you've guessed it) ...the Sebastopol Clasp.

As with all books there are many people who devote their time, skills and finance to its publication. Watson's original literary agent was supported by the *Strand* magazine and other journals that helped bring Watson's writings to the masses. My approach was slightly different – I relied on the support of many through the Kickstarter programme to facilitate this particular volume. I thank them all. Special mention and praise must go to Steve Emecz for his tireless work and his continued interest in the adventures of all things Sherlockian. Thanks also to Brian Belanger for channelling his inner-Paget once more to produce a stunning front cover, and to my friend Christophe Vever who proof-read many of the stories. Finally, my thanks to David Marcum and especially to my wife Wendy who have both been great sources of inspiration independently of one another with their knowledge and support respectively over the years.

Martin Daley
Kirkcudbrightshire
Scotland
2023

Milton Keynes UK
Ingram Content Group UK Ltd.
UKHW012203221123
433027UK00009B/173/J

9 781804 243213